RESILIENCE OF CHARLOTTE LAKE

By D. L. Reavis

ISBN:978-1-968792-02-2

Chapter One

— • ● • —

"Mayday, mayday, mayday." The pilot's voice echoed in Ethan's headset as the Blackhawk helicopter plunged deeper into the storm. Darkness swallowed the aircraft, its spinning blades drowned by the violent winds. The crushing weight of positive G-forces gave way to weightlessness as they spiraled toward the ground. Every instinct screamed: *this is the end.*

How long had they been falling? They couldn't have been too high; they were still in the mountains. Ethan braced himself for impact as the helicopter spun out of control, blood draining from his head as gravity pressed him hard into the seat. He searched the window for any point of reference but found only black clouds. It was like being trapped in a tiny boat tossed about in a stormy sea. He glanced at Steven, sitting calmly with his eyes closed. *How could he sleep through this?*

Then, through the swirling fog, Ethan spotted treetops flash by in fleeting glimpses. For what had felt like an eternity, they had been hugging the western slopes of the

Sierra Nevada's. Terror gripped, when the Blackhawk banked sharply to the right, exposing a sheer granite wall off the starboard. Out the other window—another mountain face loomed only about a hundred yards away.

Where are we going? The G-force indicated they were in a steep climb. Suddenly, negative G's pulled Ethan from his seat. The helicopter shot over a small plateau. Steven stirred, glanced over, and said calmly, "Get ready. The fun's about to start."

Before Ethan could react, a bright flash filled the cabin, followed by a deafening explosion. The Blackhawk lurched violently, smoke flooding the cockpit.

"Brace for impact, Ethan. We're going down!"

"What the…" Ethan started, but Steven cut him off.

"Don't worry, it's all part of the plan," Steven said, tightening his seatbelt as the helicopter dropped. "We'll be fine."

The ground rose rapidly. At the last second, the pilot arrested the descent, slamming the helicopter down hard. The bird tipped, and the blades tore into the earth. Ethan's head smashed against the shattering window, his helmet saving him from a fatal blow. Ears ringing, he hung suspended as everything went still.

Disoriented, Ethan dangled by the seatbelt, struggling to process what happened. *Did they crash on purpose?* If so, why? They could have been killed. His thoughts were cut short when someone grabbed him, released his belt, and pulled him through a mangled door. They moved quickly away from the smoking wreckage.

As they cleared the smoke Ethan looked around at the activity on the mountain plateau. "I'm not hurt, where's Steven?"

"He's fine. Come on, we have to go," said the rescuer.

Ethan's head was spinning. He needed to lie down. He reached for his helmet, but stopped at the sound of an approaching helicopter.

"Leave that on, Mr. Dalton. Your ride is here."

Another Blackhawk touched down on the plateau. His vision flickered in and out as his rescuer strapped him into the new seat. The door slid shut, and Ethan watched his rescuer back away as the twin turbines spun up. The ground fell away beneath them, and they made a sweeping turn to the northwest.

Through the haze in his mind, Ethan saw the wreckage of the first Blackhawk shrink below. Moments later, it exploded in a fireball. Ethan slumped into his seat, shaking his head just before unconsciousness took him.

Ethan had no idea how long he had been out when he was jolted awake. The thump of the rotor blades' frequency had changed. The sky was clearing, and the sun had just disappeared behind a ridge. The rising snow-covered ridge line confirmed the feeling in his stomach that they were on a gradual descent. As they started to make a turn through the evening haze, he spotted a flashing red light go solid red, and then slowly turned green. He felt the negative G's as the pilot increased the descent and turned towards the light.

A helicopter approach path indicator, hidden out here in the wilderness. How convenient. Ethan's thoughts were still muddled, and he wished he'd been given more of a briefing—*"no longer hunted by the outside world"* was vague at best.

As they descended into darkness, the ridge disappeared from view. The thumping of the blades deepened as he felt the G force of an arrested descent. Ethan exhaled, heart pounding, as the ridgeline swallowed them. He wasn't sure if he was being rescued or delivered.

Chapter Two

The door slid open and two men in camouflage helped Ethan out of the helicopter and onto a gurney. "Good evening, Mr. Dawson. I pray your trip went well."

A controlled crash doesn't count as a good trip. Ethan kept the thought to himself as he stepped out of the Blackhawk.

"We have been ordered to escort you to the sickbay. You feeling alright?"

"Just a nasty headache and considerable dizziness. Other than that, nothing feels broken."

He shivered briefly as a cold gust of wind blew down from the snowpacks. The men rolled him through a dimly lit maze of shipping containers to one marked with a small red cross.

The squeak of the door revealed a small room with a couple of chairs. A door leading deeper into the container was shut. No sooner had they arrived when a young man in scrubs opened the door.

"Good evening Mr. Dawson. I'm Doctor Winegard. Men bring him back."

At the door Ethan looked around the brightly lit room. A

fully functioning urgent care facility all tucked away in a portable shipping container. Even a hospital bed pushed against the side wall.

"You have a lot of regular customers here?" He asked.

Doctor Winegard laughed as he motioned the orderlies to place Ethan under a bright light. "More than you might think. It seems like some people are prone to accidents. And then there are the unexpected ones like yourself."

"Unexpected? You didn't know I was coming?"

"Oh yeah. We knew you were on your way. You just weren't supposed to take out a window with your head. Thank goodness you had that helmet on or we would be using a spatula to scrape up your brains."

"Ouch, that doesn't sound good. You think I might have a concussion?"

"Without a question. We'll get you checked out, and then you can get some rest." He dismissed the orderlies and started getting Ethan's vitals. After checking his pulse and looking into his eyes he pulled an I.V. kit off the shelf. I'm going to start you on an I.V. just to keep you hydrated. You can plan on spending the night."

Ethan tried to sit up. "Is that really necessary? I'm not feeling all that bad."

"You may not be right now, but if that brain of yours starts swelling, a lot could happen. We wouldn't want that, would we?"

Ethan's head started spinning, causing him to lay back down on the gurney and nod.

Ten minutes later Doctor Winegard pulled off his gloves. "No lasting damage from what I can tell. You're going to be stiff and sore for a few days, so take it easy."

"No problem, Doc. Is the bed comfortable?"

Doctor Winegard laughed. "It's a hospital bed. From my understanding, there's still a little vinegar left in you. Andrew is the nurse on night shift, he will help you get settled."

Ethan laid back in the hospital bed and let out a deep sigh. Even though it had only been a few hours since he had departed Charlotte Lake, it felt like a lifetime. He watched Dr. Winegard insert a syringe into the I.V. "Something for the pain, doc?"

"You could say that." The doctor answered. "Blink your eyes a couple of times and you won't feel a thing."

What followed was no ordinary dream.

• ● •

Ethan smelled the smoke before he heard the children running through the forest. He tried to stand, but found his captors had tied him securely to the tree. No matter how hard he twisted and pulled, he could not loosen the bindings. Where were the children coming from? What were they doing in the mountains? He tensed as a crashing sound brought with it a huge beast. Its fangs protruded in his direction and it bellowed a snarl that told of Ethan's demise. After slowly circling the tree it stopped in front of him, its cavernous mouth just inches from his face. Ethan screamed but no sound was heard. The beast let out a thunderous sound as it spoke, "Who's going to save you now, Ethan Dawson? Where is this God you say you serve? You know God isn't real. Why did you trust Him?"

Was it the stench coming from the throat of the beast or the thought of denying God that caused Ethan to stiffen and try to melt into the bark. He shut his eyes but could still see. He turned his head away, but the beast was there, snarling. He could see flames start to flicker through the trees, as gusting hot wind competed with the beast. The fire would be here soon. He jerked at his bindings to no avail. Finally, in a state of surrendered desperation, he yelled. "My trust is in You God, only You can save me."

Silence. The fire, the beast, the bindings. Gone. Thick fog enveloped his vision. He lifted his hands to his face. He realized he was no longer tied to the tree. He slowly got to his feet, but had no idea where he was going. Nothing but a quiet, peaceful haze.

Voices, someone was whispering. Were they coming for him? He looked down at his hands again, they looked old, but I'm just a child. More voices. This time they were louder, and he could hear someone saying he was waking up. What's that supposed to mean?

— • ● • —

A few moments later consciousness returned and Ethan opened his eyes. Doctor Winegard and Andrew were scanning a computer monitor when he stirred.

"Welcome back," Doctor Winegard said. "Thought you were going to sleep all day."

Ethan tried to answer the doctor but his mouth felt like it was full of cotton. It tasted like he had eaten a skunk. He mumbled an unintelligible request. The doctor seemed to know what he wanted and handed him a small cup with a straw.

Ethan lifted his arm to take a drink and looked at the attached I.V. "When's this coming off?" He mumbled.

"Now that you're awake, Andrew can remove it. Have to say, you were hit or miss for awhile. Everything went stable about an hour ago. Once you feel strong enough to take care of yourself we'll release you into the wild."

A couple hours later, Andrew removed the I.V. and unhooked the monitors. "Let's get you over to your rehab room. It's a little more comfortable."

The sun was hidden by the clouds rolling over the ridge. Ethan silently followed Andrew through the maze of converted shipping containers, most of which appeared to be for housing personnel. *Why is this place here?* Again, he should have requested more information when Steven had told him that he would be protected. His head sure didn't feel it. If the FBI owned this place, it was definitely black ops. He had no reason not to believe his old friend, but this was getting slightly sinister. A distant howl resounding off the granite walls caused every muscle in his body to tighten.

"Here you go, Mr. Dawson." Andrew punched a code into the cyber lock and the door popped open. A light came on inside the shipping container, revealing a small but well-laid-out room.

"Thank you, Andrew. Will I be seeing you in the morning?'

"Most likely not, sir. Dinner will be delivered shortly. Sleep well."

The door slammed shut, leaving Ethan alone somewhere in the High Sierra Mountains, with a very clandestine feel. He looked at the deadbolt and shuddered as he turned the knob. *Was this his prison? Did he really think he could somehow escape justice?* He dropped his backpack on the bed and headed for a shower.

The steaming water battled against what had transpired over the last thirty-six hours. Yesterday morning he had been sitting on Mount Bago surveying Charlotte Lake. Then, Steven had arrived in the Blackhawk.

He had stayed on top of the mountain, hoping Steven would go away. He had watched as Steven climbed the mountain. He should have done the right thing and started down. But, he didn't. He was hollow. Not a shred left inside his chest.

Steven hadn't yelled at him. He didn't even complain about the twenty-minute climb. He just sat down beside him and put a hand on his shoulder.

Ethan had no idea how long the two of them had stared into the valley, but finally Steven had told him it was time to go.

He had followed Steven back down the mountain to the waiting helicopter with a lump in his throat and cloudy consciousness. That was before the storm.

Ethan shut his eyes, all he could see were Krystal and her children waving at the departing helicopter. Sure, he would miss the stone cabin in the crater and the frequent visits with his friends in the village, but the empty void in his chest would come from what almost was.

The water turned cold as Ethan felt pulsating blades, followed by the sound of the departing Blackhawk. Shutting off the shower, he banged his fist against the wall. "I said I trusted you God. What are you doing? Please tell me."

Chapter Three

A stiff cold breeze whipped up the camouflage netting stretched over the common area between two shipping containers. Ethan turned up the collar of his coat and took a sip of coffee, the warmth barely cutting through the chill.

The place looked deserted. Ethan sat at a weathered picnic table, the metal chilled beneath his fingers. He unfolded the note from his pocket. This had to be the place.

"Good morning, Mr. Dawson."

Ethan turned to greet a man with sandy brown hair, dressed in camouflage. No insignia markings, but his demeanor spoke volumes.

"Colonel Whitlock," the man said, offering his hand. "Welcome to the White Chief Camp. The doc patch you up?"

Ethan returned the firm handshake with relief. "Didn't need much, but he grounded me for a few days. I've got questions."

"Fair enough," Whitlock sat down across from him. "What's on your mind?"

"What do you know about the crash?"

Whitlock's expression was unreadable. "I know a Blackhawk helicopter disappeared on the western slopes of the Sierra Nevada Mountains. No wreckage has been found. Once it is, the story will be that you and the crew perished. It's as simple as that."

Ethan raised an eyebrow. "That's extreme. Whose idea was it?"

"We had to make it convincing," Whitlock said with a shrug. "Otherwise, some would have doubted it. Seriously, look around you, Ethan. You're just one piece of a much bigger picture. The last thing we need are bounty hunters combing these mountains."

Ethan frowned. "What about the lack of human remains? Won't that raise questions?"

Whitlock's gaze hardened. "You ask to many questions, Dawson. For the sake of the deceased, there will be human remains. They won't be yours." He leaned forward. "Now, let's get down to business. Do you know why you're here?

"From the looks of things, I'd say you need to hide me until things cool off. But why here, in a metal box in the middle of nowhere? Where are all the plush FBI safe houses?"

Colonel Whitlock laughed. "Don't get too comfortable. Once the doctor clears you, we've got a mission lined up. The sooner the better. And as for the FBI. You will not be working directly with them anymore."

Ethan tilted his head. "Black Ops?"

"That is *exactly* what it is. And since it is Black Ops, you wouldn't have heard of this place. Let's just say the FBI doesn't know everything we're doing here."

"So, they're funding you without any oversight?"

"The money keeps coming, and no one's asking questions. It works for us."

Ethan stretched his neck around. "I expected more activity considering your operation at Charlotte Lake. Where is everyone?"

"They're either on a mission or down at Willow Creek. This place is used for high-altitude training and a recovery spot for our operatives. That's the reason for the medical pod."

Ethan nodded, starting to piece things together. "What is this job you mentioned?"

Whitlock's eyes narrowed. "Not today, Dawson. You'll be briefed once we have all the pieces in place."

Ethan folded his hands behind his neck and stared into the clouds. Whatever was coming was bigger than him, and here he was stuck in the middle of it. Colonel Whitlock didn't seem concerned about the gray area between official duty and what needed to be done. Ethan questioned his ability to do the same. In war, he had done some things for the good of humanity that kept him up at night. This sounded like something darker, more sinister.

"So why me?"

Whitlock's chiseled smile showed no compassion. "Thanks to Steven you have been on our radar for a long time. When you pulled that vigilante stunt in New York, we knew you were our man. We just had to get to you. Then you pulled that disappearing act. Thanks to a young love-struck lady at Charlotte Lake you were found. Unfortunately, someone in the agency was actively looking for you. Once we got a name, Steven took over. That was why he paid you a visit."

Ethan fumed. "He wasn't alone. That intruder had no intentions of taking me alive. What would have happened if I had been sleeping when they came calling? I would have been dead."

Whitlock frowned. "I guess Steven chose not to tell you. When the intruder broke the window, Steven was on his way around the cabin to terminate him. When he heard the muffled shot fired he knew it was you. He wrote in his report that he just wanted to mess with you and returned to the front porch. You can blame him for that."

Ethan still wasn't happy. "Why didn't you extract me at that time? It might have saved a lot of heart burn."

"We were dealing with a lot of negative things going down surrounding Charlotte Lake and felt it best to keep you there for insurance. I'm sure you noticed that our operative there is not a warrior."

"She saved my life."

"That she did and it won her a promotion. Let's just say, she misses you but now carries some cold metal for protection."

Ethan couldn't imagine sweet little Anna with a concealed weapon. "I'm sure Charlotte Lake leadership approves."

Whitlock shook his head. "As far as we know, no one in security is aware of her extracurricular activities."

"So, when Anna contacted you with the Mayday call you decided to use it as an excuse to get me out of there? Killing off three hundred violent criminals to cover pulling out a washed-up

Ranger. That was really civil of you."

"If we hadn't, you would still be a wanted man. At last count there isn't a soul out there looking for you. That's why we have recruited you for the job."

"The one you're not telling me about? What if I don't accept?"

"I suppose it would mean you would be here a long time. We can't just let you back into civilization. One sighting of you and the whole ops goes up in flames."

Looking down into his rapidly chilling coffee, the statement hit Ethan like a brick.

He wasn't here by choice. He was here because someone decided he belonged in a box on a mountain. Somehow, he would get a message back to Krystal that he was alive. As soon as he could, he would escape this high-altitude-minimum-security prison. He wanted his freedom.

"Are we through here?" he asked the Colonel.

"For now. When you feel you're strong enough, you will be given a laptop. In it you will find the file explaining your mission. Have a good day, Ethan."

Whitlock stood, nodded at Ethan, "It's a pleasure having you aboard. Take care of yourself." With that, he turned and walked towards the Bell 407M sitting on the helipad, its blades slowly starting to spin.

Ethan sat staring at the mountains. His thoughts were not on the helicopter with rotors spinning. His memories took him back to the time his parents had sent him off to camp. He remembered how scared he was to leave the city and go to the mountains. His parents had told him, he didn't have to go. But, they constantly reminded him how much they had paid.

His first day at camp, he only did what he was told and made no attempt to meet the other boys. His childish introverted attitude caused him to despise youth camps. It had felt more like a prison camp. Kind of like this.

His dizziness reminded him the concussion still hadn't worn off. Yes, he still needed a few days to heal, but as soon as his head was clear, he was going to get on with this mission.

As the Colonel departed over the ridge to the south Ethan's stomach growled. He stood up and headed for the mess hall. "Beef Stew" was scribbled across the handwritten sign taped to the door.

He pulled the door open and was hit with the aroma of the promised hearty lunch.

A couple of tables with a handful of folding chairs graced the dining area. Not much of a mess hall, but what do you expect to find in a shipping container. A counter separated the business end of the forty-foot metal box from the dining area.

At the sink a young man wearing fatigue pants and a dark green tee shirt looked up. "Be with you in a minute sir."

Ethan remained silent as he took in the business end of the shipping container turned mess hall. It looked more like the inside of the food trucks he had frequented near Hanover Square in New York. Clean, compact, and functional. He picked up a laminated menu sitting on the counter. Besides the soup du jour, they offered the standard freezer-to-fryer menu. He took a deep breath, letting the stew's aroma make the decision for him.

Chapter Four

The wind howled as Ethan stood looking through the only window in his shipping container-turned-living quarters. It wasn't much of a window - more like a porthole to nothingness. Outside, a blinding whiteness stretched on forever.

He was supposed to be getting out of here. But no helicopter was landing in this, not unless the crew was on a suicide mission.

Frustrated, he turned back to the laptop the IT specialist had delivered. He'd thought it was his connection to the outside world. But it offered no weather report, no news, no access to email. Just a single app inviting him to "explore".

At first, Ethan had resisted out of stubbornness. But now, out of sheer boredom and mild curiosity, he scrolled over the icon and double-tapped.

The next hour was spent reading and re-reading the mission file. The more he studied it, the less it made sense. What was the intended outcome? A feeling of desperation filled his stomach as he studied the maps. It had the makings of a one-way trip to the nation's capital.

Why him? Of all the operatives, he was the least familiar with the agency's internal workings. Maybe that was the point. Did they want him to get caught? Was failure built into the plan?

From his days as an investigative reporter, Ethan knew every covert operation carried risk, but this felt different. This wasn't just some foreign embassy or even a remote cartel. This mission was deep inside the heart of the FBI headquarters.

The more he thought about the mission, the more he questioned the goal. It had to be more than the infiltration of the FBI's database. Could it be that they were testing him? Fingers hovering over the keyboard, Ethan scrolled through the mission details again, scanning for details he might have missed. No matter how hard he looked, gaps remained.

Two weeks had passed since his arrival at White Chief Camp. During the first week, he spent his days soaking up the sun on the granite rocks overlooking the lake. Then the mild fall weather gave way to this winter wonderland. Last evening, the message came that he would be picked up at 11:30 this morning.

When his stomach growled, he checked his watch. Plenty of time to grab something to eat.

The icy wind slapped his face as he shoved open the door. He pulled the strings tighter on this parka hood as he surveyed the surrounding mountains emerging through the blowing snow. The flashing strobes from the helipad reflected off the snow laden pine trees. As he pushed his way up the trail to the mess hall, he could see the wind blowing snow across the helipad. The circles of green and yellow lights framed by strobes, created a contrast to the solid white surrounding.

With a gloved hand on the mess hall door, Ethan paused, watching the landing zone until the chill of isolation seeped into his bones.

"Good morning, Mr. Dawson, the usual?" Stewart asked

from behind the counter.

"Thanks. Any interesting news this morning?"

"Overheard a couple of the guys talking about an incoming flight. Might be yours," Stewart said, cracking eggs into a skillet.

Ethan poured himself a cup of coffee and took a seat. "You see the weather? Not sure anything's flying in that."

"You don't need to fret about the snowstorm. I've seen them fly in here in worse." Stewart slid the bacon, eggs and hash browns in front of Ethan. "I don't think they even need to see the ground to land that thing. Sure scares me."

"I wasn't able to get the weather forecast this morning. Is the internet down?" Ethan asked.

Stewart frowned. "I don't think so. Mine was working earlier." He pulled out his phone and after a couple of clicks said, "Working just fine. Want to use mine?" He tossed his phone to Ethan.

Ethan clicked on the web browser and entered his email account username. Immediately, the phone froze. He tried to exit the web browser but nothing happened.

"I think I broke your phone," he said, tossing it back.

Stewart restarted it. "Says 'unauthorized use detected.' What did you try to access?"

"Just my email," Ethan replied, realization dawning. "I'm guessing everything has to go through a local server?"

Stewart scratched his head. "I don't know, but I can direct you to IT."

"Not necessary," Ethan muttered. "I already know."

He sat in silence, his anger kindling over the extent of his captivity. At least he would be leaving soon. The first thing he would do on the outside is acquire a new phone. He finished eating and was nursing a second cup of coffee when an orderly in white coveralls stepped into the mess hall.

"Thought I might find you here, Mr. Dawson. Your flight is twenty minutes out. They're asking you be ready for a quick departure."

Ethan nodded and pulled on his parka. Halfway back to his quarters, he noticed the man following him.

"Anything I can help you with?"

"Orders are to stay with you until you board the chopper," the orderly said nervously. "I will wait outside."

"I imagine you will," Ethan said.

Inside, he packed quickly. The laptop was the last thing in his backpack. He would be off the mountain before they knew it was missing.

He felt the deep thumping before he heard the helicopter approaching. The orderly knocked on the door. "Hurry up, Mr. Dawson your ride's here.

The sound of the approaching Blackhawk intensified as they made their way towards the lighted landing pad. Ethan scanned the storm filled sky. They were still about a hundred yards from the pad when the dark shape emerged out of the storm. It was anything but stable as it slowly descended towards its target. The blowing snow became a blizzard as pitch of the rotor blades increased for landing.

Ethan was holding his breath as he fought back against the stinging ice particles. Turning away as the Blackhawk touched down on the frozen pad. As the outwash subsided, the orderly grabbed his arm and pulled him towards the helicopter. The door slid back, and the crew chief pulled him aboard. The orderly saluted, and backed away. Ethan was still fastening his harness as the thumping of the blades deepened. The earth fell away. Ethan accepted the headset from the crew chief shutting out the noisy decibels.

"Welcome aboard, Mr. Dawson. Flight time's about thirty-five minutes. The weather at our destination is overcast and light rain. No food or drink service, so sit back and enjoy the ride."

"Where are we headed?"

"We're taking you to Fresno. That's all I know. Sorry."

As they climbed over the ridge, deja vu struck. It had only been two weeks since he had lived through a chaotic roller coaster ride into the mountains. Way too soon. Ethan took a deep breath and felt his head spinning.

Am I passing out?

He leaned forward against the harness. Shutting his eyes, he tried to maintain consciousness. *What's happening?* It wasn't fear. Something physical? Couldn't be PTSD… the crash wasn't that bad.

Ethan woke to negative G force and assumed they had cleared the mountains. The ride had smoothed out and he could hear the pilot chattering with Fresno Approach. The rain streaming across the side window confirmed their lower altitude. He stared into the fog.

He could hear the controller giving them their approach clearance. "Thunder six, cleared for RNAV 29R approach, maintain 3,000 until established."

Thunder six, Ethan thought. What a name. "Concrete Mixer" felt more accurate.

At least he was thinking clearly now. Clearly enough to know that someone needed to answer his questions. He was not ready to go busting into the FBI headquarters unannounced and unwelcome.

His equilibrium spun as he felt the turn onto the approach. Maybe he would just hijack his ride east and leave the country. Where would he go? Maybe Canada. No, that wouldn't work. They would send him back. Not only that, it's too cold. He would go to somewhere tropical.

He laughed under his breath. No. He was going to do what he was told.

Through the thinning fog, he could see traffic slowly moving on a freeway. He tightened his harness. Krystal had told him to trust God. He grimaced. The Bible she gave him hadn't been read since Charlotte Lake. The last two weeks had been a struggle. He needed help.

The helicopter touched down with a jolt. Rain pelted the windows as they taxied to the ramp. He looked up at the Signature Flight Support sign shining from the side of a large hangar.

Well, at least they'll have a restroom. Maybe even a phone.

Chapter Five

Ethan gave up on getting a phone after the crew chief followed him into the men's room. *He must have his orders not to let me out of his sight. This has to stop. I am not a prisoner.*

Back outside, they sat at a patio table, overlooking the rain-swept tarmac. The pit in his stomach deepened, and his rising blood pressure was approaching a boiling point.

"Where's my ride?"

The crew chief picked up his phone and clicked open Flight Tracker. "Looks like they're about ten minutes out. Care for a cup of coffee?"

Ethan huffed. "I can wait. Thanks."

"Suit yourself. I'm ordering one."

A couple minutes later, a sharply dressed attendant brought a steaming cup of coffee. The aroma made Ethan instantly regret his decision. He needed something to shake the weariness clouding his judgment.

He looked up just as the landing lights of an arriving aircraft appeared beneath the low-hanging clouds.

"There's your ride, Mr. Dawson," the crew chief said,

standing up. "Should be a lot more comfortable than the Blackhawk. Quieter, too."

Ethan's attention was on the sleek Citation Latitude as it rolled gracefully onto the tarmac. The soft whine of its jets slowly spinning down was a far cry from the deafening roar he'd grown used to.

He slowly got to his feet. *Are they sending me to the lion's den in the lap of luxury? Who in the nation's capital is aware of my pending arrival?* He hated the thought of being without a weapon.

They waited beneath the canopy until the aircraft door opened, and the stairs lowered.

"Have a great trip, Mr. Dawson," the crew chief said, extending his hand. "It's been a pleasure."

Ethan hesitated. The man's face showed no malice, just professionalism. He was just doing his job. The real problem lay with whoever was pulling the strings.

Ethan clasped his hand firmly. "Thanks for your hospitality. Stay safe."

Then he stepped out into the rain. The umbrella did little in the blowing rain. He splashed through shallow puddles, as he quickly crossed the tarmac. He took the steps two at a time and ducked into the jet.

A professionally dressed young lady greeted him at the door.

"Welcome aboard, Mr. Dawson. I'm First Officer Laney. Would you care for a beverage?"

"Nice to meet you. Don't happen to have a fresh cup of coffee?" Ethan asked as he settled into a soft leather seat.

"No problem." She opened the galley and popped in a pod. Soon, the rich scent of brewing coffee mingled with new leather and cleaning solution.

"We'll be out of here shortly," she added. "Just waiting on two more passengers."

Ethan tensed. Who else was on this flight? No doubt a handler and his backup.

For now, he'd enjoy the coffee and watch the fuel truck servicing the aircraft in the rain.

Five minutes later, a dark SUV pulled up to the jet. Two men jumped out, shielding themselves against the rain.

Ethan stiffened. No way… He couldn't tell. As the first man stuck his head through the door, Ethan knew his attitude was about to change.

"Good to see you have recovered," Steven said. "Any lingering dizziness?"

"Not until you showed up. Didn't think the Colonel would be reckless enough to make you my handler."

Steven slid into the seat across from Ethan. The second man stepped in behind him and removed his hat.

"I don't," said Colonel Whitlock, his voice carrying quiet authority. He gave a nod and dropped into the seat across the aisle. "That's why I'm tagging along."

The increasing whine of the turbines interrupted the awkward silence. Ethan sipped his coffee and eyed the men across from him. He had four and a half hours to turn this hostile situation into something productive.

He trusted Steven. But the lack of transparency was taking its toll.

I'm not even sure I have a dog in this fight. But they do. And they're not telling me everything.

As the jet taxied towards the runway, small talk filled the cabin between Ethan and Steven. Colonel Whitlock reclined, eyes shut, silent.

Ethan, knowing what was to come, got tired of the small talk and folded his arms. Steven nodded at his boss, smiled, and crossed his arms.

The Mexican standoff was on.

The pilot advanced the throttles to the takeoff detent, and the autothrottle took over. The twin Pratt Whitney engines spooled up creating a deep muffled roar as they accelerated down the runway. The whine of the bypass fans intensified as the aircraft rotated, and the periodic light bumps of the runway disappeared and they transitioned into a smooth steep climb.

Ethan felt a fog press in on his mind. He opened the overhead vent. The hiss of air hit his face and he leaned back and shut his eyes.

I'm not ready to play their game.

Ten minutes later, he opened his eyes and found himself staring at the moving map behind Steven's head. He looked over the Sierra Mountains depicted on the map. Somewhere out there was Charlotte Lake. According to the map their flight path took them directly over the mountain community.

His gaze drifted out the window. Jagged snow-covered peaks reached up at them. He tried to find the lake, but they were frozen and buried beneath the snow. Somewhere, nestled amongst the wilderness was a home. In that home was a family that owned his heart.

It was almost four. The girls would be home from school, probably gathered around the kitchen table, doing homework. Jonah was either irritating his sisters or playing with his toys on the rug. And Krystal…

His chest constricted. She'd be keeping the girls focused, and fixing dinner.

His eyes stung. He shut them again and tried to breathe.

I can't do this. He laid back in his seat and struggled to steady his breathing and rein in his thoughts.

He did what he knew Krystal would want him to do. He prayed. Was it selfish? Probably, as he wanted to wake up from this bad dream and find himself in the cabin.

He had let Krystal down, and now he was just a couple small flashing lights climbing higher above the mountains, slowly moving east in the star saturated sky.

"I will do whatever you want, God. But, please let me return to Charlotte Lake." Ethan whispered.

"What did you say?"

Ethan opened his eyes. Steven was watching him.

"Did I say something?"

"You mumbled something, but I was half asleep and didn't catch it."

"Probably for the best. We need to talk."

Steven nodded and pulled a small notepad from his backpack. He scribbled a message and slid it across the glossy mahogany table. Ethan picked up the note and glanced at Colonel Whitlock. His eyes were closed and mouth open.

Pay attention, my friend. You are intentionally being kept in the dark. I talked them into letting me stay in Washington as your backup, but you're not supposed to know. Keep your head. Do what you're trained to do.

Ethan looked up, eyebrows raised. He jotted a reply.

Kept in the dark. Why?

Steven glanced at the Colonel and scribbled.

There are informants inside the agency. We need to insure you have zero knowledge to what's going on. It's a security firewall for the organization per chance you get caught. Hope you understand.

Ethan's jaw clenched. He scribbled one more note.

Of course, I understand. I'm dispensable. Thanks, friend.

He slid the note back to Steven and looked out the window, past the curved-up wingtip, staring into the darkening sky.

Chapter Six

Thirty minutes after the wheels had left the runway, they had leveled off at flight level four-five-zero and were halfway across Nevada. Ethan and Steven were casually reminiscing about their time in Afghanistan. It wasn't until the captain made his way back through the cabin that Colonel Whitlock stirred.

Stretching and looking around the cabin, he finally spoke. "Maybe it's time we got down to business." He rose and made his way to the galley.

Steven glanced at Ethan with a chuckle. "Sir, we've got it under control. Bring me back a Dr. Pepper?"

When the Colonel returned, he opened up his table, brightened the overhead lights, and pulled a file out of his pack. "Ethan, did you bring the laptop we gave you?"

"Was I supposed to?" Ethan said dryly, already planning on ranting about its worthlessness. He was interrupted by the captain returning from the lavatory.

"Evening gentlemen. Should be a good flight all the way to Washington National. Anything you need?"

"Just a little privacy." Colonel Whitlock said his scowl unmistakable.

The captain raised an eyebrow. "Of course, sir. We'll be up front if you need us."

Steven gave the Colonel a side glance. "You could use a lesson or two in human decency, unless you plan on landing this plane."

The Colonel didn't respond. Ethan reached behind his seat, pulled out the laptop, and slid it onto the table in front of Whitlock. "Might be worth something if you'd unlocked the internet access."

Whitlock's scowl faded into a grin. "We're not doing that. You're officially dead to the world. One wrong search and the hounds will be barking up your tree. We cannot let that happen. Let's run the program."

He handed the laptop over to Steven.

Steven opened the laptop and waited for it to boot.

"There's a lot more on here than you're aware of. You've been kept in the dark for your protection." He connected a wireless mouse.

Ethan rolled his eyes. "My protection or yours?"

Steven just arched an eyebrow, then tapped a few keys and spun the laptop towards Ethan. "There you go. Unlocked and ready."

The screen displayed a half-dozen icons. None were familiar.

Steven clicked one, a window opened, displaying lines of data. "This is the program you'll be installing on the FBI mainframe."

Ethan tried to read the data but it didn't make sense. "Is this encrypted?"

Steven tapped a couple more keys and watched as additional windows opened. "I guess you could say that. It's in a format that the main frame will accept. You don't need to know what it says. You only need to know how you're going to get it in the system."

Ethan leaned forward trying to see what was coming up on the screen. A prompt appeared. *Activate device.*

"Ethan, let me see your left hand." Reaching over, Steven flipped the pad of Ethan's left hand just below the thumb. "Now watch."

The busy wheel spun briefly before confirming. *Device connected.*

Ethan pulled back, his eyes narrowing. He looked at his hand and then back to the laptop. Messaging the pad on his hand he frowned. Then shock turned to anger.

"What audacity do you have inserting a chip in my hand? What kind of a friend does that? When did you pull this stunt?"

Steven raised his hands. "Cool down. It's not all bad. There was no way you were going to get into the FBI headquarters with a thumb drive. This is the only way." He pointed to the mouse. "The agency uses these. Your chip will pair with the receiver. Right now, we need to upload the program to it."

He typed a few commands. The progress wheel started spinning.

"Can't feel a thing, can you?" Steven grinned.

Ethan glared. "You violated my body. How about I put something unauthorized in your brain? Something in the nine-millimeter range." His eyes cut to Colonel Whitlock. "Was this your brilliant idea?"

Steven gave Ethan a strained smile as Whitlock just shrugged and turned to look out the window into the darkness.

Typical, Ethan thought. Avoiding accountability.

He slumped back against the seat, closing his eyes. His thoughts were a storm of betrayal and disbelief. They knew he would never approve of the chip. When did they do it? He opened his eyes, staring at Steven.

"So, that night at the medical unit... it wasn't necessary?"

Steven showed his resignation and straight lined his smile. "Don't blame the doctor. He was under orders. The chip isn't dangerous and can be removed once the mission's over."

"If I make it out." Ethan's voice was tight. "There's a good chance I won't leave headquarters alive."

"That's being a little pessimistic," Steven said gently. "I, for one, am confident you'll succeed. Let's go over the ingress and egress plan. It's complex, and you can't take notes. You'll be searched, and we can't risk anything compromising the mission."

— • ⬤ • —

For the next ninety minutes, Steven and Colonel Whitlock walked Ethan through the plan, step by step. No detail was spared. Ethan listened, asked questions, mentally mapping out the plan. When they finished, he repeated back the instructions with precision.

Whitlock nodded at Steven, who pulled a manila envelope from his pack. "This is your identification pack."

He slid a badge across the table. Ethan picked it up and studied the photo. It was him in a navy-blue blazer, white shirt, top button undone. A genuine smile softened his otherwise hard features.

"When was this taken?"

"It wasn't. It was created," Steven said. "With the right program, anything can appear real. You notice the hazel eyes?"

"Should I to assume you have color-enhancing contacts?" Ethan asked.

Steven nodded, pulling out a small box. "Right here. Also, gray hair dye. You're going to be ten years older for a couple of days. Think you can act like it?"

"If it helps, I sure feel ten years older."

Ethan eyed the items. "Do I get a professional makeup

artist?"

Steven smirked. "Not a chance. We don't need additional people involved,"

He held up the contact lenses. "You need to wear these all the time you are in the building. They're engineered to pass iris recognition in the sublevel passageways. The I.D. will match that of a software engineer who has access to that department."

"What happens if he shows up while I'm there?" Ethan asked.

"The system won't accept duplicate iris patterns. If he's in there, you will not gain entrance. It could raise red flags and possibly lock out further access. It would be best to check his schedule prior to reaching that level."

Just another thing to remember. Ethan shut his eyes and tried to picture the layout of the headquarters. "And how am I going to find the schedule?"

Steven glanced at Colonel Whitlock for an answer, only to find him snoozing. Steven shook his head and brought up the map. "The easiest, yet most dangerous, is to ask the attendant at the entrance desk. Your iris double is Keegan Garland. If he's there, just make your way out the building via a different exit and come back later."

Ethan leaned back and crossed his arms. "Where will you two be while I'm committing treason?"

Colonel Whitlock snorted awake. "It's none of your business. Whatever it is, it won't involve getting caught. Best you don't know." He stood up and headed for the lavatory.

Ethan watched the door close behind him. "If that latrine had an ejection seat, this ride would be a lot more enjoyable."

Steven laughed. "He's not always that grumpy. A lot's riding on this. Successfully complete the mission, and you'll find one happy Colonel. I'll be nearby."

Ethan reclined his seat and turned off the overhead light.

A hand on his shoulder woke him. Ethan blinked, stretching.

"We've started our descent. The captain said we have about ten minutes before we need to fasten our seat belts."

Ethan headed to the lavatory, splashing cold water on his face. The flight barely five hours, felt more like twenty. Was it the flying or the weight of what lay ahead? He wasn't sure. All he knew was that he needed sleep before heading into the belly of the beast.

Back in his seat, he gazed out the window. The soft glow of the nation's capital flickered between the clouds. The moving map showed that they were following the Potomac River to the airport. As they descended beneath the clouds, the National Mall came into view, stretching toward the Capital, with the Washington Monument standing tall across the Tidal Basin. A gentle turn aligned them with the runway. Everything seemed to accelerate, the ground, the fear, the mission. As the engines reversed their thrust, Ethan took a long breath and let it out slowly.

The Citation came to a stop and the jet engines wound down with a high-pitched whine.

"Well, Ethan, it looks like your ride's here." Colonel Whitlock extended his hand. "We will be monitoring your progress. If all goes well, we'll see you back at camp."

Ethan firmly gripped Whitlock's hand, meeting his gaze with unwavering intensity. "If I make it back, I expect more than a shipping container for lodging."

"That depends on your attitude," Whitlock replied with a smirk.

Ethan shook his head. "That really makes me want to come back."

He dropped Whitlock's hand, nodded to Steven, and descended the steps.

The icy wind cut through him, urging him towards the black SUV waiting off the wing. Without hesitation, he slid into the back seat, shutting the door.

The driver pulled away without a word. Ethan glanced back at the plane, just in time to see Steven heading for the hangar and the aircraft door closing.

Why does everything have to be a mystery?

Chapter Seven

Ethan tried to get his bearings, but with the SUV's constant turns from one road unto another, he was totally disoriented. A few minutes later, they crossed the Potomac River, and the Washington Memorial came into view on his left. As they passed the National Mall and the Treasury Building, the driver made a right turn. A few blocks later, they pulled into the Grand Hyatt Hotel.

Well, this beats the shipping container, Ethan thought.

As the SUV came to a stop, the driver handed Ethan an envelope. "Sir, this is your key. Go straight to the elevator-eighth floor. Enjoy your stay here in D.C."

Ethan stepped into the lobby, too tired to appreciate the grandeur of the soaring atrium. He did as the driver instructed, taking the elevator to the eighth floor. On the way up, he opened the envelope and retrieved the key card, checking the room number. He was struggling, exhaustion weighing him down. He knew better than to make any life-altering decision without a good night's sleep.

Inside the room, he dropped his backpack and collapsed onto the mattress.

———•●•———

They were screaming across the sky. Low enough that Ethan could make out details in the early morning haze. The horizon off the wing swayed wildly, the aircraft lurching in an unsettling rhythm. It was obvious the pilot no longer had control.

The ground was coming into sharp focus, rushing up far too fast.

Is this how my life is going to end?

He looked toward the cockpit. The flight crew worked feverishly, their faces tight with fear. The intercom crackled.

"Prepare to crash."

What a message to give your passengers. The people who trusted you with their lives, and now you're letting them down.

Ethan leaned back in his seat, surprisingly calm.

Oh Well, he thought. It's been a good life.

His mind turned to his wife and daughters, brutally murdered. Sadness was followed by a flicker of peace.

It's a good thing I put my faith in Jesus. I'll be seeing them soon.

A piercing light filled the sky, growing brighter by the second. It streaked toward the aircraft, impossibly fast, before erupting into the cabin with an explosive brilliance.

———•●•———

Ethan jolted awake, his breath ragged, heart pounding. Morning sunlight flooded the room through the open drapes. His shoulders tensed at the sight of the flashing light on the hotel phone. He hesitated before picking up the phone and pressing the message button.

A computerized voice crackled through the speaker. "You have four new messages. First message, 6:45 a.m."

"Ethan, this is Steven. Meet me down in the Cabinet in fifteen minutes. They've got a great buffet."

Twenty minutes later, "Where are you?"

Ten minutes after that, "It's important, Ethan. Don't stand me up."

The last message came about fifteen minutes ago. "Okay, my friend. You win. Get here as soon as you can. I'll stay until you do."

Ethan shrugged and decided to take a shower.

— • ● • —

Half an hour later, the host escorted Ethan to Steven's table. He was nursing a cup of coffee.

"I was about to call out the search and rescue dogs," Steven said. "Did you have a good night's sleep?"

"The mattress was comfortable," Ethan said, scanning the room for the buffet. "What are you doing here? I thought you'd be fluffing your pillow in California by now."

"I should be, but someone thinks you need babysitting. They don't know you like I do." Steven motioned for the waiter. "Good thing I stayed. I came across some pertinent information this morning. Not gonna make you happy."

Ethan returned with a plate stacked with protein. "Let's hear it."

"They're expecting you. They don't know your name or what you look like, but they know someone's coming," Steven made air quotes. "A 'reliable source' tipped them off. They believe someone is trying to infiltrate their mainframe from the outside. They're reinforcing firewalls and pulling in extra resources to protect their data files."

Ethan's eyes narrowed as he chewed on a slice of bacon. "And that's supposed to ruin my day? Isn't our mission just copying files?"

Steven fidgeted, a sign of something deeper was coming.

"Yes… and no. It's true we are retrieving FBI data, but there are other commands embedded in the program. Let's just say, they're not so… passive."

Ethan put his fork down and crossed his arms. "We're not inserting a virus, are we? Because if that's the case, I'm out. I'm not destroying the nation's intelligence infrastructure."

"Simmer down, brother." Steven held up his hands. "We're not destroying anything. One command opens a portal for our organization to access the system. Our mission is to protect U.S. citizens from tyrants and cartels. To do this effectively, we need the latest intel. Setting up our own network takes time and resources we don't have. So, we're piggy backing on theirs."

Ethan chewed thoughtfully. "Why not just ask for a portal? Why the spy act?"

"They don't know we exist. At least, not officially. There are rumors, but no paper trail. We want to keep it that way. A long-distance relationship, if you know what I mean?"

"Of course. Will this patch trigger any alarms?"

"No idea. It's a stealth coding, should appear like an authorized update. But I'm not a software engineer. If it does, you'll know."

"Great. Then what? Throw my hands up and hope for mercy? Five to ten for breaking and entering, and another ten for tampering with government property. Thanks, brother. If this is the easy part, what about the other command?"

"It erases your digital tracks," Steven said, shrugging. But the twitch in his cheek betrayed his unease.

"Nothing at all to worry about. Sure. What's my ingress time?"

Steven looked at his watch, "Same as planned. Just… be

ready to get out of town fast. The entire intelligence community will be looking for you." Steven stood. "Good luck, my friend."

Without another word, he left.

Ethan stared at his half-finished breakfast. Suddenly, he wasn't hungry anymore.

<hr>

Back in the room, Ethan organized his backpack. He would not be taking it with him to the headquarters, but he wanted it ready for a quick departure. Dropping it off at the front desk, he was assured that they would keep it secure.

The sidewalks along 10th Street were filled with federal workers and tourists, some gawking, others hurrying along. Ethan maintained the casual pace of someone on their way to work. Dressed in khakis and a navy-blue blazer, his identification badge swung from a lanyard. He would soon find out if it worked.

Fifteen minutes later, he passed through the concrete planters, clearly there to protect against vehicles. He nodded at the security guards like he belonged. Inside, he pulled off his gloves and approached the reception desk.

A middle-aged lady looked up and smiled. "Good morning, may I help you?"

Ethan glanced at her badge. "Good morning, Beth. Has Keegan Garland arrived yet? He hasn't replied to my text."

Beth looked at her screen. "Looks like he got called out on a last-minute trip. He won't be back until tomorrow. Anything else I can help you with, Mr. ...?"

"Sorry, I should have introduced myself." Ethan lifted his badge. "Ted Dillon. Temporary detail from the west coast. Thought Keegan and I could get together and catch up on life. Thanks. Maybe you could just point me to the conference room."

Beth gave directions. He nodded politely and thanked her again. Security scanned his I.D. and waved him through. He hummed "It is well" as he moved along the typical sterile government building corridor.

At the elevator, he pushed the down button and stepped aside. The first elevator opened, revealing two agents deep in conversation. He waved them off and waited. The next one was empty.

Holding his badge to the reader, he pressed "B" for the subterranean level. A green light flashed. The elevator jerked into motion, starting down. Ethan breathed a sigh of relief.

The muted hum of fans greeted Ethan in the cool, empty hallway. He briefly shut his eyes, visualizing the map in his head. Turning right, he soon reached a locked door with an iris scanner.

Ethan blinked his eyes a couple times, hoping the hazel contacts had stayed in place. Leaning in, he stared at the scanner.

"Access Denied" lit up in bold red letters.

His chest tightened. What was the backup plan? Could he have been set up. Was Keegan really out of town?

Ethan blinked again, glancing nervously down the hallway. He noticed the security cameras looking at him. It wouldn't take long before someone questioned his legitimacy. One more try.

Blinking to moisten the contacts, he stared into the scanner. Time seemed to freeze. He heard the sound of footsteps echoing down the hallway. He only had a few seconds.

"Come on."

Click. A green check mark appeared.

Letting out a sigh, Ethan slipped in and let the heavy steel door softly close behind him. Holding the handle to prevent it from slamming, he waited until he heard the soft click of the lock reengaging. Pressing his ear against the door, he listened intently as his heart pounded in his chest. The footsteps rapidly approached and then faded down the hallway.

He flipped a switch and surveyed the room. It matched the briefing. He pulled up a rickety office chair and slid up to the monitor. It was definitely last decade's model.

He was relieved to see that even though the computer was old, the mouse had been updated. He picked it up, looking it over. Sliding the toggle switch to on he ran it across the desk until the screen came alive.

A login window appeared asking for his username and password.

He looked at his left hand, shrugged, and gave it a hard flick.

Just like on his laptop a wheel started turning and a few moments later, he was logged in.

Chapter Eight

It took ten seconds for the system to synchronize the requested files with the chip buried in Ethan's hand. He didn't know how long he had before alarms rang, but he had a couple of questions of his own.

Typing his name, he pulled up a large file. Hundreds of pages, but he only cared about one thing. The people behind his family's murder.

He scrolled through the list, finding the answer.

The kingpin was retired, living in the Poconos. He had been apprehended but was released due to lack of evidence. Ethan recognized the picture of the retired congressman.

Ethan's blood boiled. *This man is living in peace while I'm running for my life. If I could just get my hands around his neck…*

Wait a minute. You're not supposed to have these feelings. You've changed. Haven't you?

His shoulders dropped and he looked around. He didn't have time to read more, but he would take the file.

He hit the copy button and then paused. *Why am I leaving this here? It's an opportunity of a lifetime.* Backing up, he hit cut. Navigating to the chip's active memory, he pasted the file. The transfer wheel spun.

A strange sensation crossed his mind. He felt as if all the wrongs he had done were being injected into his body. A weird feeling for sure.

When the wheel stopped, he quickly searched Charlotte Lake. Another massive file. The same thing. Cut. Paste. Another spinning wheel. Most likely, there was a backup somewhere, but maybe it would slow down the interference.

Once the wheel stopped turning, Ethan clicked on the Motor Pool icon, scheduling an agency vehicle. Then he checked out a sniper rifle, a 9mm handgun, and a small supply of ammunition. He requested it be in his vehicle.

He blinked when a message popped up. Ready in 10 minutes.

Ethan flicked the chip in his hand. The connection severed. So far, so good.

He shut off the light. Stepped into the hallway and almost collided with a young man.

"Sir, that's a restricted area. Could I see you identification?"

Ethan glanced at the man's badge. "Who are you, and what gives you the authority to question my access? Only a few of us have access to this area, and I don't think you're one of them." Ethan briefly lifted his badge, not giving the young man time to read it.

"Sir, I'm Keegan Garland. I do have access. Now, if you want to come back in there and show me what you were up to, I would appreciate it."

"Good to meet you, Mr. Garland. I would love to chat, but I have a car waiting. You have a nice day."

Ethan didn't wait for a response. He walked calmly down the hallway, resisting the urge to run.

Two minutes later, he stepped into the garage, where an attendant stood in front of a gray sedan.

"Mr. Dillon, I assume?" the attendant asked.

Ethan said nothing, simply holding up his badge.

"Great. It's all ready. The sniper rifle is in the trunk with the ammo, and the 9mm in the glove compartment with two clips. Have a great day and stay safe."

Ethan took the keys and nodded a silent thank-you before slipping into the driver's seat. Wasting no time, he started the car and made for the exit.

As he approached the exit, his pulse quickened. A security arm extended across the exit, and a guard was motioning him to stop.

Had the alarm been sounded? Do they know who I am?

He forced himself to stay calm, slowing the car and rolling down the window.

The guard leaned down and looked into the car. "Sir, may I see your I.D.?"

"Of course." Ethan lifted his badge for the guard to see.

"Could you remove it, please?" the guard asked, his voice faltering. "We've had a security breach, and I'm required to run checks on anyone leaving the facility. It won't take long"

Ethan's mind raced, "Certainly. Please hurry. There's a situation developing north of town, and I need to get there before it blows up. You understand?"

His voice carried a balance of authority and impatience.

The guard nodded. "Got it, Mr. Dillon, I'll hurry."

Ethan watched intently as the guard's eyes darted back and forth between his badge and a computer screen.

The guard's raised eyebrows told a story Ethan did not

want to hear. When the guard picked up the phone, Ethan knew it was time to act.

Ethan shifted the car into gear, his heart pounding. The moment the guard nodded and his right hand dropped to his holstered weapon, Ethan slammed his foot on the gas.

The sedan surged forward, slamming through the gate.

Almost immediately, Ethan was on the street, tires squealing, as he made a sharp left turn. He sped past two parked police cars, relieved to see they were unoccupied. Without slowing down, he careened through a red light and made a hard right turn onto Pennsylvania Avenue, narrowly avoiding oncoming traffic. His focus sharpened. He had to escape.

A hundred yards down the road, he jerked the wheel right onto 11th Street, the tires screeching as they struggled to maintain traction. *I might be able to get away, but not in this car,* Ethan thought grimly. This sedan was a liability in a town crawling with law enforcement. Dumping it out in the open would be suicide. He searched for a parking garage.

Weaving through traffic, Ethan created chaos, cars honking and tires skidding to avoid collisions. Sirens echoed in the distance, but no flashing lights in his rear-view mirror. Four blocks up 11th Street, he passed the Grand Hyatt. Have to get my backpack.

Crossing H Street, he spotted an underground parking garage and whipped into the entrance. He pulled the ticket and anxiously waited for the gate to raise. He needed to make sure not to draw attention.

The parking garage was nearly full, but after a tense search, he spotted an empty handicap spot and pulled in.

For a moment, he sat in silence, his white knuckles still gripping the steering wheel and his chest heaving.

Ethan grabbed the 9mm and the clips from the glove box, sliding them into his blazer. He hopped out, the sound of approaching sirens filling the parking garage. The wailing grew louder, coming up 11th Street. A cruiser flew past the entrance. He knew, however, it was only a matter of time.

He pulled the sniper case and ammo from the trunk, taking the stairs to the street level. The seconds ticked down as he stood at the crosswalk, his intense focus watching for trouble. Another cruiser flew by. The light changed and Ethan walked across H Street to the Grand Hyatt.

The host looked up and smiled. "Ready for your backpack, Mr. Dawson."

Ethan's stomach tightened, but he forced a polite nod. "Yes, thank you."

With his backpack slung over one shoulder and the gun case in hand, he scanned the street.

Across the way, a tour bus. Ethan joined the line of passengers waiting to slide their luggage into the compartments. He gave the driver the gun case, and boarded the bus with his backpack over his shoulder.

Finding a seat in the back, he transferred the handgun to his backpack and stuffed the blazer under the seat. Digging into his backpack he pulled out a light-weight jacket, blending in with the tourists.

The door closed.

Ethan's chest was tight as he nervously looked up and down the sidewalk. Sirens were blaring as a police car sped by. Uniformed policemen were coming towards the bus on the sidewalk. He had to hide. But, where? All he could do was slouch down in his seat and look the other way. It looked like the officers were moving in the direction of the bus. What am I going to do?

A door slammed and a passenger passed by returning to his seat.

The restroom!

Ethan stood, backpack in hand, and ducked into the cramped latrine. Whoa, it sure didn't smell great, but maybe it would keep him out of jail.

He didn't know how long he waited. Four, maybe five minutes. He had no idea what was going on outside the door, but finally the bus started moving. He waited until the bus stopped for a minute and then started up again. They must be past the first stop light.

Ethan cracked the door and peeked out.

No sirens. No cops.

He slid back in his seat.

They crossed the mall and the Capital building stood large on the left. Shortly, they took the ramp onto 395.

Ethan's breath finally eased.

He didn't know where the bus was going. He didn't care.

Anywhere was better than here.

His head slumped against the window, and before long, exhaustion pulled him under.

Chapter Nine

Ethan stirred as he became aware that the bus had stopped. Subconsciously, he registered the sound of passengers disembarking. Stretching and opening his eyes, he noticed the bus was half empty. He sat alone at the back.

I guess we're getting off here… Wherever here is.

He stared out the window, searching for a clue. Fairfield Inn. But what town?

Didn't matter.

He grabbed his backpack and joined the others heading for the exit.

A woman with a clipboard stood outside, greeting each passenger, checking names, and handing out room keys. Ethan perked up.

This could get interesting.

When her eyes met his, she paused, looked at her clipboard, then back at him. "I can't for the life of me remember your name."

Ethan offered a disarming smile. "Ethan Dawson, ma'am. Is there a problem?"

She frowned, flipping through several pages. "You're

not on my list. Do you have your itinerary?"

Ethan's mind raced. Time to improvise. He furrowed his brow, exhaled deeply, and feigned confusion.

"Did I get on the wrong bus? We are heading for Stroudsburg, right?"

Her eyes widened. "Oh my goodness, no. This is Lancaster, Pennsylvania. I don't know how I missed you. I'm so sorry."

She was clearly on the verge of a meltdown.

Ethan softened his tone, switching from potential villain to misunderstood victim. "Well, I suppose it's not your fault. I just need to find a way to the Stroudsburg." He checked his watch. "I don't suppose there's a bus heading that way?"

She shook her head, visibly distressed. "There aren't any buses going that direction. You would have to go into Philadelphia and catch the train. I don't know what we're going to do."

Ethan shrugged casually. "Well, that's a real mess. I guess I'll have to rent a car and drive up in the morning. Just have to find a place to spend the night."

Her face brightened. "We can help you with that! We had two cancellations, so I still have a couple of rooms." She handed him a key. "I am so sorry, sir. If there's anything else you need, please don't hesitate to ask."

Ethan looked at the key and had a thought. "Those cancellations wouldn't have left behind some meal vouchers, would they?"

"Oh, of course! I hadn't thought of that." She rummaged through her clip board and pulled out a couple of meal tickets. "Here you go. These are for the Longhorn Steakhouse and IHOP. Oh, our group is also going to the Sight and Sound Theater tonight, if you would like to join us."

Ethan felt he had pushed their hospitality as far as he should. "Thank you for the offer. Tempting, but I need to get some rest. Big day tomorrow."

He slung his backpack over his shoulder, grabbed the case containing the sniper rifle, and walked into the hotel.

* * *

Ethan wanted nothing more than to collapse on the bed, but there was work to do.

He booted up the laptop and tried to connect to the internet. No luck. After thirty minutes of trying to bypass the block, he gave up.

He opened the secure app, flicked the implanted chip in his left hand. The transfer wheel spun, and a file window popped open. He transferred all the data from the chip to the laptop. With the transfer completed, he started sifting through the remaining files. Something didn't add up.

Why would there be more than just the access and cover programs?

He scrolled through the directory, scrutinizing each file. About halfway down, a word in the syntax stopped him cold. Tracking.

No way. Why didn't I think of this sooner?

Ethan rubbed the chip beneath the skin on his hand. Can I even remove it? The thought made him wince.

It'll hurt, but it has to come out.

* * *

Ethan picked up the phone and ordered a taxi. After washing his face, he pulled on his coat and grabbed some cash from the bottom of his backpack.

Outside, tourists milled around, filling the streets, eager to get a glimpse of the Amish lifestyle.

Ten minutes later, Ethan walked into Walmart for the

first time in over a year. He hated the place. Too many people, too little awareness. As he moved through the aisles towards electronics, the anxiety in his chest climbed. Every camera felt like it was aimed at him.

He waited impatiently at the counter while an associate activated his new phone.

Then he swung by the crafts aisle for an Exacto knife and the pharmacy for bandages and hydrogen peroxide.

He waited another fifteen minutes for the taxi. For a moment, he considered using one of those steak house vouchers. But no, every minute counted. He had to get it done.

***

Back at the hotel, Ethan sat at the desk with the lamp close, illuminating his hand. A damp washcloth lay beside the sterilized knife and tweezers.

He poured hydrogen peroxide over the soft pad of his left hand. Taking a deep breath, he clenched his teeth and made the first cut.

The razor-sharp blade sliced through his skin. Blood welled up instantly as he worked the tweezers into the incision, hunting for the tiny chip. Pain radiated up his arm as his fingers cramped.

Finally, the rice-sized chip slid free. He set it on the cloth.

The incision, barely a quarter of an inch, was deep and angry. It stung when he rinsed it with the hydrogen peroxide and applied the bandage. It would take a few days to heal, but the foreign object was out.

Later, Ethan pulled on his coat and headed out for dinner.

Outside the Longhorn Steakhouse, two Amish horse-drawn buggies were tied to a hitching post. He reached into his coat pocket and pulled out a tissue. Inside was the microchip.

Glancing around to make sure no one was watching, he walked to one of the buggies, opened a small storage box in the rear, and dropped the chip inside.

He stepped back, brushing his hands against his coat.

Whatever the FBI's capabilities, they're now following a slow-moving target headed deep into the countryside.

The sun had set by the time Ethan walked out of the steak house. The buggies were gone. Colonel Whitlock's team would be tracking the wrong man.

Back at the hotel, he stopped by the business center and opened a web browser. For five minutes, he just sat there staring at the home page.

Do I really want to do this?

He had everything he needed on his laptop. It wasn't like he could call Krystal.

His offshore accounts crossed his mind, but he had enough cash for now. No need to trigger any red flags.

What he needed was a ride to the Poconos. A rental car was out without a major credit card. Uber was his only option.

He installed the app on his phone, added his prepaid card, and requested a pickup first thing in the morning. A woman by the name of Beth accepted the request.

Now, for a place to stay. A few clicks later he found a vacation rental in the Poconos within walking distance of his target. The word target made him pause.

Do I really want to do this? Should I be doing this? What does it mean to be a changed man? I'm still a soldier. I still need to protect the innocent.

He started justifying his plan, determining he wasn't doing it for revenge, but that it would make the world safer.

Safer for who?

He shut out his conscience and scrolled through current events. After scanning a dozen headlines, he concluded that the world would be better off without constant noise.

It was time to rest.

At the front desk, he waited to purchase a bottle of water. The host was on the phone getting annoyed with someone. Ethan almost choked when the host told the caller that Ethan Dawson was not registered at the hotel.

They must have pinged the tracker earlier. Was it safe to stay? Are they watching the hotel now? Should I get out of here tonight?

He considered leaving right then, but decided against it. They were already chasing the decoy. He just needed to stay alert.

And besides, he was tired.

Thankfully, the room was under someone else's name.

Chapter Ten

Ethan woke early. He needed to spend some time on the treadmill before breakfast. An hour later, soaked with sweat, he hit the shower. The workout left him invigorated, and he found himself looking forward to breakfast.

He checked the time and decided to go through his backpack. Every ounce he could shed was that much less he had to carry. Dumping everything out on the bed, he started sorting and repacking. A few items were no longer needed for the mission, so he set them aside.

Then he picked up a small, round, white object, about a quarter-inch thick. What the…? He turned it over. An apple symbol was printed on the face. Realization dawned. It was an AirTag.

They weren't just tracing him with a microchip. Someone had planted this in his pack. But who? The FBI was after him, sure, but they wouldn't have had the opportunity. Most likely, it was Colonel Whitlock's team. They needed to keep him in their sights. Eventually, he would reconnect with them, but for now, he had other plans. The one consolation, whoever it was, they likely wanted him alive.

He pulled back the corner of the drapes and froze. His worst nightmare was unfolding in real time. Three dark blue SUVs were pulling into the parking lot. They had found him.

Snatching his backpack and rifle case, Ethan headed out the door for the back stairs. He had two minutes, maybe less, before they would surround the place. He took the steps three at a time, exiting out the back and sprinting across the parking lot to the dumpsters. Hidden in the shadows, he crouched low, watching as one SUV crept around the building and stopped near the rear exit.

The tinted windows hid the occupants. Hopefully, they were focused on the hotel exit. Ethan crawled through the brush, dragging the rifle case behind him, working his way up the hill. At the top, he reached a stone block wall surrounding the property. A glance back at the SUV confirmed he was still hidden.

He dropped the rifle case over the wall. The thud it made told him it was a long drop. He slowly removed his backpack and dropped it on top of the case.

Two men got out of the SUV. It wasn't the black ops group. It had to be FBI. He didn't want anything to do with them. How did they find him? He would have to be more diligent to not leave a trail.

Sliding over the wall, he dropped to the ground. He landed in a wooded area, well out of sight. Dusting himself off, he shouldered his pack, picked up the case, and moved out through the trees.

Casually, Ethan walked down the convention center driveway, crossed the street, and entered the IHOP. He was shaking and hungry.

He opened the Uber app and rescheduled his pickup for an hour earlier. That gave him thirty minutes to eat. Sitting at a booth with a clear view of the road, he ordered a high-protein breakfast and lingered over an extra cup of coffee.

Five minutes before his ride was due, he paid his bill.

Not seeing any action from the feds, he headed for the door. A maroon Honda Civic pulled up right on time. He slid into the back seat.

Beth, the driver, greeted him with a professional smile. "Not every day I get a trip this far. Looking forward to seeing the Poconos."

Ethan wasn't in the mood for conversation, but gave her a polite nod. "Thanks for your willingness to take me. There aren't many options for public transportation from here to Emerald Lakes."

Beth chatted briefly, mentioning how she was doing this part-time to help with her upcoming wedding. As they wound through the countryside and merged onto the state highway, the conversation faded. Ethan closed his eyes.

He thought of Kendra. They had saved for a year to afford a decent wedding. Her parents were dirt poor, and there was no way he and Kendra wanted to burden them with that expense. He missed her and their daughters more than he could bear. Would he ever have closure? Maybe once he drove the final nail in this coffin.

By noon, they crossed Interstate 80 and entered the Emerald Lakes community.

"Is this where you want to be dropped off?" Beth questioned, as they pulled up near the beach area.

Ethan nodded. He didn't want her knowing exactly where he was headed. "Yeah. It's too early to check in. I'll just walk to the house when it's ready.

Getting out of the car, he handed Beth a roll of bills. "Thanks for taking the time to bring me up here. Here's something to help you with your wedding. Have a safe trip home."

Her eyes widened. "Thank you so much. This really makes it worth it."

As Beth drove away with a smile, Ethan scanned the quiet surroundings. The area was deserted. It was off season and the place was pretty much vacated. A gust of cold wind blew in off the lake, making him shiver. He picked up his gear and set out.

Half an hour later he arrived at the vacation rental. It sat next to a small pond, with a deck stretching around the back. He punched in the access code. Finally, he could rest.

It looked small but had a full basement and all the essentials. It had to be busy in the summertime. For now, it was his refuge.

Downstairs, he kicked back on the couch with his laptop and opened up the FBI files. He wanted to read all of them, but his time was limited. He narrowed in on the documents concerning Congressman Eduard Adams. His gut churned. This was an emotional tsunami waiting to hit.

It didn't matter; he was committed to taking the guy out. It was playing on his conscience, but the hatred fermented in his thoughts was stronger than he allowed his conscience to overcome. He started reading.

Hours passed as he read. When he shut the laptop, darkness had fallen. Nothing he had seen changed his mind. The congressman had resigned after the ethics committee had brought charges against him. He had been indicted on a number of charges. Then, he flipped and was given witness protection status. He obviously had turned state evidence.

Rage welled up. This man, who by all visual evidence had ordered the murder of his family, was sitting comfortably in his home, with FBI protection.

That was about to change. Ethan would take care of business and then find a way back to Charlotte Lake.

The night was bitter. Ethan had assembled the Remington 700. He had no way to test the accuracy of the scope. The first shot would have to be the last shot.

His coat was hardly enough protection against the chilly fall night. Silently, he slipped into the woods behind the rental. It was only a five-hundred-yard hike through the dense landscape before he reached the road.

Fifty yards to the west, he found the entrance to the golf

course. The placard read, Eighteenth Hole. The final hole. How ironic.

He passed the tee box and veered into the hillside. Twenty minutes of slow deliberate movement brought him to a fallen log overlooking the target. Nestled down in the brush, he positioned himself behind the log for cover.

He had a clear view of the house. Through the glass patio doors, he saw a man in a recliner, reading.

That was his target, but he must verify. He couldn't risk killing the wrong person. After all, he wasn't a murderer. Just a soldier, delivering justice.

Turning on the night vision scope, he scanned the yard. All quiet. That would change as soon as he pulled the trigger.

He shut off the night vision capability and looked back through the scope into the house. The lights inside were bright, and the crosshairs centered on the congressman's chest. As long as the sites were aligned, this will be an easy shot.

He made a few adjustments for stability. Flipped off the safety.

Just as he exhaled and touched the trigger, two children darted into the frame.

What the..?

They ran to the man and climbed into his lap.

Ethan froze. Slowly, he raised the rifle barrel and re-engaged the safety.

He placed the rifle on the log and started shaking uncontrollably.

Sitting on the damp leaves, with his back up against the log, his chest pounded. The reality of what almost happened hit him like a freight train.

What if he had fired? At best, a grandfather would have been killed. At worst… a child.

Ethan's throat constricted as he silently screamed out to God as he fell face down in the leaves. "Why did you let me come here? Why did this almost happen? You know, God, that I am Yours. I am not even supposed to think of doing something like this. Take me home God. I no longer to deserve to live."

Face down in the leaves he sobbed until a howl of a coyote in the distance, interrupted his disparaging state of mind. Silence rolled over him like an incoming tidal wave as he rolled over.

Wet, snow landed on his face like a divine whisper. *I can make all things new.*

Ethan... you need to forgive the man who killed your family. You will never be at peace until you do.

He lifted his head, checked the safety, and again looked through the scope.

The man was still sitting in the chair with the two young girls. A woman, likely his wife, had joined them.

Ethan watched in silence, taking in the whole room before returning to the occupants. Staring at the Hallmark moment with a twist, he noticed a Bible sitting on the end table next to the congressman's chair.

Doubt sprung up as Ethan was hit with mixed feelings. Was it possible that this guy was a believer? How could a believer have done the things he had done?

A verse surfaced in Ethan's mind. "Be kind and compassionate to one another, forgiving each other, just as in Christ God forgave you."

His shoulders tensed. *Where did that come from?*

Then another. "For if you forgive other people when they sin against you, your heavenly Father will also forgive you. But if you do not forgive others their sins, your Father will not forgive your sins."

Ethan knew what he had to do.

He had no choice, it would not go away until he did.

Chapter Eleven

●

Thick snow was falling when Ethan arrived at his vacation rental. At least the snow would cover his tracks. Yet it did nothing to hide the scars on his heart. Only a serious, face-to-face act of forgiveness could heal that wound.

He asked God why it had to be so personal. There was no audible answer, but deep down, Ethan knew the truth. The burden he carried would not be lifted until he listened to what God was telling him. Tonight, he would pray about it. Pray that God might offer another way.

All night, Ethan tossed and turned, plagued with dreams of violence and screaming. Fragments of his past, fears of the future. Peace and joy had once been a part of his life, but those memories felt distant and hazy, clouded by years of pain.

At five o'clock, he gave up on sleep and crawled onto the treadmill. Exercise would clear his head, though it couldn't touch the deeper ache. An hour later, after a hot shower, he sat on the couch with the Bible Krystal had given him. This was the same Bible he had carried into the mountains last year, trying to escape his past. He ran his fingers over the cover before opening it to Matthew. He read through the Sermon on the Mount, letting the words of Jesus sink in.

Closing the Bible, Ethan shut his eyes and begged God for forgiveness. He prayed for protection, not from others, but from himself. As the minutes passed, a profound peace began to settle over him. The weight on his chest started to lift.

Just one more thing to do and I can go home.

When the sun rose, Ethan could see he would be making new tracks through six inches of snow. The roads hadn't been plowed, and with so few residents, he doubted they would be cleared anytime soon. He sighed, resigning himself to the truth, things don't always go as planned.

He stared at the rifle case by the door. It was now a liability. After some searching, he found a closet under the stairs filled with summer sports gear. He pulled everything out, shoved the rifle case into the back corner, and packed the gear tightly over it. No one would find it until summer.

• ● •

As he walked through woods towards Congressman Adam's house, Ethan's thoughts were conflicted. The 9mm handgun was hidden in the pocket of his coat. He had considered leaving it behind, but doubt had overpowered his faith. Not so much about the congressman, but because of the world. Too many times lately, he'd found himself in danger without the proper tools. At least that's what he told himself.

When he emerged from the woods onto Pinecrest Drive, Ethan was relieved to see it had been plowed. His pulse quickened as he neared the congressman's road. The house came into view, along with an SUV backing out of the driveway. Ethan stepped aside, his hand instinctively gripping the handgun. The young woman driving glanced his way and waved. He reluctantly waved back, noticing two toddlers strapped in the backseat.

He let out a breath he hadn't realized he had been holding.

Just as he was about to turn up the driveway, the side door opened. Congressman Adams stepped out, carrying a bag of trash. He spotted Ethan and waved.

"Good morning. Enjoying an early winter walk?" he asked as they met at the trash can by the street.

"Early winter, indeed." Ethan replied, voice calm though his hand still gripped the gun in his pocket. "Actually, I was on my way to see you. Do you have time to talk?"

The congressman's expression turned cautious as he extended his hand. "I suppose so. Do I know you?"

Ethan released his grip on the gun and extended his hand. "We haven't formally met. But I'm certain you've heard of me. I'm Ethan Dawson."

Adams froze, color draining from his face. His eyes darted nervously, scanning the empty street.

Ethan offered a disarming smile. "Sir, you don't need to be afraid. I am not here to harm you."

"I-I'm having trouble believing this. Ethan Dawson died in a helicopter crash in California. I saw the photos. The official report. So, who are you, really? A reporter?"

"I was a reporter once," Ethan said, scratching his beard. "I gave it up after you had my family murdered."

Panic flickered across the congressman's face. "That was only an accusation. I was cleared of any involvement. Where are you getting this… false information?"

"You call it false, but you know it's true. Do you even read the Bible sitting next to your chair? Or is it just for show?"

Adams visibly shivered, his gaze shifting towards the house, "When were you in my home? What else do you know?"

Ethan raised his hand, calming his tone. "Sir, we don't need to continue with this kind of conversation. Let's just say, that you may want to close your drapes at night. There are people out there that want to do you harm. That's what brought me here. I had you in my crosshairs and was about to avenge my family. But when the two girls climbed into your lap. I couldn't do it. I needed to see you face-to-face."

Adams slumped as he dropped his head. When he looked back up, his eyes were swollen with emotion.

"I'll prove who I am," Ethan said quietly. "Last year, when you had your driver take out the gangster, I was sitting in the brush watching. You had been sitting on the porch in a rocking chair. You were walking back to your car when the shot was fired."

"Enough," Congressman Adams raised his voice. "I have heard enough. How could you know this?"

"Like I told you, I was there. Sorry to upset you. Just tell me what's changed in your life to bring you here?"

Adams hesitated. Then he looked back at the house. "Come inside where it's warm, I'll tell you." He extended his hand again, "And please, I don't deserve to be respected. Call me Eduard."

Ethan wasn't sure if it was a good idea, but with the reassurance of the hard steel in his pocket, he followed Eduard into the house.

Eduard's wife looked puzzled at first, and then sadness swept over her face when her husband introduced Ethan.

She stepped forward and wrapped her arms around him. "I am so sorry for what happened. We've been praying for you every day since…, well, since Eduard came to know the Lord. We never imagined he would get the chance to ask your forgiveness. We heard you were killed in a helicopter crash. What happened?"

Ethan looked into the tearful sadness. He had no idea what to think. It was obvious Eduard had shared his checkered past with his wife. He felt a lot of anger flowing out of his body. What was he to do?

"Thank you, Maggie," he said. "Some days are harder than others. I am not perfect. But like Eduard, I too have come to believe in God. And I have accepted Jesus as my Savior. Let me start at the beginning."

They sat down at the kitchen table, and for the next hour, Ethan shared the loss of his family, his hatred for the killers, and his revenge. Eduard choked up when Ethan spoke about the rage he had felt when justice failed. Ethan left out his time at Charlotte Lake, but shared his journey of faith.

"How did you find us?" Eduard asked.

"I hacked the FBI," Ethan said with a wry smile. "Wasn't even looking for you, but there you were in my file. You can thank them for that."

Ethan took a deep breath as his face tightened. "Which brings me to why I'm really here. I had a plan when I walked through the woods. I meant to kill you. But behind a fallen tree, I broke down and wrestled with God. He firmly told me that I had to forgive you. I told Him I would. He told me it had to be face to face. Now, I know why."

The sadness in Maggie's face was turning to tears of understanding. Ethan inhaled deeply and turned to Eduard. "Eduard, I am so sorry for the hatred I have had for you since I found out about your involvement. Having come to know the Lord, I'm supposed to forgive. Last night, that happened, not by my strength, but that of my risen Savior who has forgiven me. Eduard, I no longer hate you or have any hard feelings, because you are my brother."

Eduard stood, tears streaming down his face. They met half-way around the table, embracing in the kind of reconciliation that only faith can bring.

Chapter Twelve

Walking back through the woods, Ethan felt as though the weight of the past year had been lifted. He still missed his family, but the bitterness he had carried was gone. He found himself humming songs from the church at Charlotte Lake. It was time to get his things together and start the long trip west.

Exiting the woods, Ethan walked around the deck to the stairs. He had climbed two steps when he noticed additional footprints in the snow. He froze. Slowly, he reached into his coat pocket and gripped the handgun.

"Good morning, Ethan. For a friend, you are one pain in the neck."

Ethan, shaking his head, looked up to see Steven sitting on a wiped-off deck chair.

"Welcome to the Poconos. What brings you up here?" Ethan brushed off a chair and sat down, grinning.

Steven was still shaking his head. "Do you know how hard it was to find you?"

"I'm kind of surprised you did. I had the FBI on my back for a while. Almost caught me in Lancaster. Gave 'em the slip out the back door. Thought it was you guys at first. How did you find me?"

"You have a bad habit of sharing your wealth, and that generosity is going to get you killed. Your cute little friend spilled the beans."

"If you found me, what about the FBI?" Ethan started considering his options.

"They'll be here soon, but you don't need to worry. We picked up the social media post immediately. We posted a ton of misinformation to throw them off. Eventually, they'll figure it out and come hunting." Steven stood. "Is it any warmer inside? I could use some coffee before we take off."

Sipping on his fresh cup of coffee, Steven watched Ethan load his backpack.

"You know Colonel Whitlock is going to send you to the brig for this little shenanigan? I don't know how much more of this I can take, bro. I know we spent a lot of time in the trenches, but you're going to have to be a team player."

Ethan just smiled and kept packing. He figured as much. Maybe he should just head out the back door and let them catch him at Charlotte Lake.

Steven continued his rant. "Whitlock's also not thrilled about your DIY chip extraction surgery. That was one hardcore thing you did there. Not so sure I could've done that. We tracked it down a country road at two miles an hour to a farm a couple of miles north of town. That alone might have worked without the AirTag backup."

Steven glanced at his phone. "You about ready? Our ride's five minutes out. And get the rifle, we don't want to leave any clues."

"How did you know about the rifle? What else do you know?" Ethan asked.

"We know you didn't shoot the congressman. What happened?"

"It's complicated. You wouldn't understand." Ethan headed downstairs for the rifle. What should he tell Steven?

Could he get him to understand what it was like to have faith in God? Could he even try?

When he came back upstairs, Steven was looking out the door. "They're here. Let's go."

Ethan watched a white Jeep Wrangler pull into the driveway. "What happened to the black Suburban, you run out of them?"

"It's hard to be choosy when you're relegated to a rental car. Unlike the FBI, we don't have agents all over the country. Fortunately, we could get something that could handle the snow."

They both slid into the back of the Jeep. Steven introduced Ethan to Tanner, the driver and his partner, Conrad, as they backed out of the drive.

"Is our plane already here?" Ethan asked as they pulled into the Pocono Mountain airport.

Steven rolled his eyes. "If you're talking about the jet we brought out, the answer is yes. If I had any say, you'd be riding back in a C-130."

"If you hadn't showed up, I would be looking forward to a few days on the train."

Ethan spotted the sleek Citation Latitude sitting on the ramp with the door open. The fuel truck pulled away as they arrived. After dropping them off, Tanner left to return the rental.

Ethan greeted the flight crew as he boarded and slid back in his seat. It had only been three days since they had left Fresno for Washington. He seriously hadn't expected to be making the return flight. "God is good," he muttered.

"How's that?" Steven asked, sitting across the aisle.

Ethan had to collect his thoughts. "I was just thinking about all that has happened in the last seventy-two hours. Just thinking about how God has protected me during the whole mess. Despite my rebellion."

"Rebellion? Yes, sometimes I think you are your worst enemy. I remember back in the service, you were not really religious. What happened?"

Ethan's gaze drifted out the window. "When you spend as much time as I have with people who know God and love Jesus, it doesn't take long before that truth wears off on you. I have to say, I believe it would be healthier for me to go back to Charlotte Lake. After this week, I sure could use some more of what they're selling."

"I don't think that's in your cards, for the foreseeable future anyhow. Speaking of Charlotte Lake, we have some work to do on the flight home."

With the rest of the team on board, the turbines started spinning.

"What's going on at Charlotte Lake?" Ethan gave Steven a concerned stare.

"A.I. found anomalies in the Charlotte Lake files. Something strange is coming from the community's security team. It's going to take someone familiar with the people to find it. You and Anna are the only ones that meet that description."

They had just started moving, when Ethan noticed two black SUVs pulling into the airport parking lot. "If we don't get out of here soon, neither one of us will be looking through files." He pointed out the window. "We have company."

Steven followed Ethan's gaze. "Looks like the FBI doesn't want us leaving." He jumped up and stuck his head in the cockpit. Moments later, the captain pushed the throttles forward, and the jet surged ahead. The periodic bump of the runway increased as they back taxied to the end of the runway.

Ethan could feel his heart beating. He looked over at Steven who looked relaxed and unconcerned. He must have noticed Ethan's uneasiness. "It will be two to three minutes."

"Can the tower stop us from taking off?" Ethan asked.

"This airport is uncontrolled, no air traffic controllers work here."

They were approaching the north end of the runway, when the first officer motioned for Steven to come forward. Ethan couldn't hear, but felt the intensity. Returning to his seat, Steven's eyes were glued out the window. "We just lit a fuse."

"What happened?" Ethan asked.

"The FBI broadcast on the unicom frequency, demanding we return to the ramp. Captain told them, they were broken and unreadable."

As they lined up on the active runway, Ethan spotted both FBI vehicles speeding across the ramp in their direction. The soft hum of the engines increased to a high-pitched whine as the captain advanced the throttles to the takeoff detent.

"Looks like we're in for a game of high-stakes chicken," Ethan said. "Surely, they won't take that chance."

"Depends on how agitated they are." Steven said.

Their closure rate increased rapidly as the aircraft rocketed down the runway and the SUVs sped toward the intersection. Two hundred yards before impact, the captain rotated, and they left the ground as the passengers watched the SUVs slide to a stop just shy of the crossing runway.

Steven saluted them as they flew by. "So long, boys. Enjoy your debrief."

They made a sweeping right turn and continued climbing into the clear afternoon sky. Ethan lay back in his seat and exhaled.

— • ● • —

Leveling off at 43,000 feet, Ethan got up and fixed himself a cup of coffee. Returning to his seat, he noticed Steven deep into his laptop. "Anything interesting?" he asked.

"Yeah, you will need to go over this. I sent it to your laptop."

Ethan pulled out the footrest and sat back scrolling through the files. It took him back memory lane as the papers showed pictures of the village, the people, and the leadership. He read through each of the reports. His attention sharpened when he came across a file describing the underpinnings of the community. It described a lot of what Ethan had seen once he was taken into the inner circle of the security team.

How do they know this? Only a score of people know these things. Last year while he was part of the team, the security chief felt that someone was leaking information to the outside world. Could Anna be the mole? He didn't think so. Even though she was in contact with Steven, she didn't have access to the information in the files.

Ethan got up and fixed another cup of coffee. He returned to the files, running a search on Anna, all he found was a blurb, describing her adoption and move to Charlotte Lake. That was good, at least she was not on their radar.

He had seen enough, but out of curiosity, did a search on Krystal. A whole slew of hits appeared. He started reading, the more he read, the more rapid his heart beat. Her parents had reported her missing, she was last seen by a friend in Utah who had dropped her off at an airport where she boarded a small plane with her children. No word of where she went. The pilot or plane has not been identified. It is suspected that she was on her way to meet Ethan Dawson somewhere in the west. No verification as of this time.

Ethan's heart pounded as he searched the files for information on the intel going to a foreign organization. The source was unknown. Who were they feeding? The FBI had tracked it to a camp ran by a cartel fifty miles south of the Mexican border. His chest tightened. They were gathering information on the infrastructure of the community, and the gold mine.

Could it be that the cartel was planning a takeover of the mountain community?

He closed the laptop.

Steven looked over at Ethan, lost in thought. "Who's spilling the beans?"

"I don't know." Ethan's perplexed stare.

"What's this underpinning that's mentioned in the leaks?" Steven asked.

"I'm not sure I want to divulge that information. It's classified."

"By who? Obviously not the government."

"The community leadership have their own governing board. They decide. Don't push me, Anna doesn't even know." Ethan's thoughts were scattering all over the place.

"How can we help if we don't know what we're dealing with?" Steve asked.

"When the time's right, I'll tell you what you need to know."

Ethan sipped his coffee and looked out the window. He could see Lake Michigan stretching north. Maybe he could escape to Canada with Krystal and the children. He drifted off to sleep thinking of them.

He awoke to the captain speaking with Steven. "No doubt, we're being tracked. The FBI knows the aircraft call sign, and our departure airport. I would say, they will be waiting at Fresno when we arrive."

"What can we do to throw them off track?" Steven asked. "Do we have to land at Fresno?"

"We could change our destination airport. But they will see the new destination as soon as we make the change."

"We could crash. That's one of Steven's favorite past times." Ethan stood up to stretch.

The captain's eyes lit up. "We could simulate one. Not comfortable with it, but it would work."

"How?" Steven asked.

"Deception. We request a fuel stop over Nebraska. We

descend into uncontrolled airspace, cancel our flight plan, fly low for awhile, then file a new plan under an assumed call sign. Bingo. We disappear."

"Won't they still be waiting at Fresno?" Ethan asked.

Steven looked questionably at the captain. "What about Willow Creek? Can we land there?"

"I'll check the weather. It's sketchy, no IFR approach, short runway. We will run the numbers."

The captain returned to the cockpit. Steven turned to Ethan. "What are you thinking?"

"I'm thinking I'm in this pretty deep and want to be dropped off somewhere safe."

Steven laughed. "Right. My question was in reference to Charlotte Lake. We agreed to provide them security. Should we be concerned about the leak?"

"Yeah, probably," Ethan said. "I'm thinking I should pay them a visit and see what I can find out."

"I agree that an in-person visit is necessary, but not from you. Not yet. I'll discuss it with Colonel Whitlock, but someone needs to tell Anna. She's likely our best hope of finding the mole."

"We're in trouble." Ethan mumbled.

"Maybe. But we need to try."

The moving map showed them over Oxford, Nebraska, when the engines changed tone and the descent began.

"Looks like we're heading down." Steven said.

Chapter Thirteen

Ethan looked out the window as the Nebraska farmland blurred beneath them. The jet leveled off at five hundred feet, skimming low over the landscape as they maneuvered around small towns. He wondered how the locals might react to the impromptu barnstorming. Would they report it to the FAA? Or, more likely out here, enjoy the spectacle and go about their day.

For twenty minutes, they screamed over fields, rivers, and rolling hills. As they approached Wray, Colorado, the jet began a gradual climb. By the time they crossed the eastern slope of the Rocky Mountains, they had regained cruising altitude. Ethan glanced at the moving map. Mariposa airport was depicted as their destination, but he doubted that was where they would actually land.

Two uneventful hours passed as they flew west, high above the Nevada desert. Then the Sierra Nevada Mountains rose on the horizon, jagged and snow-covered, majestic and forbidding. Yet to Ethan, they felt like home. A strange emotion welled up. These mountains, massive and timeless, seemed to welcome him back.

—————— • ● • ——————

The jet banked slightly right, revealing Yosemite Valley stretching out like a serene painting. As they turned southeast, the peaks filled the windows. The map showed seven thousand feet and flying towards Oakhurst. Ethan tensed. They were preparing to land. But where? They had mentioned a camp, but what camp could accommodate a jet this size.

Crossing over Oakhurst, the aircraft made a sharp left turn. He heard the mechanical whine of the landing gear. Though it didn't feel like they were descending, the ground surged upward. The hills narrowed around them as they navigated the terrain with surgical precision. Relief washed over Ethan when a runway finally appeared beneath them.

The tires chirped on contact. The roar of the Pratt & Whitney engines in reverse thrust, slamming Ethan against his seatbelt. At the end of the short runway, the pilot executed a tight 180. He saw just how little runway remained. No wonder they had questioned landing here.

As they taxied, Ethan spotted a cluster of Quonset hangars near the edge of the airstrip. Most were open-ended and housed Blackhawk helicopters. His eyes widened at the sight of a couple F-16s tucked into the shadows.

"What's a rogue black ops squadron doing with fighter jets?" he muttered. This operation was becoming more complex, and dangerous, than he'd anticipated. Whoever these people were, they had enough firepower to start a war.

They rolled to a stop inside one of the open-ended hangars. The engines powered down, leaving an uneasy silence.

"How convenient," Ethan said under his breath as he unbuckled. "This isn't just a camp, it's a fortress."

A cold wind swept down from the mountains as they followed the colonel's aide toward a cluster of temporary structures behind the hangars. It had already been a long day, but Ethan still had to face Colonel Whitlock. He checked his watch, it was almost dinnertime. Maybe that would temper the rant.

The building's exterior was weathered and unimpressive. Inside, however, was a brightly lit conference room, warm and inviting. A couple of men in camouflage sat at the table. Ethan shrugged off his coat, poured himself a cup of stale coffee from a side table, and introduced himself. Roland and Lewis were both former military commandos.

The door banged open. Colonel Whitlock strode in.

"Ten-hut! "barked the aide. Everyone rose.

"At ease, gentlemen. We've got work to do," Whitlock said, his voice sharp as frostbite. His gaze landed on Ethan. "Welcome back. Enjoy your little detour?"

Ethan noted the sarcasm. "Thank you, sir. Glad to be back in the mountains. It's been a long four days."

"And whose fault is that?" Whitlock shot back, his tone rising. "Stealing an FBI vehicle, a sniper rifle, and a handgun. Are you out of your mind? You're lucky you're not rotting in a brig somewhere. I considered leaving you to clean up your own mess. It's guys like you that threaten our operation."

Ethan winced. "Sorry sir. Won't happen again."

"You're right it won't." Whitlock's tone was icy. "While you were creating chaos at the headquarters, I was in D.C. justifying our existence to someone at 1600 Pennsylvania Avenue. Your stunt set off alarms from Langley to the White House. If you had been caught, we would have denied knowing you."

"Sorry, sir. I don't know what I was thinking." Ethan murmured.

Whitlock sighed, frustration still burning. "Keep your emotions in check, Dawson. I was going to send you back to

White Chief, but we have a situation. Riley, brief them."

The aide stepped forward, with a laser pointer and activated a flat-screen.

"Gentlemen, we have a hostage situation. Normally, this would be handled by FBI or local law enforcement. But the location is fifty miles south of the U.S. border. That puts them beyond the jurisdiction of any U.S. agency, and the kidnappers know it."

"And we can intervene?" Steven asked.

"Not legally," Whitlock cut in. "But we don't technically exist. So, we make our own rules. Go ahead, Riley."

The screen displayed an overhead view of a compound.

"This is an international missionary outpost," Riley explained. "Over the past two decades, it's housed dozens of missionaries and their families. We estimate fifty-three U.S. and Canadian citizens are currently on-site.

"Two weeks ago, the Morego Cartel took over. Surveillance shows about twenty armed enforcers in the compound. The hostages appear to be confined to the dining hall."

He clicked to the next image of a shallow grave containing two bodies.

"We believe these are missionaries who have already been executed. Given the groups nonresistant beliefs…"

"That's enough," Whitlock interjected. "Here's the bottom line. We're going in there to neutralize the cartel and extract the hostages. This will happen swiftly and we will not be taking prisoners. The enemy has sealed their fate."

"How are we getting in there undetected with the border locked down?" Steven asked.

Riley clicked to the next slide, showing a high-altitude

shot of the compound.

"To maintain the element of surprise, you will be conducting a HALO jump from 20,000 feet."

"A daylight HALO?" Steven asked skeptically.

"Night jump," Riley replied. "You will be equipped with NVGs. It's a dangerous nighttime operation, but necessary under these circumstances. Everyone here is certified."

The colonel turned to Ethan. "Your records say you've done a few of these. What's your status?"

Ethan considered downplaying his experience. Looking down, he wasn't sure he still had what it took for a night jump. Spotting his bandaged hand, he raised it. "I'd love to help, sir, but I'm injured."

The room erupted in laughter. Even Whitlock cracked a smile.

"Nice try, Dawson. You're going. All six of you. I would love to join you, but Riley and I will be flying the jump plane."

Riley stepped back in. "Let's talk about the evac plan. Four Blackhawks will be flying along the border. Once you hit the ground, the first chopper will turn towards the compound. You'll have seven minutes to neutralize all threats and get the hostages into the courtyard. Any questions?"

Ethan had plenty, but exhaustion and hunger kept him quiet. Answers would come soon enough.

Whitlock stood. "Alright, boys. Grab some chow. Rest up. We meet here at 0900 for last-minute assignments."

Chapter Fourteen

It was still dark when Ethan stepped out into the ice-cold morning breeze. He turned on his headlamp and headed for the fire road outside the camp. After a couple hundred yards, his brisk walk turned into a steady jog. The road climbed gently towards the distant mountains, and as the dawn crept in, their jagged silhouettes began to sharpen against the sky.

Patches of snow grew more frequent until they completely covered the road. Ethan followed the tire tracks of some adventurous backcountry driver, slowing to a walk as he reached Kelty Meadows. From this vantage point, five hundred feet above the camp, he could see the runway lights stretching to the west through the thinning mist. He brushed off a log and sat down.

He had hoped the morning run would clear his mind, but it hadn't. The next twenty-four hours weighed heavily on him. Was he losing the edge? HALO jumps used to thrill him. Now, the adrenaline was mixed with unease.

His thoughts drifted back to Afghanistan, dropping into a village at night from 25,000 feet to take out Taliban fighters torturing the locals. The mission had lasted ten minutes. The fighters never knew what hit them.

This mission felt eerily similar. Same odds, one to five. Certainly, the cartel enforcers had no problem killing, but how trained were they in military combat?

He thought of Abram, the spiritual leader back at Charlotte Lake. What would he think of Ethan using force to free the missionaries? How would the pacifist missionaries react when their captors were neutralized?

Ethan checked his watch. That debate would have to wait. Brushing snow from his pants, he headed back to camp. No way he was missing breakfast after this climb.

— • ● • —

After a quick shower, Ethan, pulled on a fresh BDU. It was his first time in uniform since Afghanistan. He was a little surprised when he walked into the crowded mess hall. For a place that looked practically deserted last night, there were probably a hundred men and women. They were carrying on conversations at a decibel level above Ethan's preference. He made his way through the chow line and found Steven and the team.

"About time you got out of bed." Steven jabbed.

Ethan just smiled at his friend. No need in one upping him, by telling him about the six-mile run. He was really more interested in the bacon on his plate.

"Any of you seen the ops order for tonight?" he asked.

They shook their heads.

He turned to Steven. "Remember the HALO into that village in the Kandahar Province?"

Steven grimaced. "Hard to forget. Took out fifty Taliban in ten minutes. I thought the villagers were going to smother us with gratitude. Couldn't eat goat meat for a year after that feast."

Once the laughing stopped, Ethan got serious.

"Guys, we had a one to five ratio and took care of business in ten minutes. Tonight, it's the same, one to five, but we only have seven minutes."

Steven shrugged. "These aren't hardened fighters. Just a bunch of slap shot criminals."

Ethan shook his head. "That's what makes them dangerous. They shoot before they think. Don't get cocky, or you'll end up in a body bag."

"Thanks for the downer." Steven grinned. "But you're right, this is a dangerous mission, regardless of the enemy's ability. Let's see that ops order."

— • ● • —

The sun had risen over the mountain ridge, flooding the camp in warm sunshine. Silently they crossed the compound to the conference room.

"Good morning, gentlemen," Colonel Whitlock greeted. "Hope you had a healthy breakfast. Weather at the drop zone is overcast at 5,000 feet, visibility fifteen miles. You will still be jumping from twenty thousand feet. Open at three. That gives you three minutes to stick your landing. Each of you have the map and need to verify you landing zone. No, mid-air collisions."

He hesitated as he studied and looked over the operation details.

"Once shooting starts, we will detonate flash grenades a mile west of the compound. That should disorient their forces and pull focus away from the mission. Let's go over individual stations. Riley."

Riley stepped forward and used his laser pointer to detail responsibilities. Ethan was happy to be assigned overwatch with his sniper rifle. He needed some time on the shooting range before departure.

Once the questions were answered, Colonel Whitlock took over.

"Gentlemen, you have a couple of hours to get your packs together. Make sure you double-check your weapons. At 12:30, we will be doing a practice HALO jump. Some of you are a little rusty. Chutes and oxygen equipment are in hangar two. Get an early lunch and be ready when the King Air lands. Dismissed."

The low whine of the PT6A turboprops turned Ethan's head. The King Air was executing shallow snake turns through the valley, lining up for the runway. It touched down and rolled to a stop, using far less runway than the Latitude.

He stepped into his quarters and grabbed his pack. It was everything he needed for the mission.

By the time the props stopped turning, the team had assembled on the tarmac. Colonel Whitlock walked up behind them.

"Just got news that the Morego has arrived at the compound along with ten of his lieutenants. There are now a confirmed sixty combatants and the king pin. You boys wanna back out?"

Steven frowned. "We'll talk about it after we're back on the ground. Let's go get some fresh air."

Inside the King Air, Ethan sat on the floor, pack in his lap, chute against his back. The plane climbed slowly in a racetrack pattern over the valley. The turbine hum inside his helmet was strangely calming.

His mind drifted to all the times in war he had waited for the green light. When he left the military, he was sure those days were over. Yet here he was. Tanner elbowed him. Looking over, he saw the rest of the team strapping on their oxygen masks. It was about time.

Everyone stood and lined up for the exit. Riley slid open the door, and the cabin roared with wind. Time stood still as they watched the light over the door. When the light flashed a couple of times and turned green, all six men exited in six seconds, disappearing into the sky.

For the next ninety seconds, they maneuvered into a formation. As the ground rushed closer, they fanned out and deployed their chutes. Ethan's chute had opened first, so he followed the others into a line. The grass alongside the runway came up fast, he flared the chute arresting his descent. He did a two-step landing before rolling into the grass. His heart pounded as he gathered up his chute. If this was just a warm-up, tonight would be intense.

The team dropped their gear in the hangar and headed for the debriefing room. Ethan could feel the adrenaline still coursing through him, and judging by the energy in the room, he wasn't alone. They grabbed drinks from the fridge and gathered around the table.

Steven clapped Ethan on the back. "Still got it in you, old man?"

Ethan placed his hand over his heart. "Haven't been that amped in years."

"Wait until tonight. You'll wet your pants."

But Steven's smile faded. "Seriously, we should rethink

this."

Their conversation was interrupted by the rumble of the King Air returning to the ramp.

"There's no question we need to strategize," Ethan said. "We're facing a one-to-ten ratio. The only way we walk out of this is by putting the odds in our favor."

The door opened, and Colonel Whitlock entered, followed by Riley.

"Well done boys. Good to see you all made it." Whitlock said, pulling a Coke out of the fridge.

"What's your take on tonight? Should we call it off?" he asked.

The men exchanged glances, a mix of concern and determination.

Steven leaned forward. "I wouldn't say, call it off. We just need to tweak the plan. Riley, show us the latest intel."

Riley pulled up a satellite image. "This picture was taken two hours ago. You can see the difference from yesterday. A lot more activity and vehicles around the buildings."

"Where's Morego? How many are guarding the hostages?" Steven asked.

Riley zoomed in on the compound.

"As I showed you this morning, all signs indicate the hostages are still in the dining hall. That hasn't changed."

He moved the laser to a cluster of houses along the west wall.

"These six houses are active. We have seen a lot of the cartel moving in and out. For some reason, they're avoiding these other six on the east wall."

The pointer moved to a large structure at the center of the screen.

"They seem to congregate around the building here in the center. We're thinking this is the command center."

Ethan's mind drifted back to Charlotte Lake and the hostage crisis there. The captors had planned to burn down the meeting house with the people inside. His jaw tightened.

The cartel could be just as ruthless.

"What are their demands?" He asked.

Colonel Whitlock spoke up. "No ransom. They want a prisoner swap. It seems that we have two of Morego's brothers in custody and he wants them returned to Mexico."

"So, where's the president on this swap?"

"Not happening. That's why we're here. No media. No paper trail. No credit. We go in, get the job done, and vanish. Even the hostages won't know who saved them. They'll be taken to a secure detox location for medical evaluations and… a bit of disinformation indoctrination. You know the drill."

Tanner spoke up. "Is that why we're not taking prisoners?"

"Exactly," Whitlock said. "Can't look like a U.S. military strike. Needs to look like a cartel gang war."

He turned to Steven. "You're the team leader. Any final instructions?"

Steven stood motioning the laser pointer.

"Make sure you keep your eyes open. Sixty targets means one can slip through. Tanner, once you have secured the dining hall, the rest of us will reign terror on anything else that moves. Watch each other's backs. These guys aren't Taliban fighters, but all it takes is one lucky shot."

The room went silent.

Steven handed the pointer to Conrad. "Everyone, walk through your movement and responsibilities."

Each team member outlined their approach and tasks.

By late afternoon, they were aligned. But the weight of the coming mission hung heavily over the room.

Chapter Fifteen

Ethan rolled over and grabbed the ringing phone. "Good morning, sir. This is your wake-up call. Acknowledge."

"Yeah, yeah, I'm awake. Thanks," Ethan muttered, hanging up.

He glanced at his watch. He had an hour.

After a hot shower, he dressed in a solid black uniform and then sat on the edge of the bed with Krystal's Bible in his hands. Flipping to Psalms, he found a message of hope, not in his own strength, but in the Lord's. The words steadied his nerves in a way nothing else could.

The hangar lights blazed overhead when Ethan arrived. Colonel Whitlock and Riley huddled over a monitor, faces tight with concern. Outside, their copilot performed a preflight inspection on the King Air. Ethan found his gear and began a procedural check.

One by one, the rest of the team arrived, double-checking their packs before gathering near the aircraft stairs.

"Good morning, gentlemen," Colonel Whitlock greeted. "Hope you've got your big boy pants on. Two hours ago we received intel that Morego's been joined by Venezuela gang leader, José Rafael. He showed up late last night with ten of his lieutenants."

Steven frowned. "What do we know about them?"

"Not much. Snippets have been coming in over the last six months, but nothing concrete until last night. Drones picked them up crossing the border into Mexico. It was confirmed by a border cam."

A nagging question arose in Ethan's chest. It didn't make sense. Could it be that they were joining forces to take down another gang, or did they have something more sinister in mind?

"Do we know why he's there? That's a risky move for a casual visit."

Whitlock's expression hardened. "We don't know yet. The gang is new, likely springing up with the recent influx of illegal immigrants. It's not officially our problem, but their presence adds complexity. If they engage, they're collateral. Don't take unnecessary risks. I want every one of you coming home alive."

— • ● • —

The turboprop engines droned as Ethan leaned against the side of the aircraft's interior, his pack cradled in his arms. They followed the Sierra Nevada's western edge, heading south.

The copilot's voice crackled through the speakers, "Forty minutes to the drop zone."

Ethan's thoughts drifted as fitful sleep tugged at him. Returning to combat after his conversion to Christianity weighed on him. He missed his conversations with Abram. Those times spent sitting in the rugged chairs in front of the fireplace. Abram sharing Bible verses in answer to Ethan's questions. He drifted off to sleep.

"Fifteen minutes!" Riley barked, loud enough for the six men to jerk to attention.

● ● ●

From the cockpit, Colonel Whitlock could make out the border below. Their flight plan showed Mexico City as their destination. A deliberate misdirection to get them over the border. The moving map display showed five minutes to the target. It was time to act.

"Mazatlan Center, this is King Air 511 Sierra Charley. We need to change our destination to Palm Springs."

"Roger, King Air 511. Please stand by."

Seconds crawled. Whitlock's eyes stayed locked on the target moving ten miles off their left side.

"King Air 511, you are cleared to Palm Springs via right turn, direct Thermal, direct Palm Springs, maintain flight level two-zero-zero."

"Mazatlan Center, King Air 511. Any chance we can make a left turn? Mechanical situation, it would be safer."

"Roger, King Air 511. Left turn approved. Contact Los Angeles Center, one-two-eight point six."

Whitlock acknowledged the clearance, switched frequency, and started a sweeping left turn. One last look at the winds aloft, he reached up and hit the switch.

In the back a red light flashed above the door. They struggled to their feet, lining up for the exit. The light went solid red, and Riley slid open the door. The cold night air rushed in. Two minutes later, the light flashed green.

———————•●•———————

Darkness swallowed Ethan as he plummeted through the air. He stabilized in the butterfly position and located the Chem strips on the other five. One close by and the other four lower.

Ethan checked his altitude, seventeen thousand feet. Pulling his arms in slightly, increased his descent rate, closing the gap with the others. To his right, the remaining team members converged.

As had been one of his old habits, Ethan hummed the lyrics of an old song, as he fell through the night sky.

Earth below us, drifting, falling, floating, weightless, coming home.

Steven made an adjustment, setting them up for their opening. Ethan checked his altitude, five thousand feet. Steven signaled: three, two, one.

The group burst apart, pulling ripcords at three thousand feet.

Ethan's chute deployed with a sharp jerk, the straps snapping tight around his thighs. He pulled down his NVGs. He could see the others.

Two minutes before impact. He scanned the ground. Still dark. A few dim bulbs gave off enough light to see the compound five hundred yards to the west. Back to the ground.

Objects began to take shape. He spotted two teammates below and to the right. He followed their descent. Scanning for a clear landing. Shrubs and cacti dotted the terrain. *Avoid the cacti.*

He turned towards a bare spot, coming in fast, too fast. He pulled down hard on the toggles, braking his descent. His feet hit the desert floor, momentum sending him into a roll. He yanked his chute down and quickly stuffed it into its bag. *Leave no trace.*

After insuring nothing was left behind, he assembled his sniper rifle. Scanning the area, he counted off the team members. All accounted for.

Steven raised a hand and signaled forward.

It was time to free the hostages.

———— • ● • ————

A small rise hid them from the compound. As they approached the ridge, Steven and Conrad veered right around the north side of the compound. Lewis and Roland to the south. Ethan and Tanner continued straight up the hill to the crest.

Reaching the ridge, Tanner fist-bumped Ethan and descended towards the dining hall. Ethan positioned himself behind a three-foot-high boulder, with an unobstructed view of the compound.

Switching from the NVGs to his night vision scope, he scanned the compound. Two guards stood watch outside the dining hall. They were Tanner's targets to start the chaos.

Ethan checked his watch. They had been on the ground for ten minutes. He looked back through his scope and listened.

"South ready."

"North ready."

"Ridge ready." Ethan whispered.

Through the scope, he watched Tanner circle the conference center. Tanner raised this silenced Luger and fired two quick shots. The guards crumpled to the ground. Slipping through the door, Tanner disappeared inside.

Ethan held his breath. No movement. Silence.

"All clear hostages secure." Tanner's firm voice confirmed.

Relief washed over Ethan, but not for long.

Two pops shattered the night, followed by thunderous explosions as the incendiary grenades did their job. Within seconds flames engulfed all six houses.

A mile west, flash grenades ignited in rapid bursts, lighting up the sky. Cartel enforcers bolted from the houses, only to be cut down by the assault teams.

Just as quickly as it began, it was over.

"All clear," came the call. But then…

Ethan froze. The conference door opened. Morego emerged, pushing a girl, a gun pressed to her head.

"Hostage situation," Ethan whispered. "Morego has a girl. Gun to her head."

"Do you have a clear shot?" Steven's voice sounded clearly in his ear.

"Maybe. Not clean."

"We're on our way."

Two tense minutes later, Steven and Conrad crouched in the dark on the north side of the dining hall.

"Status?" Steven asked.

"Still there. He's looking around." Ethan gasp. "Wait! He's now moving towards the dining hall, pushing the girl. He sees the downed guards."

"Take the shot Ethan. Now!" Steven ordered.

"I don't have a clean shot. I might hit the girl."

"Do it now, Ethan!" Steven barked. "He's going to kill more than her."

Ethan's hands trembled. His daughters' faces. Krystal's voice. Abram's counsel. The weight of the Words of Jesus pressed in.

This wasn't about saving himself. It was about saving that little girl and everyone inside.

He opened his eyes. Crosshairs steady.

God, guide this shot.

He squeezed the trigger.

Morego crumpled to the ground.

Ethan kept the crosshairs locked on the target as Steven and Conrad swept in and pulled the girl to safety.

The distant thrum of approaching helicopters cut through the night. Time was running out.

Ethan's eyes shot skyward at the faint whistle slicing through the air. His gut clinched. It couldn't be real. Where was it coming from? "Incoming! Incoming mortars!" He yelled into his mic.

The whistle intensified until a deafening explosion hit the ground a hundred yards south of the conference center. Dirt and flames erupted into the sky.

Ethan spotted a distant flash. "Incoming!" he warned again, shifting his sniper rifle south focusing his scope.

"Two launchers, six combatants."

"Tanner, get out of there! Stat!" Steven's voice exploded with panic.

Ethan watched Steven running towards the dining hall as hostages poured out in confusion, their movements frantic and aimless.

Steven's voice boomed, cutting through the chaos, guiding them towards safety just as the south end of the conference center exploded in a fireball.

Ethan returned to his scope just in time to see another flash from the launchers. He chambered a round, aimed thirty feet above the group, and squeezed the trigger.

It was too far to be accurate, but a close shot would distract the combatants. Just as the combatants hit the deck from his projectile hitting close by, the mortar exploded into the south end of the dining hall. Debris and bodies flew everywhere.

Ethan's chest constricted. He couldn't think about casualties now. He had to keep them pinned down.

One after another, he sent rounds towards the combatants, forcing them to take cover. But they began to rise, emboldened by the realization that his shots lacked accuracy. They went back to reloading their launchers.

The roar of an approaching Blackhawk cut through the night.

"Hold your fire, Dawson." The unfamiliar voice commanded in his ear.

Ethan turned as the helicopter screamed overhead. He shifted back to his scope. The combatants had heard the incoming Blackhawk and were scrambling for cover.

The tracers from the GAU-19 Gatling Gun lit up the sky, tearing through the launchers and cutting down the remaining fighters.

Ethan exhaled, lowering his rifle.

The chaos intensified as more helicopters descended. Flames flickered against the night, casting eerie shadows over the carnage.

Bodies were scattered among the debris. Cries of pain echoed as the injured struggled to their feet or were carried by others.

Ethan's instinct as a warrior yielded to that of a medic, but the place was a battle zone. There could still be enemy combatants lurking. He stayed on high ground, pulling out his night vision goggles.

The burning buildings provided enough light to illuminate the remains of the compound. The injured were being carried towards the four Blackhawks.

Ethan scanned for his team. Steven was in the thick of it, encouraging the hostages to keep moving. Conrad, Roland, and Lewis were returning from assisting the first evacuees.

But where was Tanner.

A voice came over the radio. "Mexican military

helicopters have just departed Tijuana. ETA thirty minutes."

Ethan decided his overwatch was done. He descended the hill, reaching the compound as the last of the survivors were being loaded onto the helicopters.

Inside the remains of the dining hall, he found Steven kneeling beside Tanner.

Steven looked up, his face grim. Fear flickered in his eyes. "We need to get him out of here now. He's banged up pretty bad."

"Vitals?" Ethan asked.

"No external bleeding, but his pulse is weak. He must have been hit by something."

Together, they lifted Tanner, supporting him on either side. They carried him towards one of the Blackhawks, moving through the courtyard littered with devastation.

A lump formed in Ethan's throat as he passed the extraction team removing five hostages in body bags.

"We let them down." Ethan said quietly. "Where did we go wrong?"

"Don't go there! We did what we could." Steven's sharp command cut through his guilt.

An intuition hit Ethan. He stopped and looked around. They were missing something.

"Come on Ethan, we need to get out of here." Steven urged them on.

Ethan spotted Conrad coming their way. "Conrad, help Steven, I need to check something."

Handing Tanner off to Conrad, Ethan ran towards the burning conference center.

Thick smoke was filling the building as he ran down the hall looking in each of the rooms. Flames were moving up the hallway. He heard the screaming plea for help and ran into the smoke, literally feet from the flames.

Opening a door, he found a young girl tied to a chair behind a small desk. On the desk was an open laptop. Ethan shut the laptop and stuffed it under the girl.

Picking up the chair, the girl, and the laptop, he threw them over his shoulder and headed down the hall towards the exit. He struggled as smoke filled his lungs. *Hang in there Ethan. You're almost clear.* His eyes burned as he flew through the exit door.

Steven was motioning for Ethan to hurry as the sound of the Blackhawk's turbines were picking up. The girl screamed as Ethan slid her and the chair into the helicopter on its back. He pulled himself in behind her and Steven pulled the door shut.

The Blackhawk lifted off into a smoke-filled sky. Ethan fell back into a seat, the weight of the mission heavy on his shoulders.

He felt a hand on his shoulder and turned to Steven pointing to the headset hanging overhead. Ethan looked up and shook his head. He didn't want to talk to anyone right now. He watched Conrad remove the girl from the chair, before he pressed back against the headrest and shut his eyes.

Chapter Sixteen

Ethan's morning run left fresh footprints in the two inches of snow that had fallen overnight. His thoughts churned with the events of the last forty-eight hours. Flames from the burning houses cast flickering reflections on the arriving Blackhawks, sent to evacuate the hostages. He could still see them, running from the dining hall to the waiting helicopters. Still hear the incoming mortar shells. Still feel the thunder of the explosions as they struck the conference center and dining hall.

He picked up his pace as he jogged back down the trail towards the camp. How could they have been so careless? It was planned, but not executed. Maybe the debriefing this morning would sort it out. Did I let my team down? Morego coming out of the conference center was the interruption that shattered their plan.

Ethan was five minutes late for the debrief. He made his way through the room, brushing past a few unfamiliar faces to get to the coffee pot. Colonel Whitlock's voice was already raised, laying into someone, and judging by the tone, it was him. Ethan ignored it. His gaze drifted to the nearly empty box of donuts. Way to ruin a perfectly good morning run.

They were kind enough to leave him a seat at the table. Sitting down he turned towards the Colonel. "What happened to the Venezuelans?"

Colonel Whitlock squared his shoulders. "I'll be the one asking questions, if you don't mind."

"Actually, sir, I do mind." Ethan voice, strong yet measured, brought the room to attention. "We went into a rat's nest last night. We earned the right to know. I'm retired military, not here to be barked at. Now, if you want us to be on your side, it's time you showed a little respect. So, what happened to the additional threat last night?"

Whitlock's face turned red, reaching for his coffee cup. He tried to take a sip only to find it empty. He tried again before setting it back down.

"Sorry, Ethan. You're right. You've earned that much. As we were approaching the target, the drone picked up Rafael's entourage leaving the compound, heading northwest. We didn't get that intel to your team in time."

"Thank you, sir. Do we know where they are now?"

"No. We lost them during the battle." Whitlock's paused. "But there's good news. Thanks to your, let's say, heroic, and admittedly dangerous, stunt, we know where they're heading. The laptop you retrieved gave us a trove of data. It appears Rafael has taken a particular interest in Charlotte Lake."

"You call that good news?"

"Poor choice of words," Whitlock admitted. "But it's helping us connect the dots. Once we finish the debrief, I need to meet with the five of you to discuss the next mission.

For now, let's focus on yesterday's events.

He looked Ethan in the eye. "The girl you rescued is Heidi Quintella. She's under medical care here at the camp. She has suffered both physically and emotionally, but the doctors think she'll recover in time. By the way, she's asked to speak with you."

"How long before we return her to her family?"

"She doesn't remember her family. She was kidnapped by Rafael and sold to Morego." Whitlock answered. "Let's discuss that after the debrief."

Whitlock nodded at Riley who brought up the overhead shot of a now destroyed compound.

"Good job making it back. According to medical, Tanner had a rough night but woke up this morning and wanted to attend this meeting. I nixed that idea. He has a nasty concussion and will be non op for a few weeks.

"As for the group operating south of the compound, we still haven't identified them. Chatter on social media suggests Rafael had enemies tracking him and assumed he was still at the compound. The missionaries were lucky you guys were there."

"Luck had nothing to do with it," Ethan muttered.

Whitlock's frown, prompted Ethan to continue.

"There were too many coincidences to call it luck. I believe the Almighty used us to answer the prayers of the hostages."

"God, luck, happenstance, whatever you want to call it," Whitlock said, glaring back at the screen. "It worked. But the aftermath has been almost as explosive. The Mexican government is accusing the U.S. of a military attack on their soil. The State Department is denying involvement. Fortunately, we were long gone before they arrived. Our intel was accurate, There's nothing on radar showing Blackhawks crossing the border either direction. A few jackrabbits and a couple of desperadoes might have caught a glimpse of low level flights, but nothing official."

"What about the missionaries, are they going to talk?" Steven asked.

"They're safe at an undisclosed location and well cared for. They have no idea who rescued them. All they remember is chaos and being lifted out in black helicopters.

Whitlock turned to Steven. "Okay, start with you. Walk us through it."

For the next hour, each man detailed what he had witnessed and the actions he had taken. The slaughter of the cartel enforcers had been brutal. How do we justify taking those lives? Ethan wondered. Then he remembered the bodies of the missionaries in the pit. Heidi tied to a chair. Guilty by association, he thought grimly.

When the debrief concluded, Whitlock dismissed the staff and sat down with the five operatives.

"Let's talk about Ethan's favorite place. Our specialist ran an A.I. analysis on the data Ethan extracted from the FBI. It confirmed what you already suspected, there is a mole in the community. We didn't know to what extent…"

"Didn't?" Ethan asked.

"Until you stole Morego's laptop." Whitlock continued. "This morning, we found extensive communication between someone at Charlotte Lake and Morego. The leaked information from Charlotte Lake was then traded to Rafael for the young girl."

Angered boiled inside Ethan. How could anyone do this to a young innocent life. Did this trader have any idea how far-reaching their betrayal was? He ached to return to Charlotte Lake and find this mole. But could he trust himself not to act out in anger?

"Ethan." Whitlock's voice brought him back.

"Sorry, sir. What did you say?"

Whitlock rolled his eyes. "Based on your time at Charlotte Lake, do you have any idea who the mole might be?"

"No, sir. I have racked my brain. We had one person

leaking information, but he was killed by his outside contact."

Whitlock nodded. "I think it's time we have a face-to-face meeting with Anna. She might be able to help."

Ethan's heart raced. This was his chance. "I volunteer to go." He said quickly.

Colonel Whitlock laughed. "I bet you would. But you're still dead, remember? It's too soon for your resurrection at Charlotte Lake."

Ethan slumped back. He knew Whitlock was right. When the danger of retribution passed, maybe then. He prayed that day would come soon.

Colonel Whitlock started gathering his things.

"Steven, I had planned on you and Tanner making the trip, but now with Tanner on medical leave, find a volunteer. As soon as you're ready send Anna a message. We don't want to wait too long.

"Ethan, I want you to take the lead on finding Rafael and his gang. We need to know his whereabouts. Gentlemen we have work to do, stay safe."

Chapter Seventeen

Anna reached into the pocket of her smock and pushed the acknowledge button, silencing the vibration. She glanced around the greenhouse; none of the women seemed to have noticed. Pulling on her coat, she announced she'd be right back and stepped outside.

The cold bit at her cheeks as she trudged through the snow, her breath rising in quick puffs of fog. Her mind raced. The pager's signal was a code she had hoped to never see again.

The FBI had a job for her.

Her cabin, nestled among the trees, came into view. The familiar scent of pine and wood smoke greeted her as she stepped inside, doing little to calm her nerves. She peeled off her coat, fingers trembling, and made her way to a small writing desk. After a final glance around, she pressed her index finger against a hidden sensor beneath the desk.

With a soft click, a concealed compartment opened, revealing a compact satellite messenger. She hadn't used it since sending an SOS in the fall. She could only hope the batteries still had a charge.

She sat staring blankly as the device searched for a satellite connection. Six months had passed since the violent attack had shaken the community. The harsh winter had shielded them from further danger, but no one believed the threat was gone.

Anna stood and walked to the window, pulling aside the heavy curtain to peer out at the snow-covered forest surrounding her cabin. It all looked so peaceful. How deceptive.

The messenger beeped, connection established.

Authenticate.

Her stomach tightened as she typed in her code. A few agonizing seconds passed before the device vibrated with an incoming message.

Potential threat identified. Stand by for further instructions.

Anna sat the messenger down, her heart pounding. What did they want her to do? She couldn't go to security. It would blow her cover. If only Ethan were here, he would know what to do.

She could still visualize the Blackhawk helicopter flying low over the village that stormy afternoon. It had never been found.

The messenger lit up again. Anna wiped away the tear sliding down her cheek before reading the message. How she missed him. They had never agreed on what their relationship should look like. She wanted to be more than friends. He didn't. Now, he was gone.

Be in the crater meadow at 2130 hours. Come alone.

She stared at the screen. She had expected more. Like a detailed instruction on how to thwart the potential threat. Maybe someone would meet her there. Why wasn't the FBI willing to involve the Charlotte Lake security?

Back in the greenhouse, Anna had trouble focusing on her task of setting plants. She was relieved that no one questioned her short absence.

It was eight thirty when Anna pulled her white insulated snowsuit over thermal underwear. It was going to be a cold night, and she had no idea how long she would be up in the crater. Her backpack, filled with survival gear, was strapped tightly to her back.

She retrieved the 9mm Beretta from her dresser. It was just like the one she'd used to save Ethan's life. Nightmares of that harrowing night still haunted her.

Strapping on snowshoes, she stepped out into the darkness, bypassing the cleared path to avoid the security cameras. Dogs barked as she passed behind the cabins, but no lights flickered. No curtains moved. She intercepted the crater trail just beyond the reach of the last camera.

The ascent was grueling. She had always prided herself on staying in top physical shape, but even she wasn't immune to the toll of a long winter. Her calves burned, her breathing labored. Still, no matter how acclimated she was, it took a lot of endurance at this altitude.

The moon had not yet risen as she made her way up the mountain towards the crater. She followed the switchbacks even though they were buried three feet under the snow. Soon, the longer days would start the spring thaw. The lonely howl of a coyote came from down in the valley. She shivered.

With still a half mile to go and four hundred feet of vertical climb, she was exhausted. I should be home in a warm bed. The stars appeared sharper and brighter up here. As she studied the stars looking for constellations she noticed a soft yellow light moving across the sky from the north. She expected it was a satellite, but as it moved closer, she could see the occasional flicker of red and green lights.

She tensed, though the aircraft had to be thousands of feet above her. She pushed it out of her thoughts and continued up the trail.

As the trail leveled off, she checked her watch. Twenty minutes early. If only Ethan still lived up here in the stone house. Her memories drifted to the times she sat in his favorite chair with her hands wrapped around a warm cup of coffee. She could see the dark outline of the stone house now. No beckoning glow in the window. No smell of wood smoke coming from the chimney. It looked cold and forlorn. Her heart ached.

Anna's first thought was to wait inside, but hadn't she suffered enough. The protection the four stone walls provided was nothing to the mental anguish they would cause. She would just stay on the north side of the frozen creek. Brushing off a boulder sticking out of the snow she sat down to wait.

She was running.

A two-track gravel lane stretched before her. She didn't know where it was but she could picture the tall rag weeds along its narrow width. Her pigtails bouncing on her shoulders. Where was she? She could not recall but felt that she was heading home. The shadows were long. She pushed back the memory. It was too painful. Like a vapor of fog floating up from the farm pond came vision of that night. As she rounded the corner she could see the flashing lights. Who were they? Why were they there? She ran towards the house. They heard her coming and stopped her on the broken down porch. She didn't know who he was but he was wearing a uniform with a red plus sign on his sleeve. He wrapped his arms around her and stopped her from going inside. She never saw her mom and dad again.

Anna bolted upright, her muscles tense. She stared into the night sky. Something was up there. The stars seemed to betray its presence, disappearing, shifting, returning, as if signaling the movement of something descending rapidly. A muted rush of wind startled her. Her eyes widened as a dark shape emerged from the sky.

She was on her feet as the fluttering of the canopy folded down around the skydiver. Without thinking, she pulled the Beretta from her pocket. It was awkward in her hand. There was no way she could pull the trigger with the insulated gloves. She slid it back in her pocket. Anyone that jumps from that altitude wouldn't be intimidated by her sidearm.

The jumper pulled the parachute in and quickly shoved it in his backpack. It was only then that she became aware of a red dot as it bounced off her arm and stopped on her chest. That could be only one thing. She held up her hands to show she was not armed and looked around. A hundred feet up the trail was another jumper. His parachute was settling around him as he was on one knee with an assault rifle fastened on her. Anna froze.

Chapter Eighteen

---•●•---

Anna watched the first jumper as he scanned the surrounding area with night vision goggles. She hoped it didn't take too long as she was not happy with the red dot frozen on her chest. Once it appeared that the area was secure he pulled off his helmet and smiled.

Anna felt her chest explode. The projectile was not one of lead, but one of recognition.

"Steven!"

His grin didn't waver as he wrapped his arms around her in a big bear hug. "Who did you think it would be?"

She trembled as she pounded against his chest. "You scared the living daylight out of me. I thought you were dead!" Then, a spark of hope lit her face. She turned towards the second jumper. "Ethan?"

Steven's arms tightened around her. "Sorry, Anna, it's not him."

Her shoulders dropped. "I had hoped…"

He gave her hand a gentle squeeze. "Let's get inside where it's warmer."

They passed the other jumper, who was packing up his

chute without a word.

"Who is he?" Anna asked. "Someone I know?"

"You don't. And it's best it stays that way. Anonymity is one our greatest assets."

"He scared me. I didn't even realize there was a second jumper."

"That was the plan. I came across your line of sight to draw your attention. Works every time."

They crossed the frozen creek, avoiding the log bridge. Anna cringed as they approached the dark stone house.

Steven brushed snow away from the door and pushed it open.

At least she wouldn't be alone.

He lit a lantern, and the scent of kerosene mingled with the musky air. Dust puffed into the air as Anna sank into what used to be her favorite chair.

"Why all the precautions?" she asked. "Did you think you were jumping into hostile territory? I thought the mountain was under perimeter security."

Steven nodded. "It is. And yes, we assume every job is hostile. It's protocol. Why do you think we're here?"

"I figured you missed me." She tried to smile, but her voice was tight. "How bad is it?"

"We don't know for sure. What we do know is someone here is selling information. That's where you come in. Anna, we need you to locate the source."

Anna stared at the dark fireplace. She wasn't the kind to meddle in other people's lives.

"You have an open line to security," she said. "Why not go through them? They would be better suited for this."

Steven's expression turned serious. "We believe the leak is coming from inside the security team. The intel that was compromised is classified level."

Anna raised an eyebrow. "How do you know that I'm not the guilty one? Do you think you really know me that well."

Steven didn't hesitate. "Simple. You don't have access

to the classified information we intercepted. If you did, you wouldn't have come up here tonight. Do you have any clues on who it might be?"

Anna frowned. "Not off hand, but if it's someone working for security it narrows down the suspects. Does the FBI have any clues that might help? What was in the classified information? That might help."

"I wish I did. But the contents of the intel are too sensitive to share. At least not right now. Maybe never."

Anna huffed, frustrated. "Real helpful."

"Sorry, Anna. That's just how it has to be. We've done all we can. It's up to you now. Once you have found the traitor, we will leave it up to you on how you reveal it to the community."

He leaned forward, voice low. "The clock's ticking. We believe the community's anonymity will be compromised before summer. If that happens, you can expect a massive influx of not only adventure seekers, but those that wish to destroy your community."

Anna's chest tightened. Her heart pounded. What if she failed? Was there someone out there that had her back? It didn't sound like it.

What kind of information was so classified that she wasn't allowed to know it, yet she was expected to find the mole.

Steven stood, slinging his pack over his shoulder.

"We need to get going."

Not wanting to be left alone in the cabin, Anna forced herself out of the chair and zipped up her snowsuit. "If I do find this traitor, do I contact you?"

"You won't have to. We'll know. Be careful out here. Things could go south, fast."

He snuffed out the lantern and the room went dark. She grabbed his arm and followed him to the door.

Her voice was barely a whisper. "You were in the helicopter with him. Did he suffer?"

Steven stopped and gave her a long, tight hug. "Let's not talk about Ethan. It will only bring more pain. Focus on your mission, Anna. It's for the best."

A blast of freezing wind swept through the doorway, the old hinges squeaking in protest. Anna pulled her hood tighter against the cold.

Steven's silent partner was seated on the edge of the porch, weapon resting against his leg, night vision goggles still fixed to his eyes.

"Seeing anything out there?" Steven asked.

The man stood, adjusting his gear. "Nothing. Too cold for anything up here, except three crazies. You ready to head for lower altitude?"

"Where's your extraction point?" Anna asked.

"Not your concern," Steven said. "You'll be home by the time we catch our ride."

"Nice to be trusted," she muttered. "I suppose it's for my protection. Right?"

He chuckled. "Not everything's about you, girl. This one's for our safety."

They walked together across the meadow to where the trail headed down to Charlotte Lake.

Steven stopped and turned to her. "Well Anna. This is where we say goodbye. Be safe out there."

She took a deep breath as she watched Steven and his partner vanish into the night. The cold stillness of the night was biting into her skin. She shivered at the thought of her mission.

As Anna made her way down the dim trail, her thoughts grew heavier with each step. Ethan had warned her about corruption in the FBI. The fact that her curiosity about Ethan inadvertently brought about the attack on the community bothered her. Sure, God had forgiven her, but as far as the community, they didn't know she had anything to do with it.

Would she need to confess to the community before she was truly forgiven? Was it the weight of her guilt that was depressing her or just the winter gloom?

She longed for someone she could confide in, someone who wouldn't judge her but help her work through the guilt.

As Anna approached the tree line the shadows seemed to reach out for her. She shivered as she entered the darkened woods, moonlight flickering through the pine boughs casting eerie patterns on the snow.

Leaving the trail, she retraced her tracks through the thick underbrush. Dogs barked in the distance, but she wasn't concerned. Wildlife often stirred them at night.

Finally, her cabin came into view. She let out a long breath as she stepped inside, closing the door behind her.

The comforting scent of wood smoke greeted her. She lit a lantern, peeled off her snowsuit, and collapsed into her chair, exhausted.

It was almost midnight.

Chapter Nineteen

"You seem a little distracted this morning, Anna. Are you feeling okay?" Sandra asked.

Anna barely heard. She moved mechanically, pouring water over the freshly planted seeds, her mind tangled in thoughts she couldn't shake.

"I'm fine," she said, but the words lacked conviction.

Sandra gave her a knowing look. "You don't sound fine."

Anna sighed and turned away, continuing down the row. Maybe it was exhaustion, or maybe it was something deeper. Seeing Steven last night surfaced memories of Ethan, and worse, suspicions of betrayal reminded her of Cody. She needed someone to confide in. But trust was a dangerous thing.

By the time Anna left the greenhouse, the sun was dipping behind Mount Bago, casting golden streaks across the sky. The trail had turned to slush. Rather than head straight to her cabin, she took the long way around the lake, drawn to the quiet cemetery nestled against the hillside.

The wind whispered through the trees as she knelt before

the newest stone, brushing away the snow with gloved fingers.

Cody Edward Turner.

Her heart cried out as she traced the letters chiseled into the stone. Memories came in waves, crashing against the walls she had built around them.

Cody had been her best friend since childhood, her partner in adventure, the boy who taught her to hunt, to fish, who knew the woods and the mountains. He had been her world.

And then he left.

The day he ran away from the village, he took a piece of her with him. Six years of silence. Questions with no answers.

When he finally returned, he was different. The boy she had loved was gone, replaced by someone darker, someone she barely recognized.

And yet, sometimes… there were flickers. The old Cody, hiding behind wary eyes and quiet gestures. The way he looked at her when he thought she wasn't watching, the way his touch lingered when he brushed a stray lock of hair from her face. She had hoped they might find their way back to each other. But fate had other plans.

Now, all she had left were whispered prayers and the bitter ache of what might have been.

She rested her forehead on the cold stone, closing her eyes. "I miss you," she whispered, her breath forming a cloud in the evening air. "I still miss you."

A gust of wind sent a shiver, but she didn't move. Somewhere deep inside, she wished for a sign. A whisper. A flicker of warmth in the cold.

But the wind only carried silence.

All she had left was her faith in God.

———•●•———

The next day, Anna walked around the lake to the meeting house, enjoying the warmth of the spring sun. She softly sang songs of praise as she met up with others on their way to church. She clung to the hope that spending time in God's house might renew her strength. Yet, the knowledge that someone among them was betraying their community cast a shadow over her spirit. It was Palm Sunday, the day Jesus rode into Jerusalem, just days before He was betrayed.

Abram met the worshipers as they filed into the log meeting house. Anna noticed how frail he had become in his old age. She appreciated his wisdom and made a note to visit him soon.

Only a couple of benches in the back of the church were empty. Lantern light flickered across bonnets as Anna scanned for her friends. "If only they were color-coded," she thought with a faint smile.

Just as she was about to take a seat in the back, a small hand tugged hers. Looking down, she met Christiana's smiling eyes. "Come sit with us, Anna."

———•●•———

"You seem a little down." Krystal told Anna once the service was over. "Why don't you come up to our house for lunch? The children would love it."

Anna hesitated and then nodded gratefully.

As the congregation dispersed, Anna lingered outside, lost in thought. She was grateful that Krystal invited her to lunch. Perhaps companionship was what she needed.

They walked together up the trail. The children running

ahead laughing and splashing in the slush.

Krystal's log home, perched on a natural shelf above the lake, was meant for her and Ethan. Now, with Ethan gone, she lived there alone with the children.

Anna sat comfortably in the living room, looking out across the lake. She felt a tinge of envy as she watched Krystal with her children. What would it be like to have someone to care for, or someone to care for you?

She turned. "Krystal, I need someone to talk to."

Krystal sat beside her. "What's bothering you, my dear?"

Anna glanced at the children playing. "I think a lot of you, and I trust you. Are you okay with helping me through a serious challenge?"

Krystal took her hand. "Of course, I am. But first, let me pray."

Tears welled as Anna listened to Krystal pray for Anna's peace and for wisdom in their conversation.

Anna wiped the tears from her eyes as she tried to speak. Krystal got up and brought her a glass of water. "Take your time, Anna. I'm here for you."

Anna finally found her voice. "Now I understand why I could never steal Ethan. You are a true friend."

Krystal smiled with a tinge of sadness. "He was special. But God had other plans. You're shaking, Anna. Is the problem that bad?"

Anna wrung her hands. "I've been in contact with the FBI... and we're in danger."

Krystal's only reaction was raised eyebrows and a stoic smile.

Anna hugged herself before continuing.

"They said that someone here has been selling information about the community to some really bad people."

"How can we be certain of this information?" Krystal asked. "Naturally, we wouldn't want to falsely accuse someone."

"Oh, I trust my contact. Let me start from the beginning."

Anna shared everything, even the night of the attack, and the part she played. The weight of many years of confinement lifted from her shoulders as she released her past.

"Now, you understand my dilemma. I've lived a double life for years, but I never intended to hurt anyone... but now we're at risk. Can you help me?"

Krystal sat motionless, for what seemed like an eternity. The furrowed lines on her brow were frozen. Fear tightened Anna's chest as her imagination read Krystal's reaction. Was it a mistake telling Krystal? Was her world about to fall apart? Anna exhaled. Whatever happened she was ready for this to be over.

"My dear, I am so sorry you have such a burden to carry. Yes, you have made mistakes, but they are forgivable. The commitment you made to the FBI must be taken seriously. For the security of the community, and because of your Christian testimony."

Anna smiled weakly. "I know, but it's difficult to do the right thing, when you know it's because of your own poor decisions. Do you have any ideas on how we identify the person doing this?"

"I'm not a private detective, Anna. But, we can pray about it, put our heads together, and just maybe we can come up with a plan. Let's go sit on the porch for a bit."

Bundled in their coats, they rocked quietly looking down at Charlotte Lake. The breeze was a little chilly, but just the thought of springtime brought with it the feeling of renewal. Soon the snow would melt and the flowers would bring color to the mountain.

"Anna, I want you to pray this time. Ask God for forgiveness, and for wisdom in finding the person that's doing harm. Please remember, we are seeking restoration, not retaliation."

Anna reached over for her friend's hand, bowed her head

and prayed with a broken heart. When she finished, she was filled, not with certainty, but with peace.

"Thank you," she whispered. "I'll be back soon. I need to start by making a list of who has access to that kind of information."

Krystal hugged her. "Go. Be careful. And remember, you're not alone."

Anna stepped onto the trail, the burden lighter, the path ahead a little clearer.

Chapter Twenty

The squirrels scampered from tree to tree as Anna sloshed around the lake toward the storehouse. If she remembered right, Sarah had a list of the residents.

Abram's cabin, just off her right, stopped her in her tracks. Should she? If not now, when?

Turning up the trail, she knocked on the door.

"Greetings, my dear Anna. Come on in." Abram said warmly as he opened the door. "What are you up to this afternoon?"

"I was on my way to the storehouse, when your cabin drew me in." Anna smiled. "Figured God wanted me to stop."

"I'm certain that He has His reasons. Have a seat by the fire."

She settled into a comfortable old chair, memories rushing back to childhood visits. Ellie, Abram's late wife, always had time to teach her the cultural ways of the community.

Abram sat across from her, his kind eyes studying her. "Tell me, my dear, what have you been up to lately?"

"Just working and waiting for spring," Anna replied. "Looking forward to Easter. Are you preaching on Sunday?"

"No, I have decided to leave it to the younger ones this year. Time has taken its toll on this earthly body. But more importantly, how are you, Anna? It's been about six months since we lost Cody. Are you okay?"

Anna choked up. She hadn't expected anyone to mention his name.

"Not really. I had a good cry at his grave the other day. I miss him. The old Cody, before he…"

Abram reached over and squeezed her hand. "I know. God knows too. Trust Him, Anna."

"I try. But sometimes it feels like I'm being punished for all the things I've done wrong. Does He really forgive us?"

"Of course He does. First John 1:9 reminds us: If we confess our sins, He is faithful and just to forgive us our sins and to cleanse us from all unrighteousness. Confess your sins to Him, Anna. It doesn't mean you can blatantly go on sinning. That would be an indication you haven't really repented. Spend less time worrying and more time reading your Bible. Someday, I'll tell you my story of redemption."

Anna gave a faint smile. "And you think you're getting too old to preach. Thank you for the advice. Krystal's been telling me some of the same things."

"She's a wise counselor. It would be good for you two to spend more time together."

A knock interrupted their conversation. Anna stood reluctantly, not ready to leave, but knew their conversation was over.

She opened the door to a young man holding a bag of groceries. "Good afternoon, Jonathan. Come on in. Your grandpa will be glad to see you."

"Hi, Anna." Jonathan smiled as he placed the groceries on the table. "You don't have to leave just because I'm here."

Anna hesitated. She glanced at Abram, who was already watching his grandson with quiet affection.

"I need to get going anyhow." she said, forcing a smile. As she reached for the door, Abram's voice stopped her.

"Anna, remember, truth has its way of revealing itself. Trust God's timing."

She nodded and, with a slight wave, said goodbye. His words settled over her like a warm blanket against the cold wind.

• ● •

The storehouse, nestled up against the granite mountain, buzzed with activity. The spring weather had stirred the community to life. Anna gathered a few supplies and took a seat near the counter, scanning faces. Could it be one of them? Her senses sharpened. A man she barely knew lingered near the back. Was he watching her?

It had to someone she didn't know. Or… was it?

When the last customer left, Sarah finally joined her, wiping her brow.

"Busy afternoon, with Easter Sunday coming up. What can I do for you, Anna?"

"I'll take a loving husband, two wonderful children, and a happy life." Anna said with a grin.

"I only know of one of those, and he's taken." Sarah paused. "I've been in your shoes, trusted God had a plan and look at me now."

Anna clenched her jaw. Enough already. She knew Sarah meant well, but she was hurting, and wanted a practical solution, not a spiritual one.

"Do you have a community directory? I'm doing some research, and it would help."

"Sure, we keep those behind the counter." Sarah retrieved a small booklet. "Just updated in January, so as far as I know it's current. What are you researching?"

Anna tensed. She couldn't lie. But she also couldn't say. So, she smiled as she replied, "Well, I had better get home before dark. Thanks for your help."

As she stepped outside, a gust of wind swept in off the lake, cutting through her coat. The ice would soon break, and the deep alpine blue would return, as it always did. Seasons changed. Life moved forward.

It had been a year since Ethan's arrival at Charlotte Lake. A smile touched her lips as the memory surfaced. He had brought strength, steady, unshaken. She'd fallen for him before she even knew him, drawn to the quiet storm that lingered in his eyes.

Why did I think that was okay?

She had convinced herself it was God's plan. They were meant to heal each other. The way he looked at her back then… it wasn't rejection, it was restraint. As if he saw something in her she couldn't see in herself.

She had imagined it so many times. Of Ethan finally giving in, reaching for her hand, pulling her close. She longed to be the one to ease his pain.

If only he had listened. Maybe he would still be alive. They could have built a life together.

But even if he had stayed, he would have never looked at her the way he looked at Krystal.

She remembered the first time she spotted him in church, sitting quietly in the back, hands clasped, eyes distant. There had been something different about him, something broken yet unbreakable. And she had wanted to be the one to put him back together.

Now, he was gone.

A lump formed in her throat.

Passing the meeting house, she felt drawn inside. The room was empty and quiet. She sat on a rugged bench and closed her eyes.

She was nine again, newly adopted and scared. It was their first Sunday at Charlotte Lake and she felt hollow inside. She was still heartbroken, missing her friends from the city. The long bus ride and the hard hike up the trail. She didn't understand why her new parents were bringing her to this place.

That warm summer day, when they came to the meeting house, everyone welcomed them. She didn't want anything to do with them. She wanted to go home. Now, this was home.

She pushed the painful memories aside, replacing them with a truth more lasting. God was her Father. She was His child. She bowed her head and told Him everything. Tears slipped down her cheeks, not of heartbreak or fear, but of joy.

When she stepped back outside, the sun had set. Darkness was closing in, but Anna barely noticed. She walked briskly around the lake.

Tomorrow, once her chores were done, she would go see Krystal.

Chapter Twenty-One

Anna sprinkled a small portion of water over each of the sprouting plants. Spring was always an exciting time in the mountains. Snow melting off the valley floor, the flowers bringing bursts of color, birds singing. Even the livestock seemed to sense the change, giving birth to new life. It was a season of renewal.

But what was the source of her joy this morning? She shook her head at the thought.

Her mind went to her encounter with God in the meeting house. She had told Him everything, and in return, He had given her peace. She could move forward, knowing that He was watching over her. She still needed to find the traitor, but now it wasn't out of hate. It was a desire for justice, for reconciliation.

By the time she finished her chores, it was nearly eleven. After changing into a clean dress at her cabin, she made her way around the lake, stopping at the bakery for a fresh loaf of bread before heading up the path to Krystal's.

Krystal sat on the porch in a rocking chair, watching Jonah play with his toys.

"I wondered if I would see you today. Figured you'd be biting your nails to get started." Krystal motioned for Jonah to pick up his toys. "Let's go inside. It's still a little chilly to just be sitting out here."

Inside, Anna dropped the booklet on the table and picked up the cup of coffee Krystal sat in front of her.

"According to this list, there are 253 people living here in the community," Anna said, "That's more than I expected."

Krystal wrapped her hands around her warm cup. "I've only been here for a few months, and most of that has been wintertime. It never felt like that many. Not everyone shows up on Sundays."

Anna thumbed down through the list. "For sure. Church is not mandatory here in the village. You can bet that there are a few that find it unnecessary."

"Why would anyone want to live here without being part of the fellowship?"

"I'm not sure that has ever been addressed." Anna answered. "It could be that they just don't believe, or it's not important to them."

"I think our first step should be to divide them into two groups. Not saying the church attendees are exonerated, but we have to start somewhere."

Anna agreed.

Krystal returned with a notebook and a pen, together, they began organizing the names. Some of the names caused them to laugh at the thought, but the task was serious. When they finished the first round, they had divided the residents into two broad categories: 140 who regularly attended church, and 113 who did not.

Krystal grabbed the list of churchgoers. "We can't ignore any group, but I think we should narrow down the list as much as possible first."

"I have to say, I don't know a lot of these personally," Anna said, studying the names of the non-attenders.

Krystal tapped her pen against the notebook. "How about we break all of them down by probability?"

They divided the names into three groups: likely, possible, and unlikely. As they worked through the church list, Anna felt a familiar guilt creeping in. How could she even think that one of them would do such a thing?

She came across Sandra's name and hesitated. She and Sandra had been friends almost as long as she'd known Cody. The idea of Sandra being a mole seemed laughable... but hadn't Cody also seemed trustworthy once? Sandra had always been vocal with her frustration with community rules, but that didn't make her a traitor... did it?

Anna swallowed the thought. *What am I doing? Am I any better than the person I'm hunting, casting suspicion based on feelings?* She tried to justify it. She was doing this to protect the community, not tear it down, but the doubt still gnawed at her.

She closed her eyes, silencing the voice of conviction pressing against her conscience. She remembered how it felt when Cody ran off just weeks before their wedding. The whispers, the sideway glances, the unspoken judgment. For the longest time, she had been trapped under the weight of her own self-condemnation. Was she now going to put someone else through the same thing?

Krystal broke the silence. "Anna, do you know George Winston? Says he lives over on your side of the lake."

Anna blinked, caught off guard. "Yeah. I don't remember which cabin is his, but it's close to his parents. You know, Doctor Winston?"

"Of course. I don't know how I missed that. What's your impression of him?"

"Don't really know him. He's older than me, we never spent time together. Why do you ask?"

"Aw, just wondering."

Krystal's vague answer didn't go unnoticed by Anna. *Does she know something?*

By the time all 253 residents had been divided into their respective categories, Anna felt more focused. The most likely suspect, she believed, would be among those who didn't attend church and had the ability to cause damage discreetly.

"Thanks for helping break this down." Anna said. "I know you can't do much undercover work, with the children and all, but anything you can do to help eliminate names will make a difference."

Chapter Twenty-Two

Anna lay back in her sleeping bag, nestled among the rugged rock formations. Above her, the Milky Way stretched across the sky, a glowing river of light. It had been two weeks since she and Krystal had worked on the list. She longed to talk to Steven. He might have insight on how to proceed.

It was too late in the season to meet in the crater, so she had sent a message for him to meet her at Kearsarge Pass. He had questioned the need for them to meet, but finally gave in. She checked her watch, thirty minutes to go. She scanned the sky, wondering if he would use the same aerial approach as before.

Ten minutes before the meeting time, she heard footsteps crunching up the trail from the east. It had to be Steven. She watched as two men topped the pass. She started to crawl out of her cocoon. The voices were unfamiliar and sharp, speaking in a language she didn't recognize. She slid back into her sleeping bag and wiggled behind the boulders.

The men stopped right in front of her, their voices heated. Anna's heart pounded as she peeked around the rock. Are they just a couple hikers? Not likely.

She looked at her watch. Five minutes.

She surveyed the sky for an aircraft. Nothing but stars. Looking back at the two men, her heart stopped. One of the men had pulled a gun from his pack and was waving it angrily, displaying his displeasure. She shrank deeper into her sleeping bag, pulse racing. If Steven walked into this unprepared, he might not walk out.

Anna shivered when the sound of a night owl drifted through the pass. Something was about to happen. Peaking around the rock she could see the hikers were aware of something moving in the night. Her shoulders relaxed. She had seen this before.

A red dot appeared on the gunman's chest. Anna barely had time to register it before the man jerked backward, a muffled shot breaking the silence.

The other man's hands shot into the air. He babbled frantically in his native tongue.

Out of the darkness, an image emerged, clad in winter military gear. Night vision goggles in place, rifle steady, moving methodically towards his target.

"Get on the ground, now!" the voice barked

Anna didn't know if the man understood English, but the tone, and the weapon, spoke universally. He dropped to the ground whimpering.

The aggressor cautiously approached. He kicked away the fallen man's weapon, then addressed the survivor in short, clipped phrases. The man rolled over and sat up.

After a brief exchange, the hiker got up and ran over the pass towards Onion Valley. The man in battle gear watched him go, before picking up the guy's backpack and set it on a boulder.

"Okay, Anna, you can come out." He said.

Anna was shaking so hard, she wasn't sure she could. "What if I don't want to?"

Steven laughed, "Then, I'm coming in after you."

The laughter caused Anna's panic to subside. "Not sure there's room in here for you and your gun," she replied. "I'll come out."

She crawled from her cocoon, and Steven wrapped his arms around her in a big bear hug.

"Girl, you sure know how to attract trouble. How did you know those guys were going to be here?"

"I didn't. I came up here early so I wouldn't keep you waiting. Good thing, or I would have run into them on the trail." She hesitated. "Who were they?"

"Venezuelans. Not part of the gang we're expecting, but I have a hunch they're connected."

Steven scanned the area with his night vision goggles and then turned back to Anna. "Well, no cozy stone cabin tonight. Let's take care of business and get out of here. What's the latest on the traitor?"

Anna wrapped the sleeping bag around her shoulders. "We've narrowed it down to thirty-five suspects, but we're stuck on how to go further."

"Who is this we? And, are you certain it's one of these thirty-five?"

"Krystal. She's been helping me. She's an outsider, and I trust her. We aren't certain of anything, but we had to start somewhere. Any advice?"

Anna started shivering.

Steven wrapped his arms around her and pulled her close. "Start getting nosey. As I told you last time, our analyst believes your mole is part of the security team. If you can get your hands on the roster, it would help narrow it down."

"I forgot about that. Not so sure I can get nosey. I will try."

He grinned. "Sure, you can. I know you better than that."

Anna pulled away and punched him in the chest. "Very funny. I'm just a serious, God-fearing, mountain girl living a double life in a conservative community."

"You had better get home before you freeze. Need an escort?"

"Thanks for the offer, but I'm afraid the community elders wouldn't approve."

Steven laughed. "Be careful. I would hate for something to happen to you. Now get gone. I have a dead thug to disappear."

The snow crust crunched under her snowshoes as she descended. A lot was spinning in her head. What was Steven doing? The warmth of his arms still lingered. Was it the memory or the cold making her shiver, she wasn't sure

She had forgotten about the suspect being part of the security team. That would have saved some time. But who exactly was on the security team? That had to be classified. If only Ethan were here…

The Milky Way had vanished behind thin clouds by the time she approached the lake. Footsteps ahead made her freeze. Slowly, she stepped off the trail into the undergrowth. Who would be out here this time of night? She crouched silently watching and waiting. It could be security. There it was again.

The footsteps quickened, and a man she didn't recognize walked briskly by. He was carrying an assault rifle and wearing night vision goggles. It had to be security. Why was he headed towards the pass? Could he be the one?

Once she could no longer hear the footsteps, she made her way on down to the village. Waiting just outside the view of the cameras, she tucked herself in behind some rocks. The dampnight air chilled her as she waited.

Eventually, she could hear the man returning. Could she trail him to his home? It wasn't worth the risk.

In the darkness she made out his shape. His thin build eliminated a number of suspects. He stopped about ten feet from her hiding place. She ducked behind the rock as he pulled down his night vision goggles and scanned the area ahead. She breathed a sigh of relief when he didn't check out the brush. When he flipped up his goggles she got a glimpse of his face in the moonlight. Her heart stopped. Oliver?

Anna wanted to jump out of the rocks and run to him. He was one of the few men who had not avoided her when she was down. He had been one that assured her that she had done nothing wrong. It can't be him. Or can it?

She stayed hidden until Oliver was well down the trail before working her way around the cameras into the village. One day, they were going to catch her doing her nocturnal activities. But not tonight.

Inside her cabin, she lit a lantern and pulled off her snowsuit. One day, she'd leave the danger, and the secrets behind. Maybe she would be a wife, a mother. Live a quiet life.

She smirked. Right. Dream on, girl. You're not getting any younger.

Chapter Twenty-Three

Anna stopped by the greenhouse just long enough to talk one of her coworkers into watering her plants. She decided to cross the outlet and ended up knee deep in the water.

"It sure would be nice if they built a bridge." Anna muttered as she worked her way up the north bank. She wasn't happy with herself. A quarter-mile savings wasn't worth wet feet. She could stop at the bakery to dry her socks and boots, but she was anxious to get to Krystal's. They had a lot to talk about.

As Anna neared Krystal's path, a familiar voice called out. "Good morning, Anna."

Though eager to see Krystal, Anna couldn't resist a moment with William and Claire.

She gave William a brief hug. She had strong feelings for Cody's grandparents. They had lost their son and daughter-in-law a few years ago, and then their grandson last year. It had to be heart breaking.

"How's grandma feeling this morning?" she asked.

"Old and cantankerous. Why do you think I'm out here?"

He smiled. "Really, she's doing just fine. She's knitting a sweater and needed me to stop talking, so I decided to enjoy a little spring weather. I have to say, it doesn't feel very spring out here. Haven't seen much of you lately. How are you doing?"

Anna fiddled with her fingers. There was so much she wanted to share with her adopted grandpa, but it was too soon. Someday she would tell him everything, and hopefully he would forgive her.

"All I can do," she said. "I wake up in the morning, go about my day, and trust God will help me through my sorrows." Anna knew that she had much to be thankful for, but she still had days of sadness.

"Anna, I'm sure I'm not the only one to tell you that God has a plan for your life. Trust Him and be willing to listen for His voice. He provides in mysterious ways. Don't shut yourself off from others. Open your heart and share His love."

Anna pondered William's words. She had been spending a lot of time alone, but in her defense, it had been winter.

She stood. "Thank you for the advice, Grandpa. I'm on my way up to Krystal's, I have been enjoying her friendship."

William smiled. "She sure is a godly woman. Her children come down and bring us cookies. We don't need the calories, but the love they bring us old people is priceless."

She turned back and squeezed William's hand. "Tell Grandma, I'll stop in and see her soon."

"She would like that, Anna. You be careful out there."

As Anna carefully worked her way up the slippery path, she thought about how the children blessed William and Claire. What resilience the couple showed. They had been the first ones to settle here, building their cabin by the lake. All these years later, were still living in it. Now surrounded by the people they love.

Anna had a lot to think about. She needed to spend more

time talking to God and less time chasing criminals. She was getting way out of her lane.

———————— •●• ————————

"So, tell me what's new?" Krystal asked, drying the last of the breakfast dishes. "What have you been doing the last two weeks?"

Anna sat at the table with papers spread out around her cup of coffee. "You don't want to know. It would have you on your knees praying for my healing."

"I'm not so sure. I already pray for you a whole lot and more. You take up a lot of prayer time. With three children, that's saying something."

Anna couldn't miss Krystal's big smile. "How much do you want to hear?"

Krystal sat down with her own steaming mug. "All of it, of course."

Anna scooted closer to the table, glancing at Jonah playing in the living room. "It was scary…"

Krystal's face was drawn tight as Anna finished sharing everything that had happened. "So… do you think it's Oliver?"

Anna looked down at her feet. "Not really… but I don't know."

"That doesn't sound like a confident answer. You need to know for sure before you even think about accusing someone. Could we arrange a casual meeting? I'm not sure I know him. Does he have a family?"

"He does. A wife and two young boys. They attend church, but not every Sunday. I could take you to meet his wife. We could do it under the pretense that you just want to get to know other moms."

Krystal raised an eyebrow. "You want to go now? I love

the idea of meeting other moms. The girls are at school, and Jonah would love to meet new friends."

"Good with me. They live on this side of the lake, so it shouldn't take long."

———— • ● • ————

A woman about Anna's age opened the door.

"Anna, come on in." She turned to Krystal and held out her hand. "Hello. I don't think we've met. I'm Louise. What brings you ladies here this morning?"

"I wanted to introduce Krystal to other mothers in the community," Anna said. "Figured you would be a good place to start. Would now be a good time?"

"Oh, most certainly." Louise smiled down at Jonah, who clung tightly to Krystal's skirt. "Jonah, the boys are playing in their room. Would you like to join them?"

Jonah looked up at his mother. She nodded, and he slowly followed the sound of children playing in the adjoining room.

The women sat down in the sparsely furnished living room. There were only a few pieces, an old sofa, an overstuffed chair, and two side tables. But the place was cluttered with books, papers, and half-sorted laundry. Still, it was clean.

Anna scanned the room, noting details for later conversation with Krystal. Nothing obvious suggested secrets or betrayal. She turned her attention back to the women, who were hitting it off. Krystal was interested in learning how to fit into a remote community and Louise wanted to hear about the outside world. Anna? She wanted to know if Oliver was a traitor.

Be patient, girl.

She caught Krystal's eye and raised her brows. Krystal

gave a subtle nod.

"How did you and Oliver meet?" Krystal asked. "Have you always lived at Charlotte Lake?"

"Oh, no," Louise answered. "We moved here five years ago. That was soon after we met. We worked together, he was a field agent, I was in the office. Bit of an office romance, I guess."

"I hadn't heard that," Anna said, leaning in. "Where was this? What made you leave and move here?"

"We worked for the FBI. Denver field office." Louise dropped her voice. "We're under witness protection. Maybe someday I can tell you what happened."

Anna thought she was going to explode. Witness protection? What are they doing here? That was like leaving cheesecake out in a New York alley. It was bound to attract rodents.

"Do you plan on going back once the threat passes?" She asked.

"We love it here. What was supposed to be temporary grew on us. Oliver loves working security. I love raising the boys. We hope, God willing," Louise said, patting her belly, "for a baby girl before the summer's over."

Krystal smiled warmly. "Congratulations. Is Oliver at work today?"

"No, he's sleeping," Louise said, glancing at a closed door. "He covered a shift last night."

"Oh, sorry. We won't stay long," Krystal said, speaking with a muted tone.

"You don't need to worry. With two boys in the house, he can sleep through anything."

As the conversation turned to sleepless nights and endless diapers, Anna's fingers brushed her flat stomach. A quiet ache settled in her chest. Maybe one day she'd share in that joy.

Her eyes wandered, then froze on a photograph lying on the end table. Steven and Ethan, standing beside a sleek business jet.

Her pulse quickened. She casually picked up a book and the paper. Using the book to hide the paper she started reading. What was this doing here?

A cough came from behind the closed door. She quickly closed the book and laid it back down.

She had trouble maintaining her composure. It had to be an old picture. Ethan was dead and Oliver had nothing to do with Steven. Could it be that he knew something she didn't?

Anna stood up reaching for her coat. "Sounds like someone is waking up."

Krystal followed suit. "Thank you for your hospitality, Louise. Bring the boys up sometime. Spend the day."

— • ● • —

Back on the trail, the uncertainty lingered.

"I don't think he's the one," Krystal finally said as they climbed the switchbacks on the path.

"I'm not sure," Anna replied. "I tend to agree, but are we just hoping for Louise's sake?"

She didn't mention the picture. If only she had been able to read what it was about. When was the picture taken? Is Ethan still alive? One thing for sure, Oliver had interest in the two guys.

"Hard question to answer." Anna said. "Why did he go up the trail towards the pass last night? I think I need to talk to him alone."

"Do you think that's safe? If he's guilty, it could be dangerous."

"I've known Oliver since they got here. He wouldn't hurt me."

"I've heard of criminals turning on family to keep them from talking. I hope you're right."

At Krystal's, Anna grabbed her pack and gave Krystal a hug. "I'll be careful. I guess I'll have to trust God just a little more. Someday, I'll be like you, sister. Thank you."

Anna was halfway down the mountain when she started questioning why she hadn't told Krystal about the photo. Maybe she just hadn't sorted through the confusion yet.

Next time I see Steven, there will be questions, that's for sure.

Turning north to go the long way around the lake, she had only gone a hundred yards when she passed George Winston heading south. She nodded a greeting as they passed.

That's strange. So close to Krystal's, after she had just asked about him.

Was she seeing him?

No way would those two get along.

She was overcome at the thought of anyone other than Ethan being with Krystal.

Chapter Twenty-four

The vegetable plants were six inches tall and growing every day. Soon, the soil would warm enough to transplant them into the garden. Anna knew she had to get to the bottom of the threat before that happened.

She would talk to the security chief, Arnold was an old friend of her dad's. He would help her. Could she even get inside City Hall? She hadn't been there since she lost her father. As a little girl, he used to bring her to work. She remembered being in awe of the place, with its blinking lights, rows of computers, and walls full of camera monitors. So different from the rest of the community. Sometimes, she even wondered what it would be like to have electricity in their cabins.

She could see the stepping stones across the lake's outlet were completely submerged under the water rushing out of Charlotte Lake. No way was she going that route. Anna finished her chores and headed around the long way.

Who's in charge of bridge-building around here? She thought. Most of the year, it wasn't a problem, but right now it added fifteen minutes to every trip she made.

It was close to noon when she arrived at the barn and found Robert, the farm manager.

"Well, hello Anna! Haven't seen you around in awhile. Ready for spring?" Robert called out.

Anna always found Robert friendly and helpful. If something needed doing, he was the man to ask.

"I'm ready for someone to build a bridge across the outlet, so I don't wear out my feet. You got a minute to talk?"

"On my way home for lunch. You're welcome to come along. I'm sure the wife's cooked plenty." Robert answered.

"Thanks. I'll walk and talk, but I've got a lot to do."

They started north towards Robert's cabin.

"What's on your mind, girl?" he asked.

"You know my dad was on the security team. I've been thinking… maybe I'd like to get involved somehow. Could you help me get my foot in the door?"

Robert didn't answer right away. He just gave her a sidelong look as they walked. When they reached the path leading up to his cabin, he stopped, turned, and took Anna's hands.

"Anna," he said gently, "you don't belong in security. That life is far from the one you know. I understand wanting to try something different, but… I'm not sure this is it."

Anna's heart sank. She had been sure Robert would help her. She started to tear up.

"I guess I'm not good enough to work there," she said, her voice cracking. "Everybody just thinks of me as a gardener. It's not like I'd be shooting anyone! Can't I at least try?"

She wondered if her teary performance was working. Robert looked so stoic standing there in his Stetson, but finally, she saw a tiny crack in his armor. She wiped off the tears to push him over the edge.

Robert sighed and dropped her hands.

"Okay, I will talk to Arnold. Maybe, and I repeat, maybe we can find something for you part-time."

"Oh, thank you, thank you!" Anna cried, throwing her arms around him.

Robert just shook his head as Anna skipped happily down the trail.

———— • ● • ————

For two days, Anna tended her plants and worked on her list. She had her doubts. Did she even really want to work in security? No, she didn't. Could she do the job if she had to? Of course.

She knew the only reason she was doing this was to get the roster. Surely, there had to be another way. Too late now. If Arnold called for her, she was committed.

It was Saturday afternoon, and she finished watering plants and headed home. She wanted to shower, curl up by the fire, and read. She would see Arnold in the morning at church, maybe he would say something there. Probably not, he never mixes work with church.

Freshly showered and in her housecoat, Anna had just settled down with her book when someone knocked on the door. She frowned and glanced at the old clock on the mantel, only 7:30. Shrugging, she pulled back the edge of the curtain and froze.

Oliver stood on her front porch, dressed in battle gear, an assault rifle slung over his shoulder.

What should she do? Did he see her the other night? She could just ignore him, like she wasn't home. She backed away from the window, hands trembling.

Knock, knock, knock.

She jumped as the knuckles hit the solid door.

I have to answer the door. He knows I'm here.

Wiping the sweat from her brow, she forced a smile and opened the door.

She stepped back with a feigned look of surprise. "Good evening, Oliver. Are we under attack?" She forced a concerned look.

"Good evening, Anna. Sorry to scare you. I was just going on duty when the chief asked me to bring you in."

"Bring me where?"

"He wants to see you in his office. Go ahead and get dressed. I will wait out here."

Anna shook her head, "I've had a big day, and am ready for bed, Oliver. Tell your boss I'll see him at church in the morning."

She started closing the door, but Oliver stuck his boot in, stopping it.

"Anna, this is serious. It's not an option. If you're not out here in ten minutes, I'm coming in after you. Please don't make me do that."

Terror surged through her. She nodded silently and shut the door. Did Arnold really send him? Or had Oliver found out she was snooping? At least Krystal knew. Maybe Steven was lurking behind a tree somewhere, waiting to save her.

Steven!

Anna moved quickly. She knelt under her desk, pressing the secret button to release the compact satellite messenger. Powering it on, she retreated into her bedroom, closing the door behind her.

"Hurry up in there." Oliver barked from outside.

"Hold your horses! You ever tried putting on a dress?" she called back.

The device finally connected with a soft beep. Anna quickly typed out a short message. "Oliver came for me. Might be suspect." She hit send and finished dressing.

"Two minutes!" Oliver said.

Anna ignored him, watching until the message showed sent. Finally, she powered off the device and returned to its hiding place under her desk.

With a sigh, she pulled on her coat and opened the door.

"About time, young lady. Was afraid you were going to cause me trouble. Let's go."

The darkness deepened as they made their way around the lake. Anna was relieved when they passed the trail, leading up to the pass. At least he wasn't dragging her out there.

Her pulse quickened when they passed the storehouse. Isn't that the way into City Hall? Where are we going now?

Another hundred yards brought them to the hardware store and woodworking shop. Oliver opened the walk-in door. The dark building pressed in as she struggled to follow Oliver through the shop. He stopped and pulled open a hidden trapdoor, causing light to flood the room.

"Go ahead," Oliver said. "I'm right behind you."

The stone steps slowly spiraled to the right as they descended into the mountain. The solid granite chilled the air, growing colder with every step. Turning left, they came to a room that appeared to have no exits. Anna came to an abrupt stop.

"What is this place?" Anna asked. "My final resting place?"

"A little overdramatic, girl." Oliver chuckled. "You should be so lucky. Now, it's time for you to have a little patience."

A grinding sound came from the ceiling causing Anna to look up. A four-foot section slowly descended.

"Speaking of over dramatic. Who came up with this idea?" she asked, eyebrow raised.

"You like it?" Oliver grinned. "Something from my past."

"Go figure," Anna said, shaking her head. "Not bad. A

primitive community with a hidden elevator. How's it activated?"

"Face recognition. Even has your pretty mug is in the database."

"And how do you know that?" Anna asked as they stepped onto the platform.

"Simple. It scans everyone in the room before activating the lift."

They ascended into a well-lit control room and the elevator clunked to a stop. Specialists sat in front of monitors wearing headsets. Anna recognized a few faces and nodded greetings as she followed Oliver into a hallway leading deeper into the center.

A plaque next to a heavy door simply read "Chief". Anna inhaled deeply as they entered.

Arnold stood up respectfully and motioned toward a chair. "Good evening, Anna. Thanks for coming. Please have a seat."

"Thanks for coming? Are you kidding? You sent the Gestapo to drag me here. Not sure I had a choice. You're welcome," Anna said, her Irish roots starting to show.

Arnold laughed. "You're right. You didn't have a choice. I had hoped to wait until next week, but something came up."

He nodded at Oliver. "Before I dismiss Oliver, I want to go over something. Sit down, Oliver."

Oliver leaned his weapon against the wall and sat down next to Anna.

Arnold leaned forward and slid a paper across the desk. Anna's heart skipped. It was the same paper she had seen at Oliver's home just days ago.

"Anna, have you seen this picture?" he asked.

Anna craned her neck, like she was trying to see.

"You can pick it up. It won't bite."

She picked it up and studied it, her mind racing. What was she to tell them? She had to tell the truth, but struggled to find the words. She bowed her head and shut her eyes.

God, please help me say the right thing.

She raised her head and met Arnold's gaze. "Yes. I was at Oliver and Louise's the other day. I saw it sitting on the end table. Did I do something wrong?"

"We're not sure yet. Do you know who these men are?"

Anna stared at the photo, searching for an out. "One of them looks like Ethan. Is it his brother?"

"Come on Anna. You know that's Ethan," Arnold scolded. "Who's the other guy?"

Anna looked intently at the paper for a way out. "It says here… Steven McMillan, an associate of Ethan Dawson. That's…"

"We know who it is," Arnold interrupted. "We want to know what you know about him."

Anna shrugged her shoulders. "I don't remember Ethan ever mentioning Steven. Did he die in the storm too?"

Arnold looked extremely annoyed. "I think you're not telling us everything. But we don't have proof." He glanced at Oliver. "Go ahead and make your rounds. I'm sure Anna will tell me if she remembers anything else."

"Will do boss. Watch her, she's a spitfire." Oliver joked, grabbing his weapon and leaving.

Arnold tipped his head, making sure Oliver was gone. He leaned in, his tone softer. "Anna, I've known you since you were a little girl. I have watched you go through a lot of bad stuff, some self-inflicted, but I respect your resilience. You're a strong, godly woman who just needs a little guidance."

Anna sat with her hands folded in her lap, emotions swirling, and conviction flowing through her soul. She trusted Arnold. She had to.

He gave her a kind look. "Anna, what didn't you tell us while Oliver was here? I know you're holding back, and it pains me that you don't trust us. What's going on?"

Tears pricked her eyes. She needed Krystal. Krystal always knew what to say. Just have faith. "I do know Steven.

It's a long story… and one I'm not proud of. It'll take a while to explain everything, but right now, we have a bigger problem."

"Yes, we do," Arnold said. "That's why I called you here tonight. But why couldn't you say that in front of Oliver?"

Anna hesitated. The truth was dangerous. "Because… he may be a traitor."

Arnold sat back, silent for a long minute. "Anna," he said finally, "who else have you told?"

"Just Krystal. She's been helping me."

"Helping you do what?"

"Find the traitor," Anna said, confusion creeping into her voice.

Arnold shook his head. "Oliver is not the mole. When Ethan and I discovered classified information was leaking, Oliver was the first person we cleared. He's now my right-hand man. Until last week, you were a prime suspect. You can thank your friend for clearing that up."

"Krystal?" Anna asked.

"Not even close," Arnold said, almost amused. "Steven."

Anna reeled. "You were up at the pass?"

"Of course not. We have drones. Our intel had tagged the hikers as foreign spies and were certain you were their source. We watched them arrive and when you didn't come out, it left us puzzled. That was when we noticed a fourth person coming in from the side of the mountain. Thermal imaging revealed it as a military operative so we waited, not knowing what to do.

When Steven took out the one hiker and sent the other guy running, I sent Oliver to bring you in, but you disappeared. You're good at that."

He paused. "Bottom line, Anna. We now know Steven is your contact. That you've been the FBI's insider here. And most importantly, that you're not a traitor, just a misguided informant."

Anna trembled, her legs shaking. "Yes. I am guilty of

that, but I would never hurt our community."

"Thank you for your honesty," Arnold said. "Now listen. You can keep working undercover, but you need to be smarter. One wrong move could get you killed."

Anna offered a weak smile. "I'm sorry for being such a problem. I never wanted it to turn out that way. Can I tell Krystal?"

Arnold raised an eyebrow. "She's already been briefed."

"What?" Anna slid forward in her seat, furious. "She said she wouldn't tell anyone! Why would she do this to me?" Anna dropped her face in her hands and cried.

"Stop it, Anna. Krystal did not squeal on you. We knew you had been spending time up there and approached her after the pass incident. She's on your side."

Anna wiped her eyes. "Can I at least go see her? I need someone."

"Sure. But it's late."

"I'll see if she's awake." Anna stood up. "Oh, what was so urgent that it couldn't wait until tomorrow?"

Arnold smiled. "I didn't want to ruin church service by having this on my mind."

They walked together through the woodworking shop toward the exit.

"Will I be working in City Hall?" Anna asked.

"No," Arnold said. "You will continue working in the garden. Your security employment is classified. Only Oliver and I will know. Just help us find the traitor."

"Good night, Anna."

The night air was cold as Anna stepped outside. She headed toward Krystal's cabin. The moon barely filtered through the trees, casting faint silver patterns on the forest floor. Maybe she should wait until tomorrow after church. She heard the sound of something coming down the path. She ducked into the shadows expecting to see Oliver in his combat gear. At least he wasn't the enemy.

Instead, she heard whistling. That's not Oliver.

She held her breath as George Winston crossed the creek and headed east down the trail. What was he doing at Krystal's at this time of night? She cringed at the thought.

Well, If George just left, Krystal must be awake. Anna turned up the path and crossed the creek. At the top of the hill the dark cabin came into view. Not a light to be seen. Anna turned around and headed back down the path.

Chapter Twenty-five

Anna found a place to sit, in the crowded meeting house. The sunshine and warmer weather was encouraging more of the folks to get out of their cabins and attend the Sunday morning service. She spotted Krystal next to Louise about halfway to the front. A sinking feeling hit her stomach. All of a sudden, she felt very alone.

She struggled to find peace in the singing and instead found herself analyzing the men in the meeting house. Was one of them the traitor? She shook her head. Was this how Satan worked? Was she the problem? Her chest tightened under the weight of the previous evening's events. Everything she had done wrong seemed to be coming to light.

Her gaze landed on Arnold, sitting there, singing like he didn't have a care in the world. By his actions, he proved that you could spend your weekdays at City Hall and live the rest of your life in a primitive, remote community. The contrast overwhelmed her. Could she do it? At least she was able to spend most of her time in the garden.

After the singing, Eli stood and read the story of Joseph,

reassuring his brothers after their father's death. When the reading finished, Abram stood up to speak. His trembling yet strong voice filled the room.

"I would like to thank my brother for sharing with us the story we have heard many times. Joseph was favored by his father, and it created envy with his brothers. Envy can cause us to do things that we normally wouldn't consider. It destroys relationships. It leads to strife, division, and bitterness. Fortunately, here in our community, we all have access to the same material blessings. But envy doesn't just apply to possessions, it also relates to the life that someone else is experiencing.

"It is important to thank God for the life He has given us. He has a plan."

Abram paused, his gaze steady.

"The Bible urges us to guard against envy. It's destructive to each of us and to our community. My brothers and sisters beware. Satan is cunning; he finds the smallest crack to work his way into your heart.

"Finally, envy is a contrast to love. True love, as Jesus told us, does not envy or seeks to outdo others."

As Abram slowly sat down, Anna pondered his words. It was as if he knew what she was thinking. Was she being envious of the life that others were living? Mothers, daughters, sisters, wives? All she could do was acknowledge that, yes, she was still lonely.

Eli, asked one of the deacons to read from Romans chapter twelve. Anna tried to stay focused as she heard, "Do not be conformed to this world, but be transformed by the renewing of your mind."

Did she even know what the renewing of her mind would look like? Now she would have to listen to Eli explain it for an hour. He had a way of getting under her skin. Why couldn't he be more like Abram? Maybe he will when he gets older and wiser.

The deacon continued, "Be kindly affectionate to one

another with brotherly love, in honor giving preference to one another."

The words struck her like a clapper against a bell. Was she kind to others? Was this whole idea of weeding out the traitor, even if there really was one, being judgmental and mean? She didn't hate anyone, and she wasn't doing it out of selfish ambition. Maybe she was being too hard on Krystal.

"Do not be overcome by evil, but overcome evil with good."

Wow, what a way to end. She had started as an informant to help the community. Had she allowed evil to twist her mission? Anna shook her head slightly. Still, she felt alone.

Eli stood to his feet and surveyed the congregation. "Vengeance is mine, says the Lord." His booming voice echoed off the whitewashed walls.

"It is with humility and by the grace of our Lord and Savior, Jesus Christ, that I stand here today. I pray that God will speak through us as we share His message of justice and mercy."

He paused for a moment and looked down at his Bible.

"In first Samuel chapter twenty-four we are told of the account of King Saul going out into the wilderness in search of David. He was filled with envy, knowing that David was to be the next King. King Saul came across a cave and went inside to rest. It just so happened that it was the same cave where David and his warriors where hiding. While King Saul rested, David's men wanted him to kill King Saul. But, David knew that there was a cost to unrighteous vengeance. He asked the men, 'Who am I to stretch out my hand against the Lord's anointed one?' David would not let his men take vengeance on the King. He trusted that God would bring justice in his time.

"But when vengeance takes over, we become prisoners of our own anger. We think punishing others will set us free, but in reality, it only deepens the wounds. What we need is not revenge, but healing."

Eli wasn't done yet. He thumbed through his Bible, finally finding what he wanted. "We need to trust God's justice. As we read in Genesis, Joseph's brothers had concern about their plight once their father died. They were certain that Joseph would take revenge on them. What did Joseph tell them? He reminded them that they had meant evil against him, but that God meant it for good. Justice delayed is not justice denied. God's justice is perfect and will come in His time. The question I have for each of you, do you trust Him enough to let go of your anger?"

Anna was feeling the pressure pushing down on her. Was Eli aware of her situation? Did Arnold tell him about her past? Or was this a happenstance? What was God trying to tell her? Her attention turned back to Eli.

"Redemption comes through forgiveness. Jesus tells us to love our enemies and pray for those who persecute us. Forgiveness is not easy, but it does give us freedom. Forgiveness allows God to work in the hearts of both, the offender and the offended.

"Are there wounds in your life that need healing? Are you holding onto bitterness, waiting on justice to be served? Today, God is asking you to give it to Him. You need to let go."

It looked as if Eli was looking her in the eyes. She didn't know what to do, so she gave a wry smile and looked down.

"Letting go of vengeance does not mean ignoring wrongdoing." Eli continued. "There is a difference between seeking justice and seeking revenge. Justice is about righteousness and restoration. Seeking revenge is about making others suffer.

"Sometimes we are required to uncover the truth. Sometimes we are required to stand up to injustice. But, always are we called to do so with a heart that seeks God's will and strive for restoration. Justice in God's hands leads to redemption. Justice in our hands often leads to destruction."

Finally, Eli closed his Bible and sat down. Anna exhaled.

Arwel Brannon, the youngest minister, stood.

"You are faced with choices in your life. Will you hold onto your anger, or will you release it into the hands of a just and loving God?

"You will be wronged, trust that God sees you. If you are struggling with bitterness, ask God to help you forgive. If you are fighting for justice, seek it with wisdom and love, not hatred. God is the ultimate judge. It is our responsibility to trust Him, live in righteousness, and let go of the burden of vengeance. Just as God has forgiven us, so are we to forgive those who have wronged us."

After singing another hymn, Arwel closed in prayer.

Anna exhaled slowly, putting her finger against her temple. The sermon clung to her like a winter chill, working its way into places she didn't want to acknowledge. She let the sunlight warm her face as she sat on the outdoor bench, waiting for Krystal. When would the truth come out?

Krystal spotted her and hurried over, smiling. "You're looking forlorn today. Are you okay?" She asked, sitting down next to Anna.

"I'm not sure how I'm doing. We have a lot we need to talk about. Are you busy this afternoon?" Anna asked.

"Louise and the boys are coming up for lunch. You're welcome to join us."

Anna gave Krystal a grim smile. "Not very conducive to the conversation we need. I can come up this evening, unless George will to be there."

Kristal jerked around, startled. "Who?"

"Don't give me that," Anna said, trying to keep her tone soft. "I was on my way to see you last night when I saw George Winston coming down from your place."

Krystal looked shocked. "No one was at the house last night. I put the children to bed when it got dark and turned in myself shortly after that."

"If he wasn't up at your place, what was he doing coming down your path?" Anna asked.

Fear flickered in Krystal's eyes. "Come to think of it, Growler was agitated around eight. I let him out, and he took off into the woods. Wasn't gone long. I just figured he heard an animal. Do you think George was out there?"

"I'm almost certain. Why did you ask me about him the other day?"

Krystal hesitated and then lowered her voice. "Can we talk about that when you come up?"

Anna nodded, softening her tone. "Sorry for coming across so harsh. I'll see you this evening."

Chapter Twenty -six

Maps were spread across the conference table in the briefing room. Ethan and the rest of their team were studying the terrain around Charlotte Lake. Over breakfast they'd heard rumors of a credible threat against the primitive, off-grid community.

"What's the plan?" Colonel Whitlock asked as he walked into the room.

"Identify and eliminate the enemy, sir." Tanner answered.

"Good to see you back, Tanner. You still seeing double?"

"Just one of you, sir. Fortunately."

"Thank goodness," the rest of the room echoed.

"Alright, gentlemen. Thanks for all your love. Let's get started."

Riley brought the satellite view of Charlotte Lake up on the large screen. Pointer in hand, he circled the lake. "Most of you have been here. None more than Ethan. We're not going into the community but doing what we're calling Operation Overwatch."

Steven interrupted. "Rumor is that there is a credible threat. Who are we dealing with?"

"We're still not sure, but we suspect it has to do with Rafael and his gang. We have resources working night and day in hopes of uncovering the threat. We know there were only ten of them at the mission, but that doesn't mean much. With so much illegal movement across the border, Rafael's had plenty of opportunity to recruit. We don't know if we're dealing with a dozen, or an army. The analyst estimates five to six hundred."

Ethan spoke up. "Last time it was three hundred hardened street gang members, and you took them out with air-to-surface rockets. You have any more if we need them?"

Colonel Whitlock half-raised a hand to interject. "We have everything we need. But remember, that's the number the analyst came up with. Scientifically, the number is considerably lower. The A.I. probability report has the threat number down around seventy-five."

"So, A.I. calculates that Rafael will only bring the men he thinks he needs?" Ethan asked.

"My take is that Rafael thinks Charlotte Lake is a small, unguarded village," Whitlock answered. "We won't know until it happens. In the meantime, let's get on with today's mission. Go ahead, Riley."

Riley clicked to the next slide. "We'll be splitting the six of you into three teams. The primary route into Charlotte Lake is Kearsarge Pass. Secondary is Charlotte Creek. The third, highly unlikely, is Glen Pass. We propose the Glen Pass team set up on the ridge overlooking the trail and lake, giving us backup for the other two."

"I volunteer for Glen Pass," Ethan said eagerly.

"We figured as much," Colonel Whitlock said. "We don't want you too close to the community. But it makes sense to have you there. You're more likely to spot abnormalities, given your time there."

"Thank you, sir." Ethan felt the tinge of excitement.

"Just remember, Ethan, you are not to go into the community unless they are under fire," Whitlock added, reading Ethan's mind. "I think it best if Steven joins you. He might be the only one capable of stopping you from starting a war."

Ethan grinned, raising both hands, palms out. "Nobody's perfect."

"Let's get with it, gentlemen. We are not notifying Charlotte Lake security about our presence," Whitlock said, locking eyes with Ethan, "and let's keep it that way. Understood?"

"Yes, sir," the team echoed.

Riley returned to the monitor, bringing up an overhead of the basin below Glen Pass. "Due to the proximity, you two will drop in right here. As you can see, there are a lot of boulders sticking out of the snowpack. Use caution, we don't need to do a medevac at that altitude."

Ethan and Steven nodded.

"Tanner and Roland, you'll be at Kearsarge Pass. You will jump in under silk too. It's pretty straight forward, except you're the most likely to see action."

"No problem, other than Roland gets airsick." Tanner laughed, punching Roland's shoulder.

"Keep that up, Tanner, and you will be the action," Roland shot back rubbing his shoulder.

"Okay children, behave." Riley clicked the mouse, bringing up another image. "Lewis, Conrad, you'll cover Charlotte Creek, where it dumps into Bubbs Creek. This spot above the valley looks good. But if it looks too risky, we'll drop you at Cooper Creek trailhead and you can hike up. That would be about six miles."

Lewis and Conrad shrugged. "We'll find a drop zone."

"Alright," Riley said. "We will be flying nighttime drone missions, so Ethan, don't shoot everything you see out of the sky."

Ethan looked around with an innocent question mark on

his face, causing the team to burst into laughter.

Riley raised his voice to be heard. "Depending on the winds aloft, we're looking at a 3 a.m. departure. You'll be notified if that changes. Jump altitude will be fifteen thousand feet, no oxygen needed. That's all I got. Colonel?"

"Gear up and rest while you can. This mission is going to test every one of you." Whitlock stretched and got to his feet.

* ● *

The afternoon sun reflected off the runway as Steven and Ethan exited the building. "Let's get a hot meal before we go on a MRE diet," Steven said.

"I know a great bakery about seven hundred yards from our overwatch position," Ethan smiled. "Most of which is vertical."

Inside the mess hall, the clanging of dishes and banging of pans competed with dinner conversations. Steven looked around, shaking his head.

"If you don't mind, let's get our food to go and head back to the briefing room. There's stuff I'd like to discuss, and don't need the whole camp hearing it. Not that they could in here."

"Yeah, it's not exactly a peaceful place tonight. The briefing room sounds good."

Food in hand, they walked out into the evening. The sun had just disappeared below the tree line. A cold breeze off the mountains reminded Ethan of being in the crater at Charlotte Lake. He missed sitting on the front porch, watching the arrival of the night sky. He felt the hidden joy of tonight's mission.

Unfortunately, they would not be in the stone cabin by the fireplace tonight.

"This is much better," Steven said as they stepped inside the empty briefing room.

"Do you have any reservations about tonight's mission?" Ethan asked, pulling a couple of water bottles from the fridge.

Steven finished chewing on a mouthful of meatloaf. "No reservations, but I have a personal question. Do you mind?"

Ethan laughed. "Everything you ask me is personal. What's on your mind?"

"I have known Anna for a long time. She was so strong-willed and determined, I called her Tiger, until you came into town."

"What's changed?" Ethan asked.

"Before you, she was so ingrained in the community culture that it was almost impossible to get useful information. We go back about fifteen years. She was adventurous, innocent and vulnerable. I was eighteen months into the FBI and was tasked with infiltrating Charlotte Lake.

"I loved the mountains, so I backpacked into the community. Back then, there had been some trouble, and they weren't letting anyone in. So, I hiked across Glen Pass, met one of the rangers, and, to shorten the story, met Anna through him."

"You still haven't told me what changed," Ethan said.

"I was getting to it."

"Via Rae Lakes?" Ethan quipped.

"Yes, because it took time. Anna was getting paid, but never spent a dime. And she gave us nothing worthwhile. The Bureau wanted to know how the governing body worked. Anna either didn't know or wouldn't tell us. Even to this day, a lot of mysteries surround that lake."

"There sure are," Ethan said, chewing on a half-cooked carrot. "Beyond anyone's imagination. So, what's changed? We've got a flight to catch."

Steven sighed. "You're annoying. Okay, skipping ahead,

after you arrived, her reports shifted. They went from vague updates to actual intel we could use."

"And you blame me?"

"Of course. You inspired her to think outside the box. The shy young girl, has now become a brave outgoing, and I might add, compassionate woman."

"She's always been compassionate. You said you met with her recently. How's she doing?

"Well, pretty good. She gave me a big hug after I terminated a bad guy and ran off his buddy." Steven grinned. "For once, she didn't ask about you."

"Is that supposed to break my heart?" Ethan smiled.

"It's a good thing, Ethan. She's a little bit crazy, just like you."

Steven tossed his Styrofoam container in the trash.

"Let's get some rest. Last time in a warm bed for awhile."

Chapter Twenty -seven

The waning moon was just coming up over Madera Peak when Ethan left his quarters and made his way to the hangar. He paused for a moment, looking deep into the millions of stars mapping the night sky. The chill he felt wasn't from the cold. God willing, before the night was over, he would be within sight of Krystal's cabin.

The hangar buzzed with activity as specialists prepared for the mission. Along one wall, tables held all of their gear. Ethan found his table and started the inspection. Priority one, was his chute. Without a properly opening chute, he wouldn't need the rest of the gear. He checked it carefully, verified the packing, then patted it and moved on to his pack.

After inspecting the empty pack for abnormalities, he started packing the contents. Subzero sleeping bag, four-season tent, MREs, water filter, Jetboil, toilet paper, emergency kit, and a mix of smaller essentials.

The only things left on the table were his weapons. The usual, a sniper rifle, a 9mm Beretta, and two hundred rounds of ammunition. With everything packed, Ethan joined the rest of the team sitting around a table, the hum of last-minute preparations filling the hangar. He leaned back and stared at the softly buzzing overhead lights.

"Do you guys ever think about what happens if this is our last mission?" Tanner asked.

Roland laughed. "You think we're getting fired?"

"No, seriously," Tanner said. "What we do is dangerous. We're jumping out of a King Air in a few hours. If something goes wrong… what's next?"

Steven took a sip of coffee, his expression unreadable. "That all depends on what you believe."

"Do you go to church?" Tanner asked.

Steven shook his head. "Grew up in church. Didn't take it too seriously. Not sure what I believe now."

"Why?"

Steven shrugged. "Maybe I saw too much. Too many people get the short end of the stick. How could that happen if God is in control?"

Roland nodded. "I know what you mean. It's hard to believe when you see the worst of civilization. Feels like if God was in control, things wouldn't be so broken."

Tanner leaned forward and turned to Ethan. "So… do you believe in God?"

Ethan met his gaze. "I do."

Tanner's eyes widened. "After everything you've been through, you still believe?"

Ethan's gaze hardened slightly. "You would think everything I went through would have made me give up. But honestly… it's why I believe. For what it's worth, I made that decision just a few days before leaving Charlotte Lake."

Silence settled over the group, heavier than before.

"Do you ever pray before a mission?" Lewis asked.

Ethan smiled faintly. "Every time."

Roland exhaled. "Well… can't hurt, I guess."

Tanner chuckled. "Alright then. Do you mind praying for us now?"

Ethan sighed and ran his hand through his hair. Then,

without hesitation, he bowed his head.

"God, You made us. You know exactly what we're walking into. You know the folks at Charlotte Lake and how much they love You. We're trying to protect them, Lord. Keep us sharp, keep us strong, protect us from the enemy, whoever and whatever that enemy might be. And, God… if this is our final mission, don't let us face it alone. Amen."

A chorus of quiet "Amens" followed. No one spoke for a moment.

Roland shrugged. "Well, I guess I can't say I've never prayed before a mission now. Thank you, Ethan."

The mood seemed to have shifted, still serious, but somehow steadier. Whatever happened around Charlotte Lake. They felt as if they weren't alone.

Colonel Whitlock strolled into the hangar. "You princesses done packing, or should I call the cub scouts to help you?"

"Says the guy that gets to sleep with his teddy bear tonight?" Conrad shot back.

Whitlock smirked. "That smart remark just earned you the number one spot on tonight's jump. Hope you're wearing your thermal underwear."

"No problem, sir." Conrad laughed. "First to hit the silk, is the first one in camp."

"Alright, gentlemen, let's move." Colonel Whitlock turned and headed for the King Air.

— • ● • —

The rumble of the PT-6 turboprops shook the inside of the King Air as they back-taxied for runway 26. Deja-vu for the six combat veterans strapped in the back. It had only been a few weeks sense they had dropped into Mexico. But this time, they were jumping into friendly territory. The climate would be their enemy. A cold front was forecast to move through the area in two days.

The King Air made a teardrop turn at the end of the runway and came to a stop. The rumble of the turbines shook the airframe as Colonel Whitlock pushed the throttles forward. The rumble turned into a distinct, rhythmic chopping sound, as the high-speed propellers bit into the air. Ethan felt the plane fighting the brakes. A small jerk and the tone shifted rapidly as the prop load changed, they accelerated down the runway. The rhythm of the expansion joints on the runway quickened and then disappeared as the King Air rotated and rose into the night.

Climbing to fifteen thousand feet, they paralleled the western slope of the Sierra Nevada Mountains. Ethan checked the altimeter on his wrist as they leveled off and turned east. First drop, ten minutes out.

Riley moved to the door and clicked in his safety strap. The jump light turned red.

Conrad and Lewis stood and moved to the back, followed by Tanner and Roland. Ethan sat, staring at the light, waiting for it to turn green.

Last time he was in this position, he had landed in the desert. All he had to do was miss the cactus. Tonight, he would land on a snow-covered mountain. Anything could happen. Could he trust God to protect them as they fell through the darkness?

He exhaled and tightened the straps on his chute.

The light turned green. In two seconds, the first two jumpers disappeared into the night. Two minutes later, the Kearsarge Pass team followed.

The King Air buffeted as it crossed the ridge east of Kearsarge Pass. They made a tight right turn back toward Charlotte Lake. Ethan followed Steven to the door. Riley peered out, then stepped back. The light flashed green.

They fell into the blackness.

Ethan stabilized and checked his altimeter. Fourteen

thousand feet. This would be a quick one. Their target, ten thousand five hundred.

Three… two… one… pull.

The chute jerked him upright. He looked up. Full canopy, no rips. Flipping down his NVGs he scanned for the landing zone. Sixty seconds to touchdown. LZ located.

Where's Steven? There he was just about down. Ethan realized he would overfly the LZ. Spiral to stay in zone.

Snowpack coming up.

Miss the boulder. Brake descent. Roll into the hill.

He hit the snowpack hard, punching through the crust he post holed up to his knees. Trying to roll, he felt the chute twist his legs painfully. He threw his weight the other way and plopped down on the snow. Pain flared in his knees as he collapsed his chute.

"How you doing over here?" Steven called, laughing as he trudged across the snowpack. "Have to say, looked like you stuck the landing."

"I'll let you know once I get out of this hole. The chute tried to destroy my knees."

Ethan unhooked his packs and shoved them aside. Steven reached down and slowly pulled him out of the snow.

"Easy now. They're a little tender," Ethan said, wincing.

After moving and stretching carefully, the pain eased. Ten minutes later, Ethan was back on his feet, and they moved down the mountain toward their overwatch position.

A natural depression created the perfect camp spot. It was hidden from the village, trees provided cover from overhead drones, and they were protected from the wind.

First priority was to set up their tents and stash their gear. By the time they finished, the sky had already begun to lighten.

Moving up to the edge of the berm, they found a spot to scope the whole lake without being seen.

For twenty minutes, they lay on the edge of the berm, scanning the community below. Ethan's binoculars found

Krystal's cabin, just two hundred fifty yards away.

"Hey, you think it would be alright if I went down there for a cup of coffee?"

Steven chuckled. "That was one of the Colonel's concerns when you picked this spot. Someday, but not today."

Before Ethan could argue, Steven continued, "Before you crash, could you contact the other teams? I would like to know they're in place."

"Sure, be right back."

Sliding down from the berm, Ethan slipped his earpiece in and keyed his radio. "Glen Pass to Kearsarge, come in."

Static crackled for a moment before Tanner's voice came through. "Kearsarge in the nest. How's things there?"

"Perfect. Just like home. Have you talked to Bubbs?"

"Affirmative. They landed on the wrong side of the river. May be a bit before they're in position."

Ethan acknowledged and signed off. It was his nap time. Four hours would come too soon.

Chapter Twenty-eight

Anna had spent all afternoon in City Hall going over the list. She was in over her head trying to find the suspect, none of it made sense. Every member of the security team had been vetted and was a strong supporter of the community. She had to be missing something. Could someone have access to security without actually working there?

She glanced around the room. If anyone saw her digging through files, the suspect might get tipped off. Maybe that was the answer. Start a rumor and watch what happens.

For the next two hours, she scrolled through the entire list. One by one, she opened each file and in a box marked notes, she typed the same four words, "Suspected of adverse activities." She winced at the thought of what could happen if this backfired. At least she was logged in under Arnold's account. He will be furious, but get over it if she found the mole.

Anna slipped out of City Hall through the storehouse exit and headed for Krystal's. The question still nagged. Why had Krystal asked about George Winston?

She didn't think George had the mental capacity to sell out the community, and he didn't work for security. But maybe Krystal was working with him. Could Krystal have outside contacts? George might have classified access through his dad. She was certain Doctor Winston was on the leadership team. That could be a possibility. No, that didn't sit right. Krystal wouldn't risk doing something like that, not with the kids.

The mountain stream ran full and tumbled down beside the switchbacks. The trail was slick with moss and mud. Anna noticed large boot prints on the trail. Someone else had come this way recently. Was George up here? No way. His boots weren't this big. She would find out soon enough.

"Good morning, Anna. What brings you up here today?" Krystal greeted her at the door as Growler sniffed around Anna's boots, tail wagging with recognition.

"I thought maybe I would update you on what's going on. Are you busy?"

"Busy as in raising three children? I would guess I'm busy. But I've got time for a good chat. Want to enjoy this warm afternoon out here?"

The sun felt good as they settled into the rocking chairs on the front porch, overlooking the lake. After a quiet minute, Anna broke the silence.

"So, the other day you asked about George Winston. Why?"

Krystal gave her a knowing smile. "You're relentless. George came up here and asked if I was interested in seeing someone, namely, him."

"And what did you say?"

Krystal shifted uncomfortably. "I told him it's too soon since Ethan left. And honestly, I don't really know him."

"But what did you tell him?"

"I said I would think about it. That was the last time I saw him. He hasn't been back and avoids me at church."

"You sure he hasn't been up here since? I saw someone

coming down the path from your cabin. I think it was George."

Krystal took a long breath. "Anna, as I told you. That was the only time. And we stood right here on the porch. I remember because I wasn't wearing a coat and it was freezing. He didn't come back after that."

Anna considered what Krystal had said. Could George be spying on Krystal? If he was interested in her, would he do something that stupid?

"Strange. I'd keep my doors locked if I were you. I'll tell security to keep a watch on the area." Anna paused. "Let me fill you in on what I've been doing."

She told Krystal everything, starting with Oliver taking her to City Hall.

Krystal shook her head. "Do you know what kind of hornets' nest you stirred up by marking everyone in security as suspect? You probably just alienated everyone except the person you're after."

Anna winced. "Maybe. But I had to try something."

"You remind me of someone I used to know. God only knows how much I miss him."

"Me too. We wouldn't be in this mess if he was here."

"It's getting chilly. Do you want to come in for dinner?"

"If you don't mind. I get lonesome at home every night."

"Not at all. It will make the children happy. They love you."

• ● •

The sun had set by the time Anna left Krystal's. Stars glimmered overhead and a chill had replaced the warmth of the day. The sound of the stream tumbling beside the path was hypnotic.

She stopped at a fallen log and sat in the darkness, letting her eyes close. The cool, rushing water as it carved its way over the stones, gurgling, and chattering like a secret whisper to the trees. The sound, both constant and ever changing. A soft murmur in a shallow eddy, and a sudden rush where the water spilled over rocky ledges. It filled her senses, completely washing away the noise of anxiety, leaving only this moment. Pure, unbroken, infinite.

Then…

A rustle behind her.

Too close.

She jerked around.

A dark figure loomed. Something heavy struck her head. Pain exploded, then darkness.

———•●•———

"Ethan, get up here now." The crackle in his earpiece snapped him awake.

Sliding from his sleeping bag, Ethan grabbed his night vision goggles and climbed the berm where Steven lay prone, scope to his eye.

"What's happening?"

"Someone's carrying a woman. Two hundred and fifty yards out. You will see him come out of the trees shortly."

Ethan trained his NVGs. A shape emerged. His pulse spiked.

"It's Anna. I'd recognize her from a thousand yards. What happened?"

"She left Krystal's half an hour ago. I lost her when she entered the trees heading toward the lake. Then this guy appeared carrying her. She's out cold."

"She needs our help."

"Not yet, Ethan. We need to see where he's taking her. If we jump too early, we might lose them both."

Ethan gritted his teeth. Watching Anna being treated like that was more than he could handle. Where were they going? He searched the side of the mountain in the direction they were moving.

"There are more of them. A small camp, four hundred yards, just below our elevation."

Steven trained his rifle in that direction. "Yeah… that's not good. Call in backup."

Ethan slid down the bank and grabbed the radio. "Glen Pass to Base, come in."

Static.

He tried again. Nothing.

"Ethan, you may want to see this."

Back on the berm, Ethan saw Anna was just being carried into camp. Three guys were standing around a small fire and turned towards the arrival. Two of the men drug Anna into one of the tents.

Ethan felt the anger rise inside. "No response from base. You do what you must, but I can't sit here and watch them treat her like that. I'm going in."

He slid down the bank and was pulling on his combat vest when Steven slid down to join him. "You're not going it alone brother. Just try not to kill them all. It would be nice to have someone to interrogate."

"Sure. I'll try, but don't get your hopes up. Remember Marghozar?"

"Who could forget? That was horrible, and you didn't even know her. Let's just hope this doesn't turn out that way."

"That depends on our approach. What you thinking?" Ethan asked.

"What about Amir Mahbata?" Steven said, referring to a surprise attack they experienced in Afghanistan.

"We need a flash grenade for that to work." Ethan said.

"I have us covered." Steven patted his side. "Let's go."

They moved out of camp and crossed the contour of the

mountain, staying well above the abductors. "I'm guessing Venezuelan gang. They're ruthless." Steven whispered at a hundred yards out. "We have only one shot at this."

They advanced stealthily through the trees, their senses sharpened as they closed in on the enemy camp. The soft glow of the fire illuminated the three men. One of them was standing near the tent Anna was in. The other two were conversing by the fire, their rifles resting on a log nearby.

Behind a cluster of trees, they verified their plan in hushed whispers. The objective was clear, rescue Anna, and if possible, capture at least one of the assailants for interrogation.

Ethan would circle around to approach the guard next to the tent. Steven indicated he would handle the other two. Ethan held up two fingers and pointed to his watch.

The seconds ticked as Ethan moved silently, footsteps muffled by the pine needles. He reached the rear of the tent and heard muffled struggle inside the tent. His muscles tightened with anger induced adrenaline. He spotted Steven on the other side of the campfire slowly coming out of the trees, his suppressed handgun extended. Ethan glanced at his watch. Ten seconds. Silently he started the countdown. Three, two, now.

Ethan's movement was swift; his left arm wrapped around the assailant's neck, and he shoved his silenced Beretta into the man's side. He yanked the man into the darkness. The man's left hand went for his weapon. The sound of Ethan's muffled shot was echoed.

Ethan watched Steven dragging one of the assailants away from the fire. The other lay crumpled on the ground. He could see Steven in the woods with a weapon trained on the entrance to the tent.

Then, the tent flap zipped open.

A burly unshaven man stepped out, dragging a dazed Anna. Even from his position in the trees, Ethan could see the flicker from the fire, reflect off the Bowie knife held to

Anna's throat.

The man's eyes widened as he saw his friend lying face down on the other side of the fire. He started dragging Anna towards the trees. It was apparent that he wanted out of the light. It was time for the reveal.

Ethan stepped out of the shadow with his arm at full extension, the Beretta pointed at the captor's head.

"Alto" he commanded.

The man froze as he turned towards Ethan. "Stay back!" he shouted in Spanish.

Ethan's Spanish wasn't good, but he knew what the man said by the fear in his eyes. Out of the corner of his eye he could see Steven approaching through the trees.

"Suelta la pistola!" The captor yelled as he pressed the knife tighter. Ethan could see a small amount of blood starting to run down Anna's throat. He slowly lowered his Beretta and laid it on the ground. He raised his hands. "Let her go. She's not done anything to you."

"Shut up and get on the ground." The man was bouncing back and forth from English to Spanish. Another sign he was about to panic.

Ethan had to challenge the captor's ego. "Look at her. She's so weak she can't even stand up. Why don't you fight someone your own size. You're nothing but a big gorilla" Ethan mocked as he started to approach them, his hands held out to his side preparing to fight. That's all it took, the man dropped Anna to the ground and started forward.

A red dot appeared on his temple.

A muffled shot.

He collapsed at Ethan's feet.

Ethan flipped down his NVGs and surveyed the area. No movement on the ridge. No backup from town. The threat was neutralized.

Steven knelt beside Anna, checking her pulse. Ethan silently prayed for her as Steven checked her vitals.

"We got here in time." Steven said. "Other than a lump

on the head, she appears to be okay."

"There's a doctor in the community. If you want to maintain overwatch, I'll take her there." Ethan said.

"Nice try, Ethan. You are not going into the village. We can call in help."

"What about Krystal's?"

"Not a bad idea, but I'm taking her. You clean up this mess."

Ethan sighed as Steven carried Anna away. "Probably for the best."

He doused the fire and wrapped the bodies in sleeping bags, dragging them to a ravine.

"Next time," he mumbled, "we make this a downhill thing."

He had just returned from dragging the third body into a ravine when Steven returned.

"How's Anna?"

"She was still quite groggy when I set her down on the porch. I knocked on the door to wake Growler and got out of there."

"Did you see Krystal?"

"I waited in the shadows until Krystal opened the door. Growler came after me but Krystal's attention was focused on Anna. I petted the old hound for a bit while Krystal helped Anna into the house. When Krystal called for Growler he took off and so did I."

"Thanks. I really miss her. Maybe someday. Let's finish cleaning this stuff up and get this prisoner up to camp."

Chapter Twenty-Nine

Where was she?

Why was he carrying her? It felt so good to be in his arms. Could she stay here forever? Why was he sitting her down?

Moonlight spilled across the cabin. It looked familiar. Had she had been before?

A dog barked. She'd heard it before, where? Things began to sharpen in her mind.

Then a bright light hit her face.

"Oh no, Anna."

The voice was close. Someone she knew.

She felt strong but gentle hands checking her pulse. She knew those hands.

"Krystal," she muttered weakly.

"Let's get you inside, dear." Krystal said, lifting her carefully.

She laid Anna on the couch and gently ran a cool washcloth over her forehead and cheeks. The soothing touch quieted the chaos in Anna's chest. Dirt and grime faded with each gentle wipe.

"What happened?" Krystal asked.

Anna tried to answer, but no words came. Panic turned to tears, she could feel running down her face.

"It's okay, my dear. Just relax."

Krystal's voice wrapped around her like a warm blanket. Anna melted into the cushions and drifted off to sleep.

● ● ●

Voices.

Who was talking? It wasn't Krystal.

How long had she been asleep?

Anna opened her eyes. Blurry shapes slowly came into focus. Krystal… and someone else.

Doctor Winston.

He was seated beside her, holding her hand. Was he counting her pulse? Did she even have one?

She blinked her eyes. Things were clearer now.

He placed his stethoscope on her chest. He was checking her heart. It was broken.

Tears filled her eyes.

"Doctor," she whispered.

No response.

"Doctor," she tried again, her voice a feeble rasp.

He smiled. "Anna, you're awake. Welcome back."

"Where have I been?" she asked, voice soft but audible.

"That's what we would like to know," he said gently.

"How did you end up here at Krystal's?"

She opened her eyes wider, pain pulsing through her skull. She tried to sit up, but the doctor's hand stopped her.

"Stay lying down. You were hit on the head, hard. Do you remember what happened?"

She winced, trying to piece the fragments together. "I… I was sitting by the stream. Then… I think Ethan was carrying me. He was strong. I remember… they fought the bad guys."

Her vision tunneled again. Darkness crept back in. She struggled to stay awake, finally succumbing to the darkness.

— • ● • —

She was floating, just above the treetops. A thickening haze rose from the lake, reaching for her. She reached out, touching the approaching fog. The wind descended from the mountain tops, pushing her out across the water.

Her heart filled with fear as she watched the waves churning below. Whitecaps tumbling over each other, thunderstorms towered overhead. She saw slanting rain moving across the lake before pounding her with stinging pinpricks.

"Where are you?" she cried out to God. Only the howling wind responded. She felt herself descending towards the angry waves. Desperation clawed at her. "Jesus, please save me."

Through the oppressive darkness, a small light appeared, distant but growing brighter. She reached for the light. Hope arising within her as the light drew near.

She reached for it, hope rising. It expanded, pushing back the shadows.

Crashing waves reverberated in her ears. Her body shook, jolting her awake.

Her eyes shot open.

— • ● • —

"Anna, wake up!" Doctor Winston shook her shoulder.
"I'm awake," She mumbled.

175

"I thought we were losing you, girl. You can't shut down on us."

Anna sat up as her awareness slowly returned. "Can I have a drink of water?"

She sat staring into space as she sipped water through a straw. Trying to piece together the night's events.

She remembered leaving Krystal's… walking toward the stream… the sound of the rushing water… Sitting on the log...

Then. The picture became clearer.

A dark figure from the shadows.

A stick in his hand.

The look in his eyes.

No.

He wouldn't do that.

Would he?

Her chest tightened. Her stomach twisted. She shut her eyes, but his face remained. Was it real?

She pushed the hurt aside. Her head still throbbed. She needed to talk to Steven.

She looked up at Doctor Winston. "How long before I can go home?"

"Not for awhile, my dear." Doctor Winston replied. "Krystal's going to take care of you. I'll be back this evening."

Morning light filtered through the window as the doctor left instructions and grabbed his bag.

Anna patted the couch beside her. "Krystal… I need to tell you something."

Krystal sighed as she plopped down next to Anna. "You really should rest. We can talk later. I'm exhausted."

"I saw his face. The man who attacked me."

"How could you? It was dark."

"I don't know. But, when I shut my eyes, that's all I see. The stick raised above his head… and the moonlight… I saw his face. I don't understand. He must hate me." Anna sobbed.

"Who's face, dear?"

"I don't want to say his name," Anna whispered, burying her face in Krystal's shoulder.

Krystal wrapped her arms around her. "Only God can take away this pain, Anna. But you're in danger, Arnold needs to know."

— • ● • —

"Is he ready to talk?" Ethan asked Steven, nodding toward the zip-tied man propped against a boulder.

"He's said a couple of things about his rights. I explained that illegal criminals are not blessed with rights." Steven said.

"Anything about why Anna was kidnapped?"

"Not yet. Maybe a little enhanced interrogation will help."

Steven crouched beside the prisoner, speaking in low Spanish. Ethan couldn't hear the words, but the fear on the man's face told him everything.

"Well, that was interesting." Steven said when he sat back down. "He said his name is Pablo. Claims they weren't here to kidnap anyone. They were to meet their contact from the village. He showed up with Anna and said to dispose of her. They didn't want to, but the man said he couldn't do it himself... because he is a 'godly man.'"

"What?" Ethan's anger rose. "A godly man clubs a defenseless woman, and then turns her over to a vicious gang?"

Steven shrugged. "I have a feeling he's not as godly as he claims. If he'd stayed in camp, he could've explained it to his Maker."

Ethan's eyes narrowed. "You took Anna to Krystal's. He doesn't know she's alive. We need to keep it that way."

"The doctor came and went. Think he told anyone?"

"Not necessarily. He keeps people's personal information close to his chest. The sooner we shut this down, the better."

"You stay here, and I'll go." Steven got to his feet.

"No way, brother. Krystal needs to know. We can swear her to secrecy. Don't even try to stop me." Ethan stood. "Is Pablo secure?"

Fear returned to Pablo's face as Steven practiced his Spanish. "He's not going anywhere."

They moved through the trees, careful not to be seen in the early morning light.

"What did you tell him?"

Steven laughed. "I just told him, that the rock he thinks he's sitting on is a grenade without the safety pin."

"I wondered what that Spanish word kaboom meant."

Ethan's heart pounded as they approached the cabin. It had been over six months since that Sunday afternoon with Krystal. She had told him she would pray for him every day and anxiously wait for his return. But the world believed he died in the crash. Did she?

"Wait here," Steven said, as they came to the edge of the clearing. "Let me explain before she sees you."

"What's the point?"

"Dude, once she sees you, logic's out the window. I need her to understand the Anna situation before that happens."

Ethan nodded reluctantly. "I suppose you're right."

"Give me five minutes. When she comes out on the porch, she's all yours." Steven grinned. "Go easy on her. She's been through a lot."

"She's not the only one."

Steven walked through the clearing and stepped onto the porch. Growler barked from inside.

Ethan watched as the door opened, and Krystal greeted Steven. He watched as they shook hands, then went inside.

Growler burst across the clearing. He barked a couple of

times and ran circles around his old master. Finally, stopping to mark a tree Growler returned to Ethan sniffing around his legs.

Ethan talked softly to the dog as he reached down and scratched his ears.

"How's she been? You been protecting them like I told you to?"

He moved through the trees to where he had a direct view of the front porch. His pulse quickened. Just a few more minutes.

What's that? Someone was coming up the path.

Ethan clicked his mic. "Steven, we've got company coming up the path. Get out of there."

Two clicks confirmed Steven had heard. Ethan waited, but Steven didn't come out.

"Change of plans. Stay put." Steven whispered. "Krystal's meeting our visitor on the porch."

The door opened. Krystal stepped onto the porch… with a broom.

She looked around and then started sweeping and whistling.

He wanted so bad to run to her, but the impending arrival of the visitor caused him to hold his ground.

A familiar figure emerged from the trees, Eli. Ethan tensed. Anyone but him.

Ethan slid further back into the trees and listened.

"Good morning, Eli. What brings you up here?" Krystal asked casually as she leaned on her broom.

Ethan's heart pounded as he thought of her in his arms. All he had to do was get the preacher to head on down the trail. For now, all he could do was eavesdrop.

Eli pulled his hat off and stepped up on the porch. "I was just down at the Lindbergh's and they were saying they heard a ruckus up on the mountain last night. Is everything okay?" He moved toward the door.

Krystal blocked his way. "Everything's just fine. As far

as fine can be with three little ones. We didn't hear anything. I'm sure if there's a problem Growler can handle it."

———— • ● • ————

"Good move." Ethan whispered. He looked down and realized he had pulled out his Beretta and the safety was off. *What am I doing? He's a preacher. Habit I guess.* He flipped on the safety and returned the gun to its holster.

———— • ● • ————

Eli looked around Krystal at the closed door. "Well, William and Claire are concerned. Maybe you should move down by the lake."

"We're fine here. We just made it through the winter and the children are looking forward to playing in the stream." Krystal started sweeping. "You have a good day now, Eli. We'll see you on Sunday."

Eli stepped off the porch and put on his hat. "Krystal, you do know that you are only a visitor here. Where you live is up to the community leadership. This was supposed to be for you and Ethan. Without him, we may need to open it up for a family. Good day."

Ethan was fuming as Eli passed by his hiding spot. He wanted to step out and teach the preacher man a little humility. But he kept still and whispered a prayer for strength.

His attention turned back to Krystal, who stood scanning the trees. Did she feel him. His heart raced. Was God speaking to her? Not sure.

Ethan slowly retreated into the trees as he watched Krystal turn and walk back into the house. He keyed his mic.

"Abort reunion, I say again, abort. I'm not coming in."

Two clicks.

Steven and Krystal stepped back onto the porch. She crossed her arms, listening to Steven's quiet explanation.

Ethan turned and walked away. His heart stayed behind.

Chapter Thirty

Anna looked up as Krystal closed the door, struggling to contain her excitement. She still couldn't believe what Steven had told her. Was he really alive? She wanted to share it with Krystal, but Steven had given her stern instructions not to tell. No one could know.

They had planned to meet on the porch, until Eli's unexpected appearance forced them into hiding. She tensed at even the thought of Eli outside the cabin. If he had pushed his way in, everything could have unraveled. Steven had helped her to the bedroom where they hid until Eli left.

She rubbed the knot on her head, it still throbbed. Anna lay back down as Krystal sat beside her and placed a cool hand on her forehead.

"Still running a little fever," Krystal said gently. "You rest. I'll get you some tea."

"What did Steven tell you?" Anna asked.

"Probably what you already know. We need to keep you hidden. Whoever hit you is still in the community."

"I'm certain he is. Can I stay here?"

"Of course. The children will love it. Speaking of which,

I'm surprised they slept through all the activity. Did you hear anything out of them?"

"Not a peep."

"Good. The last thing we need is to explain why a soldier was in the living room with his arms around their Anna." Krystal gave a sly smile. "Who, I might add, looked like she was enjoying it."

Anna blushed. "He was just comforting me."

"Okay." Krystal rolled her eyes and grinned.

• ● •

Ethan sat on the rock, working his way through an MRE when Steven emerged from the trees.

"Well, that didn't go as planned," Steven said, collapsing beside him.

Steven leaned back against the cold boulder. "I think Eli was the one who attacked Anna."

Ethan's head jerked up. He wouldn't be surprised, but if true, it would shock the community. Eli was next in line to be their spiritual leader. Ethan thought back to some of their encounters. Eli had been cold to him since day one, resistant to his arrival, suspicious of his friendship with Anna, and that night by the lake still haunted him. Mysterious, yes. But capable of this?

"Anna told you that?" Ethan asked.

"Not directly," Steven said. But she panicked when he came through the clearing. When I asked if he had ever laid a hand on her, she just shut down. If he didn't attack her, he's hurt her in the past."

Ethan clenched his jaw. "This will devastate the community. We need to be absolutely sure before accusing him. But we can't sit on this. We need to talk to someone."

"As in?"

"Abram."

"Who?"

"Oh, I guess you haven't met Abram. He's their oldest spiritual leader. He took me in when I first arrived at Charlotte Lake. I spent my first night in his loft. Quite an interesting man. He prays about everything, and his wisdom shows it."

"Wouldn't Arnold, the security chief, be better?

"Not for this. Because of Eli's position, we need spiritual guidance, not firepower."

Steven hesitated. "Yeah, about that. I'm not so sure I agree with the whole spiritual thing, but I do see your point. Eli kinda works for Abram. Shouldn't we clear this with the colonel?"

Ethan stood, pulling out his knife. He approached Pablo, who stiffened in fear.

"Relax," Ethan muttered, cutting the zip ties on his wrists. Pablo looked stunned, rubbed his wrist, still chattering. Ethan tossed him an MRE and then returned to Steven.

"What did he say?"

"He was begging for his life. He was sure you were about to gut him." Steven said, laughing.

"Could've. But sometimes we show compassion, even when it's not deserved. What are we going to do with him?"

"Can't leave him here. How about we take him to Kearsarge Pass? Tanner and Roland will enjoy the company."

Ethan nodded toward Kearsarge Peak. "That's about three miles. If we leave now, we can make it to Abram's in time for dinner."

"I thought we were waiting until dark?"

"We're better off going in during daylight. I know where the cameras are." Ethan was already on his feet getting prepped to go.

"Sounds good to me. Wouldn't mind some home

cooking." Steven tossed the remains of his MRE into his pack.

Pablo groaned when Steven explained the plan. Soon, they joined the Pacific Crest Trail and were exposed to Charlotte Lake as they descended to the southeast.

Their prisoner muttered curses in his native language, and occasionally spitting at his captors. Every time he did, Steven tugged the rope leash hard.

"He's complaining about his rights." Steven told Ethan. "Says, when he gets back to civilization, he's going to hire a good attorney and sue us for torture."

"Does he realize, with that attitude, he may not make it to civilization?" Ethan asked.

Steven laughed as he relayed the message. Pablo turned and spit at Ethan, causing Steven to jerk the rope. Pablo fell flat on his face. He lay there screaming like a baby. Steven snipped something in Spanish that stopped the screaming. Pablo got to his feet whimpering.

About a half mile from the pass, they sat down for a break. Sitting on the trail Ethan looked out over Kearsarge Lakes and his thoughts went back to the first time he had come down this trail just over a year ago. Back then he had little knowledge of the mountains but was in awe at the towering peaks and pristine blue lakes. Some things never change.

He leaned back on a rock and putting his hands behind his head shut his eyes and drifted into a mystic utopia. So many things had happened over the year, but the most important was his faith. Last year when he looked down on the lakes he imagined how many millions of years it took to carve out this panoramic spectacle. Now it was simple. God spoke it.

It was time to go. Ethan keyed up his mic. "Kearsarge Pass, you there?"

A couple of clicks and Tanner answered. "Go ahead."

"We're bringing a prisoner your way. ETA twenty

minutes."

"Roger that. We've been tracking your progress. Meet you on the trail."

Ethan double clicked his mic and they moved on towards the pass. There wasn't much in the way of vegetation at this altitude and they soon spotted the team sitting in the shade of a scraggly tree.

"Looks like you boys have been busy." Tanner said as the group found a place to sit. "How did you come across this scoundrel?"

Steven explained briefly. "This guy's lucky, his friends didn't make it. He doesn't speak English."

"No hay problema, amigo." Conrad spoke up.

"You're the man, Conrad. See if Pablo can enlighten you on their interest of Charlotte Lake." Steven said.

"I'll do my best. What are we to do with him when were through?"

"Whatever you want, but that would not be nice. I would say, contact Whitlock and bring him up to speed. Just don't tell him about our dinner plans."

"I can't believe you guys are doing this." Tanner said. "We thought we were supposed to stay hidden."

"That was the plan until Pablo and his buddies showed up."

Ethan glanced at his watch. "We need to get going. Abram turns in early."

They descended toward Bullfrog Lake, taking a route that would keep them out of view. On the north side of Bullfrog Lake they stopped to enjoy the moment. Ethan squatted and cupped a handful of the icy cold water, splashing it on his face.

He pulled out his hanky and dried off. Looking out across the glassy blue lake he was mesmerized by the reflection of the snowcapped mountains. How could anyone witness this view and not believe in God? Sure, they would say that this all happened over a billion years. "To believe that would take a lot of faith."

"What would take a lot of faith?" Steven asked.

"Oh, sorry, I was just looking at God's creation." Ethan answered. "Thinking that to believe this all happed by chance, takes a lot of faith."

"So, you're saying erosion doesn't happen?"

"Oh, it happens. Just not over billions of years." Ethan said, as he clinched his backpack and walked away.

As he rounded the lake he could see Steven still sitting on the rock looking out across the lake. Was he thinking about their conversation? Ethan recalled just a year ago he was there. Not knowing for certain about anything.

Soon, he arrived at the trail junction with the PCT and sat down beside the stream. Lying back on the pine needles he shut his eyes and shortly found himself humming the words to the song they had sung in church the last time he was there. When he came to the chorus Ethan felt the lump in his throat. Was it really well with his soul?

"There you are." Ethan sat up at the sound of Steven coming down the trail. "Just about got a nap in."

"Yeah, Sorry about that. I just had to do some soul searching at the lake. You ready?"

Ethan jumped to his feet, pulling on his pack. They climbed the switchbacks and moved across the plateau before leaving the trail to follow the contour around the north side of the lake.

The sun was setting when Ethan pointed to a small cabin in the trees.

"There's Abram's."

They slowly descended through the trees, the smell of wood smoke drifting up to meet them. Coming around the side of the house they stopped and cleared the area. Not a soul in sight.

"Well, here goes. I hope he doesn't have a heart attack." Ethan said as they stepped up on the porch and knocked.

Chapter Thirty-One

"Come on in," Abram's hollered.

Ethan turned the knob and pushed open the old wooden door. Abram was sitting in his chair, reading his Bible. Ethan stepped inside, smiling at the shocked expression frozen on the old man's face.

He reached out and grasped Abram's hand. "Good evening, Abram. How have you been?"

Time seemed to stand still as Abram's bewildered expression slowly melted into tears. He squeezed Ethan's hand as best he could. "My son... my son. Ethan, we mourned your death. Sit down and tell me I'm not dreaming."

"You're not dreaming, Abram. I brought a friend with me. This is Steven."

Steven stepped forward and offered his hand. "Abram, it's an honor. Ethan speaks highly of you."

Still trying to process the shock, Abram managed a smile. "Nice to meet you too, Steven. I don't even know what to say. This is just... too much." He sobbed as realization set in.

Ethan offered Steven the other chair facing the fireplace and pulled up a kitchen chair for himself.

"Tell me Ethan, what happened? Where have you been?" Abram asked once he had regained his composure.

"We don't have time to tell you the whole story, but we can start with the important parts." Ethan said with a sigh.

"It's all important to me," Abram replied.

"That's why we're here now." Ethan reached over and squeezed Abram's hand, causing a smile to spread over Abram's face.

"I had to leave to draw the enemy away from Charlotte Lake. The powers that be believed if I wasn't here, my enemies would lose interest."

"I understand the reasoning, but we heard you died in a helicopter crash."

"I was in a crash," Ethan admitted, leaving out that it was staged. "But, I survived. That too was by design, to convince the enemy that I was dead. Unfortunately, there was no way to make it convincing without the village believing it too. That wasn't my plan, and I'm sorry for the deception."

"It wasn't your fault, Ethan," Abram said gently. "Is the enemy still a threat?"

"I will let Steven explain."

Steven leaned forward. "I arrived here the night of the New York gang's attack. Ethan and I had a long conversation about future threats and the need to get him out of here. What he didn't mention is that the helicopter crash was staged. No one was supposed to get hurt, but a gust of wind caused Ethan to slam his head against the window. His helmet saved his life, but he suffered a concussion and needed time to recover."

He paused, watching the flames dance in the hearth. "That's the beginning of a long story. But the real danger now isn't Ethan's old enemies, it's someone within the community."

Abram's brow furrowed. "The enemy within. Who? Have you talked to Arnold?"

"The security chief is aware that someone here is leaking

information to the enemy, but he doesn't know who. That knowledge has been tightly guarded until the traitor is found. That is why we came to you first."

"I guess I understand. So, have you discovered who it is?"

"We have a suspect," Steven replied. "Our team received credible intel that a Venezuelan gang was planning to take over the community. They bought information from a Mexican cartel, which included a shocking amount of classified data, including the location of the Charlotte Lake gold mines."

Abram's eyes widened. "That's serious. Not even all our people know about the mines."

"It surprised us too," Steven admitted. "We had our suspicions, but liked what you were doing up here and didn't want to upset the apple cart."

"Sounds like the apple cart has already been upset. Did you find the gang?"

"That brings us to why we're here. We have been watching the lake and surrounding area from up on the mountains. Last night, we spotted someone carrying Anna through the woods, and she appeared unconscious. We tracked their movement to where four men were camping."

"Oh my! Is she still there?"

"No. She's safe now, at Krystal's. Doctor Winston checked her out, she's going to be okay."

"You rescued her?" Abram asked, stunned.

"We couldn't let them hurt her," Steven said. "In neutralizing her captors we ended up taking one of them alive. He claims they didn't plan on kidnapping Anna, but that an informant from the village brought her to them. Said she was getting too nosy and needed taken out."

Abram's head shook rapidly, his shoulders tense. "She's always been a problem child, but this… this is horrible. God will deal with these evil men. I'm glad she's safe. You said you have a suspect, how?"

"That's the sensitive part, and why we came here," Steven said. "This morning, we returned to Krystal's to strategize on keeping her safe. I went in while Ethan stayed hidden in the woods. Eli showed up. Not wanting him to know we were there, Krystal met him on the porch. When Anna saw Eli through the window, she panicked."

Abram held up a hand. "Wait. You're saying Eli kidnapped Anna? He wouldn't do that."

"We don't know," Ethan said. "We're only telling you what we know and trusting your wisdom to help us find the truth. Steven, tell him what Pablo said."

Steven nodded solemnly. "Pablo, our prisoner, told us their informant said he was a godly man."

Abram stared into the crackling flames. His lips moved in silent prayer as the room filled with the sound of the ticking mantel clock. Ethan watched him, hoping he could bear the burden they were placing on his shoulders. His stomach rumbled.

Abram finally turned to Ethan. "Do you mind if we pray for wisdom before we say anything more?"

"Of course not," Ethan replied. "I would expect nothing less."

Abram reached out, taking their hands. His voice cracked and his hands trembled as he prayed, asking God for revelation, wisdom and grace. He paused often to sob, but continued, pleading for guidance through the storm.

After the prayer, Abram asked, "You boys hungry? There's plenty of stew."

"If you don't mind," Ethan said. "We haven't had a home-cooked meal in a week."

"Good. We'll talk about the future over supper."

As the aroma of beef stew was drifting up from their bowls, Abram voiced his concern about publicly accusing Eli. They agreed the concussion could have caused Anna to misidentify her attacker.

"How do you recommend we proceed?" Abram asked. "We somehow have to prove, one way or another, Eli's involvement."

"That depends on Doctor Winston," Ethan said. "If he hasn't spilled the beans, we can use misinformation to draw out the real traitor."

"But if he has talked," Steven added, "we can use fear to flush them out. Either way, we need to know soon."

Ethan's expression grew tense. "If her attacker knows she's at Krystal's, they both could be in danger."

Just as they were discussing how to proceed, the front door crashed open. Four armed security officers stormed into the cabin, their faces set in grim determination.

"Hands where we can see them!" barked one of the officers, weapons trained on Steven and Ethan.

Abram's eyes widened in alarm, his spoon clattering on the table. Holding up his hands he rose to his feet. "Put your weapons down! These men are friends."

"Please sit down, Abram," another officer instructed. "We have reasons to believe these men are a threat to you and the community."

Ethan slowly raised his hands, locking eyes with the lead officer. "Come on Oliver, it's only been six months. You know who I am."

Oliver's face went pale. He lowered his rifle. "Ethan? But… you're dead."

Ethan smiled. "That report was grossly exaggerated."

Realization dawned. The officers relaxed, lowering their weapons. Oliver accepted Ethan's outstretched hand. "I don't even know what to say. What happened?"

"It's a long story. One that should be told in the briefing room. Any chance of getting the team together?"

"I'm sure we can. The boss is already there."

"Good. Also, ask Doctor Winston to join us." Ethan turned to Steven. "Why don't you keep an eye on Krystal's cabin? If the word's out, they might be in danger tonight."

"Sure thing. I'll set up an overwatch," Steven said, as he got to his feet. "Abram, thank you for the stew. It was an honor to meet you."

"Wait," Oliver said. "Is there a threat we don't know about?"

Steven offered his hand. "Oliver, I'm Ethan's friend. We're part of the paramilitary team tasked with protecting your parameter. Ethan will fill you in. As for Krystal, she's not the threat. We have reasons to believe someone might try to hurt her or Anna. We're going to make sure that doesn't happen."

Oliver shook Steven's hand. "Welcome to Charlotte Lake. We appreciate what you guys do. If you don't mind, a couple of the boys will join you. They are more than happy to see some action."

"The help is appreciated, but don't expect much action."

Steven left the cabin with two of the security officers in trail.

Ethan carried his plate to the sink. "Give me a few minutes to help clean up. I'll meet you at the storehouse."

Oliver checked his watch. "Twenty minutes. See you there."

After apologizing to Abram for their abrupt arrival the security team left the cabin. Abram patted the back of the empty chair. "Sit down, Ethan. I don't mind cleaning up, but I want to spend this time to talk to you and pray."

Ten minutes later, Ethan gave Abram an emotional hug and stepped into the night, heading for the storehouse.

Chapter Thirty-Two

Ethan walked along the trail from Abram's to the storehouse. As he passed William and Claire's a flickering light shown through the window. That would be one of the first stops once he officially returned. William would have a lot to say. He loved the way William chastised him while making him feel loved. It had to be a gift.

The bakery was deserted, but smoke curled from its chimney. They must fire it the night before to keep the ovens hot. He could see the outline of the storehouse and dropped his night vision goggles as he made his way across the planked porch. The hinges creaked softly as he pulled open the door.

No one was inside.

Ethan moved to the corner and sank into an easy chair. It amazed him that the community survived. The storehouse, their only grocery, remained unlocked, because everything inside was free.

The door squeaked open.

Oliver entered and leaned up against the counter. He checked his watch and coughed.

"I'm here." Ethan said, making Oliver jump.

"Don't do that. You'll give me a heart attack. Let's go" Oliver clicked on a small flashlight.

They passed through the big oak door into the ice cave. Nothing had changed. Animal carcasses hung from the ceiling, bins of fresh produce lined the shelves. On the stone wall, Oliver lifted a flap, revealing a faint emerald glow. He pressed his thumb to the scanner. Bolts retracted with a mechanical clunk, and the door slid open.

Every time, Ethan thought, *this place amazes me.*

They moved down a sterile hallway toward the conference room.

"Arnold hasn't been told," Oliver said casually. "He's gonna flip."

"You didn't tell him?" Ethan's tensed. "This is going to be fun. You go in first."

Oliver entered while Ethan hovered by the door. He peered inside to see Arnold with his back turned.

"Evening, Oliver. Did you apprehend the intruders?" Arnold asked.

Oliver leaned back in his chair. "We got one. The other took off. Last I saw, two of our guys were following him up the mountain."

Arnold's fist slammed the table. "How could he escape? Were they still inside Abram's cabin?"

"They were. But good news is I brought the other guy in for you to question."

Ethan stepped back, as Arnold spun around looking into the hallway. "Where is he?"

"Oh, he'll be here shortly. Had to take a pit stop."

"What? He's running around in here unattended?"

Oliver nearly lost it trying to keep a straight face. "Oh, here he comes now."

Ethan strolled in and dropped into the chair next to Arnold. "Good evening, boss. Am I late again?"

Arnold's gaze locked on Ethan, his expression void. "It's

about time you get here, Ethan." The words coming out as a normal response before Arnold's brain triggered an explosion. Ethan grinned as he watched Arnold's mouth open and shut wordlessly. Arnold placed both hands on the table and pushed back. His shoulders dropped and he exhaled. He rubbed his temples trying to make sense of what he was seeing.

"I'm not surprised," he finally said. "When I read the report on your presumed death, I questioned it. Now that you've returned, you have a lot of explaining to do."

"Happy to see you too. Where should I start?"

"Well, I'm sure, a book could be written. But tonight, just tell me why you came back, and who my men are chasing up the mountain."

Oliver cut in. "That was a little white lie, boss. The guys are with Ethan's partner, Steven. They're guarding Krystal's cabin tonight. I'll let Ethan explain."

"Please do." Arnold's tone sharpened.

Ethan nodded. "Before I left, you told me you suspected a mole in the community. We found FBI files confirming a mole existed, but did not reveal a name. Steven met with Anna and tasked her with telling you. I assume she did?"

"See did. We had to force it out of her. She's a problem child."

"You can say that again. She didn't want to accuse or trust anyone until she had cleared them. Your core team was cleared first, but then things got… complicated."

Ethan took a drink of water.

"Last night, after she met with Krystal, she was attacked."

Arnold's brow furrowed. "And we're just hearing this. How bad?"

"She's in Krystal's care now, with Doctor Winston's oversight. That's the good news." Ethan detailed the attack, rescue, and the captured prisoner. "Our team at Kearsarge Pass is interrogating Pablo. He may know more."

"So, you have a prisoner?"

"Yes. We took him to our team at Kearsarge Pass."

"How about we take him off your hands?" Arnold asked.

"Fine. Just don't let him escape. Transfer him to Willow Creek when you're through questioning."

"Do your boys have a radio?"

Ethan pulled out his radio. "You can find the frequency on here. Let them know you're coming and who sent you. They could get a little trigger happy."

Arnold turned to Oliver. "Ready for another mission?"

Oliver pushed his chair back and took Ethan's radio. "Would love to hear the rest of this story, but we're on it."

Ethan scanned the room. "I would love to tell you everything, but I'm not sure I will be able to return to the community. Krystal doesn't know that I'm alive. Please keep this information classified. Thank you."

The team nodded.

"Arnold, can we speak privately?"

"Of course. Thank you, team, go get some sleep, we will have some things to work on tomorrow morning. Be here at nine."

When the room cleared Arnold reached around his back and swung the door shut. "So, who is it?"

"I will tell you what I know and let you decide." Ethan explained the clues and Anna's account. "By no means is it conclusive. Pablo may be able to confirm it."

"Or lie to get us off his back," Arnold muttered.

"It's all we have, until we come up with a sting operation. Any ideas?"

Arnold thought for a moment. "We leak the news about Anna's attack. Then we set a trap."

"She'll need protection."

"Make her appear vulnerable to draw him out. While you and Steven cover her from a distance."

"Why us?"

"I will schedule an all hands briefing during this time.

The attacker will think she's alone."

Ethan nodded. "Where are you thinking?"

"Outside the village. If it is Eli, he'll know where the cameras are. As far as that goes, almost everyone in the village knows that. I have an idea, come with me."

They entered the control room just as an assistant handed Arnold a note. He read it, pocketed it, and gestured to the screen. "We may already have our guy. I doubt it, but we'll see. Let me show you the locations first."

They were still pouring over the map when the two officers showed up with a man that Ethan recognized but couldn't name.

"Take him in the conference room." Arnold said as he turned back to the map. "I don't think he's capable of what happened. We'll find out." Arnold shut off the monitor and stood.

Arnold pulled his chair up to the conference table. "So, George, what's going on?"

George's eyes were locked on Ethan. "What's he doing here?"

"Not your concern. You know the drill. We ask the questions and you answer them."

George looked down, wringing his hands. "I have nothing to say with him here."

Arnold nodded to Ethan, who stood. "As you wish."

He returned to the control room.

"Mind if I watch?" he asked a nearby technician.

"Not at all. Welcome back. I bet Krystal was happy to see you."

"She doesn't know yet. Hopefully soon."

"Oh, okay. Something's going down. Arnold put us on high alert when you guys arrived at Abram's. We didn't know it was you. Scared us."

"Sorry. We thought we could sneak in. Guess you're just too good."

Ethan heard Arnold call his name. "Thanks ladies.

Sounds like the boss is calling."

"Have a seat, Ethan," Arnold said. "It's not George, but he has something to share."

George sat trembling, face drawn and damp with sweat.

"Ethan… I'm glad you're alive. We all thought you were gone. I made a big mistake."

Ethan leaned forward.

George started shaking his head with downcast eyes. "I…I thought maybe, with you gone, Krystal might… like me. I watched how she was with you and the children. I wanted that. She told me she still had hope that you'd come back."

Ethan found humor in what he was hearing. Poor George was lonely. He was also disillusioned. Obviously, he didn't know Krystal. There was no way she would be interested in a… what did he do? Isn't he an accountant for the community? Doesn't matter. He watched as George was struggling to get through his confession. There had to be more to this fascination.

"And then what?"

"I…I was lonely, and wanted to see her again. I started going up there. Just watching from the woods, just hoping I could see her sitting on the porch."

Ethan's rage erupted. He lunged across the table, grabbing George by his collar.

"How dare you?"

George's eyes went wide, trying to pry Ethan's hand loose.

"Ethan, let him go." Arnold's firm command brought Ethan to his senses.

Ethan dropped George in his chair and sat back, fuming.

"I wasn't trying to hurt her," George gasped, trying to get his breath. "I just…"

"You just what?" Ethan's harsh tone spat.

George swallowed hard. "I didn't mean for it to be that way. I was just lonely and thought maybe she would change her mind."

"You watched her from the shadows of the trees like some kind of stalker?"

Ethan's jaw tightened. Every bit of him wanted to pound the guy to a pulp. But, deep down, another voice whispered, this wasn't just about jealousy, he kind of felt sorry for George. It was about trust and protecting the woman he loved.

Ethan stared him down. "Stay away from her. If I catch you so much as breathe in her direction, you won't get off this easy."

George nodded, rubbing his throat. "I get it, I was out of line. It won't happen again."

"No, it won't, George." Arnold said. "As far as security is concerned, you are free to go. But you'll tell Abram what you did."

George turned to Ethan, shame covering his face. "I'm sorry Ethan. Please forgive me."

• ● •

"What do you mean, you didn't bring me any fresh bread?" Steven ribbed Ethan as he walked into camp. "Did you meet George?"

"Unfortunately. Trust me, bread would've been better." Ethan dropped his pack and slumped onto his favorite rock. "He's not our guy, just a lonely peeping tom."

Steven raised an eyebrow. "Seriously?"

"Yeah. Arnold's got doubts about Eli too." Ethan leaned forward, elbows on his knees. "You up for a sting operation?"

"Absolutely. What's the bait?"

"Anna."

Steven frowned. "She just took a blow to the head. You

really think it's safe to use her like that?"

"She won't be alone. We'll be watching the whole time," Ethan reassured him. "It's risky, but might be the only way to draw the guy out."

Steven didn't look convinced but nodded. "Alright. Who's taking first watch?"

"You are," Ethan said with a grin.

"Security's already on high alert, but I'll keep an eye out. We can discuss the plan in the morning." Steven grabbed his night vision binoculars and headed for the berm.

Chapter Thirty-Three

"You want me to do what?"

Anna's voice was tight with disbelief as Steven explained the plan. She glanced toward the kitchen, where Krystal was working. "Does she know about this?"

"Not yet," Steven said, keeping his voice low. "Once we have your attacker in custody, we'll tell her."

Anna looked uneasy. "I don't know if I can do it. I still feel lightheaded sometimes."

"I'm sorry, but there's no other way to get him to confess without you. We'll be protecting you. One wrong move, and he's history."

Anna crossed her arms. "How are you sure he'll meet me on the trail? Won't he be suspicious?"

Steven nodded. "He will. But he also knows that once you show up with evidence, he's finished."

"What evidence? It's just my word against Eli's. He's never caused trouble, and I'm the one always attracting it. Who do you think they'll believe?"

Anna was getting worried. This sounded like a crazy idea. She trusted Steven, but if only Ethan would confirm the plan.

"You don't need to worry about that. We'll plant what's needed in your backpack. Just don't open it." Steven stood to leave. "I'll pick you up just after sunset."

Anna rose slowly. "I am feeling better… but you'd better not let me get hit again." She grabbed his hand and walked him to the door.

Steven gave her a brief hug. "Get your rest. It's going to be a long night."

Anna watched him disappear into the woods, heart pounding. She continued to stare in hopes of spotting Ethan. "If only I could tell Krystal," she whispered.

"Tell me what?"

Anna jumped. Krystal stood behind her with Jonah, both looking out the window.

Great! What do I tell her? Maybe nothing. Could she really pull off this bait thing? Her head still hurt from the last attack. What if she was wrong and it wasn't Eli? No… she was sure.

"I have to meet Eli. They're setting a trap to get him to confess," Anna said, almost apologetically.

Krystal took a deep breath. "You aren't going anywhere. He can come here."

"No, it has to be this way. They need me out there as bait." Anna cringed.

Krystal's eyes narrowed. "First, who else is behind this? And why can't I go in your place? That would make more sense."

Anna rubbed her temples. There was no way she'd let Krystal take the chance at getting hurt. "I'm going to do it. I trust Steven."

"Yeah," Krystal's said with loving sarcasm. "You trust him a little too much."

Anna smiled faintly and slumped back onto the couch.

A knock stirred Anna awake.

She checked her watch, just past sunset. That had to be Steven. She heard Krystal greet him at the door. She didn't want to get up. Couldn't they postpone this one more night? But the trap was already set. The all-hands security meeting was underway. The note about her carrying evidence had been leaked. The control room would be fully staffed, eyes on every screen. And somewhere on the mountain, Ethan waited in the sniper nest, trained on the trail below.

She exhaled and sat up.

Jonah played quietly on the carpet, Christiana and Cathryn read together in the overstuffed chair. Anna rubbed her eyes and saw Steven grinning at her.

"Good evening, Anna. Ready for your stroll?"

"Ready to go back to sleep." She said, yawning, and headed to the washroom. She washed her face, brushed her hair, and tied it back in a ponytail. Straightening her dress, she sighed and walked into the living room. "Okay, let's go for a walk."

Steven helped Anna slowly climb the mountain. Twilight settled as they reached the men's camp. Anna paused to rest while Steven strapped on night vision goggles. He slung an assault rifle over his shoulder and checked the laser on his handgun, before holstering it.

"Do I get one of those?" Anna asked. "Could save my life."

"Absolutely not. That would just get someone, probably

me, killed. Don't worry, I won't let anyone hurt you."

"Too late for that," she muttered.

"Ouch." Steven said. "Let's go."

He grabbed Anna's hand and pulled her up. She didn't stop and fell into his arms. He held her briefly, before guiding her forward.

"You're relentless." He said, as he held her hand and led them into the darkness.

"Not the first time I've heard that. Take me to the trail, cowboy."

They followed the contour across the mountain to the PCT.

Steven stopped Anna as soon as they were on the tread. "Give me five minutes, then start walking toward Charlotte Lake." He whispered. "In about three hundred yards there is a wooded area. We expect he is already there, or coming that way. He should order you to stop. Obey his orders and when he shows himself, act surprised. When he wants your backpack, ask him why. Try to get him talking. We'll be listening, but you won't hear us."

Anna squeezed his hand. "I'm scared. Pray for me."

Steven faded into the shadows.

She looked up at the billions of stars blinking across the heavens, whispering a prayer.

Her watch ticked. Time to go.

What would she do if no one stopped her? Just keep on walking until she got home? It would feel good to sleep in her own bed. She felt dizzy. Maybe she could lie down here beside the trail and her attacker could come to her. No, she must push on.

Silhouette of the trees just up the trail. She clutched the straps on her backpack and slowed her pace. Her heart raced, the small flashlight she was carrying cast a dim beam on the trail. She inhaled deeply and came to a stop.

What am I doing?

Have faith.

Faith in God, Steven, Ethan up on the hill. All three are watching. But who else is watching? She reached the trees.

A sudden light blinded her.

"Stop right there, Anna," A deep voice demanded.

She froze. Her heart slammed in her chest. But oddly, she felt relief.

"Whoa, could you dim that light?" She shielded her eyes.

The beam shifted to red. She saw the silhouette now. Familiar but wrong.

"Thanks, Eli. What are you doing out here?"

"Who?"

"Come on, Eli. Did security send you up here to help me get to City Hall?"

"You could say that. You look tired. Let me take your backpack."

Anna's head hurt. That voice, familiar, but it wasn't Eli.

She wanted to see his face, but keep some distance. Who is it?

"That's okay, I've got it." She replied stalling.

"I'm not asking, Anna. Give me your backpack or I will take it. Your choice."

Recognition struck.

She stared into the red light. It was his build, his mannerism. It couldn't be. He had hung out with her and Cody when they were teenagers. She had to get him to confess, before she let him know she knew.

"You're the one that attacked me by the stream, aren't you?"

"Forget about that. What matters is that you hand over the backpack and walk back up the mountain. You're no longer welcome in our town."

He said, 'Our town'. It is him.

"You're a real man, beating a defenseless woman. You almost killed me. I'm sure God is real proud of you. Did you come up here to finish the job? Whatever you want, you're not getting my pack."

"I didn't want it to come to this, but those thugs have forced my hand. Give me that pack." He moved closer.

Anna stepped back clutching her pack, "Stay back, Arwel, or else." her voice faltering.

"Or else what?" he sneered. "Now that you know who I am, you're dead."

A red dot appeared on his chest.

"Arwel," Anna said, "You're a minister. You tell us about Jesus every Sunday. At least tell me why. Let me understand before you kill me."

An evil laugh emitted out of Arwel. "That preaching stuff is just a performance. I don't believe any of it. Took years to get the church to trust me. I won't lose it."

Anna sniffled. "We have been friends for a long time and I've always liked you."

Arwel laughed. "That's almost funny. I have known you since I got here. I really wanted to know you in a different way, but you chose Cody. You should have picked me. We could have made a great team."

"What about Rebbecca, what's going to become of her and your children?"

"That's why you must die. I can't risk my position. Not now. When the new leaders arrive, we're out. As for you, no one will miss you. A few tears, maybe they'll bury you next to Cody." Arwel laughed at his sick humor.

Anna cringed. Did Arwel have a gun? How long would Steven wait? She was certain Ethan was just waiting for a reason.

"So, let me get this straight. You sold out the community and are working with the terrorists?" Anna said, eyes locked on the red dot circling his chest. "Who's coming?"

"Was supposed to be a Mexican cartel. But they sold it to a Venezuelan gang. They've got a thousand men ready. You should be glad you won't be here when they arrive. Anyhow, it's time to get rid of you. I have to be home before the meeting's over and security is back on the trail. Move along."

"One more question," Anna said, inching back. "Then you can drag my body into a ravine. What's that red dot on your chest?"

Arwel looked down, then up at her, wide eyed.

"Move a muscle," Anna said coldly, "and that dot becomes a 9mm hole. When that happens, your wife becomes a widow, your children fatherless. And you'll meet the God you mocked."

Arwel raised his hands, trembling. Steven emerged from the trees, night vision goggles glowing green. In his hand the silencer equipped weapon emitted the laser onto Arwel's chest.

"Get on the ground, now!" Steven's harsh command thundered through the trees.

Arwel collapsed and put his hands behind his head.

Anna backed away, shaking. It was still Eli that she pictured before being struck. Was her memory that scrabbled? Arwel had confessed, but her gut still doubted.

At least it was over. Time to go home.

Time to rest.

Chapter Thirty-Four

Ethan watched from seventy yards above the trail, his crosshairs still centered on the man's chest. He didn't know who it was, but it wasn't Eli. Anna must have been seeing things. Understandable, considering everything she'd been through.

Out of the corner of his eye, Ethan noticed lights moving from the direction of the village. He shifted his attention and saw Steven zip-tying the man's hand behind his back.

Then, movement coming up the trail caught his attention. He lowered his rifle, grabbed his NVGs, and zoomed in on a team of four heavily armed men.

He keyed his mic. "You've got incoming. A team of four security personnel, ETA fifteen minutes."

Steven looked up and acknowledged with a double click.

Ethan scanned toward Kearsarge trail. Nothing moving. He would love to have an infrared drone overhead. He pulled out his earpiece and listened. Still nothing.

Movement to his right. He readjusted the NVGs, and his

heart spiked. Six men in camouflage, assault rifles in hand, were coming around the mountain toward them. As the moonlight illuminated their faces, Ethan confirmed. Not friendlies.

"Steven, you've got six armed commandos coming from the north. Get out of there, now."

He watched Steven grab the prisoner by the arm and drag him into the woods, Anna close behind. They took cover thirty yards uphill, at least giving them an advantage.

Ethan looked back at the security team making their way up the trail.

He keyed up his mic again. "You thinking what I'm thinking?"

"Two heavily armed squads about to stumble into each other." Steven whispered back. "You sure they're not friendlies?"

"I'm certain they're hostiles," Ethan replied, "but without verification, I don't feel good about taking them out. Any ideas?"

"Warn the security team. Drop a few rounds about ten feet in front of lead guy. Might scare the commandos and alert the security team at the same time. Just maybe they'll turn around and head back up the mountain."

Ethan picked up his rifle and slipped off the safety. "I have the suppressor on. The security team might not hear it."

"Take the chance. You only have about two minutes."

Ethan focused in on the lead guy. "Definitely enemy," he said softly. "I should just take him out."

"Your call." Came the reply.

Ethan shook his head. Whoever these guys are, they haven't done anything yet. He aimed four feet in front of the lead and pulled the trigger. The suppressor did its job, but in the silent mountain air, it was still loud enough for a wakeup call.

The lead commando and the next one behind him split ways diving off the trail. The other four looked around in confusion. Ethan concentrated on the lead. He was looking at his buddy who was pointing up the mountain in Ethan's direction. He knew they couldn't see him. They must be trying to figure out where the shooting was coming from. He would help them. Focusing in on the rear commando, he offset five feet right and pulled the trigger. He chuckled as the remainder of the squad scurried into the rocks.

"The security team is passing our location now. It looks like they heard the shots," Steven whispered.

Ethan turned his attention to the security team. They had their night vision goggles down, moving cautiously, scanning left down the side of the mountain and up the mountain towards his position. He needed their attention on the real threat. He pulled out his Beretta and removed the silencer.

Time to make some real noise.

He aimed just below his target and popped off a couple of shots, before hitting the dirt.

Screaming erupted from the direction of the commandos, and it wasn't English. Ethan frowned. Where do these guys come from? How many had crossed the border undetected? Could it be that they wanted Charlotte Lake for a base? Its remoteness, resources, and lack of oversight?

Why the screaming? It sounded like one of them was in pain. Ethan slid his rifle barrel around the boulder and peered through the scope. Four commandos had assault rifles aimed up the mountain, staring into the darkness. One man was down, clutching his leg.

"Ricochet," Ethan muttered. "My bad."

The last commando, clearly the leader, was using night vision goggles and scanning the mountain. Then he stopped. Ethan froze.

He's spotted me.

The man shouted in Spanish and pointed. Ethan pulled back as bullets raked the rocks around him.

"Ethan, you okay?" Steven's voice was tight in his

earpiece.

"I'm fine. Just pinned down."

"You think. What was that all about?"

"Security was looking up the mountain. Had to redirect their focus."

Gunfire intensified, but the bullets stopped pinging around Ethan's nest. He moved to the far side of the boulder and peered through the scope.

The security team had engaged. Both squads were taking cover behind rocks, trading potshots.

Ethan keyed up his mic. "Rules of engagement just changed. You ready?"

"I have been waiting patiently. You gonna share?"

"Start at the left and go right, I'll meet you in the middle. Leave the injured one, we'll interrogate him. On my count."

Ethan focused the crosshairs on the far-right commando. "Three… two… one… fire."

He squeezed three rapid shots and watched the dominoes fall. Silence followed.

Ethan scanned the mountain. No more movement. He looked back toward the trail. Steven was talking with the security team. Anna stood by his side.

Back in the trees, their prisoner leaned up against a tree, clearly going nowhere.

Ethan sighed, already dreading the fallout from this. He could only imagine what was going to happen at the next church business meeting.

"You coming down?" Steven asked.

Ethan double-clicked his mic and secured his weapons. As he made his way down the mountain, he spotted Anna watching for him. While she looked anxious, she was holding Steven's arm.

He stepped into the woods to retrieve their prisoner.

What he found wasn't resistance, it was a mess. The man had fallen on his side and was sobbing into the pine straw.

Ethan grimaced. Part of him wanted to end it, but his

conscience wouldn't let him.

He reached down and pulled the man upright. "What the…. Arwel!"

Shock hit him like a slap. This guy wasn't part of security. It was Arwel, a respected minister.

"What in the world possessed you?"

No answer. Ethan dragged him to his feet. Not his fight. Not now. He had met Arwel last year and liked the guy. Married, with kids. Did she know about her husband's covert dealings? Sad.

He shoved Arwel onto the trail.

"Ethan!" Anna voice rang out. She ran to him and leapt, locking her arms around his neck.

He caught her and hugged her tightly as she clung to him. Looking up, he saw Steven grinning.

Did he put her up to this? Probably didn't have to. He felt the kisses on his cheek as Anna didn't want to let go.

"Careful, Anna. You'll break my neck."

Still clinging to his hand, she led him back toward Steven. "Thanks for bringing him back. Krystal's going to go crazy."

Ethan placed her hand in Steven's "Now that this is over, I'm going to go see her."

"Can I come too?" Anna asked excitedly.

"No, I want to go alone. Anna, you're safe now. Steven will take you home."

They stood together, watching the security team escort Arwel and the injured commando down the trail. A retrieval team would come for the dead.

Fifteen minutes ago, these men had been coming down the trail, maybe chasing some twisted version of a better life. But they'd chosen violence. Chosen to kill. Ethan exhaled.

Was he any better?

He didn't kill for money, or vengeance. Not this time.

Was that justification?

He would ask Krystal.

"Give me an hour," he told Steven. "Then meet me at her place."

He picked up his rifle and disappeared into the trees.

Chapter Thirty-Five

Ethan stood at the edge of the clearing. A dim light glowed behind the curtains. He glanced at his watch. The children would be in bed by now, and most likely Krystal was reading by the lantern.

He had left the grime of the day in the stream beside their camp. With one brush across the wrinkles in his clean BDU, he took a deep breath and stepped into the clearing.

Growler's bark shattered the stillness. Through the window, Ethan saw Krystal's silhouette, turn toward the window. She had to have heard the earlier gunfire. Was she afraid? Most likely. But she would also be praying.

How do you pray for the unknown?

He knocked gently. The sound echoed in the quiet night. A corner of the curtain moved slightly, then dropped back. He tapped again, softer this time.

Growler's low growl rumbled from the other side of the door.

He took a step back in anticipation of Growler bounding out the door.

"Who is it?" Krystal's voice was muffled and cautious.

"Just one of your old friends," he replied softly.

The door creaked open, and before he could react, a hundred pounds of rock-hard dog almost knocked him to the ground.

"Whoa, Growler. Easy boy." Ethan laughed, steadying himself. Growler released him and began dancing in happy circles.

Ethan looked up at the woman he loved. She stood in the doorway, eyes squinting into the darkness, her face a mix of disbelief and hope.

Ethan stepped back onto the porch. "Hello, darling."

"Ethan?" her whisper barely audible.

He stepped closer and took her hand, feeling the tremble. "It's me, Krystal. I'm back."

Tears welled up in her eyes. She reached up, fingers brushing his face.

Her knees buckled, and Ethan caught her, cradling her in his arms as he carried her inside. He laid her gently on the couch, brushing a stray lock of hair from her forehead. His heart pounded as he looked into her stirring face. How he had missed her.

She blinked up at him. "Is it really you?"

"In the flesh." he chuckled. "Sorry for the shock."

Krystal sat up and motioned for him to sit. She nestled into his arms, trembling as the fire crackled.

"I've been praying for this moment," she whispered.

Ethan gently kissed her forehead. "And I've been fighting to make it happen."

Krystal looked up, eyes searching his. Slowly, their lips met, soft familiar, long overdue.

"Welcome home, Ethan. How long are you here?"

He exhaled. "Unfortunately, not long. There's still an adversary out there."

"I don't know how long I can keep doing this," she said, her voice breaking. "I'm lonely, Ethan. I'm thinking about taking the children home to my parents. With the East Coast gang gone we'd be safe."

His chest tightened. He understood, but hated the thought.

"Krystal, I love you more than I can ever show. I don't know when all threats will end, if they ever will. But for now, we have to trust God is working out His plan."

"I love you too." Krystal sniffled. "I'm just lonely."

Ethan held her tighter. Silence fell, until Growler raised his head and stared at the door.

Ethan went instantly alert.

"Are we always going to live like this?" Krystal's asked, watching him reach for his weapon.

Ethan ignored the question, glancing at his watch. Had it already been an hour? Not enough. What could he tell Krystal to give her hope? Was hope even possible? He had to figure it out.

A soft, coded knock tapped on the door.

Steven stood at the door, still wearing his combat vest and carrying his rifle. "Good evening, Krystal. You look a little shell-shocked."

Krystal, gripping Ethan's arm, narrowed her eyes. "Confused would be more appropriate. I don't know whether to hug you or scream. You make me so angry. Why didn't you tell me?"

Steven stepped back as if bracing himself. "Operation necessity, girl. We needed Ethan focused on the mission, not distracted by some beautiful young lady."

Krystal blushed, pulling Ethan even closer. "Where does it go from here?"

Steven's expression turned serious. "How much did you tell her?"

"Not much," Ethan said. "You could've stayed away a bit longer, like the rest of my life."

His grin earned a glare from Steven.

"Krystal," Steven said, "the community's still in danger. There's a foreign organization with knowledge of the community and its resources. Once they're dealt with, we'll wrap up our mission, and Ethan will be free to chop your wood."

Fear showed in Krystal's face. "Should I take the children to their grandparents?"

Steven shook his head. "Traveling now is more dangerous than staying. That man you're clinging to is your safest bet. He would give his life for you."

Ethan could feel Krystal trembling and her grip intensify. He wrapped his arm around her and pulled her against his side. It was a feeling he wanted to last.

"That's my fear. What's the time frame?" She asked.

"That's unknown," Steven replied. "But once the snow melts, we'll see signs of an impending attack. Security's on high alert. We'll keep you informed."

Steven turned to Ethan. "Ready to head back up to camp? It's been a long day and I need to get cleaned up."

"You need my help to wash behind the ears?" Ethan asked. "Wait on the porch. I need to tell someone goodnight."

After the door shut, Ethan wrapped his arms around Krystal again. Her eyes searched his.

"When are the conflicts going to be over?" she asked.

"This is my last fight, dear. Once the threat is gone, I'm resigning. I'm coming home."

"That scares me. 'Last fight' could mean a lot of things. Remember our conversation last fall, when you put your faith in Jesus? Has anything changed?"

Ethan held her tight. *Has anything changed?* He asked himself. So much had changed that he had no idea where to start. "We only have a couple of minutes, my darling. Let me give you the peace of mind to know that my faith in God is stronger than when we said goodbye. God has carried me through more than I can explain. He will carry us through this, too. Keep praying, Krystal."

Tears slipped down her cheeks. "Will you come back

tomorrow? The children would love to see you."

"I would love to, but do you think it's wise?"

She paused. "You're right. It'd be best if you just come back to stay."

She kissed him again, "Take care of yourself. I'll always love you."

Ethan squeezed her hand. "Love you too, my darling. Goodnight."

• ● •

Steven was rocking on the porch when Ethan stepped out.

"It's about time, soldier. I was just about to call in the cavalry."

"I was under attack," Ethan laughed. "Had to fight off the demons. Let's get out of here before I change my mind."

Clouds rolled in over the peaks as they climbed the mountain.

Back at camp, Steven dropped his gear beside his tent and headed for the stream. Ethan stirred the coals and tossed on a couple of small logs. Sure, someone might catch the scent of smoke, but with all the woodstoves burning in the village, it would go unnoticed.

He set the coffee pot by the coals and rubbed the back of his neck. Was it the stress of the day or the lack of coffee? He continued to work out the knots as the water started boiling.

Flames flickered, summoning memories unbidden, yet persistent. It was a simpler time back before violence shattered his world. He shut his eyes against the flames, only to see the sunlit faces of his late wife and daughters. He felt the pressure on his chest as he tried to experience their touch. It wasn't there. His memories didn't come with all the senses.

Were these memories fading?

Was Krystal, and her children, diluting his past?

The thoughts slipped away as quickly as they came.

The fire snapped him back.

Steven returned, wet hair dripping, shirtless. "You look lost, brother. You alright?"

Ethan poured coffee. "Hard to say. I either need a therapist or a long walk in the woods. Coffee?"

"Please. It's freezing."

"It's warmer with clothes on," Ethan said, grinning as he handed Steven a cup.

Steven reemerged, dressed and somber, sitting by the fire. "I've got an uneasy feeling about this place. Setting emotions aside, what do you think?"

"I think you are one annoying partner." Ethan smirked. "From the looks of things, I'm not the only one with emotional attachments to this place. That aside, there's a lot to be concerned about. I think..."

He stared into the flames.

"You think what?" Steven pressed.

"I think it's time we bring everyone together."

"Everyone?"

"Yeah. Now that our mole is in custody, we can stop keeping the security team in the dark. The local leaders will handle Arwel, probably some tribunal. It's a sad situation, but one of his own making." Ethan paused. "And thanks to you, Anna's cover is blown. She's now working with security."

"Speaking of security. What's the condition of their security?" Steven asked.

"Better than what you saw last year. If we get Arnold's approval, I would like you brought in on their capabilities."

"That's a novel idea," Steven said. "What about the Colonel? Should we bring him into the village for a meeting with their leaders?"

"Absolutely not," Ethan snapped. "He'd take over, that would do more harm than good."

Steven raised an eyebrow. "There are six of us. Do we bring in more?

"Maybe. But let's wait until we understand the threat better. The Colonel's probably monitoring us already. Speaking of Whitlock, let's try the radio again."

Chapter Thirty-Six

Anna curled up on her couch, journal in hand. As much as she wanted to crawl into bed, she knew some things needed to be recorded before they slipped away. It wasn't how much time had passed, it was about what had happened in the short span of two days.

She began writing about her visit to Krystal's cabin, the things they had shared. The walk down the path, the sound of the mountain stream bubbling beside her… and then, the moment.

Anna shut her eyes. Her pulse quickened.

Eli!

Her eyes snapped open. She shook her head and tried again. All she could see was Eli standing over her with that big stick. He'd been saying something. But what?

Am I going crazy?

It was Arwel who attacked me, why is Eli in my head?

She shivered and pulled the quilt tighter around her, whispering a prayer. She was struggling, emotionally, spiritually, with the mess she had become.

The answers didn't come, but as she surrendered the fear

and confusion to God, the trembling began to fade. She would trust Him and do the right thing, even if the path ahead was unclear.

Her eyes grew heavy as she picked up the journal again.

What do I write? Every detail? Or just the highlights?

What do I say about Steven? Is he… taking Ethan's place as her hero?

She laughed aloud, startling herself. No. That can't be. After all, Ethan was only a pipe dream.

She was still holding her journal when she drifted off. By the time she stirred again, the fire had burned low and a chill filled the room. Groggily, she stumbled to her bedroom and crawled into bed. Tomorrow she would return to the greenhouse. Her plants would be needing water and she needed the distraction.

At least for now, she was safe.

— • ● • —

The next morning, Anna whistled as she moved through the greenhouse, watering can in hand. It felt good to be doing something productive for a change. The days were getting longer and the wildlife more active. On the way to the greenhouse, she noticed little sprouts of green popping out of the ground. Soon wildflowers would blanket the mountainside around the lake. Spring was the perfect time of year.

If only yesterday had been a dream.

But it wasn't. And after lunch, she was expected at City Hall for a briefing.

With her plants looking happy, Anna left the greenhouse and walked down to the lake. She and Cody used to spend time sitting on this old log bench. It was tucked back into the trees and was worn smooth from years of use. The ice was almost gone, and little whitecaps bounced across the surface. A cool breeze coming off the water caused her to zip up her coat. Sounds of the day's activities floated across the lake.

A peaceful place. For now!

She bowed her head and prayed. How she longed for the carefree days of her youth. Life had never been easy, but she had been blessed. After her parents died others stepped in. When she lost childhood friends new ones found her here at Charlotte Lake.

The hardest time had been when Cody had abandoned her, but even then, the community wrapped their arms around her. It was during this time, her faith became real.

She remembered the day she gave her life to Christ. The most important day of her life. She was content with living her position in the community and went about serving the Lord.

And then, one spring day a stranger walked into church. He carried himself with confidence. She recalled him bending down to listen to Abram before slipping onto a bench in the back. She had tried to listen to the sermon, but kept stealing glances at the handsome stranger.

Anna smiled at the memory. That evening she had watched him again at the singing. She wanted to meet him, but fear stood in the way. By Monday morning rumors had spread like wildfire. The stranger was Ethan Dawson, a widower from New York, and he was moving into the stone cabin up in the crater.

On a whim, she had gone up to clean the cabin. Would she have gone if she had known she would meet him there?

She sighed. Thinking of all the times she had tried. God had other plans.

Cody's sudden return had shaken everything. She realized she still loved him. They were reconciling their relationship. An upcoming wedding planned.

Anna's eyes filled with tears. She remembered the night Ethan brought the news to her cabin. Cody had poured out his heart just hours earlier, promising to do what was right. And then Ethan stood at her door, and she knew. Cody was gone.

She wiped the tears from her cheeks and opened up her journal. Time to finish this chapter and move on.

With clarity and faith, she recorded the events leading up to the present time. Her final sentence read.

"I know that what I recall from the night of my abduction will bring pain and sadness to our church and to the Charlotte Lake community. I do so not out of anger or malice, but from a desire to share the truth."

She closed the journal with a final pat. A deep breath of cool mountain air steadied her. It was time for City Hall.

— • ● • —

"Good afternoon, Anna." Sarah's big smile welcomed her arrival at the storehouse.

"Looking for something good to eat?"

Anna smiled. She always appreciated Sarah's cheerful spirit, especially in hard times. "It is a good afternoon. I'm here to meet Arnold. Could you get him for me, please?"

"Sure. Be right back!" Sarah disappeared through the door into the ice cave.

Anna browsed idly, not really looking for anything. Maybe she would take something home for dinner.

Sarah returned with Oliver. "Good afternoon, Anna. We didn't know when we might be seeing you."

"It was a rough night, and the plants needed watering," she said, glancing at Sarah. She needed to be careful. Not everyone knew what happened. Yet.

They walked past Noah in the ice cave, he was butchering a deer. She had been here before but what she didn't expect was for Oliver to step up to a plaque on the wall. He lifted a pane and pressed his thumb on a glass plate.

A loud clank, then light spilled into the cave as a hidden door opened.

"So, this is the other entrance," Anna said. "Beats lifting the floor in the woodworking shop."

She recognized the hallway. There was a flurry of activity around the monitors as Anna and Oliver entered the conference room, barely noticed by the others.

Arnold looked up and smiled. "Good afternoon, Anna. How are you feeling?"

She shrugged. How was she supposed to feel? She felt like she didn't belong here. Maybe her work here was complete. She should go about her life, dancing through the flowers, looking for a soul mate. More likely, they were going to tell her to crawl into a hornet's nest and find a pot of gold.

"I'm doing okay." She answered, rolling her eyes. "Just hope I can get out of here in time to make the quilting bee."

"Sarcasm noted." Arnold grinned. "I'll save your fingers by keeping you busy. Take a seat."

<hr>

Arnold tapped his tablet. "Have we found them yet?"

Keenan, the scruffy tech manager, pecked away silently. Finally, as the silence became awkward, his eyes lit up. "Yep. They're on the north slope. Sending the summons now."

"How long until contact?"

"About five minutes. We're using a drone. Launching now."

The big screen lit up as the drone soared above the lake. Anna watched in awe as the image shifted. It came to a stop and the video zoomed in on a couple of tents and a smoking fire ring. She looked for signs of Steven and Ethan. Did they hear the drone and hide in the thicker trees? It wouldn't surprise her if they shot it out of the sky.

The camp grew larger as the drone descended, dropping a package, and then shot back upward.

They watched as Steven emerged from the trees and picked up the package. As much as she wanted to watch Steven, Anna knew he was not alone. Somewhere hidden by the trees and brush Ethan was staring through his sniper rifle, the drone in his crosshairs. She scanned the surrounding area. If she had Ethan's experience she would be able to pick up the slight variations in the terrain, giving away his location.

A flicker of light caught her eye. "Keenan, can you zoom in between the two tall trees to the left of the camp?"

The picture offset left and zoomed in. As the picture came into focus, Ethan, rifle aimed skyward, lay camouflaged in the underbrush.

"This is why we use drones," Keenan said.

With the note in hand, Steven looked up at the drone and gave a thumbs-up. They continued to watch as Ethan came out of the trees and the two headed down the mountain.

"Looks like they will be here in twenty minutes," Arnold said. "Let's go over what's going on with Arwel. Have we heard from Abram?"

"Yes. There will be a meeting tomorrow night." Oliver answered. "They asked that Arwel be present to tell his side of the story. Unless you override me, I think he should be in chains."

Arnold shrugged. "It sounds kind of cruel, but considering his crime, it's appropriate. Has anyone talked to Rebbecca?"

"I heard that William and Claire were taking her under their wings." Oliver said. "She's going to need a lot of prayer to get through this one."

Anna felt the tears forming in her eyes. Her heart ached

for Rebbecca. Just the thought of it caused judgmental memories of loneliness to boil in her chest. She caught a tear with the back of her hand. "When the time's appropriate, I would like to see her. I don't blame her."

Arnold's unusually compassionate nod at Anna, told her he appreciated her desire. "I'm sure that opportunity will arise, but for now, let's focus on protecting the community."

He leaned forward in his chair and gently placed a hand on her arm. "Are you going to be okay with Ethan and Steven here?"

Not only was she going to be okay, she would excel being in the company of her two favorite men. Maybe a little giddy, but she'd pull through. "Of course. If it wasn't for them, I would be in Paradise right now."

"Speaking of Paradise. What do you know about Steven? Considering you have a history with the guy, clue us in."

Anna blushed. "I told you all I know, as for our history his only concern was to protect the community from outside influences."

"Sorry Anna, I'm not buying it. Tell us who he is."

"As I wrote in my report last week, he's a really nice guy We met over at the ranger station about fifteen years ago. We were both a lot younger, well, fifteen years younger. Steven had just got out of training and was assigned our area. I had known the ranger for a long time and he thought I might be a soft contact for Steven."

"You told us all about your indiscretions, tell us about Steven. Where's he from, what's his background, most of all, why are you so in love with him?"

Anna's face turned beet red. "Who said I'm in love with him?"

Arnold waved his hand away. "Forget that part. We don't have all day. Go on with what you know."

Anna took a couple deep breaths to slow down her heart rate. "I really don't know a lot. For many years, we had very little contact. He had left his job here to go serve in the army where he met Ethan. I had thought he was gone for good, until one day he sent me a message that he had returned. We met up and I brought him up to speed. Naturally, I never revealed classified secrets, mainly because I didn't know any.

"Steven has always been nice to me and never asked me to do anything against my conscience. He never pried or tried to get me to go digging up information. I really like him, even though, I don't think he's a believer."

Arnold ran his hand through his beard. "That could be problematic if you start spending too much time together. Be careful."

Oliver stood. "Looks like our guests are here. Be right back."

Anna fidgeted. Her heart ached for Rebbecca. "Do you think Arwel could ever make things right?" she asked.

Arnold looked up, incredulous, "Anna… do you not remember that just a few hours ago, he was moments away from killing you? All you have to do is rub your head to remind yourself that he knocked you unconscious. Carried you to your enemies. And now you want redemption for him?"

He shook his head. "You amaze me. But I doubt he'll ever be free again."

Anna was still wiping tears from her face when Oliver returned, with Steven and Ethan.

Chapter Thirty-Seven

"**Thanks for coming**, gentlemen." Arnold nodded as the men filled the empty seats around the table. Anna hid a smile as Steven slid into the chair beside her.

"I gather you all rested well last night?"

"Only between watches," Ethan replied. "Someone's gotta keep you out of trouble."

Arnold laughed. "Trouble is never far behind you, my friend. Any new intel from your people?"

"Most certainly. I will let Steven tell you. He spoke with our colonel this morning."

"Glad to meet you, Steven. I've heard a lot about you, from more than one source. Thanks for spying on us all these years," Arnold said, sarcasm thick in his voice.

"Just doing my job. Anyhow, it's good to finally meet you. Our combat unit is ready to assist. Oh, and sorry about the trail last fall. We might have ruffed it up a bit with those Hydro 70's. They pack a punch."

"You guys are all the same," Arnold snapped back. "Thanks for your help. So, what are we facing with this Venezuelan gang?"

Steven scanned the table. "Does Anna need to hear this?"

Arnold didn't hesitate. "Thanks to you, she is part of the team now. She can handle it."

Steven shrugged. "All right. The intel we received this morning was not good at all. Unless we want to bring in the U.S. military, there's a real risk of losing the lake."

"Based on what?" Arnold asked, as the security team leaned in.

"Over the last few years, the country's southern border has been wide open. Millions of illegals have flooded into the United States, including thousands of Venezuelan gang members. Intel has them organized and planning on making Charlotte Lake their base."

Sweat formed on Arnold's brow. "Why hasn't the government taken them down?"

"They can't find them," Steven said flatly. "The FBI's scouring the internet, but these people are good. They leave no trace."

"We'll be ready when they cross the pass. We have firepower," Arnold said.

"Firepower alone won't be enough. From captured data, we know they learned from the New York gang's failure last fall. This time, they're coming in small groups between two and four, surrounding the lake. They trained in their own Sierra Nevada's in Venezuela for this mission."

Arnold looked grim. "How much time do we have?"

"Our Cyber Task Force narrowed it down to Tuesday or Wednesday of next week. If all that's true, we have about a week."

"Great!" Arnold leaned back. "Tomorrow night we've got a business meeting at the church to deal with Arwel. We'll brief the congregation afterwards. You guys should be there to answer questions."

Ethan frowned, recalling how discipline meetings went and really didn't want to experience this one. It was going to be bad. Real bad! "How about we brief the congregation first?"

Arnold shook his head. "That would not be good. If the people know what's coming because of Arwel's actions, they will lynch him."

"Fair point. We'll be there. Do you guys have a doomsday plan?" Ethan asked.

"Yes, naturally we do. Just not sure this justifies it though. What kind of support are your people offering?"

Steven raised his hand. "We're bringing in a full strike force. Unfortunately, we can't position the troops. Once we identify the enemy, they will be neutralized."

Arnold's eyes widened. "Please tell me, you're not blowing up the village."

Steven grinned. "Not this time. I guess the last orders got a little scrambled. We will do our best to keep them alive. Naturally, we won't endanger our troops in the process. But, we have one big problem."

"You want our people out of the way?"

"Can you evacuate the village in a week?" Steven asked.

"We can do it in three hours." Arnold said confidently.

"Three hundred people out of the mountains in three hours, on foot?

"Follow me," Arnold said, standing. Ethan and Steven followed him out.

Behind the command center, they passed through a set of fire doors into a six-foot-wide hallway lit by dim blue lights. Two hundred yards in, Arnold opened a heavy steel door.

Ethan sensed a cavernous room on the other side. As soon as they walked through the door, motion sensors lit up a large room, filled with rows of tables. It reminded Ethan of his high school cafeteria.

"How long can you keep three hundred people in here?" Ethan asked.

"As long as needed. They would get antsy after a few days, but we've got enough supplies for a few months."

"So… are you a doomsday prepper?"

"Not exactly. Just wanted a secure place in case of an emergency. It was built as a safe room in case of a fast-moving forest fire."

Arnold led them to a hallway lined with doors. Opening one, they found a simple room with four bunk beds along each side.

"Fifty rooms like this. Not ideal, but it works."

Steven tested a mattress. "Better than what I slept on last night. I've been watching this place for fifteen years and had no idea."

"We kept it that way, especially from the government. Too much corruption."

"Well, thanks for trusting me."

"We don't. Anna does. You can thank her."

"I'll try and remember. She's... an interesting character."

"She's an emotional powerhouse," Arnold warned. "She will draw you into her net with kindness, and before you know it, you will be carrying in the firewood. Be careful."

Back in the conference room, an overhead map of the community was on the screen. Keenan and Oliver were talking to two other specialists that Ethan hadn't met.

Oliver turned to Arnold. "I was thinking we could set up a perimeter but the math doesn't add up. We can cover the trail passes, but if they arrive cross-country, we don't have the resources."

"Do you think we need to go to occupation zero?" Arnold asked.

"I think we should. I don't mind the fight, but there will be casualties. Our wives don't want that."

"I suppose you're right. Either way, there will be physical loss."

Arnold sighed, fiddling with his tablet. "Steven, can your strike force crush them once they're concentrated in the village?"

"We'll surround the village and then rain terror down on

them. And we will take them with us when we leave."

"Then that's what we will do." Arnold pushed his chair back. "Keenan, activate the plan. Oliver, come with me. We need to go see Abram and Eli."

Arnold looked at Steven. "If we could have some assurance of a battle plan from your commander before the meeting tomorrow night, I would appreciate it. I don't want to spend the rest of my life in a cave."

"Will do." Steven said. "But before we go, we're going to check on our other two teams, bringing them up to speed."

Keenan headed for his workstation and the rest made their way out of City Hall.

"Where are we going first?" Anna asked Steven.

"We aren't going anywhere," Steven said gently. "Ethan and I have things to tend to before tomorrow." He reached out and took her hand. "Unfortunately, you can't come with us."

"That hurts, but I guess I understand." Anna pouted. "Maybe I'll go see Krystal. We have a lot to talk about."

"Speaking of hurting," Ethan said, "I noticed you flinch when Eli was mentioned. Do you still believe he was the one that hit you?"

Anna's shoulders tightened. "He did hit me. Can we talk later?"

"Okay. If you're going up to Krystal's, could you let her know we will be stopping by later this evening?"

"I will. She will be excited. We'll have dinner ready."

"We?" Steven asked.

"If you guys are coming, I'm there."

"You never give up, Anna," Ethan smiled. "We weren't going to let the children know yet, so if Krystal wants me to come in, have her put a quilt on a rocking chair on the porch."

"Aw, that's so romantic." Anna said. "It will be so fun." She gave Ethan a peck on the cheek and took off.

They watched Anna skip up the trail, her skirt fluttering

in the breeze.

"She didn't kiss me." Steven said.

"Your time's coming," Ethan replied. "Let's stop at the bakery, for some fresh bread. The guys will love us for it."

"Yeah right. How about we stop by McDonald's and get them a cheeseburger as well." Steven joked, as they headed south around the lake.

"For this being your area, you sure have a lot to learn, my friend." Ethan turned up the path towards a log structure. The smell of the morning baking was still strong in the air.

Steven's eyes got big. "Something's in the oven."

Ethan introduced Steven to the girls finishing up the day's work, and they were soon on their way down the trail with a backpack full of baked goods.

"That's the woodworking shop," Ethan pointed towards a large barn tucked back in the trees. "It doubles as a hardware store. You really should spend more time up here."

"Can't say I haven't thought about it. I can retire in a couple of years."

Ethan stopped and looked over at Steven chewing on a chunk of bread. "Maybe you didn't notice, but this is not a retirement center. Could be a good place to find a wife and raise a family."

Steven choked on his bread. "Sorry, you caught me off guard. For a moment, I thought you were talking about me."

Ethan laughed. "Don't kid yourself, Lieutenant McMillan. You're about to trade that military uniform for some homemade duds."

"I could, as long as they're not made of wool. And they come with someone to keep me company."

"I knew it. You're waiting for Anna to drop a hint."

"I reckon so. But, I'm gonna play hard to get. All kidding aside, I'm starting to like her. Actually, I always have, but the timing's never been right."

They walked in silence for a few minutes before Steven inhaled deeply and sighed. "I guess it still isn't."

"Yeah. We should be setting up terrorist war plans. Not, performing for some reality show. Let's stay focused."

They passed the livestock barn. Steven wrinkled his nose. "This the fertilizer plant?"

Ethan pointed behind the barn at the pasture full of livestock. "And the protein factory."

The spring runoff had the stream rushing down the valley, and thundering into the ravine. A mile west of the lake Ethan pointed to a tree lying across the stream.

"I don't think there's a trail on that side, but the lower we go the harder it is to cross."

They angled along the north slope and after 45 minutes of scrambling over granite, reached an overlook above Bubbs Creek.

Ethan stuck his head over the edge of the cliff hunting for their comrades. "Wherever they're at, they know how to hide. See if you can bring them up on the radio."

Steven tried the radio. "Bubbs Creek, Overwatch, come in."

Static.

Steven adjusted the squelch and tried again. "They must not have it on. I'll try Kearsarge Pass."

"No need, I think I see their camp." Ethan stood up. "We just need to get down off the cliff without killing ourselves."

They worked their way down through a crevice. They were halfway to the camp when a strange feeling swept over Ethan. He stopped and held up his hand. Turning to Steven he whispered. "Something's not right. Go overwatch."

Steven climbed higher along the face of the cliff. Ethan drew his Beretta, clicked off the safety, and crept toward the camp. Slowly looking down the sites of his handgun he moved around the brush and trees.

He froze as his stomach lurched. Conrad lay face down in a pool of dried blood. It was evident that he had been gone for a few days. Where was Lewis? He backed up and moved around the camp, approaching from a different direction. He was on full alert. With his left hand he reached down and switched on his radio and clicked a couple of times.

"Conrad's dead, looking for Lewis. Keep your eyes open."

Ethan heard the clicks. Steven had to be scanning the surroundings, but that might not be enough. Keep your head down. Going around the lower side of the camp he came to a ravine. He hoped he was wrong but the boots sticking out from the rocks, told him otherwise.

"Found Lewis, he's been shot, execution style."

Two clicks. Now he knew Steven would not only be on alert, but would shoot at anything moving. "Get out of there, Ethan! Now!"

Ethan backed out of the area, keeping his head low. The guys had been dead for a few days. They must have been hit soon after they set up camp.

"Let's get to high ground." He whispered to Steven when they met at the base of the cliff. Slowly and deliberately, they made their way up the crevice to the top of the rock face. Surveying their surroundings, they sat down hidden from the valley.

Steven pulled out his Satellite Messenger. "We're sitting ducks. I'm calling in a Blackhawk."

Ethan pulled out his field glasses and moved to the edge of the cliff. Lying on his stomach he searched for anything out of the ordinary. How could this have happened? He might understand if they had been sleeping. But, it looked like Conrad was surprised and Lewis was executed. Whoever did this was trained in Guerrilla warfare. They may be up against their equals.

Steven slid up beside him. "See anything?"

"Not a thing. I just don't want to be here after dark. We need to get a message to Tanner and Roland."

"Just got a message back from headquarters. They're spinning the blades now. ETA, twenty-five minutes."

Chapter Thirty-Eight

Steven pulled out his signaling mirror as Ethan scanned the valley through his binoculars. If anyone was nearby, they most likely would be along Bubbs Creek trail.

Zooming in, Ethan swept the valley. He had come down this trail last year and knew it well. He followed it up the valley and spotted movement. Four hikers. Young men, dressed like backpackers, even using trekking poles. At first glance, they looked legit.

He grabbed his sniper rifle. He could bring them in closer with the high-powered scope. At a half mile the magnification showed every detail. He tensed. It was four young males in their twenties. One looked like he could be a little older. That alone didn't prove anything. Then Ethan noticed something strange hanging off one of the backpacks.

"I have them." He told Steven. "Four men hiking up Bubbs Creek trail. About a half mile out."

"Confirmation?" Steven asked.

"Let's just say, they have night vision goggles hanging off their backpacks. Not your normal hiking gear."

"You're going to terminate them on that evidence? That

will get you in the slammer."

"Not taking them out, but I have a way of getting the proof."

"No, don't do it." Steven knew what Ethan was thinking. They had done it many times in Afghanistan.

"I'm going to do it. Where's our ride?" Ethan asked.

"Ten minutes out. Let it go, they're probably just hikers."

"You wanna watch this through the sighting scope? Firing in fifteen."

Steven sighed and grabbed his spotting scope, peering down Ethan's rifle line. "Got 'em. Yeah… wolves in sheep's clothing. What's your target?"

"Five paces in front of the lead. The second shot, five paces to the rear."

"The bracket. Sounds good." Steven braced for the shot.

Ethan exhaled and squeezed the trigger. The .338 Lapua roared, echoing down the valley. Dust erupted in front of the lead hiker. They stumbled back falling over each other. Two seconds later, another shot kicked up dirt behind them.

Instantly, the four dove for cover.

"We will know shortly." Ethan said as he chambered another round, wiping the sweat off his brow.

"Bingo." Steven said. "Weapons out, two ARs, two handguns." He could hear the sound of a chopper coming up the valley from the west.

They're here. Grab your gear," Steven said.

Ethan remained prone, eye on his scope. "Keep signaling. I want to see their reaction to the Blackhawk."

As the thumping intensified, the "hikers" turned their gaze down the valley.

"Two Apaches coming in hot. Blackhawks two miles in trail." Steven reported. "Let the Apaches handle it."

Ethan didn't answer. His crosshairs tracked the oldest one, now raising a weapon toward the incoming chopper.

As the AH-64's screamed overhead, all four of the hikers trained their weapons on the incoming helicopters.

That was enough.

He slowly let out his breath and pulled the trigger. The 250-grain bullet did its job, and his target dropped to the ground. One down, one to go. He shifted, found the target, and pulled the trigger. Another down.

"Eye for an eye." He muttered, backing away from the cliff.

"You get 'em?" Steven asked, as he holstered his handgun and strapped on his rifle.

"You had to ask?" Ethan replied, already prepping for a pickup.

The Apaches slowed into a standoff position, as the first Blackhawk approached. Gusty winds coming up the valley created turbulent conditions. Finally, the pilot got it stabilized overhead. A rope dropped, followed by a crew member who tossed harnesses to the men.

Steven clipped in first. Within seconds, he was airborne.

Two minutes later, the winch returned. Ethan hooked in and began rising. He had been the recipient of a couple extractions under fire in Afghanistan. This time, he had taken out the individuals capable of firing on them. Or he thought. About halfway up, a bullet pinged off the belly of the Blackhawk.

Where did that come from?

Twisting midair, Ethan watched an Apache dive toward the trail, Gatling guns blazing.

Should have taken them all out.

The crew chief pulled him through the door and with both men in the Blackhawk, they swung left and flew away from the threat. Not that it was a threat anymore, but who knew what else was out there. They climbed to a safe altitude and flew around Charlotte Dome and Mount Gardiner.

Strapped in their seats they pulled on headsets. "What's going on back at the extraction site?" Steven asked the crew chief.

"Cleanup crew is inbound. Don't worry about any threat.

The Apache pilots are itching for action."

"Thanks for the lift. Any chance you could drop us off at Kearsarge Pass? Our boys up there could be in danger."

The crew chief relayed the request. The response came as they turned toward the pass.

Three minutes later, they were slowly circling around their comrades, as the Blackhawk buffeted in the turbulent wind coming through the pass.

"Hope you don't mind hoofing it." The crew chief hollered over the intercom. "The pilots are going to set you down about eight hundred yards below the pass."

"Not ideal," Ethan answered. "But, we can handle it." The last thing he wanted to experience was another helicopter crash.

The pilot did a big teardrop and entered the landing zone at a 45-degree angle to the mountain. Setting it down firmly on a grassy patch, between the rocks. As soon as the wheels hit the ground, the guys jumped out and moved rapidly away. They had just cleared the rotors when the deafening scream of the turbines lifted off and peeled away to the right, dropping down across Kearsarge Lakes.

They started up the trail and soon spotted Tanner jogging down to meet them.

"What happened?" he asked.

"Bad news," Steven said flatly. "Conrad and Lewis were killed in their camp. Ambushed. We spotted the terrorists, likely Rafael's gang."

"Are they headed here or to the village?"

"Neither," Steven said. "Ethan took care of that, with a little Apache backup. But where there's one nest of scorpions…"

"There's more," Ethan finished.

"Have you seen anyone else coming over the pass?" Steven asked.

"Just backpackers. Roland did say ten groups came through two nights ago. Camped at Kearsarge Lake, gone by morning. If you didn't see them, they must be south bounders."

"Were there any women in the groups?"

"Can't say he mentioned gender. Of the hikers I seen, they were all men."

Steven looked at Ethan. "What do you think?"

"I think they are sneaking in here looking like long-distance backpackers. We need to find out where they're hiding."

"I agree. Tanner, get back up to Roland and make sure you secure your position. Keep us informed on the number of hikers coming over the pass, either direction. I'll get in touch with the DOE and have the rangers close the PCT and all the other local trails."

"What about Charlotte Lake. Are they ready for this?" Tanner asked.

"They're vanishing. It'll be a ghost town by the time Rafael arrives. We will be using the secondary channel, so keep your radio on."

Ethan glanced at his watch. "Hate to break this up boys, but we need to go now."

Without another word, the two men turned down the trail toward Charlotte Lake, three miles away.

Chapter Thirty-Nine

Krystal and Anna sat on the porch, watching the children play in the clearing.

"So, are you going to tell them, or just wait until he shows up?" Anna asked.

Krystal rocked slowly with the quilt draped across her lap. She hadn't said much since Anna told her about Ethan planning to stop by later. Her only response had been to quietly retrieve the quilt from the closet.

"I really don't know if I want him to show up," Krystal finally said.

"Your actions say otherwise," Anna said, pointing at the quilt.

Krystal gave a faint smile. "That's true. But how many times can a heart break before it turns to stone?"

"As many times as that heart is willing to forgive. Are you ready to give Ethan another chance?"

Krystal smoothed a wrinkle from the quilt. "Another… and another… and another. As long as there is hope."

They sat in silence, contemplating what the evening might bring, when the sound of a helicopter broke the silence. A Blackhawk emerged from the valley below Charlotte Dome, headed in their direction.

"There are two of them." Anna pointed.

"Looks like more than that," Krystal said. "Something must be happening. Maybe we should pray for the guys."

"Good idea." Anna reached over and took Krystal's trembling hand. "I'll pray."

She jumped right in asking God to watch over Ethan and Steven, and everyone involved in whatever was happening down in the valley. Then she prayed for Krystal, that she would find peace regarding Ethan, and if it was God's will, that they would be brought together forever. She finished her prayer just as the Blackhawk roared over the ridge behind the cabin.

The women watched the Blackhawk bank east towards Kearsarge Pass. It circled a couple of times before descending out of view.

Jonah came running over to the porch and grabbed his mother's arm. "Mommy, did you see that helicopter? It's the one Ethan flew away in! Is it bringing him back?"

Krystal ruffled his hair. "We don't know if he's in that helicopter. It'll be time to go inside soon, so you had better go play."

"I see it's still not time to tell them," Anna said, as Jonah ran off.

The Blackhawk rose off the pass and headed west down the valley. Jonah stopped and waved as it passed overhead.

"Considering what we're seeing, I don't think there's going to be a need." Krystal sighed. "Do you think things will ever get back to normal here?"

"I think Charlotte Lake will return to normal. But not us."

Krystal shivered. "I'm getting cold. Let's go inside."

She called out to the children, who came running, chased by Growler. Anna watched as Krystal stood and gently laid the quilt across the back of the rocking chair. She smoothed the fabric and patted it twice. Anna's heart ached for her friend.

At the door, Anna lingered for a moment, listening to the children's laughter spill from inside. She glanced back at the porch. The quilt sat quietly on the rocker. A symbol of a decision not made lightly.

Inside, the freshly stoked fire crackled as Krystal set the kettle on. "Care for a cup of tea?"

"Sure," Anna replied softly. "You know, I didn't think telling you about Ethan coming tonight would shake you up so much."

Krystal leaned against the kitchen counter, her eyes a million miles away. "He always shakes me, even when he's not here."

They stood in thoughtful silence until the kettle began to hiss.

"I keep thinking I'm ready," Krystal said as she poured steaming water over the teabags.

"Ready for what?" Anna asked.

Krystal shrugged. "Whatever God's will is for my relationship with Ethan. I feel safe when he's here."

"Ethan or God?" Anna smiled.

Krystal didn't take the bait. "God, of course. But He's always here. I just think… I would like to add Ethan, to make our family complete."

"So… you're ready to marry him?"

"Of course. He just needs to ask."

Anna laughed. "Good luck. You may need to propose to him."

"Like you did?" Krystal raised a brow.

"Hey, that was before I knew about you. Do you blame me?"

"Not at all. I'm just surprised he turned you down."

Krystal led Anna to the couch. They sat with their tea, wrapped in warmth and shared memories.

Chapter Forty

The sun was dropping below Mount Bago as Ethan and Steven walked into the village. Ethan pointed out the meeting house. "That's where the meeting is tomorrow night. If there is one."

"Do you have access to City Hall?" Steven asked as they got closer to the storehouse.

"Used to, but we'll find out."

Sarah was sweeping out the store when they entered.

"Good evening, boys. You needing some things?"

Ethan waved his hand. "Always your cheerful self. We're just on our way to see Arnold. Do you know if he's still in his office?"

"You know I'm not allowed to give you that information. Do you want me to get him?" She asked.

Ethan laughed. "You're right about keeping secrets, but thanks for letting me know he's there. I think I'm still in the system."

They pulled open the big wooden door and were greeted by the aroma of the butcher's walk-in cooler.

"Follow close," Ethan said.

The system accepted Ethan's thumbprint, and the dark cavern gave way to the sterile hallway.

Arnold was sitting alone in the conference room when they arrived.

"Come on in, troublemakers, and don't tell me you had nothing to do with the helicopters flying around here this afternoon."

"Great, we won't." Ethan said, as he sat down, crossing his hands behind his head. "What we will tell you is that somewhere in this, or surrounding valleys, there's a large number of trained militia. We just don't know where they're hiding."

Arnold looked behind him, as if expecting someone. "I would like for Oliver and Keenan to get here before we start, but I can tell you. We launched a couple of drones when your buddies arrived in their whirlybirds. While we were watching them clean up the mess, we noticed a lot of activity down by the mines."

Ethan looked over at Steven. Did he know? If not, he was about to find out.

"Are the miners in danger?" Ethan asked.

"No, we closed the mines for the winter. No one's supposed to be there."

Ethan remembered sneaking into the mines last summer. There was plenty of room in the shafts to hide thousands of militia. They could have a platoon of military-trained soldiers ready to march the three miles into Charlotte Lake. In two hours, they could have it surrounded. How much firepower would it take to stop an invasion like that?

Keenan and Oliver hurried into the room.

"It's activated." Keenan said as he slid into a chair. "Welcome back, guys. Sounds like you had an exciting afternoon."

Ethan popped the kinks in his neck. "Not our choice. What's activated?"

"We're evacuating Charlotte Lake," Keenan replied.

"Sorry, I thought you guys knew."

Ethan and Steven exchanged a look as the screen on the wall lit up.

Arnold was fiddling with his tablet. "Guys, you may want to see this. This is a live feed over the mine shafts."

All eyes turned to the monitor. What looked like hundreds of ants were moving about the clearing in front of the doors. Some were going in and out of the shafts.

"Can you zoom in a bit?" Ethan asked.

Arnold fiddled with the controls and the ants started growing until it was visibly people.

"Sir," Keenan said, "You're not zooming in, you're descending. They can probably hear the drone now."

He had no more got it out of his mouth when flashes came from the clearing.

Arnold hit the altitude button, but it was too late. Multiple flashes and the picture went haywire.

"I think I'm hit," Arnold said, struggling to regain control.

"You think?" Keenan shook his head, reaching for his tablet. "I've got number three. Maybe we can keep this one alive."

Ethan watched as number four continued an uncontrolled descent toward the clearing. Just before it hit, a clear picture of the militia crossed the screen.

"Can you back up the video?" he asked.

Arnold complied, revealing a clear picture of about three hundred men dressed in BDUs gathered in the clearing. Each one had a strange flag on their sleeve.

"Can anyone identify the flag?" Ethan asked.

"Hold on," Oliver said, typing rapidly on his tablet. "A.I. says it's a Venezuelan gang identification marking, normally as a tattoo on its members."

The men sat stunned until Steven spoke.

"I can have a couple of Hellfire missiles take them all out in a matter of minutes. Just say the word."

Ethan held up his hand. "We don't know if this is all of them. I can't imagine someone as smart as Rafael putting all his eggs in one basket. There are probably three more groups this size scattered throughout the mountains. You blow this one to smithereens and the rest will torch this place. No, I say we stick to the plan. What do you think Arnold?"

Arnold did the normal thing of pretending to remove all foreign objects from his beard. "Yes, stick to the evacuation plan. What about your people, Steven? Have you had a chance to tell them?"

"No, we haven't. Do you have outside communications in here? We need to arrange an extraction."

"Yes. Oliver will help you. Once the counterattack is in place, do you plan on coming back?"

"Wouldn't miss it for the world," Ethan answered. "Everyone I love is in this valley."

Arnold nodded, glancing at his watch. "Okay, gentlemen, let's vacate the village. Lockdown happens in less than two hours."

Ethan and Steven followed Oliver to a console in the control room.

"This computer is connected to a secure server. Willow Creek dispatch is in the directory."

Steven clicked through the steps. They waited. Seconds turned into minutes. Ethan checked his watch. They needed to be out of there before the militia arrived at the village. Most likely, there were already spotters on the hills watching people heading for the storehouse. What happens when the militia finds the storehouse vacated? Will they break down the door going into the ice cave?

"Hello, Steven. Where you at?" a voice snapped Ethan's attention back to the screen. He didn't recognize the dispatcher, but clearly, he knew Steven.

"No time to chat, sir. We need an extract out of Charlotte Lake stat."

"Didn't we just extract you earlier?" the dispatcher

asked.

"Yes, you did. We'll be in the meadow below the barn. Enemy militia are in the area, so use extreme caution."

"They're refueling the Blackhawks now. It'll be dark by the time they get there." The dispatcher paused. "Hold on."

Steven turned to Oliver. "Can you find out if the militia are moving?"

"Sure" Oliver headed back to the conference room.

The dispatcher returned. "We have a Blackhawk coming up from Fresno with a VIP. They're rerouting for the extract. ETA, twenty minutes."

"You sure you want to bring a VIP in here? They could take on small arms fire."

"They understand and will use caution. We'll launch a backup as soon as they finish refueling."

"Roger that. We'll activate our locator beacon when we hear them coming up the valley. Thanks."

"Anytime, Lieutenant McMillan. Stay safe."

Steven disconnected the link. "Let's get out of here while we can."

"They're still at the mine," Oliver said, returning with a tablet. "Looks like they're organizing and getting ready to move out."

"Thanks Oliver," Steven said as he pulled on his pack. "Has your family made it here yet?"

"I watched them go through security a few of minutes ago. Thanks for asking?"

"Has Krystal and the children arrived yet?" Ethan asked.

"I haven't seen them, but they're farther out. I'll let them know you had to go back to camp. Any messages you want relayed?"

Ethan thought of many messages. "Just tell her I love her and will see her soon."

"Love her and see her soon." Steven chided as they walked through the ice cave to the storehouse.

"What? Are you jealous?" Ethan pushed open the door

and was greeted by Robert and Hugo.

"You guys heading out?" Robert asked. "We'll be sealing this off in about fifteen minutes."

"We have to go back to Willow Creek. Arnold will explain," Ethan answered. "Lord willing, we'll see you tomorrow."

"We can only pray. Take care, guys."

⎯⎯⎯⎯⎯⎯ • ● • ⎯⎯⎯⎯⎯⎯

On the way down the trail to the barn, they met a number of people rushing toward the storehouse. The last of the daylight was fading fast. They had just passed the barnyard when Ethan heard the helicopter. Still a long way off, but it was coming their way.

He activated the locator on his shoulder.

The wind whipped up as they crawled over the fence into the meadow.

"They sound low," Ethan said as the thumping increased.

"That could be dangerous." Steven turned on his radio. "Maybe they're on our frequency."

"Blackhawk inbound for Charlotte Lake, Come in." Steven tried again. No response.

"I see him," Ethan said, pointing at flashing navigation lights coming around Charlotte Dome. "Not good."

"Charlotte Lake to Blackhawk! Get out of there!" Steven screamed into the radio.

Too late. They stood in horror as a flash came from the ground. The Blackhawk exploded and fell into Charlotte creek.

Steven switched to their secondary frequency. "Overwatch to Kearsarge, Come in."

A shaken voice lit up the speaker. "Kearsarge here. What was that?"

"Our ride out of here. Can you reach base?"

"Affirmative. Good connection. What do you need?"

"There's a backup on the way. Have them come in from the east, low over the lake. Let them know it's a war zone with enemy RPGs. Have the Apaches annihilate the area 100 yards north of the crash site."

"Will do. Also, about thirty more backpackers came over the pass. All young males. Do you want us to shut off the trail?"

Ethan rapidly shook his head. They would rather have them all in the valley.

"Let them in," Steven replied. "It's better we fight this fight on one front."

"Roger that. Stand by."

"Maybe we should just stay and fight," Ethan said.

"Sounds like you. We could, but we need artillery, and a strike team."

They sat silently as darkness consumed the meadow, and the stars appeared overhead.

"Do you believe God is watching what's going on down here?" Steven asked.

"Where did that come from?" Ethan asked after he recovered from the shock.

"Oh, I don't know. It's just, Anna has gone through a lot of stuff, yet she has this faith that God is watching over her. I just question if it's real."

It was like déjà vu for Ethan. He understood completely what Steven was going through. Anna didn't make it any easier. "It's real as the stars in the sky, my friend. Anna's not lying. It's just going to take you some time to accept it."

"Speaking of Anna, do you think the girls will forgive us for not showing up tonight?"

"I just pray they made it to the cave." Ethan said.

Silence fell again as they searched the sky for signs of an arriving Blackhawk.

The first sound outside of nature itself was the whistling

of wings slicing the air. A sharp-bladed shadow darkened the stars for a millisecond, and then a thunderous roar shattered the silence. A second later, a massive explosion lit up the sky at the base of Charlotte Dome.

"Well, there go the mines." Ethan said as the thunder of the F-16 was replaced by thumping of rotor blades.

They pulled down their night vision goggles and spotted a Blackhawk coming low across Charlotte Lake. It wasted no time coming around the barn and setting down fifty yards away from where they were standing.

They ran toward the open door and dove into the cabin as the wheels settled into the dew-covered grass. The red interior lights cast a glow on the crew chief yelling at them to strap in. Ethan heard him yell into the mic. "Go! Go!"

The deafening rotors intensified as turbines screamed. They lifted off the meadow as the crew chief slammed the door shut. The Blackhawk banked hard back over the lake as it climbed into the dark sky.

* ● *

The house shook as a jet screamed above the cabin, followed by a massive explosion. The floor shook and a picture fell off the wall.

Anna rushed to the door. She could see a flume of smoke in the darkening sky.

"Someone bombed the mines at Charlotte Dome."

Krystal and the children joined her on the porch, trembling. The children clung to their mother's skirt.

"Mommy, hold me," Jonah begged.

Anna felt a small hand slip into hers. She looked down into a pair eyes, filled with uncertainty. Anna knelt down and wrapped her arms around Christiana.

"It's going to be okay, dear. They aren't going to hurt us

up here."

"Let's go inside children. I'll read you some books." Krystal said, ushering them through the door.

"I'll be in shortly," Anna said, shutting the door. She sat back in a rocking chair. She wished she had her Satellite Messenger.

Something bad was happening. Were they in danger? Should she check in with security? She was part of that team now.

Anna stuck her head in the door. "I'm going down to see if Arnold knows what's going on. I will stop back by on the way home."

"Thanks. That'll help me sleep tonight," Krystal said, turning back to the children's book.

Chapter Forty-One

Anna practically ran down the path to the trail. She was surprised that William and Claire's cabin was dark. She ran on towards the storehouse, quickly noticing none of the cabins had their usual flickering lights. Something was wrong.

A Blackhawk helicopter came roaring across the lake. Anna froze, watching it disappear behind the barn. It sounded like it landed. Was it bringing the boys back? She could only hope. She was nearly to the storehouse when it took off and came back across the lake, climbing into the night sky.

Moonlight guided her as she followed the path to the storehouse. Inside, it was complete darkness. She pulled off her pack and retrieved a small flashlight. Where was the door? The heavy wooden entrance to the ice cave was gone, replaced by ceiling-high shelves filled with dry goods.

"Oh no," she whispered. "They must be under attack. Why weren't we contacted?"

She had to get Krystal and the children. But first, she'd check the other entrance.

Anna ran to the woodworking shop. How much time did she have? She shined her light around the shop. Where was the trapdoor? It had to be… there! But a heavy workbench sat over the area. No way of moving that. She was out of options.

She ran all the way back to Krystal's cabin. Her heart pounded as she burst through the door.

Krystal was sitting alone on the couch, the children already in bed.

"We need to go, now!" she panted.

"Where?" Krystal asked.

"I don't know. We just need to get out of here right away. Get the children. I'll explain later."

Fortunately, the children were still awake. Within minutes, the five of them and Growler were making their way down the path.

"We need to get out of the village," Anna whispered to Krystal as they joined the trail and turned towards the east. "The stone cabin might be the best place to go."

"Is it safe there?" Krystal remembered Ethan taking her and the children up there last year.

"Safer than here. If what they feared is happening, this place will be crawling with militia within the hour. And they're not nice people." Anna cringed as she led them past the meeting house and across the bridge. The children bravely climbed the switchbacks without complaining. Twenty minutes later they were on the plateau and walking along the meadow.

Gunfire erupted in the valley below, followed by explosions.

"It's started." Anna said.

"Will they come up here?" Krystal tried to control her breathing.

"They might, but Growler will warn us."

"Warn us that we're about to die?" Krystal's voice trembled.

"There might be something in the cabin to help. Remember, Ethan lived here once."

The silhouette of the cabin came into view, its dark outline brought some relief, while the sound of tumbling water tried to counter their fear.

"Careful children," Krystal warned as they made their way across the rugged bridge.

The familiar squeak of the hinges greeted them. Inside, the fresh smell of cleaner surprised them.

"Someone's been here recently and cleaned this place. Must be getting it ready for summer." Anna said, switching on her flashlight.

Once the door was shut and the lock put in place, Anna lit an oil lantern and turned down the wick.

"Go ahead and put the children in the bed," she told Krystal. "I'll cover the windows with blankets."

By the time Krystal returned to the living room, Anna had moved the rugged coffee table to one side and rolled back the rug.

"What are you doing?" Krystal asked as Anna was struggling with the floorboards.

"Ethan hid stuff down here. If we're lucky, the radios are still here."

With Krystal's help, they were able to get the first board out, and then the rest came easily. Under the floor, they found a box full of miscellaneous equipment. Anna started pulling it out and handing it to Krystal. Most of it was unfamiliar, except the one thing Anna had been searching for, a security-issued handheld radio.

"This may be just what we need. Ethan must have figured he wouldn't need it if he wasn't here. Turn it on."

As Anna sorted through the rest of the items, an ammo box caught her eye. Setting it on the edge of the floor, she opened it to find the handgun Ethan had given her the night the community had come under attack. She pulled it out, checked the magazine, and was flooded with memories.

Walking down the trail that night, keeping off the main path.

She shuddered briefly, remembering one of the gangsters as he went from cabin to cabin.

Anna looked over at Krystal playing with the radio. Could she have prevented Krystal from being taken hostage that night? She had watched as the assailants pulled Krystal and the children from Elena's cabin. She followed them to the dry goods store.

She could have shot him. Why didn't she? Was it fear? Doubt? Or something darker?

She cringed at the thought that she might have wanted Krystal out of the way. That wasn't her. At least she didn't think so.

She remembered how it had bothered her as she stood behind the tree watching the door shut. One of the assailants came out of the door and started west down the trail toward the garden. For some unknown reason she had followed this gangster. It must have been God using her in a way she was unable to comprehend. When the gangster stopped and spoke to someone down the trail, she heard the name Ethan Dawson.

She remembered pulling the trigger, the deafening explosion. And then, she was in Ethan's arms trying to figure out what she had done.

Anna exhaled and slammed the magazine into the gun.

Krystal tensed. "What are you going to do with that?"

"Protect us. Believe it or not, I know how to use this thing."

"The way it sounds down in the valley, we may need more than that. Do you know how to use this?" Krystal handed Anna the radio. "It looks like the batteries are working."

Anna turned up the volume, adjusted the squelch and pressed the button.

"Is anyone out there?" She asked in a soft shaky voice. She looked at Krystal with questioning eyes.

The radio crackled briefly and went silent.

"Is anyone out there? Please help us."

Anna held the radio up against her head. Please God let there be someone out there who can help us. Once again, a crackle came out of the speaker. Anna adjusted the squelch and tried again.

In the middle of the ensuing crackle an audible voice was heard. "Individual calling for help. Identify yourself."

Anna adjusted the squelch a little bit more. "This is a resident of Charlotte Lake. Who is this?"

"Community security. Please authenticate."

Oh great! What was her number. It was something she should remember. It's Cody's birth month and day. She keyed the mic and hoped she had it right.

"Zero, three, one, seven."

A few seconds later the radio came alive. "Anna, this is S.C. Where are you, and how did you get a radio?"

Anna sighed with relief. "We're in the crater at the stone house. This radio must have been Ethan's. Can you send someone to help us?"

There was a long hesitation before Arnold spoke. "That's impossible right now. There are over five hundred militia in the village. You need to shelter in place. Who's with you?

"Krystal and her children. We were at her cabin. We were not notified."

"That was a mistake. It will be dealt with. For now, we need to keep you safe." Anna heard the anger in his voice. "I'm turning you over to Keenan. He's working on something for you."

"Thanks, Chief. Sorry we didn't make it in."

Why had she apologized?

"Anna, this is Keenan. How much battery power do you have left?"

Anna inspected the radio. "It doesn't say, but we found extra batteries."

"Good. Stay with me. Don't give away your location, the

militia may be listening. We've got drones overhead and have confirmed the area's clear for now."

"Thanks, Keenan. What should we do?"

"Just stay there and rest. We're contacting Willow Creek for assistance. Put your radio on standby to save the batteries. I'll be back in ten minutes with an update."

"Roger. Going on standby." Anna found the setting and switched it over. She set the radio down on the table and rubbed the stress out of her eyes.

A clicking drew her attention, Krystal lighting a butane burner.

"I found some tea bags. It's time we finish our tea." Krystal said with a small smile. "Just trying to adjust to the new normal."

Anna shivered. "In that case, I will light a fire in the stove. A little heat would do us good."

Chapter Forty-Two

"What? How could that happen?" Ethan was livid. "How long before we can be airborne?"

"The Blackhawks are being equipped for the mission. Colonel Whitlock took the King Air down to Fresno to meet the Homeland Security Secretary. We don't expect him back until morning."

"I know!" Ethan slammed his hand on the table. He scrolled through his phone contacts and found Junior. Last he knew, Junior was flying charters out of San Jose. Ethan fired off an SOS message.

To his relief, Junior replied almost instantly.

Mr. Dawson. Good to hear from you. I'm over Carson City, deadheading back to the coast. Where can I pick you up?

Ethan sent his location and instructions. *The only way in is from the west. Clear skies tonight, so you shouldn't have any problems. What are you flying?*

A minute later, his phone lit up.

Cessna Caravan, Be there in about forty minutes.

Ethan looked up at Steven. "Our ride's inbound. Let's

go."

"Wait a minute." Riley raised a hand. "That's not part of the mission plan. I need to get approval."

Ethan shoved his chair back and planted both hands on the table. "You do that, Riley. While you're chasing signatures, we'll be out saving lives. Come on, Steven."

• ● •

At the hangar, they found their chutes packed, their weapons ready. After a quick inspection, they sat down at the table to wait.

"You bring oxygen?" Ethan asked.

"Always. Why?"

"I'm thinking we go in high. Last report from security shows close to six hundred militants in the village. We don't need to draw any up to the crater."

"Let's do it. What's the ceiling on the Caravan?"

"It's unpressurized so it can't be too high."

Steven checked his phone. "Looks like 25,000. Let's take it all the way up."

"Should we let the girls know we're coming?"

"No way to reach them directly. I would think Riley will notify security."

"Dude, it's Riley."

"True. We'll let them know when we get there."

Tires chirped on the runway as Junior's Caravan touched down. The men grabbed their gear and headed for the ramp.

The prop spun down. Junior hopped out and grabbed Ethan's hand. "Good to see you're still among the living. How are things going with that little lady and those sweet kids of hers?"

"As always, Junior, none of your business." Ethan laughed, slapping his back.

Junior grinned. "Yeah, well, 'none of my business' usually shows up in an envelope stuffed with lettuce. We rabbits gotta eat too."

"We need a drop seventy-five miles southeast, at 25,000 feet. How much lettuce for that?"

Junior glance at their gear and stepped back. "That high? You know that's in controlled airspace?"

"Yep. Don't care. Just get us there, we'll handle the rest."

Junior scratched his head. "We've got a roll up door for jumps, but I have never done one that high."

Junior opened the cargo door. "Toss your bag in and help me with this door."

A few pins and connectors later, the solid door was stowed and the roll-up door pulled down.

"Alright," Junior said. "It'll take about forty minutes to get to altitude. I will give you a two-minute warning by flashing the cabin lights. When I wag the wings and flash the lights again, you'll be over the target, corrected for wind. Got it?"

Ethan nodded. "You sure you're not a colonel?"

Junior chuckled. "One more thing, I don't have oxygen available back here, so bring your own."

Steven patted his belt tanks. "We already thought of that."

"Alright. Let's get going before my boss wonders where I'm at."

"What about the lettuce?" Ethan asked.

Junior scratched his head again. "Twenty pieces? Is that too much?"

"Just right." Ethan handed him an envelope. "There's five extra, just in case you find another rabbit, and need to forget where you dropped your passengers."

"Speaking of that, do you have a lat/long?"

Ethan handed him a slip of paper. "Eat it after we jump."

Junior grinned, "Never acquired the taste."

Thirty minutes later, at 25,000 feet, the cabin lights

flashed. Ethan followed Steven towards the cargo door. It had been a noisy climb out, and rolling up the jump door didn't help. Ethan checked his wrist. Altitude confirmed.

He prayed silently. "God, be with us as we drop into the night sky. Guide our fall, open our chutes, lead us to the girls."

Junior wagged the wings, the cabin lights flashed.

Steven vanished through the door. Ethan rolled out behind him.

Once stabilized, Ethan spotted Steven's Chemlight below and to his left. He adjusted his direction and looked for the landing zone. The moonlight painted the mountain ridges. He quickly identified Mount Bago. They were right on target.

He checked his wrist. Thirty seconds. Mountain peaks rising fast. Steven still in position. Ten seconds.

Ethan grabbed the deployment handle, inhaled, and pulled.

A brief change in aerodynamics just before the main chute opened with a violent jolt. His thighs screamed from the deceleration.

No time to enjoy the view. He flipped down his night vision goggles. Steven floated under a full canopy, a hundred yards away. Ethan turned east and followed Steven downwind. At 500 feet above the meadow, they banked into the wind.

He spotted the trail and adjusted slightly right. Steven stuck his landing. Ethan veered left to avoid the collapsing chute, flared hard, braking his descent.

"Thank you, God," he whispered, collapsing his own canopy and stuffing it into his pack.

"It looks clear." Steven said as he came up beside Ethan. "You see any hot spots?"

"Just smoke from the cabin."

"One of us needs to keep watch. You go in. I'll find high ground."

A distant bark echoed across the crater.

"You hear that?" Steven asked.

They paused. Another bark.

"It's coming from the cabin."

"Growler." They said in unison.

"Looks like they know someone's coming," Ethan muttered, slinging his rifle over his shoulder and heading for the log bridge.

— • ● • —

"Growler, what is it?" Anna's pulse quickened as Growler jumped and barked at the door.

"Someone's out there, or he needs to take care of business," Krystal said, rising and grabbing the handgun from the table.

Anna raised an eyebrow. "And what exactly are you planning to do with that?"

Krystal hesitated, then sighed. "Good question." She handed it over. "Here, you take it."

Anna clicked off the safety. "Let's see what Growler's excited about."

Growler's low growl deepened, making Anna pause. Gun raised in her right hand, she unbolted the door. Growler shoved through. A hand reached in and grabbed the gun, yanking it away.

Anna screamed and stumbled backward as Ethan stepped inside.

Krystal gasped and bolted for the bedroom.

Ethan blocked her path and flipped up his goggles.

"Ethan!" she cried, falling into his arms.

Anna picked herself up, tears welling in her eyes. "You scared the daylights out of me! Why do you always do that?"

"You opened the door and stuck a gun in my face. The

safest thing to do was take the gun."

Anna plopped into a chair, still shaken. "Sorry. We didn't know who was out there. Is Steven here?"

"He's nearby. We've got about six hundred enemy combatants in the valley. We need to keep them down there. Last thing we want is a surprise up here."

"Tell me about it." Anna stood and grabbed her coat.

"Stay put for now. We need to talk."

She dropped back into the chair. "Fire away, soldier boy. Girl's got things to do."

Ethan laughed. "You haven't changed. Don't worry, he'll still be out there when we're done."

Krystal let go of Ethan and put the kettle back on the stove.

"So," she said with a sly grin, "what's the plan?"

Ethan checked his watch. "Just before dawn, two hundred troops from the 10th Mountain Division will descend into Charlotte Lake. At the same time, a Blackhawk will land here in the meadow and evacuate you two and the children."

"You knew the children were here?" Krystal asked.

"Come on, dear. The way you headed for the bedroom. That's a mother's instinct."

"Aren't you guys coming with us?" Anna asked.

"Not the plan. We're staying behind to mop up. Don't worry, we'll stay safe."

Krystal shot Anna a glance and rolled her eyes.

Anna zipped her coat. "Can I go outside now?"

Ethan keyed his radio. "Your tiger's coming out," he whispered.

Chapter Forty-Three

Ethan leaned over and kissed Krystal's forehead. "It's about time, dear."

Krystal sat up and stretched. "How long did I sleep?"

"About four hours. We just received the call. They're coming."

"Should I wake the children?" Krystal yawned.

"Not yet. About an hour. I'll be on the porch."

The squeaking hinges brought back memories as he pulled the old door shut. So many mornings, he had sat on the porch trying to figure out the meaning of life. But the meaning of life was no longer on his mind. This morning, his mind juggled the upcoming counterinsurgency and the family in the stone cabin behind him.

The sound of a high-altitude aircraft pulled his eyes toward the sky. He spotted the unmanned drone in its racetrack pattern. It would be sending live images to the inbound troops. This would be a different fight. No incendiary bombs, no exploding missiles, no armed personnel carriers. It would be close-in combat, going from cabin to cabin, building to building. Rooting out militants, one at a time.

He could hear the distant thunder of multiple rotor blades slapping the air. His lungs filled with the cold night air as he looked to the heavens.

God it's show time. May Your will be done.

The door hinges squeaked as Krystal stepped outside and closed the door behind her. She set a cup of coffee down on the small table and sat down on the other rocking chair. She rocked gently, saying nothing. Ethan glanced over and saw a face filled with anxiety. He reached over and took her hand. Squeezing it softly, he whispered, "I love you."

She didn't respond, and he didn't blame her.

He took her other hand and pulled her onto his lap, wrapping his arms around her. She buried her face in his neck, and he could hear the sniffles. Why did he do this to her? The crying stopped as the sound of the helicopters increased.

Thundering vibrations echoed up through the canyon, their intensity growing as the aircraft came through the pass. The helicopters hovered briefly, long enough for ten soldiers to slide down ropes, then turned and disappeared below the canyon walls.

Ethan counted ten drops over the plateau to the east. There had to be more. He keyed up his mic. "Steven, how many did you count?"

"Ten to the east and another ten to the west. This is just the first wave. Tanner and Roland are watching a whole line of them heading towards Kearsarge Pass."

"Sounds like the girls should be getting ready. You going to send Anna down?"

"Do I have to?"

Krystal lifted her head. "It's obvious we want to stay with you guys. Can we?"

"I would love nothing more, my dear. It's just not safe, and I can't have you hurt again. We'll come to camp as soon as the community has been cleared."

"Will we be able to come back here?" Krystal wiped the moisture from her face.

"As soon as it's safe. I imagine in a few days. You'll enjoy the camp. Great people. They'll take good care of your family."

"Anna's going too?" Krystal asked.

"You bet. She may not want to, but that's not her call. You can show her all the trappings of civilization, such as it is at the camp. Unfortunately, no malls."

"Maybe I can rent a car and go to Fresno." He could see a grin forming on her face.

"Do you want to spy on them?" he asked, pointing up the mountain.

"Do what?"

He pulled off his night vision goggles and held them up to her face. "You may need to move around a bit, but look up on the ridge."

Krystal stared intently through the goggles, scanning the ridge. "Oh, my goodness." She pulled the glasses down, her blushing face had a big grin. "It doesn't look like they're spotting helicopters."

"Now you have something to talk to Anna about. Come on, let's go get the children." Ethan helped Krystal stand.

Krystal hung unto his hand and stopped short of the door. "I don't think it's a good time. They still don't know you're back. If you wake them and stick them on a helicopter, they're going to be very confused."

Ethan knew she was right, but it hurt. "I understand. I'll go relieve Steven and send them down. Love you."

Krystal turned her face up to his. When their lips parted, her reply was barely a whisper. "I love you too. Please be careful."

Ethan dropped her hand and headed up the ridge, 150 yards away. He keyed his mic and informed Steven of the plan. He watched as the couple stood up and started down from the ridge. He could see through his NVGs Steven was still holding Anna's hand, which she dropped when they were about twenty yards out.

"It's going crazy down there," Steven said when they met. "You can reach Tanner on the ridge. The next wave will be over the pass in ten minutes."

"What about security? Are you able to communicate with City Hall?" Ethan asked.

"We weren't. But, there's a ton of small drones out here. One even hovered over us for a while. Almost shot it down."

"Was it watching you two melt snow?" Ethan grinned.

Anna's face turned pink and Steven smacked his arm. "Peeping Tom. Come on down when it's clear."

Ethan saluted and continued up the mountain. The eastern sky showed signs of the coming day as the next wave of Blackhawks crested the pass. He sat with this back against a boulder and watched as elements from the Brigade Combat Team of the 10th Mountain Division infiltrated the mountain, disappearing, like wolves, into the dense terrain.

Small-arm fire echoed from both ends of the lake as opposing forces clashed. A flash, then an explosion, a rocket propelled grenade suppressing militia fire. Shouts of fear. Screams of pain. He should have slept, but adrenaline was too great. He shut his eyes, and the sound of battle conjured the villages of Afghanistan. He trembled with every blast.

Ethan raised his binoculars as the first light of dawn revealed the valley. He could pick out silhouettes hiding behind trees, cabins, and amongst the rocks. Hundreds of little ants with guns. These men weren't soldiers, just armed and desperate. They had thought taking the village would be easy. And it was.

He almost felt sorry for these young men. They had been promised a dream and were now experiencing a nightmare. He thought of all the decisions he had made in life and the price he had paid. Bad decisions led to pain and destruction.

Then came the low pulsing thump echoing off the crater wall. He looked back to see a Blackhawk rounding the eastern edge and descending into the meadow. His heart pounded as he spotted Krystal and the children, all holding hands, following Steven and Anna down the trail.

—•●•—

The blustery wind whipped up the grass in the meadow as Anna stood there holding Steven's hand. She had never been in a helicopter before. She looked back at Krystal and the children. At least she wasn't the only one afraid. They'd listened to the helicopters continuously coming and going for the last two hours. Was her home going to survive? Was the village?

Rhythmic thumping pulsed the ground like distant thunder and a Blackhawk appeared around the mountain spine, the blades churned the air with a chopping roar. It came in low, hugging the terrain.

She turned her back to the blowing dust and increasing wind. Krystal was holding tight to Jonah, while Christiana and Cathryn held onto each other, trying hard to watch.

The Blackhawk turned into the wind and descended into the meadow. A plume of dust spiraled into the air as it settled into the grass.

"Come on!" Steven shouted above the whine of the turbines and the thunder of the rotors. He pulled Anna towards the open door where the crew chief waited to help her into the cabin. She slid into a seat, with Jonah right beside her.

Anna watched Steven swing the girls into the cabin. She was falling for him, fast. But would God allow her to have another relationship? Could she commit to someone who didn't even believe in God?" She had tried for years to nudge Steven toward faith. He just never responded. Some things could only be accomplished through prayer.

The crew chief slammed the door shut. The Blackhawk pitched forward and lifted into the sky, the earth fell away beneath them. Across from her, Krystal gripped the girls, trying to keep it together as they clung to her.

Through the window, Anna caught a glimpse of a solitary figure on the ridge. Standing motionless, rifle slung over his back, staring up at them. She pressed her hand to the glass, as her breath caught in her throat. Not goodbye. Not yet.

* * *

Ethan stood, staring at the Blackhawk as it rounded the mountain and disappeared into the valley below. He exhaled and turned toward the stone cabin. Steven sat in a rocking chair, rifle across his lap.

"You ready to go duck hunting?" Steven asked.

"Haven't been since they took away my hunting license."

"Just make sure the stars and stripes are visible."

Ethan patted the flags on his sleeves. "Sounds like hunting season down at the lake. Let's go."

They had just stood up when a thundering Chinook came over Kearsarge Pass, heading their way.

"Looks like Homeland Security is here." Ethan said as they crossed the log bridge. By the time they reached the switchbacks, the first Chinook was down in the meadow, with nine more were stretching between them and the pass.

"That's a lot of hardware," Steven said. "It feels like they've been planning this for a while."

"Yeah," Ethan muttered. "It's unfortunate Charlotte Lake had to become their battleground."

His chest tightened.

Had they intentionally used Charlotte Lake to capture

these militants? Did DHS know all along that hundreds of criminals would converge on this place?

The community had been the bait.

The valley, the trap.

As they approached the bridge, a sentry waved them over to his position.

"Justin Teller, Private 1st Class," the young man said, offering his hand.

Ethan shook it. "Special Agent Ethan Dawson."

"The Ethan Dawson? I was hoping to meet you."

"Didn't know I was that popular." Ethan gestured to Steven. "This is my partner, Special Agent Steven McMillan. He's our lead."

Steven nodded and pointed toward the village. "How's the operation progressing?"

"Good to meet you, sir. It's slow going. We've lost two of our boys. Last count-150 prisoners, 45 dead militants."

Steven looked at Ethan. "That's a high ratio. Sounds like they're going to have over 400 prisoners by the time this is done."

"I thought the goal was to take them alive." Ethan said.

"Yeah," Steven growled, "well if it was up to me, we'd use fewer zip ties and more bullets."

"Easy, Rambo. Let's see where we're needed."

Private Teller pointed toward the church. "You'll find Lieutenant Carson at the meeting house. Do you know where it is?"

Ethan nodded. He thought of the sermons, the ministers sharing messages from the Bible. The rugged benches, men on one side, women on the other. Sunday night singings and the friendly conversations.

"Yes, Private Teller, I know where it is. Thank you."

They moved cautiously down the trail. Spats of gunfire echoed around the community. Near the meeting house, Ethan spotted a large group of soldiers. As they got closer, he could see, it wasn't just soldiers, but rows of militants seated on the ground, their hands zip-tied behind their back. They were young, most looked barely older than boys.

"These are the lucky ones," Steven said. "What do you think happens now?"

"With the ICE agents arriving, I doubt they'll be in the country much longer."

"It's kind of sad," Steven said. "They came here chasing a better life. If only they had followed the rules instead of a crime boss."

"All we can do is pray for them," Ethan replied. "Come on. Let's go hear what the lieutenant has to say."

• ● •

Inside the meeting house, the benches had been pushed aside and a command center set up. Officers clustered around the table going over maps. Medics treated injured on cots in the back.

They approached the table.

An officer looked up. "Can I help you?"

Ethan extended his hand. "Ethan Dawson. This is Steven McMillan. We were told you're expecting us."

"Oh, yes. Lieutenant Carson. Thanks for coming. We're about to start phase two. Having someone familiar with the village will be a big help."

Steven nodded. "Can you bring us up to speed on the progress?"

"Sure. The troops have sealed off both ends of the lake," Carson said. "We've got containment lines up both sides of the valley. Are you two trained in close-in combat?"

"Extensively," Steven said. "Cleared a number of villages in Afghanistan."

"That's been awhile. Anything lately?"

Steven glanced at Ethan. "Well, it may be classified, but

we did take down a cartel in Mexico a few weeks ago."

Carson raised an eyebrow. "So that was you guys. You're brutal."

"Only did what needed to be done. Unfortunately, we missed Rafael by twenty-four hours."

"You might still get your chance." Carson said. "If he's still alive when the smoke clears."

"Joy! Can't wait," Steven said dryly. "What's the plan?"

"Fast-moving strike teams cleared the wooded areas surrounding the lake. Now we're going to clear the structures. You two are front-line on the south side. You know the people or at least their culture. Make sure we do them right. If you're ready get over there and push west."

Chapter Forty-Four

Steven and Ethan crossed the bridge at the east end of the lake and rounded the corner into the trees. Only the occasional gun fire broke the stillness. Though they hadn't slept in over twenty-four hours, their focus was sharp. Just inside the tree line, they spotted a sergeant briefing his men. He turned and nodded as they approached.

"Okay, men," the sergeant said. "Time to move out. Keep your eyes sharp and everyone goes home."

The wooded area had technically been cleared, but danger still lurked behind every tree and rock. Both men tensed when a burst of gunfire echoed across the lake. The first three cabins were empty, and in each one they did a quick search, looking for hidden dangers.

As they stepped away from the third cabin, a shout rang out. Instinctively, Ethan grabbed Steven and yanked him behind the building just as bullets splintered the wood around them.

"Rooftop," Ethan whispered. They shouldered their rifles, and Ethan peeked around the corner. Two teenage boys were on the roof of the next cabin, assault rifles in hand, scanning for targets.

"Two armed teenagers, what are we going to do?"

Steven's face was stone. "They made their choice when they shot at us."

Ethan hesitated. "Hold on a minute."

He lowered his rifle, raised his hands, and stepped out from behind the cabin. "Don't do it, boys!" he shouted. "You're outnumbered and out of time. Put down your weapons, and you won't be killed."

He could see fear on their faces as they exchanged a glance. Ethan didn't understand their words, but he recognized the tightening grip on their weapons.

He dove for cover behind the cabin a heartbeat before gunfire erupted. He landed hard in the pine needles, pain striking from a hidden rock.

"Thank you, God." he muttered, searching for Steven.

A couple of quick bursts echoed from the other side of the cabin.

They missed." Ethan whispered into his mic. "Where you at?"

"Other side of the cabin," Steven said over the radio. "And I didn't miss. All clear."

Ethan felt sick to his stomach as he slowly approached the cabin. The boys lay sprawled on the ground, rifles beside them. "It didn't have to end this way," he whispered.

"Clear the cabin!" the sergeant ordered.

Ethan watched as the team crashed open the door. A flash grenade exploded, and they slipped inside. Shouted commands came from the cabin, followed by panicked responses.

"What are they saying?" he asked Steven.

"Just what you would expect. Don't shoot."

Ethan sighed. "Hopefully, we hear that a few more times today."

Three militants emerged with hands clasped behind their heads, escorted by the team. "This one's clear, gentlemen, it's all yours."

Inside the cabin, drawers were dumped, clothes scattered, food containers ripped open. Broken glass crunched beneath their boots.

"They were looking for something," Steven said.

"Unfortunately, they are looters at heart." Ethan replied. "They were looking for anything of value and something to eat."

"I don't know. They may have been looking for a change of clothes. Something to make them fit in." Steven said, picking up a flowery dress. "Looks to me like they picked the wrong cabin."

"Yes, they did. Whoever lives here's going to need help cleaning up," Ethan said. "She's probably not the only one."

They heard noises outside, another squad arrived. "We were sent to recover bodies," their sergeant explained.

Ethan pointed to the side of the cabin. "Sad. They chose to fight when the odds were against them."

Cabin by cabin, they moved on. Most had been vandalized, some worse than others. Mid-afternoon, they reached Doctor Winston's cabin. It had been ransacked. The medicine cabinet ripped off the wall and smashed. Pills were scattered across the floor. A photo on the mantel caught Ethan's eye. Doctor Winston, his wife, and a young child. Was that George?

Is George as innocent as he claims? Ethan mused. *It might be worth a conversation when this is over.*

"I don't even know where to start." Ethan said, surveying the next cabin.

Steven took a couple steps through the debris and retrieved a picture off the floor.

"How about here?" He handed it to Ethan.

Ethan tensed. "Who lives here?"

"Don't know, but they're obsessed." He picked up a couple more pictures of Krystal.

Ethan found a desk and started sorting through papers.

"It's George. And he's got problems."

"I know. Look at these," Steven held a handful of Anna's pictures.

"And the plot thickens." Ethan said. "Unsent love letters to Anna and Krystal. This guy's not well."

Ethan felt like he was invading George's privacy.

"Was this why he was spying on Krystal?" Steven asked. "Harmless? Or is there more to this story?"

"We may have to take him for a walk someday." Ethan said.

"Maybe convince him to explain his infatuation with our girls." Steven said. "Twist his arm a little."

"Come on, dude. We can't go breaking arms. We're not terrorists."

— • ● • —

It was heartbreaking when they reached Anna's cabin. Two soldiers were exiting with a body bag. A couple more soldiers followed, escorting two prisoners.

"Not pretty in there," the sergeant said.

"Ours or theirs?" Ethan asked, pointing at the body bag.

"Theirs. His friends moved him in here after he was shot. Poor kid, probably still a teenager."

Inside, the destruction was overwhelming. Anna's antique writing desk was smashed. Her bedroom was a disaster. Clothes tossed everywhere, blood soaking the unmade bed.

"Should we do something?" Steven asked, looking around the cabin.

Ethan shook his head. "As much as I would like to make this go away, there's nothing we can do. Leave it."

"Wait," Steven said. "She had something I gave her."

He dug through the debris, around the desk and then

headed into the bedroom. Ethan stepped outside, needing air. He dropped into a rocking chair and scanned the surroundings. Why do things like this happen? Anna had been through so much, this would be just another test of her faith.

Steven came out, holding up a satellite messenger. "Found it. This was our primary form of communication. Let's move on."

Two cabins later, they entered a larger one. It had been looted, but not destroyed. Food had been pulled from the cupboards and was littered throughout the kitchen. Home-canned food sat on the counter, untouched. Most likely the militants had no idea what to do with it.

Ethan sifted through papers strewn around a desk. "This is Arwel Brannon's cabin. We might want to do a deep dive on this one."

"Think we might find some incriminating evidence?" Steven asked.

"Already incriminated himself. I just want to make sure he acted alone."

"We need to do it quickly. There's not a lot of day left." Steven searched for anything out of the ordinary, while Ethan scanned the bookshelves. Toward the top he found some interesting stuff.

"For a preacher, Arwel sure has an interest in suspense novels," he said. "Maybe too much."

"Infatuated with the characters, leading to playing out the part? Sounds crazy, but what he did was crazy." Steven replied.

They moved to the bedroom. The bed had been roughed up and a few drawers opened.

"If you were hiding evidence in here, where would it be?" Ethan asked.

"Not under the bed. No one does that anymore." Steven went to the dresser and looked at a picture of Arwel and Rebbecca sitting on its top. Sliding his hand under the lip of the dresser he felt the trigger.

"Bingo." He said as the top of the dresser popped up and the picture slid off crashing to the floor.

"Nice," Ethan said dryly. "Destroy their wedding picture."

"Arwel already did that," Steven muttered. "Surprised it's still here."

Ethan exhaled. "She must really love him. Sad."

The hidden compartment was filled with contraband items. At least counter to the community's determination. Ethan pulled off his backpack and placed everything inside. No need for Rebbecca to experience more pain than necessary. The last thing out was a spiral-bound notebook. He flipped through it.

"No way, dude! Steven, check this out."

Steven briefly looked it over. "A treasure trove of information. Protect that."

Ethan slid the journal in his backpack. Forensic will love this.

• ● •

As the sun touched Mount Bago, they approached the dry goods store. The squad had set up a parameter and was waiting on orders.

"There's someone inside," the sergeant said. "It's going to be a dangerous ingress."

"There's another way in," Ethan said. "I'll take the lead."

The Sergeant shook his head. "I can't take a chance at you getting hurt."

"I'll take that responsibility. Give me five minutes. When you hear shooting, blow the front door."

Ethan and Steven exchanged a look and headed for the rear of the building. The old cellar door was weathered, covered with moss. Ethan grabbed the handle and pulled it open. The rusty hinges groaned as the musty air drifted up from the aged wood, and mold.

The basement was worse than he had remembered. But, the last time he was rescuing Krystal and her children. The boxes of records still occupied the shelf. They silently removed the boxes, all the time listening to the movement upstairs.

The squeaking floor and muted voices spoke of the upcoming engagement. Ethan pulled out his Beretta. Checked the clip. Seventeen rounds. He patted the extra clips. How many militants are up there? His pulse quickened.

"Let's pray." He whispered to Steven.

Steven nodded. "We need the help. Go ahead."

Ethan didn't hesitate. "God we need you. Guide our actions. We ask that you protect us as we confront our enemies. We also pray for those that we are going up against. We pray that they will lay down their arms, and that just somehow they may come to know You. We ask this all in the name of Jesus. Amen."

"Amen." Steven whispered.

Ethan slid up on the shelf, laying flat on his back. He tested the trap door, raising it slowly. It was dark in the office. He lifted it a little more and froze. Two boot heels were a foot in front of him. Slowly, he let the door back down. He glanced at his watch. Two minutes. Seconds ticked away as he listened to footsteps above him. A minute passed when footsteps walked out of the office. He silently prayed and opened the door again.

Ethan could see militants milling about in the outer room. It looked like all of them were carrying assault rifles. How many? It looked like ten, but the chattering told of more. He glanced back at Steven and nodded.

In one swift move, he swung open the trap door, and rolled out onto the floor, Beretta ready. Silence in the office.

No movement. No shots. The windowless room's only light came from the partially open door. Steven quietly handed Ethan their assault rifles and worked his way up into the office.

They listened to anxious voices from the main room. The militants had to know something was about to come down. Ethan shot Steven a questioning look.

"They think they're surrounded," Steven whispered. "Afraid they're all going to die."

Ethan nodded and grabbed a flash grenade. "Show time." He whispered as he pulled the pin. Tossing it through the slit in the door, he stepped back and counted.

Two seconds of screams before the deafening bang and blinding flash exploded from the room. Even before the flash grenade finished its work a larger explosion blew the front door off its hinges. The militants were scattered around the room, holding their heads, blindly looking towards the opening where the door used to be.

"¡No televantes! ¡Te van a disparar!" Steven shouted.

The militants obeyed, hands on heads, prone on the floor, blind and disoriented.

The squad came through the opening, guns ready. One by one they pulled the young men from the room in zip-tie handcuffs.

The store was quiet. Ethan and Steven worked their way through the store looking for anything of interest. Some books and paperwork were scattered in the office but no damage. The clothes in the main room were a mess. It looked like they had been piled up for bedding.

Ethan's started to open the dressing room door. His chest tightened, he couldn't do it.

"Steven, do you mind checking out the dressing room? It's not my favorite place."

"No problem."

Moments later, "Ethan, come in here."

Ethan forgot his hesitation. The floor was covered with

discarded militant clothing.

"They're out there." Ethan said.

Steven nodded. "Let's count the clothes, so we have a number."

Ethan felt queasy. "I'm going to let you count. I need out of here."

"No problem. See you out front."

Ethan sat down on the porch, and watched the soldiers round up the prisoners. The sergeant approached.

"You okay?"

"Yeah, I think I'm dehydrated, and tired. Thirty-six hours… One more of these and I'll be whipped."

"You have water?"

"Yeah. Just need to take the time to drink it."

Steven exited, dragging a scrawny teenager. "Got you another one. Also found four militant uniforms in the dressing room. Watch for wolves in sheep clothing."

The sergeant raised a brow. "I assume you mean civilian clothes?"

"Not just any civilian clothes. These are handmade, looking like they just time warped from the eighteenth century."

The sergeant laughed. "That won't get them far."

"Where will these guys end up?" Steven asked, nodding toward the prisoners.

"We're loading them on the Chinooks. Already sent out three loads."

"Might not be any of my business, but where are they ending up?"

"It's my understanding, there are planes waiting in Fresno to take them to Guantanamo Bay." The sergeant said, motioning for the team to move out. "You guys stay safe."

They sat on the steps and watched the procession move up the trail. There would be more.

Ethan yawned. Was it lack of sleep or the adrenaline leaving his body? He didn't seem to care. He took a long swig of water and exhaled.

"Where to next?" he asked.

An audio buzz sounded in his earpiece. "Ethan, can you hear me?"

He looked around. Steven was sitting next to him with his head in his hands.

Ethan keyed up his mic. "Roger. Loud and clear."

Steven looked over at him. Ethan pointed towards his ear.

"Ethan, this is Arnold. We have a drone overhead watching you. What's the current situation?"

"Can't tell you everything. The place is a mess and they're still removing militants."

"Is it safe to come out?"

"Negative. Stay put for now. We just finished the south side and moving around to the north."

"Sounds good. You look tired."

"We're exhausted but will finish the job tonight."

"Roger that. When you finish. Come see us via the woodworking shop."

"We'll try." Ethan stood up. It was time to get on the move.

He waved up at the drone and started back to the meeting house.

Chapter Forty-Five

Lieutenant Carson was still at the meeting house, now joined by a few more officers.

"Good job on the south side, men. Heard you had a couple hot spots."

Steven and Ethan looked at each other and shrugged. "You could say that," Ethan replied. "Where are we at over here?"

"It's clear. You can go through and inspect the damage, but the area is secure."

"What's the toll?" Ethan was almost afraid to ask.

"We have a total of 495 prisoners and 155 dead. Five of those are ours."

"I'm sorry to hear that, sir. My condolences to the families."

Lieutenant Carson looked up, his face hard. "Thanks. It's a hard truth, we live in a broken world. We'll stay until every last militant is gone. You two, get some rest."

Ethan and Steven headed for the door, but Ethan stopped and turned around.

"What about their leader, Jose Rafael? Did you find

him?"

"He's not here. Must've been in the mine when it was bombed.

That answer didn't sit right. As they walked toward the woodworking shop, a knot twisted in Ethan's gut. Something about Rafael's absence felt wrong.

"Should we inspect the cabins?" Steven asked.

Ethan sighed. He didn't want to, but a quick walk-through wouldn't take long.

"How about we do all but Krystal's? Let's make it quick."

The first cabin they entered was Abram's. Ethan's heart sank at the sight of the mess. The elderly minister's home had been ransacked. The old, rugged chair that Abram sat in had been smashed. So many things, irreplaceable, destroyed. Ethan made a mental note to return tomorrow to help.

All the cabins were a mess, but the one that hit hardest after Abram's was William and Claire's. The couple had started this community over fifty years ago. They had experienced many struggles. They all ended the same. God had seen them through.

Ethan smiled. This one wouldn't be any different.

"Let's stop in here." Ethan said as they came to the bakery.

"Don't smell baking bread." Steven said.

"No, but it will be the first place to get fired back up."

The inside of the bakery had been vandalized, but would not take long to clean.

After leaving the bakery, they moved through a cluster of smaller cabins before arriving at the woodworking shop.

Inside the woodworking shop, tools were scattered across the floor.

"Why would they do this?" Steven asked. "It serves no purpose."

"Not everything needs a purpose. Help me move this

table."

Steven put his shoulder into it and the workbench didn't budge. "This thing's heavy."

They tried a couple more times and couldn't get it to move at all.

Laughter came from somewhere. "Come on guys. Push a little harder."

"Not funny boss. What's the trick?" Ethan asked.

A soft click broke the silence, and the table began to rise on hidden casters. Three inches later, it rolled aside, revealing the trapdoor.

"Sometimes it's best to follow instructions," Arnold chuckled over the hidden speaker.

Ethan pulled open the trapdoor, and they descended into the tunnel.

"I've seen some crazy stuff," Steven said as they walked deeper into the mountain, "but this is unreal."

"Just wait."

They arrived in the small cavern, Steven looked around for the door.

Ethan laughed. "That was my reaction, too. Step over here."

They stepped aside and Ethan pointed to the ceiling. "Stare at that round spot."

A whirling noise resulted in a chunk of the ceiling starting down.

"Here's your ride."

The doors opened into City Hall and the bright lights made them blink.

Steven's stomach growled. "Let's get this briefing over with and find something to eat. I'm starving."

"I heard."

The conference room was filled to capacity with people standing around the side.

"Greetings everyone," Ethan said, waving "Looks like you're busy. We're going to find some food."

"Wait a minute." Arnold's voice was firm. "Get in here you two." He pointed to a couple of people Ethan didn't know. "Show some manners. Let our guest sit."

The two jumped up, embarrassed. "Sorry guys, we weren't thinking."

Steven smiled as he slid into the preheated seat. "No problem. We would prefer to be in the cafeteria."

Ethan looked at Arnold. "We haven't slept since yesterday morning. Haven't eaten in twenty-four hours. You have about fifteen minutes before you have a mutiny on your hands. So shoot. No pun intended."

Once the laughter died down, Arnold addressed the room.

"First of all, thank you both for your service. We felt so helpless. All we could do was watch the invasion on the monitors. It tore us up, watching them come into our community. Fortunately, we only have exterior cameras."

"That's probably for the best," Ethan replied. "There's a lot of cleanup to do inside. The meeting house is the only one that didn't get trashed. Sorry, we didn't have the ability to take pictures."

"That's okay. We'll see it soon enough. When do you think it'll be safe to start the cleanup?"

"That's not my call, but Lieutenant Carson said that they would stay until every militant is removed. I'm not sure about the ones at the mine. That was our people."

"Our people?" Arnold asked.

"Sorry. The early explosion at the mine was courtesy of Willow Creek Camp. I would imagine they will clean up that mess."

"Understood. Can we expect to exit in the morning?"

"Remember in Genesis, when Noah sent out a dove to find dry land?" Ethan asked.

"We don't have any doves."

"No, but you have drones. Send one out in the morning. If the military's gone, it's safe. Just... prepare the community. What they're going to see will be a shock."

"We'll do that in the morning after breakfast. Anything else before we wrap up?"

"Just one thing." Ethan said. "The 10th Mountain Division lost five men retaking the community. It would do well for you to spend time in prayer and be prepared to show your appreciation to the families of the lost."

Ethan stood up to leave.

"Ethan, hold on. You two stick around for a minute. The rest of you, get out of here and activate the cleanup plan."

Once the room cleared, Ethan yawned. "Boss, make it quick. Steven's hangry and I'm about to pass out."

"Sure. Arwel isn't talking. Not even to his wife. Says he'll only speak to his lawyer."

Steven pushed back his chair and pulled out his Bowie knife. "Where's he at? I can get him to talk."

Ethan laughed. "I'm thinking we wait until tomorrow. Where's the cafeteria."

"Seriously, put him in a room with us and we'll get him to talk." Steven said.

"Let me think about it. Oliver will get you fed and settled for the night."

A cheeseburger later, Ethan found his room and took a warm shower, crawled between clean sheets, and laid his head on a real pillow. His body melted into the bed.

Chapter Forty-Six

Ethan rolled over and opened his eyes. The sun shining through the window caused him to sit up.

What time is it? He looked at his watch. Only 7:30.

How could the sun be… Wait a minute. I'm in a cave. He pulled back the shades and rolled his eyes as he looked through the glass at a monitor displaying a bright, sunny day. The mountains, lake and trees looked almost real, except it was the wrong season.

He noticed his uniform sitting on the table, washed and folded. He rubbed his temples trying to fight off the nightmares that had plagued him throughout the night.

I must've been too tired to hear the door open. Guess there's no privacy.

After a quick shower, Ethan sat in the chair, opened his Bible, and began reading.

Count it all joy, my brothers, when you meet trials of various kinds, for you know that the testing of your faith produces steadfastness.

Ethan stared through the window at the faux mountain scene.

How much more testing could he handle? How much more could the community endure? No doubt their faith was stronger. Where did their resilience come from?

For the next few moments, he asked God for wisdom. He knew his faith was fragile, and James didn't mince words about doubt.

Was that why he was being tossed about?

Breakfast will be served in five minutes. A voice announced over the intercom.

Maybe, he would catch up on the local news before eating.

He picked up his Beretta, slid it in its holster, then paused before returning it to his backpack. He didn't need that here.

The cafeteria bustled with activity when Ethan walked through. He bypassed the long serving line and headed for City Hall. There he found Oliver and Keenan bent over monitors.

"Any news from the outside? Did your drone come back with an olive leaf?" Ethan asked.

"Funny," Oliver answered. "The last military helicopter left about an hour ago. As soon as it lifted off, Arnold headed out for a quick inspection.

"Is he armed?"

Oliver turned around in his chair. "Oh, yes. Too much has happened not to take precautions. So far, nothing but a ghost town."

Ethan caught sight of movement on one of the monitors and watched Arnold and two other armed security personnel on the trail by the lake.

"Have you heard from Willow Creek?" He asked.

"Not a peep." Oliver pulled up a split screen showing activity around the mine shaft entrances. "We've been receiving these video feeds. They're cleaning up the mess."

"Surprised any cameras survived."

"We're surprised anything survived that blast," Oliver replied.

Ethan watched as workers sifted through the rubble, searching for survivors and bodies. What he really wanted was to head down there and catch a ride back to Willow Creek. Arnold walked into the control center.

"Good morning, Ethan. Feeling rested?"

"A lot better, boss. What's your take?"

Arnold stroked his beard. "As you said, it's a real mess. It'll take some time to clean up, but at least they didn't burn the place down."

"So true. How did your place fare?" Ethan asked.

"Didn't go in," Arnold said. "Wanted to keep my mind on helping others."

Ethan lingered near the monitors, watching the activity near the mines. His mind drifted to the Blackhawk departing the crater yesterday morning. Would it bring the girls back?

Oliver glanced up from the console, "Let's get some breakfast before we turn the folks loose."

They stepped into the dining hall to the drone of conversations, the racket of children playing, and the aroma of a hot breakfast.

Ethan grabbed a tray, and though his appetite wasn't there, he loaded his plate with sausage, eggs, and hash browns. He added a couple of pieces of toast and some orange juice. Maybe he was hungry.

He spotted Steven and slid into a seat across the table.

Steven looked him over. "Waiting on you for breakfast is becoming a habit. Sleep well last night?"

"I slept until the sun shone through my window. Thought it was noon."

"You like that?" Oliver asked, joining the group. "It was one of the ladies' ideas."

"For a bunch of off-the-grid primitive people, it's jaw dropping." Ethan replied.

They had just taken a bite when Arnold made his way to the front. The room hushed before he even touched the microphone.

"Good morning, folks. We just completed a walk around the lake. We briefly checked out the cabins and buildings." He paused for a moment, obviously looking for the right words. "Sorry, to be the bearer of bad news, but just about every building has been vandalized. A lot of your things have been destroyed. Let's remember, these are only material things. What truly matters is that you're safe.

"Unfortunately, five very brave men lost their lives removing the militants. Please pray for their families. I haven't spoken with leadership yet, but we will make sure their families are compensated. It won't bring them back, but it's the least we can do.

"We have a couple of housekeeping things to go over before we open the doors. First of all, I would like a couple of volunteers to go with each of our elderly to clean their cabins. The other item is cleaning supplies. It's going to take a lot more than we have in stock. I have authorized a supply drop, which will be here in about twenty minutes. There will be two pallets delivered to the clearing by the meeting house.

"Tonight, we will be getting together at the meeting house for a time of prayer and praise. Please, everyone attend."

Ethan noticed Abram getting to his feet, holding up a hand. "Excuse me, could I speak for a moment?"

Arnold motioned for one of the men to take the microphone to Abram. Abram looked it over and handed it back. "I've been preaching for forty years. I don't need that thing." His voice thundered throughout the cafeteria, causing laughter to follow the thunder.

"Most of you have spent the night in a modern-day hotel room. You experienced the comfort of this facility, the satisfaction of a cafeteria. Fortunately, the food was normal. I ask you to reflect on this while you're cleaning your cabins and helping others. Tonight, most of you will return to your primitive dwellings. If you have feelings of discontent, that will be natural. God created us with a desire for conveniences. Long ago, we chose a simple life. One that is not burdened by the things of this world.

"Yes, we have the resources to turn our small mountain community into a mega resort. Would that bring you satisfaction? Maybe for a season. Then you would want more, more things. Things that would consume your time. Things that would replace the quiet, small voice that speaks in your silence. Things that steal your time with the One who died for you on the cross. Things.

"Brothers and sisters, we found comfort and shelter here in the cave, but let us not forget where we belong. Today, as we go about the task of restoring our homes, let us sing praises to God, the One who provides all things. I look forward to our time of worship and praise this evening at the meeting house.

He paused, then added, "Now, before we go, let's sing that old hymn: Great is Thy faithfulness."

Someone in the back started the hymn, their voice strong and steady.

"Great is Thy faithfulness, O God my Father."

Soon, the dining hall was filled with melody.

"Thou changest not; Thy compassions, they fail not."

Ethan sat back, listening to the harmonious voices. Something unfamiliar was stirring, an atmosphere of peace and contentment was settling over the room. Even he felt God's presence, a stillness he hadn't known in a long time.

"Morning by morning new mercies I see,"

He noticed Steven staring off into the distance. Just maybe.

Ethan closed his eyes in silent prayer as the song wound down.

"All I have needed Thy hand hath provided, Great is Thy faithfulness, Lord unto me."

Abram's soft smile spoke volumes. He held up a hand. "I have asked Eli to offer a prayer for protection and then you are dismissed."

Ethan and Steven glanced at each other, their expressions shadowed with doubt. Ethan wasn't sure he could follow Eli's prayer. It sounded heartfelt, sincere… but was it? Was Eli genuine?

As the others rose to begin clearing the tables, Ethan and Steven remained seated, deep in thought…finishing their breakfast.

"What do you think?" Steven asked once they were alone.

"He sure sounded sincere. But so did Arwel, last week."

"The community may not suspect anything, but we need to keep Eli on our radar." Steven paused. "Did you get a chance to look over Arwel's journal?"

Ethan looked up and rolled his eyes. "Sure. Read it in my sleep last night. I'll study it later today. Let's go for a walk."

"Sounds good. Meet you in the command center in ten." Steven grabbed his plate and walked off.

Back in his room, Ethan pulled on his combat vest and backpack. No way was he going out there without his weapons. Not out of fear, but because he had no idea where he would be when the sun went down. The mission was technically over, and soon, they'd need to break camp and return to Willow Creek.

When he entered the command center, Keenan was busy talking to someone on his headset, Oliver was nowhere to be seen. Ethan waited until Keenan finished the call.

"That was the dispatcher at Willow Creek," Keenan said. "He asked that you stick by the command center until Colonel Whitlock calls. Should be within ten minutes."

"Thanks. Oliver already leave?"

"He left right after breakfast. Wanted to be out there with the security detail, keeping an eye on the return."

"Not a bad idea. There's going to be a few distraught folks. Sad, but could be worse."

"No doubt." Keenan replied, just as a chime sounded. "Here's your incoming call. A little early. You want this private?"

"Nothing's private, Keenan. Speaker's fine."

The speaker crackled to life with Colonel Whitlock's voice, mid-rant. At least he sounded like his usual self.

"Good morning, sir," Ethan said, raising his voice to be heard.

"What… Who is this?" The colonel clearly wasn't paying attention.

"This is Ethan Dawson, sir. The guy you sent to Charlotte Lake."

"I didn't send you anywhere. You took off without authorization and look at the mess you made. I should have you court-martialed."

"I got a better idea. How about you send a Blackhawk over here with a couple of young ladies and three children? Then we'll both be happy." Ethan couldn't help but poke the bear.

"About that. Is Steven with you?"

"I'm here, sir," Steven said, walking up. "What's up?"

"Too much," Whitlock fumed. "You two sure know how to stir up a manure pile. Washington is imploding. Apparently, nobody had intel on Charlotte Lake before this all blew up. You wouldn't know anything about that, would you?"

Steven gave Ethan a sly grin and shrugged. "No idea, sir. We're just soldiers. When are you sending Anna and Krystal home?"

"Not before our intel people have a chance to interview them in a couple of days. They're doing just fine, and those kids remind me of my children. Get your mess cleaned up and get over here when you're done."

Ethan's face was getting hot. He had to hold it together. Were the girls being held hostage? Probably not. Still, it just wasn't right. Intel had no right to interview, or more likely, interrogate them.

"Sir, this is Ethan. There is nothing the girls can tell you that we can't. Go ahead and send them back. We'll meet them in the meadow. Just give us an ETA."

"Sure, Ethan. Wrap things up on your end. We'll pick you up when we bring the girls in about two days. I got things to do. Stay safe." The call cut off.

"Well, I'll be…." Steven shook his head. "That guy gets under my skin."

"Mine too," Ethan said. "But maybe it's best they're not here yet. Not until after the church business meeting. The Arwel mess is not going to be pretty."

"True," Steven paused. "Is the storehouse entrance open?"

Keenan gave a thumbs-up.

Without another word, Ethan and Steven turned and headed into the ice cave.

Chapter Forty-Seven

Anna and Krystal walked up the fire road following the children. After a couple of nights in the camp, they were rested and ready to enjoy the late spring sunshine. They had received news that the counterinsurgency was successful, and the community was now clear of militants. No one had heard anything from Steven or Ethan. Surely, they would check in soon.

Krystal had been quiet since Anna had shared the conversation she had with Colonel Whitlock. Why weren't they allowed to return to Charlotte Lake? That was their home. The camp had allowed them to move about freely. The food was good, and the sleeping arrangements were comfortable. There was just a mystery about the place and Anna didn't like it. She had a plan but for now would keep it to herself.

"What's on your mind?" Anna asked.

It took a moment, but finally, Krystal answered. "I called my parents this morning. They say they're coming to get us."

"I'm not surprised. Is that what you want?"

"I'm not sure which way to turn. I love my parents, but

if I go back to Colorado, I may lose Ethan."

"And if you return to Charlotte Lake?" Anna asked after a pause.

"Charlotte Lake is home. The children have gotten used to the primitive lifestyle and are making friends, and there's…" She trailed off, staring off in the distance.

"That you'll get married and live happily ever after?" Anna finished for her.

A shy smile crossed Krystal's face. "Well, yeah. There's that."

"What about you? What do you want?" Anna asked.

"I want to be sitting on the couch in Ethan's arms, watching the fire burn, sipping on a cup of hot tea. I want to kiss him when he puts another log on the fire. I want to thank God while I'm washing his clothes. I want someone to keep me warm at night and to protect us from the boogeyman. I want someone to hold my children when they get hurt and tell them it's going to be okay."

"Sounds like you're going back to Charlotte Lake."

"But, what about my parents? They miss the children." Krystal sighed.

"Invite them to Charlotte Lake. They would love it."

"They can't climb the mountain. They're too old."

"Time has a way of doing that." Anna said. "I'll pray that God will give you wisdom."

It was lunch time when they arrived back at the camp. Another Blackhawk had just landed. Anna watched the soldiers exit, but didn't see Steven or Ethan. She shuddered as the crew began unloading body bags into a truck. Who were they? Could it be?

The mess hall was unusually quiet. They all held hands as Krystal prayed for their food and for their friends at Charlotte Lake.

"Mommy, you forgot to pray for that girl," Cathryn said when Krystal finished.

"Who? What girl?" Krystal asked softly.

"The one sitting over there." Cathryn pointed.

A teenage girl sat eating lunch alone. She wore civilian clothes and had a sad expression.

"Do you know her?" Krystal asked.

"No, but we saw her yesterday in the yard. She was watching us play. I think she needs a friend."

Anna smiled. "Let's not only remember to pray for her, let's invite her to join us."

Anna walked over and offered her hand. "Hello, I'm Anna."

The young girl looked up and gave a tentative smile. "Hi, I'm Heidi."

"You're welcome to join us, if you want."

"Thank you," Heidi said with a checked smile. "No one ever sits by me."

"Well come on. I'll introduce you."

Back at the table, Anna introduced Heidi to Krystal and the children. Heidi sat next to Anna, her guarded smile softening as Cathryn began asking questions.

"Where did you come from?"

"I was brought here from Mexico. I don't really know where home is." Heidi answered softly.

"How old are you?" Christiana asked.

Heidi looked puzzled. "I don't know for sure. Maybe seventeen."

"Are your mom and dad here?"

Sadness appeared in Heidi's eyes. "I don't know my parents. I was an orphan."

Anna reached over and took her hand. "That's okay Heidi. I was too. How long have you been here?"

"A helicopter brought me here after a soldier saved me. I think it was about a month ago."

"Do you like it here?" Anna asked.

"They take good care of me. No one hurts me, and I get to eat," Heidi said choking up. "But I'm lonely. I don't know anyone."

"Well, that's about to change. You can hang out with us, Heidi. You're our new friend." Anna put her arm around Heidi and gave her a hug.

Cathryn ran around the table and hugged Heidi. "If you want, you can be my best friend."

Heidi wiped her eyes and returned the hug. "I would like that very much."

After lunch, Anna excused herself to check on updates from Charlotte Lake.

The dispatch office was bustling. It took a while before anyone noticed her. Finally, a dispatcher directed her to Colonel Whitlock's office.

Anna knocked on the closed door and got no response.

She headed outside and decided to explore the flight line. Other than two fighter jets, the hangars were empty. From what she had seen coming off the Blackhawk, she imagined clean-up was underway at the mine.

As she approached the big hangar she spotted a couple of men, entering a building. One looked like the colonel. The "authorized personnel only" sign on the door didn't stop her.

Colonel Whitlock, coffee in hand, had just sat down at a table with three other men.

"Anna," he said, looking up, "Imagine that. Showing up uninvited. Have a seat."

Anna tensed and looked around the room. "Sorry, I must have the wrong place. I'll be going now."

"No, have a seat."

Anna reluctantly slid into a chair. She looked at the men staring at her.

"What? First time seeing a woman?" she snapped.

Whitlock laughed. "Relax. They're just wondering how Steven got so lucky. Really, they're just not use to aggressive women coming in here. What's up?"

Anna blushed. "I'm trying to find out what's going on at home. Dispatch said I had to talk to you. Have you heard anything from Ethan and of course Steven?"

"Talked to both this morning. They have some things to clean up. They'll be coming home about the time you return to the lake."

"So, you're going to drop us off and pick up the guys? That is not at all what we want." Anna pouted.

"First, it's not about you. Second, it's not 'us', it's you. We just got off the phone with Child Protection Services and they recommend the children be placed under the guardianship of Krystal's parents. Once you leave, Krystal and her children will be taken to Fresno."

Anna jumped up. "That is wrong. Krystal would do anything for those children. You and CPS have a lot in common, you like to overassert your authority."

Anna headed for the door.

"Anna, get back here now!" Whitlock thundered.

Anna turned around, "Or what?"

"I'll throw you in the brig."

Anna shrugged and returned to her seat. Folding her arms she fumed.

Whitlock castled his hands, "Anna, I know you've lived at Charlotte Lake most of your life. You don't know any different. But to the rest of the world, it is a primitive community that isn't conducive to modern civilization. You don't have electricity in your homes, you don't even have running water. How can that even be sanitary? The state of California can not condone raising children in that environment. You can be thankful they aren't taking all the children out of the community. They probably would if they knew how bad it was."

"Sir, I would love to tell you what I really think of you," Anna glared at him, "but being a good Christian woman, I can't. You've never stepped foot in our community. If you did, you might respect us. Men like Ethan and Steven do. Unlike you, these men are willing to die for us. If you would only take the time to get to know us."

Anna took a deep breath. "Thank you for your

protection, even though I question if it wasn't a setup. Time will tell. As far as my employment. I resign effective immediately. Are we done?"

Colonel Whitlock's face was as red as a beet. Two of the men were holding their amusement.

The Colonel rubbed his temples and sighed. "Anna, that is not what I meant. I don't care how your community lives. It's Krystal's children. According to the CPS, the grandparents are planning to file a lawsuit for custody. If we don't turn them over, we will be in a big legal fight. One we can't win."

Anna shook her head in disgust, "Are we through?"

"Yes, you are dismissed. I hope you reconsider your resignation. We could still use you."

"I bet you could." Anna looked around the table. "Good day, gentlemen."

She walked out of the briefing room on the war path. It was time to go nocturnal.

She remembered seeing combat gear hanging on the wall in the big hangar. The aircraft doors were wide open and the place was deserted. She glanced at the camera, doubting anyone was watching.

She grabbed a pair of night vision goggles and ducked into the restroom. She stuffed the goggles into an empty trash can liner and headed for her cabin.

Chapter Forty-Eight

Ethan looked around the storehouse. The shelves were flattened, and merchandise lay scattered across the floor. Sarah and two children were busy picking up items near the counter.

"Good morning, men. It's going to be a wonderful day," she said with a warm, genuine smile. "Now, if you're looking for something, it may take awhile."

Ethan was amazed at her demeanor. "Sarah, you should be at home with Noah."

"No way. We'll be swamped in a few hours. Once folks realize what's missing, they'll come running."

"You're an example to follow, Sarah. We'll be back to help once we have made our rounds," Ethan offered.

"No need. Ten to fifteen folks will be here to help soon enough." Sarah waved them off. "Oh, have you heard from Anna or Krystal? Word is they went to the military camp."

"Not yet. I'm sure they're in good hands."

"Well, I'll be praying."

Steven was already out the door, and by the time Ethan caught up, he was passing the bakery. Smoke curled out of the chimney, and they could hear the ladies singing inside.

"Do we stop?" Steven asked.

"It would only slow them down. Let's go check on William and Claire."

As they approached the Lindbergh home. William sat on his rocking chair while young people brought broken items for inspection. He could see Claire inside giving orders.

"It's a little hectic around here, boys. Have a seat," William offered.

"We won't stay long," Ethan replied. "Just making sure you have some help. Looks like it's covered."

William smiled, "Grandchildren are a gift from God. We're blessed with five."

"A blessing it is," Ethan agreed. "Has anyone been up at Krystal's?"

"Not that we have seen. We heard they got missed. Makes me feel bad. When are they returning?"

"In a couple days or so."

Ethan turned to Steven. "I can handle Krystal's if you want to meet at Abram's in an hour."

"Works for me. I've a couple of questions for Oliver."

Ethan took off up the path, relieved to see no fresh tracks. The stream still tumbled, oblivious to all that had happened. It simply did what God created it to do.

Ten minutes later, at the edge of the clearing, he paused and scanned the cabin. Nothing looked out of place. The door was shut, no broken windows, no smoke coming from the chimney.

Still, something in his gut was telling him to proceed with caution. Hidden, he watched the cabin for fifteen minutes. Nothing moved.

Then, movement. Just the breeze? He focused on the spot. There, it did it again. Not a natural movement. It was jerky, like a cat swatting at a bug. Someone was in there.

He had been in this situation too many times. He should have brought Steven.

Another twitch. Definitely not the wind.

He approached the door, staying out of sight. Picking up a piece of firewood, he tapped it twice on the door.

Gunfire exploded through the wooden door.

He dropped the firewood and let out a loud groan. The door swung open, and someone was ready to finish the job.

Instead, the shooter found a Beretta in his face and his assault rifle knocked to the floor.

With one eye on the teenage militant and another scanning the cabin, Ethan motioned for the boy to step outside. He then motioned for him kneel and put his hands behind his head.

"How many?" Ethan asked.

"No hablo inglés."

"Well, it's your lucky day. I don't speak Spanish." Ethan's sarcasm hung heavy.

Ethan pointed at the boy and back at the cabin mimicking a counting gesture, "Uno, dos, tres?"

The kid shook his head, "Cero, señor."

Somehow, Ethan believed him. He pulled out zip ties and cinched them tightly around the boy's wrist. He helped the kid up and motioned him back inside, pointing to the couch.

"Sit." Ethan said.

The cabin looked lived in but not ransacked. While searching the cabin, in Jonah's room, a child's drawing caught his eye. A toddler and a man who looked like a soldier. "Jonah" was scribbled under the child. Ethan's name, misspelled, under the soldier. Then crossed out. Below it was scribbled "Daddy."

Ethan's heart sank.

"God is in the details," He whispered and returned to the living room.

He keyed his radio. "Steven, you copy?"

"Loud and clear. What's up?"

"I've got a language problem with a teenager up here. Where you at?"

"Just left Oliver's. I'll head back that way."

"Sounds good. I'll bring him down the mountain. Meet you at William's."

"Roger that."

Ethan pulled out some parachute cord and secured the teenager. He cleaned up the mess as best he could, then shut the bullet-ridden door.

"Let's go. Vamos."

As they made their way down the path, Ethan's eyes were drawn to the log where Anna had been sitting when she was abducted. He needed to come back and search this place more thoroughly. There could be answers here.

Steven was sitting on the porch, listening to William share about the Lord's faithfulness. Ethan motioned for the boy to sit and sat down beside him.

"So, Steven," William said, "as you can see, it was necessary for Jesus to die for our sins. And when He made that sacrifice, He did it for all mankind, for all generations."

Steven nodded. "Thanks for sharing, William. Once we get this cleaned up, I'll come back."

"Please do, my son. Just don't wait too long."

Steven turned to the boy. "¿Cómote llamas?"

The boy's face lit up. "Meteo, Senior."

Steven spoke with him for a few minutes, then turned to Ethan. "Mateo is only fourteen. When the soldiers came, he ran up to the cabin and hid behind the couch. He says, "for days." Once the helicopters stopped flying, he came out and found something to eat. He kept watch out the window afraid the soldiers would still come for him. He saw you at the edge of the clearing and panicked."

Ethan shook his head. "Does he want his diaper changed, or should I warm up a bottle? The kid shot at me! Ask him why."

"¿Por qué disparaste?" Steven asked.

Mateo answered and Steven laughed. "He said you looked scary. Thought you were a monster."

Even William chuckled, "Where you taking the lad?" he asked.

"That's Arnold's call," Steven said. "For now, we're turning him over to security."

"Sounds fair. He'll be fine sitting here until security comes by." William said.

"If you don't mind. We'd love getting him off our hands."

"Not at all. It'll give me a chance to work the rust off my Spanish. Mateo and I will be just fine. You boys be careful."

The men waved goodbye and headed east.

Abram was sitting in his overstuffed chair on the front porch. Beside him lay the pieces of the matching chair. He motioned for Ethan and Steven to join him.

"It's quite a mess inside but these girls are like a hive of bees, buzzing around."

Ethan noticed Abram holding a twisted picture frame.

"How are you holding out?" he asked.

"Thanks for asking, Ethan. We've been through a lot of struggles over the years, and God has seen us through. He will see us through this one as well. We have to trust Him."

Ethan reached over and laid his hand on Abram's arm. "I know that, Abram. But how are you doing?"

Abram choked up a bit, "I was doing fine until the girls brought me this picture. It was the last one taken of Ellie before she passed away." His fragile hands shook as he tried to straighten the creased image. "I miss her."

Ethan pushed back the lump in his throat, "Tell us one of your memories of Ellie."

Abram wiped his cheek with the back of his hand and smiled. "I would love to, but not today. Today, we mourn, tonight we give thanks, tomorrow we rejoice. After that, I would love to share the story of Ellie."

"We're going to hold you to that, my friend. See you tonight." Ethan said.

Eli was standing outside the meeting house talking to a

couple of men when they walked up. He waved them over.

"Are you guys planning on being here tonight?" he asked.

"Currently, that's the plan." Ethan answered. "What's up?"

"Would you mind not coming in military uniform?"

Ethan inhaled and rolled his eyes. "Will us showing up in uniform be a problem?"

"Well, we were just talking and think that it might make some of the people nervous. Seeing the military stuff."

"We, as in you?" Ethan said.

"That attitude's not necessary. The deacons and I decided, if you need to be in uniform it would be best if you're not here."

Ethan turned to the two men. "You guys must be the deacons he's talking about. Is this your idea or Eli's?"

The two men hung their heads.

"I thought so," Ethan said. "We'll go on over to the haberdasher's and find us some hillbilly britches. Will that make you happy?"

Eli's face got red and the deacons started laughing.

"I have to say, I look forward to you two moving on." Eli mumbled. "We could use some peace around here."

Steven tightened the grip on his rifle. "Is it peace you're after, or are you wanting us out of the way so you can administer more physical abuse?"

"Come on Steven," Ethan said, turning and moving toward the trail. "He doesn't know that we know."

"Know what?" He heard Eli yell.

"Yeah, know what?" Steven asked when they were out of hearing range.

"Just planting the seed," Ethan answered. "If he is guilty, he won't sleep tonight."

Chapter Forty-Nine

Anna woke with a jerk. She glanced at her watch, two a.m.

She crawled out of bed and dressed quickly. The brisk night air chilled her as she made her way behind the barracks. The night vision goggles lit up the area in an eerie green. Not a soul in sight as she approached the motor pool. The fence around the vehicles loomed ahead, but the gate stood wide open.

In the third row, she found the black Suburban. She slowly pulled open the latch and froze as the interior light blinked on. She quickly pushed it shut. If there was a night patrol, the light would be a beacon. She'd have to move fast.

She moved on to the next Suburban, took a deep breath, and in one quick motion, opened the door, slipped inside, and pulled it shut. The light went out. She exhaled. Everything inside was murky through the NVGs, so she took them off, pulled out her small flashlight, and shielded the beam as she searched for the keys. Nothing.

She would have to find the key box.

Sliding out, she clicked the door shut as quietly as she

could.

"Good morning, young lady."

Anna jerked and froze. A dark shadow leaned against the other Suburban.

"I thought I might find you here," the voice said. "Let's go for a walk."

She reached up to pull down her NVGs.

"You don't need those. Stay close to me."

"Where are we going?" she asked, straining to identify the voice.

"Someplace away from prying eyes and ears."

Her heart pounded. Why did everything have to be difficult?

They walked through the open gate and onto the fire road. For fifteen minutes, the only sound was the crunch of boots on the gravel.

At last, they stopped at an overlook. Dim runway lights shimmered to the west. A couple floodlights, projected across the tarmac. Otherwise, darkness.

"Anna, I need you to do something you may not feel comfortable doing."

She tensed. This was it. He'd brought her here so no one could hear her scream.

She whispered a prayer.

"What do you want?" she asked, her voice barely above a whisper as she took a cautious step back.

"I know your type," he said. "That's why I waited for you at the motor pool. Even guessed which vehicle you'd go for. That's why I removed the keys." He jingled them in his pocket.

That voice. She had heard it before. Panic swelled in her chest. She shut her eyes.

Eli. No.

"Please don't hurt me," she whimpered, retreating another step.

"Anna, snap out of it. I'm not going to hurt you."

"Colonel Whitlock?" Anna gasped.

"Yes. Who did you think it was?"

"I… I didn't know. I guess I was too shaken."

"I couldn't say anything down at the motor pool. Camp security has bugs everywhere. I know because I had them installed."

Anna pulled down her NVGs. Sure enough, it was Whitlock wearing night vision goggles as well. He waved.

"You look weird in those things," he said.

"So do you." She took a deep breath. "Now that my pulse is under control, what's going on?"

"I need you to follow through with your plan. Steal a vehicle. Head back to Charlotte Lake. Not just you, but take Krystal, her children, and Heidi too."

Anna pulled the goggles off and looked out over the runway.

"Why not just fly us out? It would be quicker."

"Like I said in the briefing room, CPS is all over this. If we make a move against them, the feds will shut us down. That last raid on Charlotte Lake was way too public."

"So, you want me to commit a crime and vanish?"

"You could say that. But don't ask me why."

"Why?"

"You're relentless."

"I've heard that before," she said. "And I'm starting to think you might have a soft heart under that turtle-hard shell. Am I right?"

Whitlock hesitated, then nodded slowly. "Anna, I'm going to tell you something, not for sympathy, but so you'll understand. Years ago, I was married and had three children about the age of Krystal's. While I was deployed, the chaplain came to find me. Worst day of my life. I went home, buried my family, and never went back."

Anna gasped. "Oh, no. I'm so sorry. I never knew."

"No one does. I never told anyone. But when I see Krystal with her children, my heart melts. As much as Ethan annoys me, he completes that family. And I regret what I said about Charlotte Lake. I wish I had it in me to live there. Modern conveniences aren't everything. What you people have, working together, living for each other, that's real. It's a wonderful place for those who can assimilate."

"Won't the CPS come looking?"

"They don't know Charlotte Lake exists. Someone deleted it from their files."

Anna stared at him. "So… when do we leave?"

"Tomorrow night," Whitlock said. "Keys will be in the first Suburban. Leave soon after midnight. You may see the two men from the briefing. They'll be watching to make sure you get away clean."

"Will you be tracking us?"

"There is a tracker on the SUV, next to the battery. Yellow tape marks the connection. When you reach the first town, unplug it. Got it?"

Anna paced. "I was going to run anyway, but this… feels crazy. I'm not sure I can do it. Will I be a hunted criminal?"

Whitlock laughed. "A little crazy? You're perfect for the job. As a bonus, I will make sure Steven keeps oversight of the area. That should make you happy."

Anna blushed in the dark. "Okay, I'm tired. Anything else?"

"Can you drive?"

— • ● • —

After breakfast the next morning, they once again took a walk up the fire road. Heidi and the children were running ahead.

"I need to tell you something important," Anna told Krystal.

"Okay. What is it?" Krystal asked.

"I can't tell you, but get everything packed. We're going to be leaving tonight."

"You want me to pack everything, wake up the children and be ready to go. "Krystal replied. "Yet, you won't tell me why. Sounds to me like the children of Israel the night of the Passover."

Anna smiled. Krystal always had a way of bringing biblical history into their situation.

"You want to go to the promised land?" she asked.

"So, we may be flying out of here tonight?"

"Something like that."

They continued on in silence, watching the children pick spring flowers and give them to Heidi. By the time they reached the lookout, Heidi had a large bouquet and a smile.

Anna studied her. The way Heidi responded to the children… it looked like this was all new to her. Had she ever experienced this kind of affection? Could she even accept love like this?

The children skipped ahead as Heidi came alongside Anna and Krystal.

"What you thinking, Heidi?" Anna asked.

Heidi hooked her arm through Anna's and smiled. "I don't know. It just seems like a dream."

"What does?"

"Walking down a gravel road in the mountains with you two and the children. Thank you for accepting me. I don't deserve it." She sniffled.

"You deserve every minute, Heidi. You are one of God's children."

Heidi's face fell. "I don't know. I just can't believe there is a God, because if there was…" She trailed off.

Only the love of Jesus could heal this shredded heart.

"Heidi, I have an extra bed in my cabin," Anna said gently. "How about you stay over tonight?"

Heidi wiped the tears away. "I would like that. Nighttime are the worst."

Chapter Fifty

At the dry goods store, two carpenters were busy repairing the front door. Inside, debris still littered the floor. Ethan and Steven spent an hour sorting through the clothing. A lot of work remained, work for someone who knew what they were doing.

Still, they found what they needed. Simple britches and shirts, with suspenders to keep the britches in place.

Retracing their route around the lake, they passed porches where residents now rested after a long day of cleaning. Everyone was friendly and waved, inviting them to the evening gathering at the meeting house. Word had gone out that, due to the exceptionally nice weather, the prayer meeting would be held outdoors. As they passed the meeting house men were moving benches into the clearing.

"We picked up these duds for nothing." Steven muttered.

"How much did they cost?" Ethan asked.

"Okay, fine… Are we wearing them anyhow?"

"Most certainly. It'll do you good to roll the clock back a hundred years."

Arnold was talking to William when they arrived at the

path. He motioned for them to stop. "Where you guys headed?"

"Up to camp," Ethan replied. "We'll be back this evening. What happened to Mateo?"

Arnold grinned. "William talked his ear off. The kid begged to go back to Venezuela."

William frowned. "It's a shame. He was promised a better life. Now look at him."

"He's in a holding cell at City Hall." Arnold said. "We're still trying to figure out what to do with him."

"William, you spent some time with Mateo. How hardened is he?" Steven asked.

William shook his head. "He's soft right now, but put a gun in his hand and it's anyone's guess."

"Suppose so. Once a dog kills a chicken, it's all over."

William held up a hand, "But as long as there's life, there's hope for redemption."

"Considering what we've seen the last few days. How do we know?" Steven asked.

"A good question," William replied. "All wisdom comes from God. We will pray for discernment."

Steven shrugged, "Not too familiar with all that. We'll just have to wait and see."

Arnold spoke up. "Speaking of redemption, Arwel broke down and is begging for leniency. All of a sudden, he's willing to cooperate."

"What changed?" Ethan asked.

"Rebbecca came to see him. They talked for about an hour. She left in tears. We found Arwel on the floor, crying out to God."

Ethan shook his head. "Go figure."

He nodded a farewell and led the way up the path. It was quieter than normal, only the trees rustling overhead.

"You believe what William said?" Steven asked suddenly. "That kids like Mateo can change?"

Ethan gave it some thought. "I do believe some people

are blessed to see the truth before it's too late. Others… don't even realize they're lost."

Steven kicked a pinecone off the path. "So, what are we?"

"I was lost, but when I accepted Christ as my Savior, all that changed. Now without a doubt, I have been redeemed."

Ethan could hear the shuffling behind him.

As they approached their camp, Ethan suddenly raised a clenched fist. Steven stopped instantly. Ethan's eyes were locked ahead.

"Movement," he whispered.

Around the fire pit, shadows shifted. Both men silently drew their sidearms. The air was thick with pine smoke. Something felt wrong.

At fifty yards, they split. Ethan angled forty-five degrees right, Steven to the left. Their silent approach would converge on the camp in a wide pincer, classic textbook maneuver, one that gave them the upper hand. Or should have.

Ethan crept forward, boots soundless on the forest floor. He kept Steven in his peripheral vision, a flicker of motion low and left, but his full attention was locked on their fire pit.

Twenty yards out.

Still no clear view. The campfire was smoldering; someone had stirred it. He felt his heart beating against his chest. He shifted to get a better angle.

"Drop it, soldier boy!"

The voice came from behind. Too close.

Ethan froze. The certainty of a weapon trained on his back. Slowly, he raised his hands. His Beretta hung in his right, loose but ready. Still, he obeyed.

Slowly turning around, he exhaled and slid the Beretta back in its holster.

"Tanner, what are you guys doing here?"

"Seeing if we could get a drop on you. Where's Steven?"

Ethan glanced in Steven's direction. Tanner turned to see Steven's fully extended gun.

"Covering my back." Ethan grinned. "Let's fix some coffee."

With coffee in hand the men found a place to sit around the fire.

"For real. What are you doing here?" Ethan asked again.

"We received a message that the threat has been eliminated." Tanner answered. "Whitlock wanted us to bring you the message and then take the rest of the day off."

"Where you headed?" Steven asked.

"Don't know. What do you guys want to do?"

Steven looked at Ethan, "I'm thinking we're going to find a couple of young ladies and have a picnic. If we can break them out of Willow Creek jail."

"Good luck with that." Tanner said. "Rumor is CPS is getting the kids. Something about grandparents ratting Krystal out."

Numbness draped Ethan before anger started melting it away. "We can't let that happen! Is that why Whitlock doesn't want us there?"

"I don't think so." Tanner replied. "Dispatch hinted that Whitlock was stalling CPS. Making them wait until Krystal had been interviewed. Speaking of the devil, he wants all of us in the crater at 0700 in the morning for an extraction."

"Best news I've heard all day." Ethan said. "You guys want to join us this evening down in the village? Give you a chance to meet the people you have been protecting."

Tanner and Roland looked at each other and shrugged. "Do they have anything to eat?" Tanner asked.

"You can count on it."

"Well, don't mind us." Tanner said. "Pack your stuff and let's get out of here."

Twenty minutes later they were making their way down the mountain.

"You're looking mighty fine with those suspenders."

Tanner chided.

"Don't get too comfortable in those BDUs boys." Ethan said. "Steven will take you to the dry goods store."

"Will do." Steven said. "Not sure there's a hat big enough for Tanner's head."

"We're good guys." Tanner said.

"No deal. Some of the folks are a little gun shy. Asked that we look a little less intimidating." Ethan said.

"Where you headed?" Steven asked Ethan.

"I'm gonna have a little private chat with Arwel."

They separated at the trail and Ethan headed for City Hall. In his backpack was Arwel's journal.

Inside the storehouse it looked like nothing had happened. Everyone was friendly and thanked him, he wasn't sure why. Maybe they just needed to thank someone. They should, and he knew they would, thank God. They had a tough road ahead.

He pulled open the big oak door and moved through the ice cave and into City Hall. He found Arnold in his office and pulled the door shut behind him.

"This must be serious." Arnold said, looking up.

"Everything's serious." Ethan replied. "I need to talk to Arwel."

"Third door on the right. Just tap on the door when you're ready to leave. Oh, and leave your weapon here. No need in getting shot with your own gun."

"Funny." Ethan pulled his Beretta out and laid in on Arnold's desk. "Don't play with it while I'm gone. Is the room bugged?"

"Of course. But, I can shut it off if you want."

"Please. Just for Rebbecca's sake. I'll brief you after the fact."

"Hum… You know something?"

Ethan shrugged and walked out.

He peered through the small window into the holding cell. Arwel was slumped in the corner, a shell of the man he used to be. How could someone with so much potential fall to such disgrace? Only God could save him now.

Was he actually feeling sorry for Arwel? Was he becoming soft, or was it God working on his heart? Just hours ago, Arwel had been in his crosshairs. The warrior within him would have pulled the trigger without hesitation.

Ethan opened the door. Arwel continued to stare at the floor.

He sat on the edge of the bed and waited.

"What do you want?" Arwel finally mumbled.

"I want you to get off the floor and talk to me like a man."

Arwel glanced up. "Why? You're nothing but a mercenary. No more a Christian than I am."

"That's where you're wrong. I haven't been paid in years. And as for faith, mine is in Jesus, and Him alone. If you think your words can shake that, you're barking up the wrong tree."

Arwel's eyes narrowed. "How do you justify all the killing?"

"I will tell you once you tell me how you justified killing Anna?"

Arwel said nothing. His hands trembled as he rubbed his fingers together, then dropping his head, he sobbed.

Ethan got up and offered his hand. "Come on. You can start by getting off the floor."

Arwel did not respond. Still weeping, he buried his head in his hands. Ethan sat back down.

"Arwel, I am not your enemy. Neither is your wife. Or your community. But do you know who is?"

Ethan waited in silence. Ten minutes passed. He was sure Arwel knew the answer. He just wasn't ready to admit it.

"I'm going now," Ethan finally said. "Just so you know, I have your journal. And the other items from your hidden compartment you thought no one would find. Let me know when you're ready to talk."

Ethan tapped on the door.

"Wait!"

Ethan turned. Arwel was struggling to his feet.

This time, when Ethan offered his hand, Arwel took it. He sat down on the bed.

"How did you find it?" he asked.

"Trade secrets," Ethan said. "What you should be asking is why we found it."

"I suppose," Arwel said. "Did you read it?"

"Enough."

"Who else knows?"

"Wrong question again. Ask yourself why I'm telling you."

Arwel lowered his gaze. "Thanks. Not that it matters. I'm history now."

"One of your making. You will stand trial tomorrow evening. Between now and then, I suggest some soul-searching. Maybe the God you used to preach about will soften that calloused heart."

"That hurts."

The door opened. Arnold stood waiting. "Ready?"

Ethan turned back to Arwel and clasped his hand firmly. "My faith is new and simple. One thing I know, Jesus died for all sin, not just the little ones. He can fix this mess. Think about it."

The latch clicked behind him. The sound of finality.

———— • ● • ————

"Sounds like all four of you are leaving in the morning." Arnold said. Leaning back in his chair.

Ethan looked at his watch and slid into a chair. "Someone's been talking."

"Just got off the line with Willow Creek. They finished cleaning up at the mines."

"Did they search the shafts?" Ethan asked.

"No way in. They were sealed by the blast."

"You mean, we could have live militants, trapped in the gold mine?"

"Yes. We have considered that and will send a team to investigate, but not for a couple of days." Arnold said.

"A couple of days! They could be dead by then." Ethan felt sick to his stomach. "Sure, these guys came to destroy the community, but..."

"If they're in the shafts alive, they will be fine." Arnold said. "There's alternate air vents and potable water caches at multiple locations."

"Well, okay. I'll try to stay in my lane." Ethan replied, a lot more relaxed.

"We're being picked up in the crater at seven in the morning. They may be bringing Anna but not Krystal."

"I heard." Arnold said. "What you going to do about it?"

"I may be married by sundown tomorrow." Ethan smiled. "If that's what it takes."

"Sounds good to me. Maybe she can get you in line. Should be a great evening at the meeting house. Go enjoy yourself and we'll see you there."

———•●•———

The peaceful evening air was refreshing as children played and people mingled. The lanterns hung around the clearing giving it a festive atmosphere. Four men stood just feet away from tables filled with cookies, cakes, and pies.

They watched as Abram came walking up the trail. His pace was slower than before. A granddaughter on his arm. Abram made his way to them.

"Good evening, gentlemen. Ethan, Steven, who are your friends?"

"Good evening, Abram." Ethan said. "This is Tanner and Roland. They're the part of our team guarding Kearsarge Pass. Right now, I think they're guarding these desserts."

"Welcome," Abram said, grasping their hands. "Thank you so much for your service. I pray that you will enjoy the evening."

Abram greeted everyone he met, slowly working his way to the front, where Eli and the deacons joined him. Was it from experience or an unspoken culture? But as soon as the leaders took their seat the people quickly made their way to a bench and sat down.

"We need to split up." Ethan whispered to Steven.

"Something going down?" Steven asked.

"Don't know. I just don't like being a fish in a shooting gallery."

"Where's security?"

"They're out there. And you can count on drones being in the air."

"Don't eat all the dessert." Steven said, motioning for Roland to follow him.

———— • ● • ————

The evening started with a song and then Abram offered a prayer of thanksgiving. Eli spoke for a few minutes. Ethan analyzed every word. He sounded sincere. His voice reflected authenticity. Was Eli for real? What about… He shook his head. Tomorrow's business meeting will be a firestorm. Hopefully, the truth will come out.

The congregation sang songs of praise, hope, and redemption. Around the edge of the clearing, the four warriors stood. Their eyes ever moving. Watching for that unexpected movement. Thankfully, it never came.

With desserts consumed, the parents gathered their children and disappeared down the trail. The four men recovered their packs and headed for the crater. It had been a long day.

Chapter Fifty-One

Anna, wearing the NVGs, silently led the line of children daisy-chained behind her, with Krystal bringing up the rear. They crept around the back of the barracks, careful to stay in the shadows. The motor pool was dark. Anna scanned the area, no movement.

At the end sat a black Suburban.

Too easy, she thought. It's like Colonel Whitlock wants us to have it.

Excitement buzzed through the children as they climbed in. Anna found the keys in the console and handed them to Krystal.

"I'm driving?" Krystal whispered, her eyes wide.

"Somebody has to. I've never driven anything before."

Krystal took a deep breath. "Oh, yeah!"

Anna passed her the goggles. "You'll need these to see anything."

The gravel crunched under the tires as they slowly pulled out of the camp, lights off.

"Oh no." Krystal whispered, slowing to a stop. "There's a soldier ahead. He has a rifle."

Anna leaned forward. "What's he doing?"

"Just standing there. Near the road."

"Probably one of Whitlock's men."

"He's waving us forward."

They rolled past slowly, hearts pounding, barely breathing. The soldier gave a nod as they eased by and disappeared into the woods behind them.

Ten minutes later, Krystal lifted the goggles and flipped on the headlights.

They wove through the forest, making their way down the mountain. Twenty minutes later they pulled onto Highway 41.

"We need to disconnect the GPS tracker," Anna reminded as they neared Oakhurst. "Colonel Whitlock said it's critical."

Krystal nodded and a mile later pulled into a shopping center parking lot.

"He said it's near the battery," Anna said. "Can you find it?"

Krystal popped the hood, and they both stepped out.

They had just lifted the hood when a car pulled up beside them. Headlights off.

"What do we do?" Krystal whispered.

"Act normal."

"What's normal?"

Anna gave a tight shrug. "I have no idea."

Two men got out and approached.

"Problem, ladies?" one of them asked.

"No, sir," Anna replied, evenly. "It sounded a little rough, so we figured we'd check the oil."

"You don't want to get all greasy," the other man said, stepping beside the engine. He pulled the dipstick, examined it, and nodded. "Looks fine to me. You should be all right."

"Thanks. Do you live around here?" Anna asked. As soon as the words left her mouth, she regretted it.

"We sure do. You girls want to come over for a drink?"

Anna stiffened. "Sorry, we don't drink. And we've got a long drive ahead. Thanks, though."

She reached up and slammed the hood.

Krystal was already in the driver's seat. As Anna turned, the man grabbed her arm.

She jerked her arm away and snarled, "Back off!"

He hesitated just long enough. She ran around the Suburban and jumped in. The locks clicked as the door slammed.

He pounded on the window. Krystal stomped on the gas.

They didn't speak until they were out of town.

Krystal exhaled hard. "That was way too close. Are all your plans like this?"

Anna rubbed her arm. "I think they were drunk."

"Probably. This time in the morning? I say we wait on the tracker."

An hour later, they pulled into a gas station north of Fresno. Everyone needed a bathroom break, and they were running on fumes.

"Do we have any money?" Krystal asked, stretching.

"I have a bunch," Anna said, "but I don't know how to get it."

Krystal blinked. "What do you mean?"

"Steven gave me a card. Said all my pay's on it. I have never used it."

"All your money?"

"Yeah, from my job. I haven't spent any of it."

"Do you have the card?"

Anna dug through her backpack and produced a debit card.

"Do you know the pin number?"

"It's written on the card," Anna said, turning it over.

Krystal groaned. "Never do that. Lucky no one searched your bag. Let's unhook the tracker first."

They found the box near the battery and disconnected the wires. The card worked, and soon the children had snacks, and the women had coffee.

Back in the car, Krystal studied the map. "It looks like we need to head east on Highway 180. All the way to the end."

The sky began to lighten as they neared Grant Grove Village. Krystal's eyes sagged behind the wheel.

"Let's stop and rest," Anna said, pointing at a sign for John Muir Lodge.

"We can't." Krystal yawned. "No driver's license."

"What?"

"They won't give us a room without proper identification. Mine's back in the cabin."

"And you know I don't have one." Anna muttered. "Can we at least try?"

"Won't hurt." Krystal yawned again, following the signs to the Lodge.

"Bring everyone inside," Anna said.

"Why?"

"Hard to turn away a family of children."

"So true. Let's go."

Whether from fatigue or quiet sympathy, the night clerk overlooked the ID. Fifteen minutes later, they were in their rooms. Exhausted, but safe. For now.

They'd rest for two nights. Enough time to recover, regroup, and ready themselves for the long climb to Charlotte Lake.

Chapter Fifty-Two

Ethan was the first one off the Blackhawk as the rotors spun down. At Colonel Whitlock's request, the four men made their way to the briefing room. Ethan was anxious to get it over with. He needed to find Krystal. It was time to talk about getting married.

Whitlock was already in his chair with his aide by his side. Two additional soldiers were seated at the table. Ethan assumed they were replacements for Conrad and Lewis. Too soon.

"Welcome home, boys. Have a seat."

"After coffee, sir." Steven replied as the four headed for the coffee maker.

After introductions to Jefferson Feeney and Ronnie Kelley, Ethan turned to Whitlock.

"Let's get this over with. I need to talk to Krystal."

Whitlock looked down at his coffee and frowned. "I got some disturbing news."

"I heard. I plan on doing something about it. What else?"

"It's not that. This morning, Krystal and the children were reported missing. A search turned up that Anna was gone too, and one of our vehicles is missing."

Ethan tried to process what he had just heard. Anna couldn't drive, and it had been a long time since Krystal had. It didn't make sense.

"So… have you found them?" he asked.

"No. The locator device pinged last at a gas station north of Fresno, around 3:00 a.m. We suspect they're heading toward the Bubbs Creek trailhead."

"Do we have resources in the air?" Steven asked.

"Not yet. We've requested a drone from China Lake. Waiting for a response."

"That's a start. How soon can we be dropped at the trailhead?" Ethan asked.

"I don't think that's a good idea. You two are too close to the girls. Let us handle this. Besides, Arnold wants you and Steven back at Charlotte Lake by seven tonight."

"Fine. I'm ready as soon as this meeting is over."

"Unfortunately, the next available flight is around four," Whitlock said. "Get some rest. We'll let you know when we have something."

"I expect nothing less." Ethan stood.

As they walked to their quarters, he muttered, "I'm about twenty-four hours away from resigning."

"Can't say I blame you," Steven replied. "I'm worried about Anna. She's not experienced with life outside the community."

"Probably not, but Krystal is. Even though it's been awhile."

"What are they doing for money?" Ethan questioned.

"Anna's loaded. Though I doubt she knows how to spend it."

"Do you have access to her account?"

"I set it up," Steven said, then paused. "Wait! Are you thinking what I'm thinking?"

"Let's go find out."

Five minutes later they reviewed the charges on Anna's

account. The first time was at the gas station where they went dark. The next was the John Muir Lodge in Grants Grove Village. The last was at the restaurant for breakfast.

"What now?" Steven asked.

"Nothing." Ethan replied. "They're clearly heading to the trailhead. We can't get to the lodge before they're gone and if Whitlock finds out, he'll bring them back here. It's best if we just go to Charlotte Lake and head down from there."

"Out of Whitlock's control."

"Exactly." Ethan said. "I'm spending the afternoon reading a journal, but not before I spend some time in the shower."

Ethan waited in the hangar as the crew prepped the Blackhawk. He was growing weary of this fast-paced life. He checked the sky, clouds were building. Were they expecting rain? His phone confirmed it. Looked like it would be raining at the lake. Didn't matter as long as they could get in.

Steven arrived clean-shaven and sharply dressed in civilian clothes.

"Feels good to be out of BDUs" he said, dropping into a chair.

"Yeah, but I hear the girls like them. You think Anna will be waiting at the landing zone?"

"No chance. I called the lodge, but they were not in. Found out they're staying another night. Judging by her spending, they're eating well."

"Good. At least they'll be rested and the weather might clear."

"Gentlemen, your whirlybird awaits," the crew chief

announced walking into the hangar. "One little pit stop and I'll join you."

"Thanks, Chief." Steven said, grabbing his pack.

Rain splattered Ethan's face as they walked toward the helicopter. His mind wasn't on the flight. It was on Krystal and the children. His heart ached. Did he deserve them? No. He could never live up to their love.

The Blackhawk lifted off, flying its familiar path. The valley off their right and the mountains on the left. They rounded Spanish Mountain and climbed toward Charlotte Lake.

The ground rose rapidly as they swung around Charlotte Dome. Ethan spotted the crater left by the bomb. It would be years before the scar would heal.

The visibility dropped as rain pelted the glass, but they were almost there.

Finally, Charlotte Lake flew by, fifty feet below them.

The Blackhawk made a tear drop turn and slid past the barn. The animals scattered as the helicopter settled onto the grass.

"Go!" the crew chief yelled, sliding open the door.

Ethan and Steven exited quickly and walked away as the thundering of the rotors intensified. The hurricane winds subsided as the Blackhawk left the meadow and flew down Charlotte Creek.

"Let's find some dinner before the meeting." Ethan said, tossing his pack over the fence.

"Sounds great. Know any good restaurants?"

"No, but I know someone who'll welcome us."

"Seriously? You remember what happened the last time we dropped in."

"You may be right. Let's go see."

They reached Abram's as the evening sky dimmed. Eli met them at the door.

"We've been expecting you. Come on in."

Expecting us? How?

Abram sat in his newly repaired chair. His face lit up when he saw them.

"Greetings boys. Pull up a chair."

"Thanks Abram. We're a little early for the meeting. Are you ready?" Ethan asked.

"The only way we can be. Through fasting and prayer."

"Oh, I'm sorry for interrupting. We can leave."

"No, no. Please stay. We were just finishing up. Unfortunately, with fasting, I don't have anything fixed."

"We'll be fine. How will this meeting be conducted?" Ethan asked.

"Straightforward. No attorneys, no judge. We'll sing, read an appropriate Bible passage, and then present the charges. Then Arwel will have the opportunity to respond."

"So, who are the jurists?" Steven asked.

"The church body."

"I remember that," Ethan said. "It wasn't fun."

Abram nodded, then added. "We do have a request. Arwel asked if you would escort him tonight. Can you do that?"

Ethan hesitated. *Why me?* Maybe Arwel had taken his words to heart.

"Sure, as long as Steven stands guard."

Eli raised an eyebrow. "Not fond of armed guards at church. But considering … and you're dressed respectfully, I'll consent."

"Done deal then," Abram said. "Ethan, go see Arnold, he will give you instructions."

Ethan turned to Steven. "You gonna to be alright without me?"

"I was going to ask you the same thing." Steven grinned.

Back at City Hall, Ethan passed through the storehouse. It looked like everything was back to normal. A bag of almonds caught his eye. That would take care of the hunger pains.

Inside, City Hall was quiet. A few specialists were busy at the monitors, not even noticing Ethan behind them. Arnold's door was open, but the office was empty. He took a seat and waited.

"You back for good?" Arnold entered, chewing on a sandwich.

"I hope. Between here and Willow Creek, I don't know which way's up."

"Understand. You got the message?"

"Escort duty. Leg chains?"

"Do you think it's necessary?" Arnold asked.

"Not really. Might not even need cuffs."

"Really? He tried to kill someone."

"I know. But if we drag him in there in handcuffs it will only harden him. If it's okay with you, I would like to evaluate his condition."

"You'll need to stay with him. I don't want a chaotic scene at the meeting."

"You mean anymore of a scene?"

"I suppose. Go ahead and see what you think." Arnold said. "Oh, yeah. For some reason, Rebbecca wants to walk in and sit with him."

"Sounds like true love. Maybe the rest of us should pay attention."

The picture was different when Ethan knocked on the cell door and walked in. Arwel was sitting on his bed, face washed and hair combed.

"Thanks for coming," he said. "I was hoping you would."

"Why?" Ethan asked, sitting down.

"I've been thinking about what you said. It's pretty easy to do when all that you've done crashes down around you.

Last night, while everyone was at the meeting house praising God, I sat here thinking about what I had done. It hit me pretty hard."

"What you had done, or that you were caught?" Ethan asked.

"Ouch. But, I deserve that. No, Ethan, for the first time, I was sorry for what I had done. I know there's no way I can fix it. Only God can do that."

"I thought you didn't believe all that?"

"I didn't think I did either, but last night I called out to Him. For the first time, it wasn't for show. It was real, Ethan, and I felt something…"

"Yes?"

"I experienced a peace that I don't understand. I found myself acknowledging my guilt and surrendering to His will." Arwel wiped the moisture off his cheeks. "All the things I have preached about, came back to me. The memorized words of the Bible spoke."

"What did they say?" Ethan asked.

Arwel held up his hands. "Ethan, I am a condemned man. Too much evil has been committed by these hands. All I can think about, is the thief on the cross. I can only ask Jesus to remember me when…"

Arwel broke down and sobbed. Ethan put his arm on Arwel's shoulder. "Do you mind if I pray?" he asked.

Chapter Fifty-Three

"You ready?" Ethan asked quietly.

"At peace," Arwel answered, getting to his feet. He held out his hands to be cuffed.

"Not needed," Ethan said. "Just don't try anything funny."

Arwel gave a faint smile. "Thank you. I promise to be on my best behavior."

Ethan shook his head. "Not certain that's good enough. I'm going to trust you until you change my mind."

"Fair enough. Let's go."

They walked together through the ice cave and into the storehouse. Outside, the air was cool and still. A woman stood waiting on the porch. Her dress graceful, her smile soft.

"Rebbecca," Arwel started toward her, then hesitated. He looked back at Ethan.

Ethan shrugged.

Rebbecca opened her arms and ran to him. They embraced, both crying, while Ethan moved to the far end of the porch to give them privacy.

After a moment, the couple joined him, hand in hand.

"Is this okay?" Arwel asked.

"As long as you don't do anything stupid," Ethan said.

"Too late. Thanks."

Ethan followed them down the darkening trail.

Could Arwel be forgiven? A lot depended on how he handled the next hour. Would he tell the whole truth? Or would he hold back to protect others?

Steven stood guard as the flicker of lanterns projected through the windows. Rebbecca and Arwel paused just before the clearing.

"Can we have a moment?" he asked Ethan.

"Sure." Ethan stepped back a few paces.

He watched them quietly. Rebbecca spoke softly, her voice full of care. Arwel nodded with slow, solemn movements. Then she kissed him gently.

"I'm ready," Arwel said to Ethan.

"I'm not," Ethan replied. "Let me pray for you first."

He took their hands and bowed his head.

"Lord, bring repentance where it's needed, healing where there's pain, and truth where there's been deception. Amen."

They echoed his amen, and together they walked to the meeting house door.

Ethan noticed Arwel wince when they heard Eli firmly preaching.

"Are you going to go all in?" Ethan asked.

Arwel nodded. "It's the only right thing to do. I just hope I can do it without malice."

Ethan patted his back. "I'm here for you."

"And so am I," Rebbecca whispered.

—————————— • ● • ——————————

They heard Abram start speaking, and shortly Jonathon opened the door. Hushed whispers scattered throughout the room as they entered. The couple walked up the aisle together while Ethan took up a position beside the door.

Ethan's eyes were locked on Arwel's demeanor. Watching for a sign of rebellion, of hate, anger. Nothing. Arwel stood still, his posture low and humbled.

Abram stood with one hand on the table to reduce his trembling. The stress flowing from his eyes. "Arwel. Rebbecca. Thank you for coming. Please remain standing. The charges will now be read."

Arnold rose with a paper in hand. He read the charges. Ethan cringed as the description of the brutal attack on Anna, moved to the night on the trail, and finished with the charge of disloyalty and deception.

The air was filled with tension. No one moved. Heads bowed. A weight settled over the room.

"How do you plead?" Abram asked.

Arwel looked at his wife, squeezed her hand.

"Guilty as charged," Arwel said, his voice clear. "May I speak?"

"As long as it's pertinent," Abram said.

"Thank you." Arwel turned toward the congregation. "First, I apologize for my deception. I am so sorry. I deserve whatever justice that is handed down. Over the last few days, I have had time to reflect on what I have done. I'll start from the beginning.

"When I came to the mountain, I was running from my past. One that was filled with sinful baggage. I tried to change but sin ran deep. I pretended to assimilate and it worked. I played the part. Everything I did was under false pretense. Through all these years the only thing real was my love for Rebbecca and my children."

He looked at Rebbecca as she squeezed his arm and showed a faint smile.

"Because of this life of deception, Satan was able to

strengthen his grip on my heart. There were moments I wasn't sure I even had a heart. I stood in front of you and shared the Gospel, all the time thinking it was a fairytale. Tonight, if nothing else, I want to assure you that what the Bible says is the truth. I was the one in the wrong."

He paused looking down at the floor. Murmuring rippled through the congregation. Hankies dabbed at eyes. Men shifted uncomfortably. A response expected by people willing to forgive while maintaining a firm conviction.

"What you have endured over the last week is my fault. I am sorry. I knew what was coming and did nothing. I tried to justify it, but there is no justification."

He swallowed hard.

"I would like to talk about Anna. It's complicated."

Ethan watched Eli's face drop. So, it was true. He looked around for George and found him sitting along the edge fiddling with his fingers. Did he even understand?

Arwel continued. "I was heading up the trail to meet my contacts when I met Eli coming down. He stopped me and…" Arwel looked down at the floor trembling. Rebbecca squeezed his arm and pulled him against her.

With raised eyebrows, Abram glanced down at Eli. "Go ahead Arwel."

Arwel pulled out a hanky and wiped his face. "Eli said that Anna was up on the trail unconscious. He was on his way to get Doctor Winston."

Premature conclusions, caused murmuring to rise among the congregation.

"Silence please!" Abram's commanding voice sounded throughout the building.

"Arwel, are you telling us that you did not hit Anna?"

"Yes, I mean no, I did not hit Anna. I only tried to get rid of her."

"I'm not sure that's any better," Abram replied, turning to Eli. "Eli, can you verify that what Arwel is saying is true?"

Eli lifted his eyes, guilt thick in his voice. "Yes, it's true.

I was on my way up to Krystal's to talk to her and Anna when I came across Anna laying beside the stream. I checked her pulse and noticed the knot on her head. At that point I didn't know what to do, but felt it best to go get Doctor Winston. At the bottom of the trail I came across Arwel. When I told him about Anna, he said he would go check on her. I went to find the doctor and was unsuccessful."

Abram rubbed his beard. "So, what did you do?"

"I made the wrong decision by thinking the doctor had already been notified and was on the way. And with Arwel assisting, I could just go home. It wasn't until later I found out what happened."

"Yet, you told no one. We will deal with you later." Abram's temper was starting to rise. "Arwel, please continue."

"I found Anna still unconscious but breathing normally. That's when I got the terrible idea to hand her over to my contacts. Thinking they would take her hostage, and she would be out of my way."

"Why was she in your way?"

"Anna had been doing a lot of snooping, trying to figure out who was selling information to the militants. I needed that to stop."

"Not sure you're winning your case, but continue." Abram said.

"I had decided not to do it and started walking on up the hill. It was then that I heard someone coming down. I stepped behind a tree and watched as George came into view and stopped next to Anna."

Gasps could be heard around the room as Ethan watched George's neck turn bright red. It looked like a meltdown coming. Ethan opened the door and motioned Steven inside. "I may need backup." He whispered, pointing at George. "He's our man."

Arwel continued. "George sat on the ground and took Anna's head in his lap and cried. He then started talking to her, telling her he was sorry for hitting her, that it was dark and he thought she was Krystal."

Ethan clenched his fists to steady his anger, while Abram raised a hand to calm the murmuring crowd.

"Watch Arwel," he whispered to Steven. "I've got George."

George jumped to his feet raging as he started toward Arwel. "He's lying!" George screamed as he barreled through the crowd.

Ethan was quicker and they met in the aisle where George found himself flat on the floor with a bloody nose. In less time than it takes to flank a cow, George was cuffed and being escorted toward the door.

"Keep him under wraps until Arnold relieves you." Ethan said.

Steven grabbed George and took him outside.

The room finally quieted down.

Abram leaned down to Eli, who nodded.

"I think it would be appropriate for us to sing a hymn at this time. Let us please focus on God and His grace. Arwel, go ahead and have a seat while we sing."

Ethan focused on Arwel as the congregation sang.

"Fear not, I am with thee, Oh, be not dismayed."

Everyone singing together was causing a calmness to spread over the crowd.

"When through the deep waters I call thee to go, the rivers of sorrow shall not overflow."

Could hymns of praise truly have such a powerful effect the human heart? Ethan could see Arwel singing as he held Rebbecca close to his side. Why did Satan have to destroy families?

"When through fiery trials thy pathway shall lie, My grace, all sufficient, shall be thy supply."

Ethan bowed his head and listened to God speak to him through song. "Thank you, God." He whispered as the singing ended.

Abram led them in prayer before turning back to Arwel. "Please stand and continue."

Arwel showed strength and humility as he stood. "After George admitted to hitting Anna, he panicked and started mumbling about needing to finish her off. I don't know why he was saying that, you will have to ask him. I didn't think he had the mental capacity to live with it. I picked up a couple of sticks and banged them together causing George to take off down the path.

"I then picked Anna up and took her to the camp. I knew at least there, she had a chance."

"Yet, in the sting, you met her on the trail to kill her?" Abram said with mild condemnation.

"Yes, I didn't want to. But I had heard that she had evidence of the traitor. On one hand I would lose my wife and children, on the other I would be guilty of murder. My godless, selfish desire caused me to make the wrong decision. I am sorry."

Abram looked around the room. "There are too many emotions to be taking questions or making a decision tonight. In time the questions will be answered and a verdict issued. For now, Arwel will remain in custody. I would encourage you to pray for him and for the others involved in this horrible act of violence. Do not gossip, do not speculate. Be of good cheer. God is good.

"Arwel, do you have any closing comments?"

Arwel looked up at the congregation with a solemn face. "Have I changed? That is a question that even I can't answer. It can only be answered in time. Abram, thank you for your leadership and wisdom. Once again to those that I have let down, I am sorry. I am unworthy of your forgiveness. Yet, I ask that you keep me in your prayers."

Arwel sat down trembling. The truth was out. For now, it was finished.

As the congregation dispersed in hushed tones, Ethan sat down on the back bench, watching Arwel and Rebbecca. It wasn't closure, not really. Too much hurt lingered. But truth had cracked open the silence. And maybe, just maybe, hope could begin its slow return.

Epilogue

Krystal pulled the SUV into the Cooper Creek trailhead along Bubbs Creek. Morning light filtered through the trees, painting shadows on the pavement. Everyone was excited to begin the long hike up to Charlotte Lake.

As soon as she parked, the children tumbled out of the vehicle, already complaining about needing to use the restroom.

"I need to clean out the car before we leave," Krystal called after them. "Just be patient a little longer."

"I'll go with them," Anna offered. "We'll be right back."

"Okay, but don't take too long," Krystal replied. "We've got nine miles to go and five thousand feet to climb."

Anna followed the children to the pit toilets tucked under the tall pine trees. She stood outside, watching squirrels dart from tree to tree. Minutes passed. Too many.

She glanced toward the vehicle. Something felt wrong.

She stepped forward instinctively, then stopped. Four men were walking toward the SUV from the opposite direction of the trail. They hadn't come from the parking lot. They'd emerged from the woods.

Her heart shuddered.

From a distance, their clothes looked like men from the Charlotte Lake community. But something was off. Their faces were set, eyes hard, hands twitching near their waists. And then she saw it, one of them lifted a weapon, leveling it at Krystal as she bent to check the back seat.

No.

Anna's breath caught in her throat. What was she going to do?

"Hurry up, children. We need to go. Now!" she frantically whispered, her voice suddenly sharp.

The children emerged slowly, confused, laughing, wiping their hands on their clothes.

"Behind the trees," Anna ordered, grabbing Jonah's arm. "Get down. Don't talk."

"Are we playing hide and seek?" Jonah asked, ducking behind a pine tree.

"For now," Anna said tightly, crouching low. "But I need you to be very quiet. Can you do that for me?"

Heidi stood frozen, staring toward the car, her chest heaving. Her mouth opened, but no sound came.

"Heidi, now." Anna grabbed her and pulled her behind the tree. The girl's whole frame was trembling. Then the sobs came, gasping, uncontrolled.

Anna held Heidi tight, trying to calm her down, her eyes locked on the men.

From behind the tree, Anna watched in horror as the men surrounded Krystal. One of them yelled something in Spanish. Krystal raised her hands in protest and tried to back away, but they forced her toward the SUV. She struggled briefly. One of the men grabbed her by the shoulders and shoved her hard into the back seat.

"No," Anna whispered.

Krystal was gone. The SUV peeled away in a spray of dust and spinning gravel, speeding down the road. The sound of the engine faded quickly, swallowed by the surrounding mountains.

Anna turned back to the children, her mind racing. Heidi was shaking uncontrollably. The girls were blinking in disbelief, and Jonah had sat down in the pine needles, staring at the ground.

"It's okay. I've got you," Anna said, hugging them close. Her arms trembled, and her breath came in shallow pulls. "You're safe. I won't let them hurt you."

But her mind screamed. What now?

No phone. No vehicle. No help.

She looked down the trail that snaked into the woods. Nine miles to Charlotte Lake. She could wait for help. But what if the men circled back? What if more were coming? Every instinct told her they had to move, and fast.

She wiped Heidi's tears, steadied the girls, and said. "We're going to walk. I need you to be brave."

Jonah nodded, trying to be brave. The girls bit their lips.

They started walking. Anna glanced over her shoulder every few seconds, every bird cry and twig snap tightening her nerves. They stayed close together.

About a mile in, the terrain steepened and the group fell silent.

Then, softly, Heidi moved up, sliding her hand into Anna's

Her voice barely a whisper. "He's the man that kidnapped me."

Anna stopped in her tracks. "Are you sure?"

Heidi's eyes welled up, but she nodded. "He was the one with the scar. I could never forget."

Anna hugged her tightly. A chill ran through her as she looked back down the trail. Who else was watching?

The trail ahead was long, and danger may be close behind. Anna had no choice but to lead them forward, step by trembling step. What lay ahead at Charlotte Lake, she couldn't say, but she wouldn't stop. Not now. Not ever.

—— • ● • ——

Thank you for reading Book Two of the Charlotte Lake Series. The journey continues in Book Three, where reconciliation at Charlotte Lake begins to blossom like a spring flower, and the search for Krystal leads Ethan down a mysterious path. One that will test his resolve, challenge his faith, and uncover secrets no one saw coming.

Acknowledgments

First and foremost, I give thanks to God. His guidance and grace have been the foundation of every step on this journey. Without His light, none of this would be possible.

To my wife, Sharla—your unwavering love, patience, and belief in me have been my greatest source of strength. Thank you for standing beside me and being my partner in every adventure. Your sharp eye for detail and ability to catch editorial errors is truly amazing, and your support has made all the difference.

A heartfelt thank you to my mentor, Colleen Coble. Your wisdom, encouragement, and generous spirit have shaped my path as a writer and continue to inspire me to reach higher.

To Cynthia Hickey of Winged Publications—thank you for your belief in my storytelling and for expanding my vision through your support.

To my friends and family who have endured countless story ideas and brainstorming sessions throughout the *Charlotte Lake* series—your patience, insight, and feedback have been invaluable. Thank you for listening, encouraging, and believing in me.

This book is a reflection of all of you. Thank you for being part of this journey.

D. L. Reavis Bio

Donald L. Reavis grew up in a conservative Christian home where reading and playing games were the primary forms of entertainment. At nineteen, he earned his pilot license and aspired to become an air traffic controller. After a 24-year career controlling aircraft in Southern California, he retired and moved back to his home state of Indiana, where he now lives with his wife, Sharla.

In 2012, his passion for backpacking took him and Sharla on an adventure along the John Muir Trail in the High Sierra Mountains. This journey sparked an even greater love for the backcountry, and the following year he hiked the Pacific Crest Trail, which led him back to Charlotte Lake. Inspired by his time in the wilderness, he began writing the *Charlotte Lake* series.

Donald is a father of three married children and a grandfather of seven grandchildren. He enjoys golfing, painting, and creating memories with his wife of over 43 years.

www.ingramcontent.com/pod-product-compliance
Lightning Source LLC
Chambersburg PA
CBHW070607300726
48975CB00006B/1738